Pursuit

Books by James Stewart Thayer

THE HESS CROSS
THE STETTIN SECRET
THE EARHART BETRAYAL

Pursuit

James Stewart Thayer

CROWN PUBLISHERS, INC.
New York

Copyright © 1986 by James Stewart Thayer

Published by Crown Publishers, Inc.
225 Park Avenue South, New York, New York 10003 and
simultaneously in Canada by
General Publishing Company Limited
Manufactured in the United States of America

CROWN is a trademark of Crown Publishers, Inc.

Library of Congress Cataloging-in-Publication Data
Thayer, James Stewart,
     Pursuit.
     I. Title.
PS3570.H347P8   1986   813'.54   85-14997
ISBN 0-517-55813-0

10 9 8 7 6 5 4 3 2 1

First Edition

To my wife
PATRICIA WALLACE THAYER

Thanks to
Judith Wederholt and John Coyne, who put this on track,

and to
John D. Reagh III, John L. Thayer, M.D.,
Joseph T. Thayer, Mark Gadsby,
David DeLuca, Stan Sims, David Teitzel, and
Emily J. Miles

Pursuit

PROLOGUE

BY THE SPRING OF 1944, THE OUTCOME of the war was bitterly clear to the German High Command.

Reconnaissance flights confirmed that two million Allied soldiers were ready to cross the English Channel. OKH's Third Branch reported that 350 warplanes were arriving in Britain from America every week. The Foreign Armies East Office estimated that Russia that spring had more than three hundred divisions—five million combat troops—grinding ever closer to the German heartland. The rebuilt Soviet armaments industry was stamping out a T-34 tank every five minutes. To all but the mystics, the war was lost.

But the mystics held sway in Berlin. And the hand of Frederick the Great crossed the centuries to steady them and offer them hope. Frederick the Great. The brilliant military campaigner. Resolute, courageous, and visionary. His portrait was the only ornament in the Fuehrer's bunker. Most nights Goebbels read to Hitler from Carlyle's massive biography of Frederick. The cult of Frederick seized Germany's leaders during the last year of the war.

Frederick offered salvation. In 1761, he and fifty thousand soldiers were surrounded by the armies of Russia. With his troops threatened with annihilation, Frederick was suicidal. His reign would end in slaughter and disgrace. Then, unexpectedly, his archenemy Empress Elizabeth died on the Russian Christmas Day. Her nephew, Czar Peter III, was a lifelong admirer of Frederick, and within hours of his ascension to the throne, he ordered his Russian troops home. Frederick was saved.

The miracle of Frederick's rescue entered German folklore. His lesson was simple: the death of one person can stop armies.

There is no doubt Hitler believed.

The death of just one person could save the Reich.

If only it could be arranged. . . .

Part one
THE ESCAPE WEST

1

AN ORDER OF TOAST WOULD SOON give him away. The Berlin office would never learn of it, but after six months of training, his life would end because he could not properly order toast with jelly.

He had been walking since midnight. His shoes had dried hours ago, but not before the damp leather raised blisters on his feet. Sand worked its way up in his clothes, and every mile or so he stopped to swat his coat and pants. He ran his hand across his forehead and along the bridge of his nose, looking for blackface he might have missed when he had washed in the salt water.

He walked awkwardly, matching his gait to the railroad ties. He was traveling north on Atlantic and East Carolina Line tracks about thirty miles inland from the North Carolina coast. The Neuse River was somewhere off to his right.

Dawn seeped into the eastern sky, and a few lights blinked on in the distance ahead of him. That would be New Bern, a fleck of a town at the confluence of the Trent and Neuse rivers. Its citizens were waking up. Because of the man walking on the tracks into their community, New Bern's farmers and merchants would remember this April morning as long as they lived.

He carried only two bags, a scuffed Samsonite suitcase in one hand and an Abercrombie and Fitch mountaineer's pack over his shoulder. The pack was too bulky, even suspicious, but Berlin had assured him it was the least noticeable way to take his equipment in. The backpack was the only expensive thing about him, as his clothes carefully matched the products of a rationed America. Berlin had studied Regulation L.85, the Ration Board's "no fabric over fabric" rule. His pants had no cuffs or back pockets. His coat was unlined and did little against the chill of the dawn wind. There were no pockets on his flannel shirt. Berlin had also learned from an article in the *Atlanta Constitution* that hats had recently become unavailable in the Southeast, so his head was bare. In his wallet were a Virginia driver's license and a draft card. Both identified the man as Paul Jacobs of Arlington.

He strode quickly from tie to tie. The meager glow of false dawn gave way to a peculiar slate-gray morning light, a color unknown in the northern latitudes of his homeland. It eerily flattened the land, robbing it of perspective, and making the steel girders of the bridge ahead of him seem insubstantial.

Wisps of fog drifted along the Trent River's edge. Dead tree branches poked through the haze and bent low over the river. Florid, broad-leafed plants, appearing tropical and sinister, quite unlike anything he'd ever seen before, grew out into the water. He shivered, surely from the wind.

Lifting the pack higher on his shoulder and judging his balance, he cautiously stepped out onto the bridge. The land quickly dropped away from the span. Through the latticework of girders below him, the gunmetal-gray water seemed still. He walked to the center of the bridge, and paused to orient himself.

The WHIT radio tower was visible to the west, just where he had been told it would be. A brick warehouse on Union Point, five hundred meters to the east of the bridge, looked even more dilapidated than it had been in the grainy photo he had studied a month earlier. He scanned the lower profile of New Bern and recognized a few other structures: the water tower and the courthouse and the Episcopal church spire.

The Greyhound terminal could not be seen from the bridge, but he knew where it was. A short walk. He glanced at his watch. He had an hour before the bus departed for Raleigh, and he was hungry. On the far side of the bridge near the waterfront was a clapboard building with glass-barrel pumps in front. A petrol station. Attached to its roof was a sign of many bulbs that spelled out "EAT," glimmering dully in the half-light of morning. He smiled at the command. His life was a series of orders. He adjusted his grip on the suitcase and began again toward the north end of the bridge. With any luck, he would leave New Bern on a full stomach.

Carolee Palmer had worked at Virgil's Esso Station and Cafe since her husband had gone off to war. He hadn't been much of a husband, Rodney Palmer, as they'd only been married three days before he shipped out. The regulars at Virgil's called her an Allotment Annie, accusing her of marrying Rodney for the fifty-dollar monthly allotment check she received as a serviceman's wife. They were funning her, she knew. She had hardly heard of the fifty dollars, or of the ten-thousand-dollar Army life-insurance policy, before she met him.

Rodney wasn't the only one sacrificing for his country. Carolee read Eleanor Roosevelt's column, "My Day," in the newspaper every time it appeared, and if that wasn't a sacrifice, nothing was. And two years ago she sold her Victrola to buy nylons. She had read that manufacturing a parachute consumed the equivalent of thirty-six pairs of nylons, so she didn't mind their scarcity, she supposed. Even stored in an airtight jar, they had deteriorated rapidly, and now she only had one pair left. She was saving them for Rodney's return, or some other very special occasion that might happen before he came back, if Bill Benson kept stopping by for lunch at one-thirty in the afternoon, instead of at noon like everyone else. Now she tanned her legs as often as she could, and every morning applied a single line of eye shadow down the back of each leg to imitate a stocking's seam.

There were other sacrifices. When the War Board announced

that the Veronica Lake peekaboo hairstyle was dangerous to women working in factories, she had lopped hers off, even though the worst thing that could have happened at Virgil's was getting her blond strands mixed in with the flapjack batter. She had shortened her skirts to the regulation size, one inch above the knee. She collected tinfoil scraps. She pasted a bumper sticker on her father's old Studebaker that read "Praise the Lord, I'll soon be ammunition," and had tacked up a "Pay your taxes, Beat the Axis" poster in the men's room at Virgil's. There was only so much one person could do.

Virgil insisted the griddle be cleaned once a week, so that morning Carolee was doubled over the stove with a tattered sock wrapped around her hand to protect her nails while she rubbed the iron slab with an encrusted Brillo pad. Despite the early hour, her full lips were painted blood-red, almost burgundy. She wore dabs of rouge high on her cheeks, and her eyes were accented with liner to make them appear round and surprised, just as Betty Grable did her eyes, according to *Hollywood Fan Magazine*. She wore a modest red blouse, a skirt without pleats, as pleats had gone to war, and black, pointed shoes. Small drops of sweat formed as she worked the grill, and she ran the back of her hand across her forehead.

Elmer DeLong was invariably her first breakfast customer, and when he entered Virgil's that morning, ringing the tin bells tacked to the door, Carolee did not bother to look up from the stove. His toast was already in the toaster. He sat where he always did, the stool second from the right, and opened that morning's *New Bern Sun-Journal*. He would shortly begin cursing the St. Louis Cardinals, National League pennant winners two years in a row mainly, DeLong believed, because they had more 4-F draft dodgers than any other team, which took some doing. DeLong wore his life in the tobacco fields like a mask. His face was permanently burned a ruddy brown, and his eyes always squinted as if against the sun. He had retired and moved into town several years ago, but he donned his farmer's overalls every day in homage to his years behind a plow.

8

"Mornin', Elmer," Carolee finally called over her shoulder. "What'll it be today?" She knew the answer, and he knew her response.

"Going to have waffles this morning, Carolee, and damned if the Cards didn't take another."

"I'm not slaving away on waffles for you, Elmer, war or no war," she said kindly, putting the toast and a dab of white margarine in front of him. "French toast is what you get, just like every morning."

"Arguing with you about breakfast is like wiping my butt with a hoop," he replied absently. "It's endless." He screwed up his eyes at the box score.

She was dipping bread into batter when the doorbells chimed again, startling her. Old Harold Shaw wasn't due for fifteen minutes. She quickly looked up from the frying pan, and her breath caught.

A stranger would have been unprecedented at Virgil's Esso and Cafe at six in the morning, but a young man—a handsome young man—was nothing short of a Baptist vision. She hurriedly wiped her hands on her apron, then ran them through her hair. She demurely dropped her eyes to the grill for as long as she could—most of a second—then smiled invitingly at the man as he negotiated his suitcase around the door. He returned the smile before placing his suitcase near a stool directly in front of her. He sat down and cast his eyes around the counter for a menu.

"There's no sense printing a menu, what with all the shortages these days," Carolee offered. "But we've got what you want, as long as it's eggs or French toast."

She renewed her grin, but it faltered when the stranger's eyes found hers. She would say later that his eyes were a blue she had never seen before, a blue never before seen in North Carolina. They were—she would pause searching for words—a fiery blue, like a sparkler on the Fourth. They were lit from within.

Elmer was also staring at the stranger, of course. What good were new folks if you couldn't eyeball them? His hair

9

was a rusty brown, long for a serviceman, although Carolee would remember he had a soldier's bearing, upright and square-shouldered. His nose was large, but thin and turned sharply. His lips were mismatched, the lower one full, while the upper lip was more severe, a thin line. His smile oddly did not soften the harsh angles on his face. The bones of his jaw and cheeks protruded slightly, making him appear hungry. And intense. Every feature of the stranger was immediate. And to look into his eyes required an act of will.

Carolee broke her gaze and dug into her apron for an order pad, unused since her first week at Virgil's. It gave her a moment to collect herself. "Eggs?" she asked finally, almost a whisper.

"Pardon?" the man asked, still wearing his crooked smile.

Before she could answer, Elmer DeLong leaned toward the stranger and asked bluntly, "Why aren't you in the service? You look tough enough."

The stranger turned to Elmer. "I am, in a way. I work for the government."

"You ain't one of them five-percenters, are you?" Elmer asked. "Damn them, anyway."

The man laughed easily. "No, I'm not a government contractor. I'm a dike inspector. I guess they figure they can use me better poking at dirt embankments than carrying a gun. Suits me fine."

Satisfied, Elmer grunted and returned to his scores.

"Can I get you something for breakfast? I'm making French toast," Carolee asked.

"Sounds good. And orange juice if you've got it. It's dried up in Arlington."

She glanced past her pad. He had elegant hands. Slender, lightly veined, and without the grime under the nails that most everyone in New Bern seemed to have been born with. For a moment she let herself fantasize about leaving New Bern, leaving it with this blue-eyed man, getting away forever from hands gnarled with work, from dirt boots and chewing tobacco. A delicious, hopeless, and very short dream. She wrestled herself back to the stranger's breakfast. "I also have bacon, but I've got to limit it to one slice a customer."

Elmer looked up from his paper and asked accusingly, "Carolee, have you been holding back bacon on us?"

The man answered, "Sure, if you've got it. I don't want to rob your regulars, though."

She ignored Elmer. "One slice it is, then. You want some regular toast along with your French toast?"

"Please."

"What kind?"

The stranger hesitated, then said quickly, "Excuse me?"

"What kind of toast?"

The man cast the smallest glance at Elmer's plate. "Well..."

A tuck of suspicion formed on Carolee's brow. A faint note of falseness, a slight shift away from the normal and expected, echoed in her mind. It was the stranger, of course. After serving the same portions to the same men at the same time for so long, a gust of wind on the door at the wrong moment would cause unease. But, still, there was something... something rehearsed about this man.

Carolee could have volunteered dark, light, or rye bread. Instead, instinctively, she asked again, "What kind?"

"Whatever you've got the most of. With marmalade, please." The man leaned forward for a glimpse of the back of Elmer's newspaper.

She would say later that this simply wasn't the proper answer, that people always know what kind of toast they like. He had deliberately avoided an easy question. And his bending close to read Elmer's *Sun-Journal* was too smooth. But in truth, the stranger's response only pulled her vague unease closer to the surface. A trace of a suspicion tugged at Carolee. There was a dissonance about the stranger that disturbed her. This fellow just didn't belong. Like everyone else, she had read in the papers about rumored landings near Savannah last month. It had prompted her to put up another poster, depicting a swastika with an enormous ear, and reading, "The less said, the less dead." But they were only rumors, they all finally agreed.

He pulled a GI paperback from his coat pocket and flipped to a page that had the corner turned down. Carolee needed time to think. She withdrew a thin packet of bacon from the cooler, peeled off a strip, and carefully placed it on the grill. She had been saving them for Bill Benson. Before the bacon's color began to turn, she cut off the fat with the edge of her spatula and flipped it into the collection can at the back of the griddle, which the Boy Scouts gathered every two weeks. The fat was made into glycerin for high explosives. Carolee did this small duty mechanically, occasionally stealing a glance at the stranger. He pulled a Camel from a pocket, scraped a match with his thumb, and inhaled deeply. He returned to his book.

She blushed at her suspicion. Unfounded, even silly. And right here in this cafe she had kidded others for their wild speculation about German saboteurs. One stranger finally visits the cafe, and she has him pegged for a Nazi. She smiled at her foolishness. And in light of her self-deprecating thoughts, what she did next was inexplicable to her, even as she did it. The FBI citation would call it "ingenious and providential."

Carolee dipped two slices of bread into the egg batter, put them on a plate, added the slice of bacon to one side, and pushed the dish across the counter to the man. The French toast was uncooked. In the moment it took him to bend down a new page and put the paperback into his pocket, batter flowed off the bread and settled to the sides of the plate, surrounding the bacon.

"Thank you, miss." The stranger lifted his fork and without another word began eating the soggy bread.

A sudden fear gripped Carolee's chest so tightly she emitted a small animal groan, lost in Elmer's shuffling of his newspaper. She backstepped toward the oven and bit down fiercely, choking off a cry. Her hand found the oven handle, and she steadied herself against it.

This man didn't know what Americans ate for breakfast. Didn't know that cold, soaking bread wasn't French toast.

Her head lightened as if from shock after a wound. The room shimmered with her fear. The stranger seemed to materialize again before Carolee's eyes. And when he was whole, he was entirely foreign. He was still leaning forward over the counter, was still wearing his friendly smile as he chewed the bread. But now he was utterly alien and terrifying.

Elmer continued to wait patiently for his breakfast, unaware of the transformation. His presence, old and solid and familiar, calmed Carolee. She turned to Elmer and with a voice that to her sounded remarkably level, she said, "I need more eggs. Be back in a minute."

She walked slowly through the door into the garage, and only when she was around the corner near Virgil's rack of patched retreads did she break into a run. A few steps brought her to the garage phone, on the wall over the desk near the lube rack. She dialed zero and after a few seconds demanded, "Hattie, get me Sheriff Henley.... Yes, it's Carolee.... Hattie, I don't have time for that now. I mean it, I've got to talk to him right away."

An age passed until Ray Henley answered. His voice was blurred with sleep, and the first thing he said was, "This better be good."

"Sheriff, this is Carolee Palmer over at Virgil's. You've got to get here right away. I've got a man here eating breakfast who I don't think is an American."

Henley brightened when he heard who the caller was. "Carolee, how are you, honey?"

"Sheriff, will you listen to me? I've got a foreigner sitting in my cafe eating breakfast."

"Carolee, you aren't listening to that old gummer Elmer, are you? He'll stir you up real good, and have a fine old time doing it."

She fought for control. "Sheriff, please, please listen. This man is a German. I swear to God he is. Please get over here."

The sheriff had never had any trouble with Carolee, and knew her to be level-headed. Maybe a bit hot in the skirt, but she was nobody's fool. And not one to take Elmer's jawing seriously. Something was wrong at Virgil's. "You keep him there, Carolee. I'll be right over. Now don't you worry none. There's a good explanation for all this, I'm sure. You just keep him there, and I'll come a-running."

Carolee replaced the receiver. Keep him there. How in good Christ would she do that? When he got done with that paste she had served him for breakfast, he'd up and leave. She pressed a fist against her forehead as if she could squeeze the fright from herself. And her answer came. Virgil was a bird man, and his wife loathed guns. She wouldn't let Virgil keep his guns in her house.

Elmer DeLong was so startled when Carolee returned that he coughed his false teeth onto the counter. Carolee raised Virgil's Remington 12-gauge so that its double snout was one foot from the stranger's eyes.

"You just sit there, and don't even think of moving."

Her words were unnaturally tranquil, and the stranger must have known that a sudden move would be the end of him. His only reaction was to lower his fork slowly. Elmer left his teeth where they had fallen and sat transfixed, incapable of uttering a sound.

"I've called the sheriff," Carolee whispered over the shotgun's cocked hammers, "and he'll be here any minute. You just sit tight."

Elmer exclaimed in a toothless lisp, "For God's sake, Carolee...."

"I know what I'm doing, Elmer," she said in a voice that was becoming unfamiliar to her. "You sit there, too. This man is dangerous."

Perhaps had he seen the blued barrels of the Remington waver even slightly, he would have lunged for her. But her arm was as steady as an infantryman's. He would be lunging into a burst of birdshot.

He exhaled slowly. "So you've called the police?"

She nodded. His vulpine eyes were trying to lock onto hers,

she knew, and she felt he was hunting her, knowing she was vulnerable. She stared down the barrels at his mouth.

"I can't wait for a policeman to come here," he said softly, as if in the presence of the dead. "If you pull those triggers, you'll kill a man who only asked you for breakfast."

The stranger slowly turned on his stool and bent to pick up his suitcase. The shotgun followed him, but he seemed oblivious to it.

Panic welled within Carolee. Oh, God, he's going to leave and the sheriff said to keep him here and I've never shot anything in my life and I can't shoot him. . . .

The man walked from the counter. With his free hand, he reached for the knob and pulled open the door.

I . . . I can't shoot him. . . .

Fire spat across the room. The thunderous peal of the shotgun blast chased itself around the cafe, rattling dishes and windows before escaping. The acrid odor of spent gunpowder filled the place. With the jerking movements of a marionette, Carolee lowered the Remington.

She must have missed. The stranger still stood at the door, suitcase in one hand. He stared balefully at her, more in sorrow than anger or fright. Only when she followed his eyes to his arm did she see the damage.

The birdshot had not missed entirely. His arm now ended several inches above the wrist. The rest of his hand and wrist had disappeared. Blood began to gush onto the floor.

The utter impossibility of what had happened immobilized Carolee and her customer. But his grievous wound did not seem to register on the stranger. His expression remained placid as he lowered the suitcase, then pulled a Walther PPK from under his coat. The short-barreled pistol was almost hidden by his hand. He brought it up without hurry, ignoring the blood splattering onto his shoes. Carolee saw the stubby gun settle on her. She awaited the impact, accepting the logic of the terrible trade, bullet for birdshot.

Still toothless, Elmer DeLong twisted off his stool and stepped toward the stranger, his arms outspread. He lisped, "Wait, you don't need..."

As if drawn to the sound, the pistol swung to DeLong. Three flat claps, insignificant after the shotgun's roar, produced a red stitching that climbed up the farmer's overalls. DeLong glanced down at the stains spreading across his overalls, then, as if the shots had only changed his mind, stepped back toward the stool he had occupied every morning since he retired. He reached for the counter, but collapsed against the stool and slid to the floor.

Carolee would tell the FBI investigators that she didn't even think about the shotgun still aimed at the stranger, didn't think about its second barrel and second trigger. Grief or fear suddenly tightened her hands. Her finger was still on the trigger of the second barrel.

The gun's unexpected recoil bounced her against the oven handle. The stranger snapped over and his legs crumpled. The Walther slid across the linoleum to the base of the Wurlitzer jukebox. A dark pool of blood seeped from beneath the body, running along the cracks in the tile.

Carolee dropped the Remington onto the counter, where it clattered against the stranger's plate. She gulped air, fighting a rising nausea. She controlled her sickness and tears until Sheriff Henley arrived a few minutes later. Then for many days Carolee wept for Elmer and the stranger and herself.

2

WALTER ARMBRUSTER'S LETTER WAS clearly a yaahu, and it came from Washington via the weekly Army Air Force's DC-3 perimeter flight to the Secret Service regional office in Seattle. "Yaahu" is an acronym for "You're under arrest, asshole, hands up."

It was the first item John Wren pulled from the courier pouch, and before he and Tom Garvin dug further into the bag they were driving the agency's Ford sedan north on Aurora Avenue to the Fremont district, where Armbruster's return address claimed he lived.

"This guy have a sheet?" Wren asked as he guided the car onto the Aurora Bridge.

"I called the Seattle police. Nothing serious. He's been arrested for tearing up his neighbor's yard with a post-hole digger. Armbruster claimed the neighbor was burying photographs of the Boeing plant in the ground near the brick barbecue."

"Spare me the rest of it," Wren said sourly as he ran a hand through his dark hair. "A dozen years in the Service, and I'm back on the yaahu patrol."

John Wren had been assigned to Seattle two years ago, rotated

17

out of the White House Detail after three heady years guarding
Roosevelt, the coveted duty in the Service. Secret Service Chief
Frank Wilson and Wren's fellow agents all conspired in pretending that the transfer was routine and had nothing to do with
the months when Wren touched madness.

In 1937, Wren had arrested and testified against a small-time
counterfeiter and big-time alcoholic named Wiley Sullivan. After
serving five of ten at Leavenworth, Sullivan was paroled. At the
end of a two-week, eastbound drunken binge, he threw Linda
Wren off the fourth-floor balcony of their Georgetown apartment
while Wren was at work.

Wren did not emerge from his darkened apartment for a month.
He and Linda had met on the walkway around the Reflecting
Pool and had known within twenty minutes they would be wed.
There had always been a thrilling inevitability about their love.
Her death was an excision of his heart. His grief reduced and
hardened him, and when he finally left the apartment, what was
left of him would not have been recognized by his wife.

From patchy evidence, Chief Wilson concluded that Wren
drove southwest, following Wiley Sullivan. Reports of Sullivan,
then of Wren, came in from Oklahoma City and Albuquerque.

Finally, a venom hunter found Sullivan's torso tied to a giant
saguaro cactus near Gila Bend. The Maricopa sheriff concluded
that Sullivan was bleeding from a hundred cactus-spine punc-
tures in his back and was not yet dead when the coyotes began
ripping at his legs.

Wren returned to work. The Arizona trip had been a palliative.
It had lessened the pain without healing the wound. Wilson had
deflected a halfhearted inquiry from the Maricopa County sheriff. Wren had only shrugged when Frank Wilson told him he
was being transferred to Seattle.

Wren downshifted and turned east on 40th. He was a large
man, over six feet two, and his knee was jammed uncomfortably
between the steering column and the stick. He rested a hand on
the shift knob. His boxing coach at UCLA had told him that
were it not for his musician's hands he would have made it in

the pros, which Wren liked to believe. His hair had recently begun to recede, not yet alarmingly, but enough to steal away the youthful appearance that had persisted obstinately into his late thirties. His eyes were ash-gray and set at hard angles. In the two years, two months, and four days of his marriage to Linda, she had often stared into those eyes, finding them bright with emotions she would delight in reading aloud. But since that time—which Wren now knew would be his only truly happy days in this life—his eyes had become shadowed and remote, mirroring the melancholy that increasingly worked on him.

His eyes were the only insight into John Wren that could be gained from his face. His chin was too large, and the ascetic mouth rarely turned up in a smile. His ears were jugged and, with his size, gave him an assertive, brawler's presence he minimized by never wearing a hat.

He glanced at Garvin. "What else have we got?"

Garvin pulled a bill from the pouch and held it up to the light. "A bogey from the home office." He laughed dryly. "Look at this. The dummies got Jackson's eyes a bit crossed." He passed the counterfeit twenty-dollar bill to Wren. "It looks like one eye is staring down at the hairs in his nose. You couldn't get a hooker to take that twenty."

"Where'd they come from?"

Garvin opened the report that had accompanied the bill. "Oshkosh, Wisconsin, a week ago. They picked up others in Madison last Thursday and Dubuque on Friday, so the artist is heading west or south." Garvin scanned the rest of the report. "From the way the bogey fades, with better artwork in the upper side and worse on the bottom, Chief Wilson thinks the artist is Lazy Charley Gow, and they've put out a warrant on him."

"He won't get out this far west," Wren said. "Not to the end of the earth."

Seattle had a two-man field office. Because Wren was the agent-in-charge, Garvin referred to himself as the agent-nowhere-near-in-charge. Whereas Wren was often woolly and detached, Garvin was animated and passionate in even the smallest of matters. Garvin's elemental joy was, as Chief Wilson had once instructed Wren, at the very limit of what would be tolerated in the Service. But Garvin had once saved Wren from a yaahu who almost had Wren's nose in a bolt cutter, so Wren put up with his eccentric enthusiasms. Garvin's red hair, round, rolling eyes, and laugh that could start a truck often led strangers to mistake him for an innocent or an incompetent. He was neither.

As Wren guided the Ford north onto Sunnyside, Garvin pulled the last item from the pouch. It was a manila envelope with the FBI insignia prominently on the front. "Secret Service—Confidential" was stamped many times over the FBI seal, almost obliterating it.

Garvin bent forward intently. He steadied the page in both hands as if words might spill off it. "I'll be damned. They've tried it again."

Wren's eyes flickered to the report. "What are you talking about?"

"They got another German. This time in some town in North Carolina." Garvin paused as his eyes slid down the page.

"Read it out loud," Wren demanded. He slowed the Ford, knowing his attention would not be on the narrow residential street.

"Will you listen to this? A fellow walks into a cafe in New Bern, North Carolina, and from some idle questions, the waitress gets suspicious. So to test her hunch, she serves him some raw French toast, and he eats it." Garvin hooted loudly.

Wren's brows rose. "Sharp lady. Paranoid, too, sounds like."

"So she figures the guy is right off the boat from the Fatherland. When the fellow gets up to leave the cafe, she blows his hand off with a shotgun. He then lets a customer have it with his pistol, so she cuts him in half with another blast."

"They sure he was a German?"

Garvin's smile widened. "His pistol was a Walther. And in his suitcase were a Krup R.V. coder and a hand-keyed Morse sender called an Afus, tuned by quartz to a preset frequency, battery-powered, generating twenty watts."

"Sounds pretty German, all right."

"He was wearing real Sears, Roebuck pants, and the chemists found traces of emery in the cloth near the knees, where they had been rubbed to look old and worn. His watch was a prewar Elgin, and from its manufacturing stamp they've determined it was sold originally somewhere in Pennsylvania. He had Gillette blue blades in his suitcase. They were careful."

"Money?"

Garvin whistled. "Eight thousand U.S. dollars. Small, used bills. And a lot of ration coupons to go with the cash."

"Any weapons or explosives?" Wren asked.

"No. So the FBI has initially concluded he was on a surveillance. They think he landed off the Carolina coast to avoid the sub nets and destroyers up around Norfolk and farther north. Submarine, probably, although there haven't been any sightings."

"That makes two German landings in the last five weeks," Wren said, slowing the Ford to look for street numbers on the small homes that lined Sunnyside. Two young ladies walked slowly on the sidewalk, leaning toward each other to whisper and giggle conspiratorially. One wore a turban, fashionable now that Rosie the Riveter was a national hero. Her friend had a military patch sewn to the arm of her blouse. Her boyfriend's unit, or, more probably, her imaginary boyfriend's unit.

Although it was a weekday, many automobiles remained parked along the street. Hupmobiles and Packards, carefully preserved. Commuters bused to the Boeing bomber plant and the Lockheed Shipyard and saved their precious gasoline points for Sunday drives along Lake Washington.

Wren remembered the earlier report aloud: "They found the first German in the woods outside Virginia Beach, spotted by an old lady bird-watcher who saw him burying a wet suit. And now this new one in North Carolina."

"Did the main office ever determine what the first one was up to?" Garvin asked, folding the report into the envelope.

"No." Wren turned the car to the curb. "But whatever either

was trying to do, it's got nothing to do with the boondocks, which is precisely where you and I are." He yanked back on the brake handle with more force than it required. "Let's go get this guy."

The house was squeezed together with a dozen other workingmen's homes on the block. With its postage-stamp yard and humble, overpruned hydrangeas guarding the short walkway to the porch, and with its stubby chimney and two-pane windows, the house seemed a miniature. Tacked to the front door was a tin sign which read "Green River Ordinance Enforced." Wren climbed three steps to the porch, then waited until Garvin had walked to the side of the house for a view of the backyard. When his partner nodded, Wren knocked loudly.

He heard the muted sounds of rustling paper. A drawer slammed, then another. A wheezy clearing of a throat. "Just a minute" came a distant cry.

"He's a collector, Tom. I can hear him in there, squirreling away his most important discoveries."

Floorboards creaked on the other side of the door. "Who is it?" The voice was an ancient rasp.

"My name is John Wren, Mr. Armbruster. May I speak with you?"

"No."

"I'm a United States Secret Service agent, Mr. Armbruster. I must insist on a few words with you."

"The Secret Service?" The voice seemed pleased. "Is it about a letter I sent to the president?"

"Yes, it is. Please open the door."

"Which letter? The one about how I discovered he rigged the 1940 election using all those Argentine pesos? Wait until the voters hear about it. No fourth term for that crook, by God."

"Open the door, Mr. Armbruster."

The bolt was wrestled open. The door cracked a few inches. Wrinkled with cunning, a small eye peered out. Wren held up his silver star, then before Armbruster could make up his mind, pushed his way into the house. Garvin hurried up the porch stairs after him.

Walter Armbruster bounced away from the door, his bathrobe flapping around his spindly knees, and was halfway across the room before he could steady himself. Armbruster was small with age, his shoulders hunched protectively. His face was a gnawed bone, white and bristling, with shaving nicks that were refusing to heal. His ferret eyes glittered wetly. His ferocious grin challenged the agents.

Armbruster drew crazed strength from his knowledge, and his scoops were on display in every corner, on every surface in his house. Filing cabinets filled the rooms, so overflowing with letters and clippings that many of the drawers could not be closed. The drawers were labeled with the names of Rothschild, Rockefeller, Pius XII, and dozens of other conspirators. The walls were covered with photos of the plotters, with Armbruster's phrenological studies tacked next to each, discussing the criminally high skulls or porcine eyes of the intriguers.

Behind Armbruster was a small dining room, just large enough for a table littered with three-by-five cards. If Armbruster held true to form, the cards would contain painfully correct penmanship tracing the world's great conspiracies and frauds, as gleaned from Armbruster's meticulous reading. Stacks of yellowed newspapers lined the dining-room wall.

There would be, Wren knew, hardly a government official or corporation president in the nation who had not received several letters from Armbruster, each revealing global networks of intrigue. On top of several cabinets were leather-bound scrapbooks, which would contain precious letters from sympathizers, those rare individuals who responded to Armbruster's messages in any way less than accusations of insanity. Yes, Walter Armbruster was a collector. Perhaps Wren's thirtieth.

Wren pulled the letter from his coat pocket. "Mr. Armbruster, may I ask if you wrote this letter to President Roosevelt." Wren stepped as near to the old man as he thought safe, what with those flailing eyes and spit bubbles at the corner of his mouth. He held the letter out.

"That looks like the one where I told him I've figured out that his true father is Count Mazzini."

Wren searched the old man's face for a hint of humor, some sign this was a grand joke. There was none. "That's the one."

"I bet I'm not the first to find out. There'll be no more hiding for that bastard."

"We're going to take you in for some questions, Mr. Armbruster. Please put on some pants and shoes."

The old man's eyes grew. "Am I being arrested?"

"Questioned. Down at our office."

"For finding out about Count Mazzini?" Armbruster asked, glowing with pride. "Roosevelt must be desperate."

Garvin said, "Your postscript says, 'Remember, I've got my old deer rifle.' Do you have a rifle?"

Wisps of white hair batted his ears when he shook his head. "Nah. I just added that to get his attention. Otherwise..." He trailed off.

"When you talk about a rifle in a letter to the president, you should expect us knocking on your door, Mr. Armbruster," Wren said tonelessly. "Your pants and shoes. Let's go."

Garvin followed the old man as he dressed. Armbruster would be questioned for several hours, then transferred to the detention ward at Maritime Hospital for psychiatric observation. Wren thought of the report out of North Carolina, of the German whose actions and motives were right then being analyzed by the FBI, the Secret Service, the OSS, and a dozen other agencies. All three thousand miles to the east.

The transfer away from the White House Detail to Seattle had taken him away from the capital's monuments, most of which reminded him of his wife. At first it had helped. But the dull work in Seattle was mutating Wren. After two years in the city, his clothes fit sloppily, and his hair would not lie right. His face sagged, and the dark shadow of his whiskers appeared earlier and earlier in the day. His joints ached in the morning. For the first time in his life, he breathed heavily after climbing a flight of stairs.

And for the first time, after twelve years, he was considering leaving the Secret Service. Kaiser Industries in Los Angeles had inquired if he wished to be considered for the job of senior security officer at twice his present pay. Wren had not yet decided, but anything was better than waiting anxiously for the Monday pouch, doing all its work that morning, then filling up the rest of the week with make-work tasks.

Armbruster returned with Tom Garvin in tow. The old man's raincoat had the same mildewy appearance as had his bathrobe. Garvin carried his small suitcase.

Armbruster stopped near his front door. "Aren't you going to put handcuffs on me?"

"You don't need them," Wren answered curtly.

Armbruster rose to his toes with indignation. "How would it look to the neighbors, me being arrested, and not even handcuffed?"

Garvin produced cuffs from his belt, gently brought Armbruster's arms around, and secured his hands.

"Now would you boys do me a favor?" Armbruster asked as they stepped onto the porch. "I got a Brownie on the mantel over the fireplace. If one of you would take a snapshot of me being arrested, I'd be mighty grateful."

Garvin gleefully ignored Wren's warning glare and returned to the front room for the camera. Working hard to suppress his laughter, he peered through the viewfinder at Wren's black scowl. He waved Armbruster closer to Wren, then closer still. The old man puffed himself up, almost to Wren's chin.

Garvin called, "Hold it," and snapped the photo.

He returned the camera and locked the door behind them. During the drive back to the office Wren decided. Two years of this was enough. He would contact Kaiser. Walter Armbruster would be his last yaahu.

3

BERLINERS CALLED THE SUDDEN changes *ein tolles Ding*, miraculous events. The overnight transformation at Berkaerstrasse 32 was certainly that.

On September 19, 1941, the building in the Charlottenburg District was, as it had been for the prior eleven years, a Jewish old folks' home. By noon the next day it was the headquarters of Department VI of the Reichssicherheitshauptamt, the Reich Security Administration. Berlin etiquette demanded that no one ask where the elderly Jews had gone.

The building sprouted quills: a rotary beam, a long-wire directive array, a trap, a quad, and other antennae that seemed appropriate atop the modern, four-story, curvilinear brick structure. Strung from posts high above the roof was a camouflage net designed to look from the air like black tar roofing. The net covered all but the tallest array antenna, which poked through. The fourth floor was recessed for a long balcony the officers used as a place to smoke and relax, where they could talk without fearing microphones in the walls.

On the sidewalk, Wehrmacht soldiers guarded the doors day and night. And behind each reinforced metal door, a black-uniformed Waffen SS storm trooper manned an MG-42, a light machine gun mounted on a bipod.

Once Heinrich Himmler's small pet project, RSHA VI had suddenly ballooned in early 1944 to become the most powerful espionage establishment in the Reich, the directorate of virtually all foreign undercover operations. In January of that year Dr. Erich Vermehren, a member of the Abwehr post in Istanbul and an opponent of the Nazi regime, had defected to the British. In a rage, Hitler signed a decree that abolished the Abwehr as an independent intelligence organization under the military and transferred its functions to Department VI, which was entirely Himmler's domain. The Department thus joined his other dreaded fiefdoms: Department III (the domestic Security Service) and Department IV (the Gestapo). The decree quickly led to the downfall of Admiral Wilhelm Canaris, who had headed the Abwehr, too independently, for nine years. Foreign espionage and intelligence were now dominated by the Nazi Party.

SS Lieutenant Colonel Dr. Theodor Paeffgen had spent the morning of June 13, 1944, hovering over his radio operators in the basement of the headquarters building. From the poor way the day was unfolding, Paeffgen could not have known that events to occur within the hour would earn him the coveted Knight's Cross.

He paced up and down the narrow walkway between the banks of equipment, frequently pausing to glance at the operators, who because of his presence nervously kept their sending hands bunched at the ready over their sets. The room was silent except for the occasional chatter from telegraph keys and the electric hum of the amplifiers.

Paeffgen let none of his anxiety cross his face. His bearing was militarily erect and squared. He was a tall man, and his wide shoulders and long neck combined to make his head look too small. His SS dossier described him as "racial type: Nordic." Blond, waving hair was controlled by a strict part on the left side. Below a high forehead were green eyes so severe that a sharp glance from him could throw off an operator's "fist"—the

signature pattern of sending Morse unique to each operator—
for the rest of his shift. On his left cheek was an angry red
dimple, courtesy of a Ukrainian partisan's grenade. His jaw protruded firmly and had an off-center cleft, and the rare smile
above it was as cold as a Prussian winter. He was called Theo
by his confidants, but there were precious few of those.

Paeffgen was thirty-four, young to command the Department's
Group D, espionage services in North and South America. He
was a doctor of law and owed his rise in the SS to being a
schoolmate of RSHA chief Walter Schellenburg at Bonn before
the war. Schellenburg took over RSHA VI in 1941. His friend
Theo Paeffgen was then in the Ukraine, where he was earning
poor marks for his work with an *Einsatzkommando* rounding up
partisans. His superior officer had written into Paeffgen's service
record that Paeffgen did not "entirely fulfill the requirements in
leadership respects," a sympathetic reference to Paeffgen's refusal
to order his men to burn, level, and salt a peasant village, peasants
and all. The cautious phrase had spared Paeffgen a court-martial.

Before the war, Paeffgen had studied at Bordeaux and Geneva
for a year and in Edinburgh for a summer. He spoke English.
And, in a department known for its internal intrigue, he would
remain faithful to Schellenburg. These were sufficient reasons
for Schellenburg to offer the RSHA VI position to Paeffgen in
1942. Paeffgen jumped at the opportunity. It got him out of
Russia and to a Berlin desk, where he proved he was formidable.

Paeffgen continued to patrol the radio room. Twelve operators
were on shift, six on each side of the room facing the banks of
instruments. On desks in front of them were their call signs,
cipher keys, and transmission codes for each agent in the field
that radioed the Berlin station. Equipment lined the walls: Ii and
tripler transmitters, crystal converters, VHF receivers, 110-MC
amplifiers, grid-dip meters, oscillators, signal generators, and
other state-of-the-art pieces of radio equipment. Their indicator
lights threw eerie green shadows across the operators' faces.

Paeffgen abruptly turned to his lead operator. "Anything yet?"
The sender lifted his headset off one ear. "No, sir."

Paeffgen could not resist asking, "Are you sure, Corporal?"

"Yes, sir. We've had empty airwaves, and Eisern Hand reports nothing."

Paeffgen nodded quickly. These operators were from Signal Regiment 506, transferred at his order from their station in Hamburg. They were the best in Germany, proven at Kursk and Leningrad. He had also posted them at the Department's backup receiving station at Eisern Hand, a village in the mountains north of Wiesbaden. Transmitters and receivers in this remote area were away from large electrical installations that created radio interference.

"When is his alternate transmission due?" Paeffgen asked, touching his upper lip with the fingers of his right hand, a habit remaining from his winter in Russia, where he had spent much of each day blowing warm air over his hands.

"He has missed the first Raleigh call time and the drop-back time. He isn't scheduled for another transmission until Tuesday, zero one hundred hours."

"What do you think, Corporal?"

The operator cleared his throat, not used to being asked his opinion. He was a Bavarian with a pulpy mountain accent. "He's dead or captured, sir. Usually if they miss the first call and the drop-back, we never hear from them again."

Paeffgen knew the percentages all too well, but he had wanted to hear them aloud. "When the slip messenger comes, have him tell Major Carstenn to meet in my office immediately. And call von Schlieffen and Rauff. We'll meet in the operations room as soon as they arrive."

The operator nodded and lowered the headset, knowing that all that remained of their agent was the faint crackling coming through his earphones.

At the knock, Paeffgen covered the phone with a hand and asked Friedrich Carstenn to enter the office. He waved his subordinate to the chair next to his desk. Unlike Paeffgen, who preferred three-piece suits, SS Major Carstenn was wearing his black uniform, with its midriff jacket belt and diagonal leather strap from the belt over his right shoulder. Over his heart were three glittering service badges, and on the left sleeve was an understated, embroidered "SD." His jodhpurs tapered down to the calf-high black riding boots. The SS skull insignia—the death's head—was centered above the silver braid on the rim of the peaked cap. The major saw that Paeffgen's eyes were locked in concentration on the opposite wall, and he lowered himself nervously into the metal chair.

"No, it's too early to be certain," Paeffgen said into the telephone. "But we cannot imagine any other circumstance under which Lieutenant Hutter would fail to transmit. We are assuming he has been taken." Paeffgen grimaced at Carstenn, lest the major have any doubt as to the tone of the conversation. "Let me assure you, Herr Reichsfuehrer, we have none better than Walther Hutter. You personally designed his training schedule."

Carstenn's eyes widened at this modest reproach. Paeffgen was not speaking with Schellenburg, Paeffgen's superior and friend, as Carstenn had first assumed. On the other end of the line was Heinrich Himmler, the nearsighted, sweet-voiced leader of the SS, a man with the cloying scent of the dead following him everywhere, a man so dangerous and unpredictable that both times he had met Himmler personally, Carstenn had almost vomited with fear. Carstenn smiled involuntarily at Paeffgen's daring, and received a friendly scowl in return, an unusual offering from the starched colonel.

Carstenn's dark uniform strengthened his features. His eyes were sloping and pensive and his mouth was gentle, almost feminine. The skin on his brow was so thin and transparent that blood vessels were visible. The major knew his face was boyish, and to compensate he set his jaw firmly and always spoke deliberately.

"On a relay from KO-Lisbon, the Eisern Hand station picked up U-513's message at zero eight hundred. Hutter disembarked as planned..." Himmler's interruption pulled back the corner's of Paeffgren's mouth with distaste. "No, sir. We are sure he didn't drown. He flashed the submarine when he reached the sand spit on the North Carolina coast. . . . No, sir. Hutter was politically correct. There is no possibility he defected when he reached the United States."

Paeffgen was silent under a torrent of abuse from Himmler. Carstenn cleared his throat tentatively, reminding the colonel he was in the room and was supporting him.

Paeffgen inhaled sharply, then plunged. "Am I to assume, then, Herr Reichsfuehrer, that the assignment remains the same?"

The colonel's face flamed red, something Carstenn had never seen before. Embarrassed, the major looked away.

"Yes, I understand. It will be done." Paeffgen shakingly returned the telephone to its cradle. He wet his lips before speaking. "Do you know what that peasant said? *'Es geht um die Wurst.'*" The sausage—everything—depends on it. Paeffgen sighed heavily "Is everyone else here, Major?"

"In the op room."

Paeffgen rose wearily from his chair. "Then let's try again, shall we?"

The Department's operations center was an interior conference room in the basement. On three walls, maps vividly displayed the Thousand-Year Empire in decline. Small pins with coded red flags marked the locations of the Department's clandestine radio transmitters. Black-flagged pins revealed stations that had failed to transmit and were presumed dead. The pins graphically showed a decimated secret force. Even more bleakly, a series of wavy ink lines told of the month-by-month retreat of German forces across the continent.

Along the east wall were cabinets containing personnel files for each agent in the field, arranged by precise code designations. An agent's designation began with a letter *V* (for *Vertrauensmann*, confidence man), a number for the country where he operated (1, indicating Afghanistan, through the alphabet to 182, for Yemen), and a personal number. Each file also included a listing of security checks on that agent, a biography, a record of his or her reports, and an evaluation on a five-number scale, from 1 for excellent to 5 for useless. When an agent was no longer functioning, his record was placed in the cabinet nearest the door, the dead file. Ominously, a second dead-file cabinet had last month been moved into the operations room and was rapidly filling.

A massive oak table filled the center of the room. When Paeffgen and Carstenn walked in, two of the high-backed chairs were already occupied. General Erich Count von Schlieffen represented the Armed Forces High Command (OKW) and reported to Chief of Staff Wilhelm Keitel. Von Schlieffen was of the *Uradel,* or ancient ancestry, whose family rank and title preceded the thirteenth century. With his scimitar nose, clipped mustache, and finely tailored uniforms, he projected refinement and superiority. Before his promotion to the OKW General Staff, the count had served under Rommel, commanding the Fifteenth Panzer Division during its assault on Sidi Omar in the Egyptian desert. Paeffgen had closely read von Schlieffen's file and was amused that Rommel, never comfortable with aristocracy, had petulantly added to an otherwise sterling report that von Schlieffen was "often preoccupied with useless acts of vanity." The count sat with his hands folded in front of him and did not look up as Paeffgen took his position at the head of the table.

Across the table from von Schlieffen was Major General Georg Rauff, the liaison with the Air Force High Command (OKL). During the Great War, he had flown with Hermann Goering in the Jagdstaffel 27, stationed at Yseghem. Rauff had saved Goering in a dogfight over Flanders, when Rauff dove out of the sun and blew off the stabilizers of a Sopwith Camel that Goering had not been able to lose. Goering had lugged Rauff up the Luftwaffe ranks behind him. Rauff was agreeably flabby — some said in purposeful imitation of his mentor Goering — and his puffiness defeated any wrinkles he might otherwise have had, making him look much younger than his fifty-five years. He smiled equally at Paeffgen.

Without preliminaries, Paeffgen began, "Hutter has missed

two contact times. We are proceeding now as if he has failed. We have been ordered by Himmler to try again."

"*Schweinerei,*" von Schlieffen swore uncharacteristically. "This absurd little dance has gone on long enough, don't you think, Colonel?"

"I was told by Reichsfuehrer Himmler a few minutes ago that what I thought was of little importance," Paeffgen replied. "Our task is to send another operative."

"We have lost two men," Rauff said, running a finger along the yellow OKL patch on his uniform collar. "What do we do now, Colonel? Reichsmarschall Goering follows these plans with more than a little interest. I must report more than abject failure to him."

Von Schlieffen said acidly, "Tell Meyer to tend to the British bombs and to get his nose out of this affair." In 1939, Goering had boasted that should one British bomb ever fall on Germany, he could be called Meyer. He was now known throughout Germany as Meyer.

Unruffled, Rauff persisted, "What about another submarine landing? Can we requisition another U-boat?"

"I have authority to use another submarine, and then another, as many as it takes." Paeffgen pulled a package of Camel cigarettes from his briefcase, a perquisite of the intelligence service. He passed them around. Not even von Schlieffen could keep the gratitude off his face. Like other Germans in 1944, he had been reduced to smoking ersatz cigarettes made of inferior Turkish tobacco and, most suspected, cow dung.

Paeffgen put a match to the Camel and continued, "But what good would it do? You are aware of our two failures this past five weeks. Submarine landings on American shores simply do not work."

"You've got several agents already in the United States," Rauff said, exhaling smoke in a huge cloud. "Terrier in Washington and Teckel in Boston. Can't we order them to carry out the assignment?"

"Terrier is valuable and loyal. However, he is an intellectual, a professor at a university. He gathers and analyzes economic data for us. He is incapable of doing what we have in mind. As far as we know, he has never even fired a rifle. Teckel's story is similar."

"Then what do you propose, Colonel?" von Schlieffen asked in English, an affectation common among General Staff officers.

Before Paeffgen could answer, a low rumble began filtering through the walls, ominous and approaching. It built quickly to a roar that filled the room. A pencil holder near von Schlieffen trembled and slid to the table's edge. He caught it before it fell and angrily gripped it so hard his knuckles turned white. The framed photograph of Hitler rattled against the wall above the filing cabinets, just as the air-raid sirens began their rising wails. These days, the sirens were barely beating the B-17s.

"Tell me, General Rauff," von Schlieffen called in German over the steady drumbeat, "how many bombers will your office's *Luegenbeurteilungen* say visited Berlin today? Four? Five?" Goering's reports to the German people on Allied air strength were so deceitfully low that Berliners were punningly changing the title of the Luftwaffe reports from *Lagebeurteilungen* to *Luegenbeurteilungen*, or "situation judgment," to "lie judgment." Many American and British bombing runs over Berlin contained a thousand planes.

Rauff ignored him. They waited tensely until the B-17s had passed. Paeffgen knew the pattern of strain. Whenever noise from the bombers offered an excuse to raise voices, the meetings dissolved into acrimony and accusation. It was easier for these General Staff officers to order thousands of men into a hopeless battle on the Soviet steppes than it was to arrange for the killing of a single man.

Paeffgen began again. "Major Carstenn and I have a new plan. Rather than have the agent come by the sea, he will come over land. We'll use a *Schleusung*." The word meant "sluice," the Department's slang for sending an agent in by an unorthodox method.

Von Schlieffen looked up, questioning clefts between his eyebrows.

34

"As you know, there are over three hundred and fifty thousand German soldiers in the United States. Regrettably, they are all in prisoner-of-war camps. Most of them were captured in North Africa."

Rauff nodded. "Our intelligence is that almost every American ship that comes to England with armaments and supplies returns to the States with German prisoners." The general paused to pull at the corner of an eye with a blunt finger, then added bitterly, "There are more German soldiers in the United States now than there were soldiers in the American army at the outbreak of the war."

"Under terms of the Geneva convention, most of them are forced to work in American factories and fields," Carstenn continued. "We understand that they were guarded very closely earlier in the war, but now it is common for ten or fifteen of them to march to work every day with only one guard. It would be fairly easy to arrange an escape and hide it long enough for the soldier to carry out his mission."

"This proposal can't be serious." Von Schlieffen opened his hands, palms up. "The difficulties would be endless. The lines of communication, arming the soldier, providing training, supplying backup, organizing his travel, and on and on."

"The major and I have much of that worked out," Paeffgen answered.

"And you are talking about a soldier apathetically sitting in a POW camp, defeated and resigned, five thousand miles from home, waiting for the war to end. Even if we could get the order in to him, he may not want to come out."

Rauff nodded. "Fat on Spam and American propaganda. An unlikely assassin."

Von Schlieffen added, "Another thing about your plan, Colonel. Our information on our Wehrmacht soldiers in American camps is very sketchy. We often don't know which soldier is in which camp. Just finding our man, much less getting him out and to the target, would be extremely difficult."

Paeffgen glanced at the major, whose chin was out defiantly, as if the generals were attacking him personally. Carstenn had hatched this plan, at which Paeffgen had at first scoffed. Slowly, very slowly, Carstenn had made it make sense.

A shrill wave of sound suddenly rushed through the op room. Paeffgen ducked. An airplane, probably a light bomber, passed a few feet over the building. The metallic shriek of its engines ended as abruptly as it had begun, immediately followed by the peculiar gurgling claps of an incendiary explosion so close and startling that Paeffgen bit deeply into his tongue. Maps shook off the wall and dust and plaster dropped from the ceiling onto the table. Von Schlieffen raised his hands over his head and quickly dropped them, perhaps thinking it undignified.

General Rauff was first to his feet. He called over his shoulder as he ran through the door, "Very close. Let's take a look."

They ran up the stairs to the fourth-floor walkway, which looked northwest over the city's low skyline. Other Department officers were already on the balcony, several pointing at flame billowing from what seconds ago had been a building a block away on Berkaerstrasse. Huge antennas that had been on the building had toppled onto the street. A cloud of flames rolled upward, dissipating in sharp tongues of fire fifty feet above the structure. A mother frantically pushed a stroller away from the crumbling building.

Disappearing west over the Grunewald Forest was a Northrop Black Widow, a twin-fuselage dive-bomber powered by two two-thousand horsepower Pratt and Whitney double Wasps, the world's most powerful airplane engines. The Americans used the Black Widow for night sorties and pinpoint bombing.

Paeffgen said around blood in his mouth, "Looks like they fell for it."

Carstenn said gravely, "That could have been us. Look at that. The building is gutted."

"What building was that?" Rauff asked, huffing heavily.

"An abandoned apartment building," Paeffgen said. "The Americans are flying in a few Black Widows with the B-17s, and while the B-17s blanket-bomb, the Black Widows go for

selected targets. The Allied bombers are searching for our intelligence units. Two weeks ago the Department's radio intercept
unit on Jagowstrasse was destroyed. So, rather than wait for a
dive-bomber to find us, we planted a decoy." Paeffgen spoke
slowly, trying to avoid tearing his tongue further. The sharp pain
was filming his eyes. "We planted several dummy antennas on
the building. Probably using the Havel River and the park as
his coordinates, the American pilot found our neighborhood and
the big antennas and released his incendiaries. It'll take them
several weeks to find out they didn't get us after all. By then
we'll have relocated."

"Was the decoy building your idea, Colonel?" Rauff asked.

Carstenn interposed loyally, "His completely."

On Rauff and von Schlieffen's recommendation, Paeffgen
would receive the Knight's Cross less than five days later. The
colonel would add it to his uniform, and leave the uniform in
his closet.

They returned to the basement. The generals raised other
objections to the operation, which Paeffgen answered with the
vagueness required by a plan that at this point was little more
than a prayer. Finally, he said, "I have listened to your many
questions, Herr Generals. Now let me ask just one. Do either
of you have an alternative suggestion?"

Fully sixty seconds passed before the colonel said quietly,
"Then by the authority given me, I am adopting this plan. We
begin today."

Paeffgen established the operations base for the POW search
in an empty warehouse on Reichenhallerstrasse several hundred
yards from the RSHA VI building. Coordinating the defense of
much of the week-old Normandy invasion, General von Schlieffen was aghast when Paeffgen requested that he transfer twenty
Wehrmacht clerks—two-thirds of the clerks at OKW—to his
command, but they were sent with the urgency that showed von
Schlieffen's appreciation of the power behind this mere colonel.

The German Red Cross's POW files were commandeered and

sent to Reichenhallerstrasse. The colonel ordered records of all captured German soldiers and sailors sent from the Reich Prisoners Office to the warehouse. Using their authority like a club, he and Major Carstenn prodded the high commands, the Operations Staff, and the Air Ministry until they were sure they had all POW records.

Ernst-Wilhelm Bohle's Auslandsorganisation had long been studying letters home from Germany's POWs. The letters were heavily edited by American censors, but much information had nevertheless been gained. The AO's files were also brought to the Reichenhallerstrasse warehouse.

The OKW and OKL staff officers railed loudest when ordered by Paeffgen to produce information regarding their commando units, the highly trained, battle-hardened battalions so secret that often one high command kept knowledge of its units from the other commands. Yet, prompted by telephone calls from Himmler's office, the generals and admirals grudgingly forwarded their files.

The long tables at the warehouse were soon covered with the records, and the sorting began. The names of snipers, munitions experts, and small-arms specialists were culled from the files and matched with the names of known POWs. Then matched with those known to be in America. Then matched with English-speakers. Then matched with those known to be at a particular camp in America. At first the sorting was chaotic and seemed to lead nowhere. But soon a few names began sifting toward Carstenn's desk.

Six days after the meeting at Department VI, a haggard Friedrich Carstenn rushed into Paeffgen's office. He placed a single folder on the colonel's desk and said tremulously, "I think we've found our man."

Paeffgen opened the folder. "And?"

"A sapper with Rommel's Third Infantry, a behind-the-lines specialist, captured in the desert by the British six months after El Alamein. Look at his record, Colonel. He is a genuine hard case. He's the man we want."

"Where is he now?" Paeffgen asked, trying to keep the excitement out of his voice.

"At the Fort Lewis POW camp, near Seattle, in the state of Washington. Northwestern United States."

"His name?"

"Captain Kurt Monck."

Paeffgen looked up from the file. His eyes met Carstenn's in a moment of shared understanding and sympathy. "Major, can this man assassinate President Roosevelt?"

"Yes. Yes, he can. I'm sure of it."

4

KURT MONCK LAY ON HIS BACK, STAR-
ing at the bunk above him. He blinked several
times, but the bunk and his imprisonment obstinately remained.
The last few minutes to the wake-up klaxon were the worst time
for him, moments when he had nothing to fight his captivity.

During his weeks at the processing station in Casablanca, he
had believed the Afrika Korps would at any moment overrun
the camp, liberating the thousands of German soldiers interned
there. Then during long hours on the deck of the Liberty ship
crossing the Atlantic, he scanned the horizon, searching for the
German cruisers or U-boats that would intercede with the American plan to take him out of the war.

Only when he disembarked at Norfolk, Virginia, and saw that
smug naval town untouched by Luftwaffe bombs did he begin
to suspect the truth. His amazement as he rolled across the
United States, through Cincinnati, Chicago, and Minneapolis,
struck him now as drollery. German soldiers had been told, and
believed as an article of faith, that much of the United States
lay in ruins, destroyed by Luftwaffe bombs in retaliation for the

massive Allied bombings of Hamburg and Berlin. All a lie. A preposterous joke.

Some of his fellow prisoners, snoring and tossing and farting in bunks around him, at first claimed the Americans had deliberately routed the train away from bombed cities. But thanks to newspapers and radios their captors freely let them have, they now knew that this mammoth country lay unscathed, and that the war was over for them and for Germany. It was only a matter of time, at most a few months. Two years in the African desert for nothing. At dawn each morning, Monck's bitterness and lethargy swarmed over him.

The horn sounded, and the two thousand POWs at the Fort Lewis camp climbed down from their bunks and began to dress. The Geneva Convention was the Bible of the American camps. The British followed it when convenient and the Russians gleefully ignored it, but the Americans, believing their soldiers in German camps would be better treated if German POWs were handled humanely, followed the Convention to the letter. The Convention stated that POWs must live in housing identical to that of their captors. Because there weren't enough barracks for the first wave of POWs to arrive at Fort Lewis, the camp's American GIs had abandoned their barracks and lived in tents identical to the Germans' for several weeks. And the Convention said enlisted men must work in the host country's nonwar industries, which the Americans took all too literally. Monck and his barracksmates were loggers.

Monck put on his ragged shirt, peppered with holes caused by twigs and saw teeth. Next came the tin pants, so called because they were stiff from dirt and pitch and saw oil. He pulled on wool socks, then his caulk (pronounced "cork") boots, which had steel toes and nail studs. He threw his duckback over his shoulder. The coat was weatherproofed with a mixture of wax and kerosene and had a huge PW painted on its back. He joined the line to the mess.

The Fort Lewis POW camp was located within the enormous

Army base a dozen miles south of Tacoma. Each prisoner compound consisted of four barracks and a mess hall, canteen, workshop, infirmary, and recreation hall. The camp at large had a hospital, chapel, showers, and a post office. Many northwesterners thought the accommodations too luxurious and referred to the camp as the Fritz Ritz.

Monck sat at the end of a table in the mess hall. As usual he sat alone, facing the door. His fellow prisoners did not know his true name or rank. A few minutes before his capture near Al-Khums, he had stripped the uniform and papers off a German corpse. The dead man's *Soldbuch*—a contraction of the German for "soldier's book," a fifteen-page booklet carried by all German soldiers, containing personal data and information on military training, transfers, and promotions—listed his new persona as Oberschuetze (Private First Class) Josef Schiller, a flak 88 loader. He had made the change because he feared the British would hang him, as they had posted a drawing of his likeness over much of North Africa. At the camp he saw no reason to revert to his prior identity.

Because letters by POWs to Wehrmacht units were not allowed, Monck had mailed a letter to Wilma Buelowius of Munich, calling her grandmother. He wrote as Schiller and said that his cousin, Kurt Monck, was the camp hygiene officer and was doing well. Monck knew the letter to General Buelowius's wife, sent to an invented Munich address, would find its way to Buelowius's headquarters and would notify them that Monck was alive. That had been enough to fulfill his duty.

He sat alone because six months ago another prisoner, an obese Wehrmacht sergeant, had insultingly imitated Monck's Swabian accent, which to Prussians sounds lisping. Monck warned the sergeant once, and the second time knocked out eight of his teeth with the handle of a Wisconsin ax. The few men in camp who still spoke with him were grateful Swabians, from Stuttgart and Freiburg.

Unlike supper, when the kitchen catered to German tastes by serving wurst or pigs' knuckles, breakfast was usually an oddity they pronounced "Veetees," which the POWs at first made palatable by adding a layer of marmalade. Then a guard told them to also put milk and sugar in the bowl, and Monck and the other Germans soon developed a taste for the flakes. He ate three bowls of them, then left the mess for the trucks at the yard gate.

He rubbed the soreness out of an elbow as he waited in the back of the truck. After living off mice and insects his last month in the desert, the logging and the Yank food had quickly put him back in shape. He had never carried much weight, and now he was back to his normal seventy-seven kilos. Swinging the ax for months had brought muscles to his arms that pushed the veins to the surface. His stomach was corded as it had been at cadet school.

In Casablanca, American doctors had tended to his sun blisters, some of which had festered for weeks and reached down to the bones of his face. His lower lip had been cracked so deeply by the African heat that stitches had been required. Monck now wore a white scar on his lip that descended to his chin and added to the sharpness of his features. There was an economy to Monck's face, with nothing wasted. It was narrow without being pinched. The nose and chin ended abruptly. The skin below his cheekbones was sunken even in well-fed times and added to his gaunt appearance. His face was a copper color, as yet not bleached by western Washington's perpetual overcast. His hazel eyes rarely registered emotion, as if ever detached and calculating, or just uncaring. Unlike many POWs, who copied the swept-back style from American magazines, Monck wore his wavy, seal-brown hair forward to hide his forehead, which had been permanently blotched by the sun.

He had been told he was handsome by a few Stuttgart women. Because of the sun's attempts to disfigure him, he didn't know if he still was. He had not been within twenty meters of a woman in three years.

The trucks began to fill. There were three men in Monck's set: the faller—usually Monck, who felled the trees—and two buckers, who sawed the downed trees into lengths with a two-man crosscut. Monck slid along the bench, making room for Hans Prahl and Ulrich Schwerin, his buckers, both Swabians.

The Speedwagon's engine cranked over, and the truck joined a line of others passing through the camp gate. When the POWs were first used as loggers, each truck was escorted by a guard jeep. Now, with the hopelessness of escape to Germany from Tacoma, Washington, frustratingly evident to each POW, only one jeep joined the convoy, trailing the last truck.

The journey east into the Cascade Mountains along the White River took an hour and a half. The trucks turned off the state highway onto the logging road, then drove by the slash of their previous day's work.

Reverence of the forest is deep in the German soul. The Saxons worshiped Yggdrasil, the great ash tree, the universal pillar upholding all things. The oak tree was sacred to the German god Donar. The majesty and solemnity of the forest still renders Germans mute. So it was each day as the POWs arrived in the Cascade wilderness. When they climbed off the trucks, the chatter ended and movement slowed as the men lifted their eyes to the firs that ranged down from Noble Knob, crossing the White River Valley, then soared skyward to the snow line of Mount Rainier. A breathtaking sight that tugged at their ancient pantheism.

The bullbuck, a kindly American and himself a man of the wilderness, gave them a moment each day before yelling, "All right, you Nazees, let's get to it."

A few minutes' work cleared the landing around the tree the bullbuck had chosen as the spar. The bullbuck, Joe Jeffries, had logged in the Cascades since he was fourteen, with a year off to fight these POWs' fathers in the Argonne. Jeffries was somewhere in his fifties, and built like a tree stump. The first day the POWs arrived at his site, he had waved away the armed military guards, then smiled benignly as he bent a crowbar into a circle with his bare hands. Jeffries wore a crew cut so close that the top of his head appeared bald. He blamed his belly, which completely hid his belt, on the six-pack of Carling he

drank every night. He spoke no German and relied on exaggerated pantomime to issue his orders.

One order was always clear: Jeffries did his own high climbing.
As the POWs sat around the trucks sharpening their axes with
stones, Jeffries slipped into a climbing belt, from which hung a
one-man saw and a topper's ax. He strapped climbing irons onto
his caulk boots. Sharp spurs protruding from the irons would
bite into a tree's bark. He walked up to the spar tree, a 160-foot-
tall Douglas fir, and rigged the climbing rope around the trunk
and to his belt.

The spar tree is the center of the area to be logged, called the
show. The spar is cleared of all limbs, then topped, and a high
lead block is strapped to the top of the tree. Through the block
runs the mainline, which drags bucked logs up the hill to the
landing. Power is provided by a gasoline engine, called a donkey,
at the base of the spar.

Jeffries began his climb, pausing to swing the topper's ax several times at each of the limbs. The POWs assembled into their
sets, with Prahl and Schwerin gathering around Monck. Schwerin
asked quietly, "Did you listen to the radio last night, Schiller?"

Monck shook his head. The camp's favorite radio show was
Your FBI.

Schwerin was a rail-thin corporal from the Fourth Armored
Brigade, captured when his parts truck threw a rod near Tell El
Eisa. "The Allies are reporting that Feldmarschall Rommel is
defending France against the invasion."

Monck's head jerked up. "Are you sure?"

"The radio said our Propaganda Ministry is releasing photos
of him preparing the interior fortifications. Pictures of him near
Rouen and Falaise. With Rommel there, maybe..."

Schwerin was cut off by a desperate cry from the spar, followed
by the dull thump of a body bouncing against the trunk. Seconds
later, Jeffries's ax hit the ground. Monck looked skyward.

What he saw was disorienting. A man, the bullbuck, 120 feet
above them, upside down.

Monck shaded his eyes against the brightness of the mountain sky. Jeffries was hanging head down, yet his spurs were still embedded in the tree. He was jackknifed at the knees, and his back was against the trunk. His arms flailed uselessly. Severed by Jeffries's ax, a length of climbing rope swayed from each belt bolt.

By the time Schwerin turned to ask what they should do, Monck had sprinted to the bullbuck's pickup truck and had lifted another set of irons, a belt, and a rope from the box behind the cab. As he ran back to the tree, he yelled at Schwerin and Prahl, "Help me rig a climbing rope."

They had done it often for Jeffries, and Schwerin and Prahl hurriedly attached the rope, ran it around the tree, and completed the connection. Monck wrapped the belt around himself, ignoring the topper's ax hanging from the belt. Monck struggled with the unfamiliar leather straps on one iron while Schwerin fastened the other iron to Monck's leg.

Other POWs stared up the tree, intoning prayers and curses, and urgently coaching Monck up the spar. A few kept their distance, not wanting to be near the trunk when the bark around Jeffries's spurs gave way under his weight.

Prahl said in a terrified whisper, "He's not moving. God, you may be too late."

Monck stepped up to the splayed roots at the tree's base. He flipped one end of the rope that circled the tree, and it bit into the bark at a higher point. He kicked his leg at the tree, and the spur caught. He stepped up. He planted his other leg, then pitched the other end of the rope higher up the tree and pulled it taut. He yanked the spur out and thrust it higher into the bark. Monck quickly found a rhythm, and Schwerin and Prahl grew smaller beneath him.

Monck concentrated on the bark passing in front of him, trying to push from his mind that he was working on instinct and had never before done any high climbing. He cinched the rope tighter as the trunk narrowed. He drew near enough to Jeffries to hear him moan. Splinters bounced off Monck as one of Jeffries's spurs began to peel away from the trunk.

Suddenly Monck's left leg collapsed and, off balance, he slid down the bark until his knee was at his chin. His spur had glanced off the hard stub of a branch Jeffries had cut a few moments before. Monck began to topple left, with his jammed left leg powerless to stop him. Helpless on the ground, Schwerin yelled an alarm.

Monck fiercely pulled the climbing rope with his right hand, taking the weight off his leg. He stabbed the left spur into the bark, and it held. He pulled himself upright and caught his breath.

He was twenty feet away from the bullbuck's face, which glowed red from blood that was suffusing it. Monck began again with his cadence up the spar. Jeffries's severed rope slapped against him, and the German quickly covered the distance to the bullbuck.

Jeffries was breathing stertorously, and he gritted his teeth in pain. He was conscious.

Monck cinched the rope to free a hand. He then pulled the bullbuck's head and shoulders away from the trunk. He climbed several steps, bringing the logger up with him.

Jeffries yelped in pain, then said quickly to cover it, "My knee. It's torn up." He stared at Monck. "I figured it'd be you, if anybody."

Monck used English for the first time since the desert. "I'm going to push you up as I climb." He flicked the belt higher up the bark and spiked up two steps, pushing Jeffries's shoulder until the bullbuck was doubled against himself. Monck climbed and again pushed the logger higher. Soon Jeffries was upright.

To take as much weight as possible off the German, Jeffries hugged the tree, which at this height had the girth of a man. "You'll have to yank my left iron out of the tree. With the knee gone, I can't do it."

Monck sank on his rigging and gripped the bullbuck's ankle. He jerked the spike free. The ground and the POWs swayed distantly beneath him.

"Can you carry my weight?" Jeffries asked.

"Yes."

"I'll free the other leg on my own, then I'm real careful-like going to turn around to face you. I'm going to be doing a lot of climbing on you, so brace yourself."

Jeffries pulled his right spur free of the bark and let himself settle back against the POW. He slowly began his pivot, letting Monck bring the damaged knee around until Jeffries was facing Monck, straddling his hips and bear-hugging him.

Monck began descending, ignoring the growing ache in his knees from the bow-legged stance.

"What happened?" Monck asked Jeffries, whose doughy face was two inches from his own. The captain was breathing heavily, and sweat coursed into his eyes.

"All my life in the woods, and it never happened until today." The bullbuck spoke with the breathless loquacity of a man who has just learned of the governor's pardon. "I was swinging at a branch, maybe being a little careless, coming in at too low an angle. My ax bounced off a knot and sank right through the climbing rope. I was upside down before I could shit. I'll tell you. . . . Say, where do you get off speaking English?"

Monck ignored the logger's question, concentrating on the unaccustomed movements of high climbing and the satisfying burn of exhaustion in his legs. Near the ground, hands reached for them and pulled the bullbuck off Monck. A dozen POWs carried him to the first-aid truck.

Monck started back up the spar. His legs churned, and his arms moved the rope with a newfound mastery. He willed strength back into his legs. Without Jeffries's weight, he felt light and confident. More than that. Joyous. And free.

The Secret Service investigation a month later would conclude that Kurt Monck stayed atop the spar—140 feet high—another full hour, gazing east across the Cascades.

5

C OLONEL ERICH HOTH WAS ABRUPTLY
picked up by a black Horch staff car in Cherbourg, where he commanded the forty-fourth Engineering Battalion, which was frantically constructing a death zone of mines
and tank traps to stop the American VII Corps. It was Tuesday,
June 20, 1944, and the Americans were only five miles from
Cherbourg. Without explanation, he was driven to the airfield
near Cap Lévy and was unceremoniously told to climb into the
Heinkel waiting there for him.

Three hours later, with mud still clinging to his boots, he was
ushered into Department VI's new headquarters in the Reichenhallerstrasse warehouse in Berlin.

"Colonel, I am Dr. Theodor Paeffgen, and this is my assistant,
Major Friedrich Carstenn. I head the Department's North American section. Please have a seat."

Hoth remained at rigid parade rest. His face was a mash of
rage and fright. Crescents were bitten into the corners of his
mouth, and his thick brows were low with anger. Only his eyes
betrayed his fear, darting between Paeffgen and Major Carstenn,
who was dressed in his black SS uniform, loathed and feared by

regular army officers. Three weeks before, SS men in a black Opel had pulled Brigadier General Guenther Hoepner off the Calais beach, and he had not been seen since. Not even Rommel could get an explanation from the SS's Prinz Albrechtstrasse headquarters.

Hoth's brown hair was wind-tossed and skewed to one side, giving him the appearance of movement even as he stood still. From the oil stains, barbed-wire tears, and four wound stripes on his uniform, Paeffgen guessed the colonel's men had for him the special respect given an officer who commands in the field.

Hoth said in a brittle voice, "There is an explanation due me, Herr Doctor."

"Yes, of course." Paeffgen returned to his desk, just moved from the abandoned headquarters on Berkaerstrasse. "First let me assure you, Colonel, that you will be back in Cherbourg with your men before nightfall, and that General Meise will be given a full and satisfactory explanation of your sudden disappearance."

Hoth shrank with relief. "I will have that chair."

"Colonel, I must ask that you answer certain questions about one of your subordinates in Africa and not ask any questions in return." Paeffgen allowed himself a small smile, gone almost before it appeared. "Is that all right with you?"

"I was bluntly told of your authority by the SS Sturmbann-fuehrer who came to Cherbourg," Hoth said testily. "It appears it has to be all right with me."

"You were under the command of Major General Karl Buelowius in Africa. His task in November 1942 was to slow the British western advance during Rommel's retreat. Apparently Buelowius and you did a masterly job, as seventy thousand Wehrmacht soldiers crossed two thousand miles of desert with surprisingly little loss of life, despite Montgomery pressing you the entire distance. You slowed the British advance by sowing anti-personnel and antitank mines behind Rommel as he retreated. Is all this fairly accurate?"

Hoth dipped his chin, not having the slightest idea where the

questions were leading and whether he was incriminating himself
in some way.

"Do you recall Captain Kurt Monck, who was under your
command?"

Hoth's mouth widened. "You bet I do."

"Do you know where he is now?" Paeffgen asked.

"His bones are baking in the desert with the others, I'd guess."

Paeffgen blew on his hands. "He is in a POW camp in the
state of Washington, in the United States."

Hoth's eyebrows lifted. "Well, I'll be goddamned." He laughed
shortly. "It just figures that he'd make it."

Carstenn was making notes behind a clipboard. "Tell us about
Monck's assignment in Africa."

"I'm not too sure what he did during the good days, during
the Afrika Korps's advances east, other than that he commanded
a sapper company. His men stole up to the enemy's lines, cut
barbed wire, defused explosives the British had planted on bridges
and ammo dumps."

"So he wasn't under your authority until the retreat?" Carstenn
asked.

"Not until after El Alamein, our great disaster." Hoth's eyes
shifted south, as if he could see the African coast through the
warehouse walls. "My men planted *Glasmine* 43s and *Schuetzen-
minen* all along the Via Balbia, the coast highway across Libya.
But Buelowius had another idea, and that was to send some men
behind the British lines to do as much damage and cause as much
confusion as possible."

"Kurt Monck?"

"And seven others. English-speakers with explosives experience. Eight were all we could find with those qualifications."

"Were they successful?" Paeffgen asked.

"They were each given an *Agentenfunk* and told a time and
band to report on...."

Paeffgen's glanced at Carstenn, whose readable face was already working the possibilities. Monck was a radio operator.
They let Hoth continue.

"Only four made the first report. Monck broadcast on the Morse that he saw two of them executed by a British firing squad. Caught behind enemy lines out of uniform."

"How long did Monck report?"

Hoth could not keep the pride out of his voice. "The others lasted less than a week. But Monck was out there six months. He crossed enemy lines November 4, 1942, near Fuka on the Egyptian coast, and we lost contact with him in early May 1943. I assumed the desert or the British got him."

Paeffgen asked dubiously, "All that time, sabotaging the British army?"

Hoth nodded.

"How is it he speaks English?"

Hoth smiled tightly. "You have much of this information on that desk in front of you, and you're verifying it. Right?"

"We never refuse information, Colonel," Paeffgen said noncommittally.

"Before we turned him into a sapper, Monck was an engineer. As I recall, he spent a year at an engineering school in England in the 1930s. Birmingham, I think."

"Where did he get the explosives?"

"He carried several pounds of plastic across the frontier with him. He probably stole the rest. Maybe made them out of artillery shells. Believe me, he knows all there is to know about iron rations. He planted more explosives in those months than a Junkers crew could have dropped."

Paeffgen asked, "Do you remember where?"

Hoth prodded his memory by pulling his chin. "In late November of 1942, he blew up an artillery dump near Mersa Matruh. A week later, he dropped grenades into the cockpits of three De Havilland Mosquitoes at the RAF airstrip at Derna. In December, he burned down a supply depot at Benghazi. He did a lot of these nasty little tricks, maybe without much effect in and of themselves. But Monck was a master at tying up an enormous amount of British resources."

Hoth stopped when a secretary, an ash-blonde no more than

seventeen years old, brought them coffee. The colonel was surprised to taste actual coffee, rather than the ground weeds he and his troops were accustomed to. He sipped slowly, savoring it.

When she left the room, he continued, "In January 1943, when Rommel counterattacked with the Twenty-first Panzer just east of Tripoli at Homs—a small feint to guard the retreat—our Panzers overran a British intelligence truck. There, in much more detail than Monck had sent over his *Agentenfunk*, was a record of his little war. It seems that each time Monck set off a charge, he left a message. Three flat rocks piled on top of each other."

Hoth tipped the cup again. "There was an entire company of British investigators searching for him. And wherever they thought Monck was, the British quarantined the area and moved men and machinery away. Pretty soon the Arabs caught on and started stacking three rocks around the desert just for the fun of seeing the British scramble. He received a couple of posthumous medals. I suppose they're not so posthumous now, with him alive."

"Was he passing as a British soldier?" Carstenn asked.

"Most of the time. He also had an Arab kaffiyeh and robe with him—not that he'd pass as an Arab at closer than a hundred meters. It must have worked, though."

"Think about this next question carefully, Colonel," Paeffgen said levelly. "Could Monck kill a man?"

Hoth laughed coldly. "Especially if there were some challenge to it."

"What about now, after more than a year in a POW camp?" Paeffgen persisted.

"Monck has taken the Wehrmacht oath. He will do what is ordered." Hoth looked scathingly at Carstenn. "Even your kind has sworn obedience to someone or something."

Paeffgen overlooked the insult to the SS. "We have nothing further, Colonel. The secretary is going to walk you to another office for a short talk with our chief radio officer. He'll want all you know about Monck's radio transmissions."

Hoth rose from his chair and placed the cup on Paeffgen's desk. He was at the door before he turned to them. "I should mention something else about Kurt Monck, Doctor." He formed his words carefully. "One night after a walking barrage by British mortars, we heard screams from a German soldier from somewhere in front of our line. He must have been injured, probably in shock, and had just wandered out into the desert toward the English positions. His cries carried to us with the howl of the desert ghibli, which had been filling our eyes and mouths with sand for several days. Suddenly Monck left the trench and began scrabbling along the desert floor. He crawled half a kilometer on his elbows, stabbing the ground with his dagger all the way, searching for British mines. Very dangerous work, and it took him two hours. By the time he found the *Landser*, the boy was dead. Monck tucked the boy's intestines back inside him, then pulled the body onto his back and started crawling back to our dugout. When Monck arrived, he was covered with the boy's blood and his own blood from the rocks and cactus. And his left hand was puffed up from a scorpion bite. I should have disciplined him for acting without orders, but everyone in that trench knew it could have been him out there, and was glad the boy had been brought back."

"An inspiring story, Colonel," Paeffgen said. "But heroism was common in Africa. We have thousands of heroes in the American POW camps."

"You have missed the point," Hoth said in a tone indicating he had expected nothing less. "His heroics were misguided at the outset. But they became utterly stupid once Monck discovered the boy was dead. What sense was there in bringing back one body when there were hundreds of others lying about? Monck did it as an impulsive exercise. He was gripped by a passion to finish an absurd task."

Paeffgen smiled narrowly.

"The man is fearless," Hoth said. "And he's resourceful, or else he wouldn't have lasted in the desert behind the British lines all those months. But there's something else there. I saw it in his eyes after his long crawl. A bit of madness. Our fabled *Todessuechligkeit*, a thirst for death. You'll need to watch him, Doctor."

After Hoth closed the door behind him, Paeffgen exulted, "You were right, Friedrich. Monck is our man."

The buzzer rang three times. The president was moving. White House Secret Service supervising agent Mike O'Brien glanced at the signal board above the desk in the tiny usher's office. On the board was listed each room, elevator, and corridor in the White House. An arrow popped up, indicating the elevator. Franklin Roosevelt was traveling from the Executive Wing to his study on the second floor and would be using the elevator.

O'Brien had been talking with Vice Admiral James McIntire, the president's bald, amiable physician, who quickly moved to the elevator to wait for Roosevelt. The few seconds of the ascent to the second floor would be all the time granted the doctor that day for the eyeball physical. McIntire would note the color of the president's skin, the brightness of his eye, and the amount of cyanosis in his fingernails and lips. Normally the doctor would also attempt to gauge Roosevelt's mood. But today he knew the president would be jubilant, because in a few moments Lucy Mercer Rutherfurd, the love of Roosevelt's life for the past thirty years, would visit for lunch.

O'Brien heard the commotion of power down the corridor. The president, his secretary Grace Tully, press secretary Steve Early, and valet Arthur Prettyman emerged from Tully's office and were immediately flanked by four Secret Service agents. Roosevelt rolled down the wooden ramp from the office, then through the large French doors. The party turned right and passed the swimming pool and the flower conservatory, then across the areaway. The president came into O'Brien's view.

The agent had seen Roosevelt several times each day for two years, yet the effect had yet to diminish. The president's vitality made O'Brien feel physically larger, as if he were being stretched. Power and confidence radiated from the president and filled anyone he was near. That three beers could do the same to O'Brien was no slight to the president.

Roosevelt rolled by at speed. His leonine head was tilted back, as if to avail himself of his bifocal pince-nez. The black Bakelite cigarette holder jutted from his jaw. He smoked twenty to thirty Camels a day, regardless of the admiral's harping. The president was smiling around the Bakelite and complimenting Grace Tully on her hair or dress, judging from her return smile.

Roosevelt's large hands confidently guided the wheelchair to the elevator door. He was wearing a blue wool suit O'Brien had seen a hundred times. Patches had been sewn onto the legs of the pants where his metal leg braces had rubbed through the wool. Prettyman, a black retired chief petty officer, lifted the wheels from the stone floor across the small gap into the elevator. McIntire followed, and the elevator door closed.

The four agents ran up the stairs to meet the president on the second floor. O'Brien looked at his schedule of the day's events. He knew almost everything that occurred in the White House before it happened. A few seconds later Grace Tully appeared again. She arranged the meetings between the president and Lucy Mercer Rutherfurd.

"She's at the gate," she said to O'Brien. "Back in a moment."

O'Brien grinned at the secretary. He had a brilliant Irish smile, full of teeth. His eyes were snared by deep lines, as if he had spent his life looking into the sun, rather than at the hands of those approaching the president. His hair had once been too black and shiny, but fashion had come around to him, thanks to Frank Sinatra. His jacket hung on him at an angle, as he could not afford to have it tailored around his .38 revolver. O'Brien waited until an agent nodded that the areaway was secure, then climbed the stairs to the first-floor north entrance.

He approached the usher. "Mrs. Rutherfurd will be here in a few moments, Edwin. Will you clear the halls?"

The usher knew the routine. Lucy Mercer Rutherfurd appeared on no White House guest lists. Her name was rarely spoken aloud by White House personnel. Those at the White House during her visits—whether they were military chiefs of staff or Eleanor Roosevelt's assorted hangers-on—were politely asked to vacate the hallways. When Roosevelt and Mrs. Rutherfurd were together he would brook no interruptions. Only once had O'Brien had to enter the Oval Office to interrupt their meal. They had switched to French and had spoken through his urgent whispers into the president's ear. Roosevelt had nodded curtly and had never mentioned the intrusion. And, by Christ, neither had O'Brien.

The buzzer on one side of the entrance hall rang once, indicating a visitor was climbing the steps to the north portico. O'Brien straightened his tie.

Lucy Mercer Rutherfurd glided into the entrance hall from the north portico. She moved with a grace that instantly made O'Brien feel a bit awkward. And she was a looker, O'Brien thought as his eyes followed her. She was tall, willowy, with a long neck and a full bosom. Her sable hair had a few gray wisps, but her face retained a youthful energy. Her smoke-colored eyes were beneath lilting eyebrows that with a slight rise could raise a laugh or break tension or send a servant scurrying off, or, O'Brien suspected, do virtually anything else. Her smile was quick and understanding. In contrast to Eleanor Roosevelt, whose perpetual energy was amplified by hands that never stilled and a trilling voice, Mrs. Rutherfurd always seemed relaxed and gay. Not that there would ever be a side-by-side comparison, as Mrs. Rutherfurd appeared at the White House only when Eleanor was away.

"Good afternoon, Mr. O'Brien," she said as she reached the stairs to the second floor. Her voice had the quality of velvet. She held his gaze a second longer than necessary, silently thanking him for his part in the rendezvous. She rounded the turn of the stairs and was gone.

The buzzer rang three times. The president and Mrs. Rutherfurd were now in the second-floor study.

The president would have summarily fired O'Brien had he known the agent had run a background check on Mrs. Rutherfurd. She had been born to wealth and station, to a prominent New England family that later lost its fortune, forcing Lucy to find work. She had been hired as Eleanor's social secretary in 1913, eight years after Eleanor and Franklin were married. Suggestions of Lucy and Franklin's enduring love darted in and out of the Secret Service report, but only a few facts were available.

She had attended each of his inaugurations, sitting at a distance in a car provided by the Service. She had married wealthy Winthrop Rutherfurd, twenty years her senior, who had died recently. Some of Roosevelt's aides—those few who knew anything at all about Lucy Rutherfurd—believed she and Roosevelt did not see each other during the marriage, but O'Brien knew different. He also knew that since Wintie Rutherfurd died, Roosevelt telephoned her almost daily, and the frequency of their visits had increased dramatically. And all but the White House visits were an unbridled panic for the Secret Service.

Roosevelt seldom announced their trysts in advance, even to O'Brien. Seemingly at the spur of the moment, the president would order his seven-passenger Ford to the gate. With hastily arranged Secret Service escort cars fore and aft, Roosevelt would be driven up Connecticut Avenue to Dupont Circle, then left on P street into Georgetown. The entourage would stop next to a sedan parked near the Oak Hill Cemetery. Mrs. Rutherfurd would emerge from the sedan and quickly flow into the backseat of the limousine with the president. The glass partition seperating them from the driver would slide up, and the procession would slowly wind around Georgetown for an hour, when she would be returned to her car.

Or, during a meticulously planned trip to the retreat at Warm Springs, Georgia, on the president's train, POTUS (for President of the United States), Roosevelt would abruptly announce a side trip to Aiken, South Carolina, where Mrs. Rutherfurd summered. The train had once sat on the rusty siding at Union Street in Aiken for fully a week. At these times, the Secret Service's iron bubble around the president was severely strained.

That most of his aides and family and the public knew nothing of these assignations amused O'Brien, whose very task it was to keep the president's movements secret. But then the press's self-censorship regarding the Allied leaders' travels during the war was almost absolute, as witnessed by Churchill's month-long stay at the White House in 1941, of which the American and English public remained in ignorance.

And surely the president's partner in his great works, his wife Eleanor, knew nothing of his meetings with Lucy Mercer Rutherfurd. Or said nothing.

O'Brien paced the hallway. He nervously ran his thumb over the empty money clip in his pocket, kept there for that purpose. He was always on edge on duty, even during an easy day, like this one. The thousand details. The gnawing suspicion he had forgotten something, had permitted one seemingly insignificant crack to appear in the president's shield, worked on him like an abrasive.

Max Smythe, O'Brien's assistant, entered the hallway carrying a briefcase with the plans for the president's journey to San Diego in three weeks for the Democratic National Convention. The two agents sat on Dolley Madison's loveseat and discussed security arrangements for the thirty-minute stop in Chicago en route to San Diego. An hour passed quickly. The buzzer rang once.

Mrs. Rutherfurd descended the stairs a few steps ahead of the usher. "Thank you, Mr. O'Brien," she said as she walked toward the north portico.

Again he returned her quick smile. He watched as she entered the backseat of a Cadillac.

Smythe, called Pancho Villa by other agents because of his black walrus mustache, whispered, "What's the boss going to do without her in San Diego?"

"Why don't you ask the president personally, next time you have tea with him?" O'Brien answered acidly. "In the meantime, let's return our attention to the Chicago stopover."

Disobeying the president's direct order, the Secret Service would later search assiduously for a connection between Lucy Mercer Rutherfurd and Captain Kurt Monck. There was none, of course. She was an unwitting accomplice.

6

"I DEMAND YOU TELL ME WHO YOU ARE," Detlef Becker yelled, his voice tight with anger. *"Das ist ein Befehl!"* That is an order.

Kurt Monck held the rumpled sheet of paper up to the candlelight. "It doesn't appear you can give me orders anymore, does it, Herr Generalmajor? Not according to this."

General Becker snatched the letter from Monck's hand. "If you think I'll risk the welfare of this entire camp for one flak-loading shit, you're dead wrong. No piece of paper can make me do that. So you'd better come up with some answers. Who are you? Why would I be ordered at all costs"—Becker's voice rose again as he repeated himself—"*at all costs* to get you out of this camp?"

Monck was silent. He had never before spoken with the Fort Lewis camp's senior POW officer. Monck had been roused from sleep by the general's aide and told to report to the general's quarters in the First Compound. It was two hours past lights out, two hours after his barrackmates' last stanza of their favorite song, "Don't Fence Me In," sung in English with great gusto. The aide had escorted Monck under Compound B's perimeter wire and through the maze of barracks in Compound A, stopping several times to let the glaring nimbus of a searchlight pass them.

The clapboard shack Becker called his headquarters contained a potbellied stove, a bunk, and a desk made of apple crates. The Americans allowed the senior POW officers to administer most of the camp's activities. On the desk was a pencil holder and shoebox containing three-by-five index cards. A duty roster was tacked to the wall above the desk.

Becker had been the ranking officer at the Afrika Korps's office of the Quartermaster General. He was captured at Tripoli and had thought it just as well, as his food warehouses had been empty for weeks.

The general was thin to the point of illness. Some thought he was starving himself, not wanting the disgrace of one day returning to Germany with more meat on his bones than his wife and children had. His hands were etched with tendons, and his Adam's apple bobbed with each syllable. He was bald, and veins mapped his head. His teeth were strong and yellow. His eyes were sunk deeply and bagged.

Becker stared down at the sheet of paper. "Do you know anything about this message, how it got here?"

"I don't know anything about it."

Becker looked at Monck as if trying to peer through a clouded window, searching for signs of deceit. He couldn't read him. He said, "The original was in an envelope tied with twine around a rock. The rock was thrown at one of our loggers. The envelope had my name on it, so it was brought to me. The message inside was in a drop code the Quartermaster Corps had used in Africa. A simple code, probably outdated now, but one Berlin would know that I had used. I had one of my radio operators from Tripoli decode it this evening."

Becker ran the back of a hand across his mouth, as if trying to wipe away the distaste caused by the meeting. "Let me ask you, Schiller, or whatever your goddam name is, does that sound like the start of a well-planned operation to you? A high-powered, top-secret mission of some sort, begun with a stone thrown at a nameless POW out in the woods?"

Monck shrugged. "How else would a message have gotten in? You haven't worked out a mail code through Red Cross deliveries. And as far as I know, there are no two-way shortwaves in camp. How else?"

Becker wanted to swing at the private's oblique grin, sitting there with his hidden knowledge and competence. This man and this letter were dangerous to his men. Nothing good could come of this. The general was about to order Monck out and put the paper in the candle's flame when the door suddenly swung open.

Goosestep Schmundt marched into the office and imperiously held his hand out for the sheet of paper. "I should have been told of this message by you, Herr General," he said as he pulled the paper out of Becker's hand. "Not by one of my men on the logging crew."

Schmundt read it with his malevolent eyes, a grin growing. Hans "Goosestep" Schmundt was the camp's senior party officer, who had crossed the Austria–Germany border to join the Nazi Party in 1930 and now held the rank of Ortsgruppenleiter, the equivalent of captain. Because he had been born in Vienna, the prisoners called him the Nazi in three-quarter time. Most captured party members were interned at the camp at Alva, Oklahoma, but a few had slipped through the screening interviews.

Schmundt was despised in the camp because he replaced the leather heels of his camp-issue shoes with wood so they would click loudly when snapped together, because he had attempted to set up a kangaroo court for POWs not adequately spouting the party line (an attempt quashed by Becker, but not without a struggle), and because he was keeping a list of prisoners who were disloyal to the Reich to be turned over to the Gestapo once the camp was liberated.

He was a short man who stood with his spine so erect it appeared to be hurting him. His tawny hair formed a widow's peak not far above his nose. His gestures were always histrionic and his words overspoken, as if he were addressing the back row of a Nuremberg rally. He had sewn epaulet straps to the shoulders of his POW coat and had dyed his camp-issue T-shirt black.

"Finally, finally we've heard." Schmundt's hands were shaking with excitement. "We haven't been forgotten. Look at this, General. It orders you to gain the freedom of one Josef Schiller"—his verminous eyes glanced at Monck—"at all costs. It puts you under his command until this is accomplished. It orders you to hide his escape for as long as possible. The signature line has the name von Schlieffen. Who is he?"

"He is at OKW," Becker said quietly. "I reported to him when I was in Africa."

"You must be Schiller," the Ortsgruppenleiter said.

Monck remained silent. Schmundt fidgeted under his stare.

"Is there a problem here, General?" Schmundt asked finally. "We have our orders. Let's start the planning."

"I'm treating the message as a hoax, Schmundt," Becker said wearily. "Some American's idea of a good time."

"It's no hoax," Schmundt insisted. "There's a confirm line on it—"

"A joke," Becker cut in. "For God's sake, Schmundt, read the newspapers they give us. Our Fatherland has about six months left. Anything Schiller is ordered to do now would be pissing into the wind."

"That attitude is typical of you, Becker," Schmundt said with a crabbed voice. "It has infected the entire camp. And it's my guess that were it not for the four names at the bottom of the page, you certainly would treat it as a prank. Ida, Paula, Angela, and Maria." He looked squarely at the general. "Those names are a message to you, General. A signal authenticating the orders. Are they not?"

Becker took a long breath. "The first two are my mother and sister's names." He turned to Monck, fearing the confirmation he was about to hear.

"And the last two are the names of my mother and sister," Monck added.

"You have no choice, General," Schmundt said triumphantly. "A POW remains a soldier in his army. These orders are absolutely binding on you, just as if you were in Germany receiving them personally from von Schlieffen."

Becker stared mournfully at Monck. There was defeat in his voice. "You bastard. You're going to hurt every man in this camp."

Schmundt lifted a sheet of paper and pencil from the desk, wet the pencil with his tongue, and drew several lines. "We'll set up task forces. We have a printer in my barrack who can forge anything. We'll have committees for uniforms, money..."

Monck interrupted, "Don't do any of that." He looked at Becker. "There must be more to the message. An address."

The general drew a rumpled envelope from his back pocket. "This was also around the rock. There's an address in here. I had my radio operator decode it. I asked him not to tell me the address, so it will be blind to me."

Goosestep Schmundt interjected, "You won't last an hour outside unless we do lots of planning. Hiding your escape will take a great amount of coordination. Faking roll calls and bed checks..."

Monck rose from his seat. "You're out of it completely, Goosestep. I don't want you to mention the message or this meeting tonight to anyone. Is that understood?"

Nobody talked to Schmundt this way, not even the general. His mouth narrowed to a stubborn line, and he drew himself up mightily to launch into a speech about National Socialism's hierarchy.

Monck's hand blurred. It appeared again, clutching Schmundt's throat high under the jawbone. Schmundt was almost lifted off the ground. He gasped feebly and clawed ineffectually at the hand.

"I don't want you meddling in this, Goosestep. You're out. Don't make me visit your barrack to tell you again." Monck waited another punishing minute, then released the Ortsgruppenleiter, who staggered onto the bench against the wall, kneading his throat. He croaked piteously trying to draw a breath.

Becker looked balefully at the pathetic caricature on the bench. In an old man's voice, he said, "*Wir wurden zum Narren gehalten, und wir haben uns selbst belogen.*" We were fooled, and we were fooling ourselves.

"General, I want only one thing from you," Monck said. "Tomorrow you are to personally tell my buckers, Prahl and Schwerlin, that they are to obey me implicitly, without question or hesitation."

"You've already planned your escape. This message only gives you a reason to go. Am I right?"

Monck opened the door. His smile was vulpine. "Nothing but a mental exercise until today. I'll be gone before the week is out." He glanced at Schmundt, whose face was still red from pain and embarrassment. "I'm afraid Goosestep won't miss me at all."

These were the last few moments of Walter Shaw's life, and had he known, he would have been glad he was spending them fishing. It was Tuesday, June 27, a cloudless day in the Cascade Mountains.

Shaw was working the White River in the morning shadow of the Noble Knob. He was using a No. 3 Colorado spinner with a worm hook and ten inches of cuttyhunk. His Orvis rod was made of Tonkin cane, the best in the world. His fly reel was a Fflueger. He stripped off about twenty feet of line and expertly lobbed the rig across the river, where it splashed down a few feet above an eddy. The line settled on the river.

Shaw knew there wasn't much in the river this time of year. Maybe a few summer-run steelhead. Small ones. But, like most steelheaders, he loved the fishing more than the fish.

Shaw's face rippled with light reflected off the river. His features were open and unaffected, and his eyes were the color of the river. He wore his favorite red-and-black mackinaw, with four pockets in front and a large game pouch in back. His felt hat had flies and spinners stuck to it. He was standing in two feet of water. The rubberized canvas hip waders kept out the water, but not the chill of the glacier-fed river. He cast again, patiently testing the same eddy.

Guilt is one of fishing's great pleasures, Shaw smiled to himself as he watched his line drift. Guilt about leaving the wife behind on fishing trips. Guilt about filling the hip flask with a couple of stiff pulls, harder to do now that the Great Whiskey Shortage of 1944 was under way. And guilt that Shaw was one of the few folks these days who could drive into the mountains to fish, as he was a C-card holder, an essential driver given a large allotment of rationed gasoline. Shaw was a physician.

He was a Portland doctor who had driven north to visit his mother in Seattle. His wife had pretended to believe his story. And he had spent several torturous hours with the old lady. But fishing in these rivers was the reason for his trip. Several times a year he came north. Sometimes with a few buddies, sometimes alone.

Standing on the banks of the White River in the lee of Mount Rainier was as close to a religious experience as he would ever have, Shaw supposed, checking the drag button on his reel. The beauty of the valley was cleansing—a communion. The river swirled and bubbled and churned downstream, pausing only at backwaters behind boulders or in deep ruts under the far bank. The shore was a jumble of rocks, uprooted stumps, and water-polished branches, deposited there during the high waters of the spring run-off. Firs and spruce lined the river with blue-green swaths. On a nearby branch, a western tanager, with its yellow belly and bright-red head, waited until a moth flew too near. The bird launched itself into the hair, snatched the insect with its beak, and flapped back to its perch.

Shaw pulled his flask from a pocket and swallowed gratefully. Why fishing and whiskey were so naturally bonded together was one of the world's great mysteries. One wouldn't do without the other.

Perhaps his shadow thrown on the water was making the fish leery. He reeled in and walked upstream. With each step, he planted his boot carefully on the damp, mossy boulders. A clump of white birch trees was upstream a few yards. He would hide in their shade.

He looked up the bank. The state road paralleled the river.

His car, a 1939 Buick, was parked against the safety railing. Occasionally a logging truck sped by, its engine screaming as the driver used compression to slow the rig. There was no other traffic.

Shaw found a spot beneath the birches. Fishing is a sport of instinct, and his instinct told him here. For balance, he wedged his boot against a rock beneath the waterline. He glanced at the worm gob beneath the spinner. Still in good shape. Once in a while he used periwinkles. Today struck him as a worm day. He pulled off some line and brought the rod back to cast.

Kurt Monck's instinct had also told him here, where the fisherman's shadow would be hidden by tree shadows and the steelhead might remain unaware of his presence. The barbed-wire garrote shot over the fisherman's head and found his neck. Monck yanked back on the tree-branch handles and crossed the wire behind the victim's head. He planted his knee in the middle of Shaw's back for leverage and savagely wrenched on the garrote. The wire sank into Shaw's neck, blood spurting from where the barbs dug deep.

Shaw scratched aimlessly at his neck for a few seconds. So embedded was the wire that his fingers never found it. His tongue extruded between his teeth. His last sight was the swift current, marbled with his own blood, carrying away his bamboo rod. His knees buckled in death. The German dragged him back into the trees.

Monck unwrapped the garrote and threw it into the middle of the river. He pulled the clothes off the body. Five minutes later, the German was wearing the fisherman's clothes. And the body was wearing tin pants and the duckback with the white "PW" painted on the back.

He lifted the body over his shoulders in a fireman's carry. With the hip waders in one hand, the German climbed away from the river. He trod carefully on the loose rocks and crumbling dirt below the guard rail. As his head gained the level of the asphalt, Monck glanced left and right around the fisherman's parked Buick for traffic. He high-stepped over the guard rail and ran across the road, the body bouncing across his back. He and the body disappeared in the forest undergrowth.

Monck stopped only once, to bury the hip waders under a shallow layer of dirt and moss. He ascended the wooded slope toward the logging show, pushing through snares of huckleberry bushes and ferns. Under the high canopy, the forest floor was murky and sodden. Bright blisters of sunlight rarely dappled the ground. The sough of the river receded behind him.

He heard a faint "Timber" ahead, the *R* rolled heavily, followed by the crash of a tree falling. His shoulders began to ache under the load.

Monck angled his way south through the trees. Prahl was felling to cover Monck's absence. Prahl and Schwerin's fright had begun four days ago, when General Becker had ordered them to obey Monck without question. It increased as they watched Monck make the garrote out of a length of barbed wire he had found. And today they were almost apoplectic with fear when Monck abruptly announced he was going for a walk and left the show with his garrote. Monck had seen the fisherman during the logging convoy's trip to the show that morning. The two American guards had been drinking coffee on the landing, their rifles in the back of a pickup and their attention on the sports page.

Hidden by a schoolmarm—a tree with a large fork—Monck surveyed the show. He could see only Prahl and Schwerin, dutifully bucking a fallen tree out of view of the bullbuck and the other loggers. Monck could hear the steady chop of a faller in the distance, but the axman was hidden behind a slight rise. With the body still draped over his shoulders, Monck ran for the mainline.

Prahl turned at the sound of Monck's heavy footfalls and was so astonished at the sight that he released his end of the two-man saw. Schwerin was on the push, and the saw—nicknamed a misery whip—buckled and slapped his chest. He stumbled on a limb, but caught himself. He, too, turned to the sound.

"Oh Jesus, no," Prahl gasped. His blond hair had been receding almost since birth. His high forehead and his round eyes made him always appear astonished. Now he looked at Monck with wild-eyed horror. "What have you done?"

Schwerin's face sagged. "I knew it. I knew it." He pulled off his blue watch cap and closed his eyes. Schwerin had seen death on the desert, but had never expected it in the protected womb of the Pacific Northwest forest. The sight of the body made terrifying memories swarm over him. He sagged against the log.

Monck carried the fisherman along the bucked log, toward the length closest to the mainline. The mainline was used to yard the logs, to drag them from the cutting strip to the landing.

"Get ready to choke it," Monck ordered. He grunted as he dumped the body in front of the log. With his foot he jammed the corpse against the log, ramming the head against the bark on the ground.

With rubbery legs, Prahl staggered toward Monck. "What are you doing? You've got a dead man there...."

"Choke the log, Prahl. And you, Schwerin, get the butt rigging ready."

Prahl glanced frantically up the mainline, fearing they were being observed. "Schiller, listen to me. I know Schwerin and I have been ordered to...."

Monck's voice was a feral snarl. "Do as I tell you. Don't think, just do it. Choke the log."

Prahl numbly lifted his choker off a limb. The choker is a short length of cable with a swivel and hook on each end. With his eyes never leaving the body, Schwerin dug a choker hole under the log. Prahl slipped the choker through the hole and noosed the log. He attached the choker to the butt rigging and it to the mainline. The log was ready.

"Blow the signal," Monck commanded, standing away from the log.

"That man, the log will..." Prahl said weakly.

Monck jerked the whistle off Prahl's neck, snapping the string it hung from. He blew shrilly.

Out of sight far up the hill, the donkey's engine fluttered a moment, then wound up. The mainline began to snake up the mountainside, pulling the butt rigging taut. The choker bit into the tree. As the log began to move, its bark squealed against the moss on the ground. It sounded like a man's scream.

The log inexorably ground against the body. Monck walked in front of it, kicking at the corpse to keep it against the log butt. The choker lifted the log fractionally, and the body was slowly squeezed under it, as if being sucked back. The bucked log—twenty feet long and weighing over three tons—began to drag over the body. The rough bark peeled away skin and hair in shaggy chunks. As the bones pulverized, the sound was like that of canvas being torn. Prahl sank to the ground, breathing in sickly wheezes.

The log slid ponderously off the body and continued its slow amble up the hill. The German bent over the crushed form. He stirred the remains, then lifted the head from the ground by the hair. It was still recognizable. He pulled it higher, but the backbone clung to it. He kicked at the vertebrae until the head came free.

He ran up the hill after the tree, carrying what remained of the head. When he came to the front of the moving log, he dropped the head and jammed it under the log with his boot. The log again began its work, mashing the skull as it moved toward the landing. When the log cleared the head, there was nothing left of the fisherman's face but loose flaps of skin.

Monck sounded the whistle twice. The log immediately stopped. He wiped his hands on the moss of a fire tree, then returned to Prahl and Schwerin. Their twisted faces showed they thought they might be next.

The captain said slowly, "Listen carefully. You will tell the bullbuck and everyone else that the body is mine, that I tripped and fell under the log as it began to move. Neither of you saw it, just heard me scream. You came running. But it was too late. Got that?"

Neither man moved.

"We don't have time to talk about this," Monck said levelly.

"I've blown the stop whistle. The chaser will be here in a minute to see what the problem is. Get your story straight, and get it now. Those are my bones over there. Do you both understand?"

"You've just killed both of us," Prahl said dully. "The Yanks will line us up against the wall."

"They'll never know." Monck looked over his shoulder at the sound of footsteps approaching in the underbrush.

Monck stared at each of them, willing them to obey. His aura of controlled violence gave him an elemental power they could not resist. The buckers nodded in unison.

The captain smiled grimly. "We may see each other again. In Schwabia."

Prahl doubled over to vomit. Gagging and spitting, he leaned heavily against Schwerin. The POW wiped his mouth and stood. Monck was gone.

7

JEFF SUTTON WAS FIFTEEN YEARS OLD,
and a star on the New Bern High School bas-
ketball team. But his folks thought he was nothing but a baby-
sitter. That's how the summer was shaping up, with his mother
every day asking him to take his little brother Bobby along.

Jeff was tall, about four inches higher than last year, when he
had lettered as a sophomore on the team. He walked like a crane
at low tide. He had a dimpled jaw, a shy smile, and hair in
sculpted black waves.

The sun was fading, the end of a dusty June day. Jeff and
Bobby were walking along Pembroke Road, just south of New
Bern. The asphalt retained the day's heat and radiated it up
through Jeff's shoes. A gentle wind tossed the fiddle-shaped
leaves of the roadside wild bamboo. A few moments ago they
had stopped at Virgil's Cafe to see the buckshot holes in the
doorframe. Now Bobby was again following Jeff like a frog's ass
follows a frog, as Jeff often complained. The kid was ten yards
behind, kicking sticks, whistling over grass reeds, throwing rocks
at stop signs, and everything else the little pukes do.

Jeff was desperate. Anna Campbell had invited him over. A

week ago Anna had put her tongue in his mouth and might do it again tonight. If only he could lose his kid brother.

"Bobby," he called. "How about a game of hide-and-seek?"

The kid was bent over, tying a shoelace. He looked up, pleased and suspicious at the same time. "Sure." He wiped his nose on his sleeve.

"You hide behind a tree in the marsh and count to two hundred. Then come looking for me. I'll be somewhere in the marsh."

Jeff led him off the road and several yards into Trent Marsh, a lowland bog bordering the river. They had played in the marsh all their lives and knew every stump and brier and path. They found a loblolly pine. Bobby stepped up to the tree and covered his eyes with his hands.

"All right, begin counting," Jeff ordered, glancing over his shoulder for a route. He'd have to walk a ways in the marsh before rejoining Pembroke Road or his brother would hear him.

Bobby began the count. Jeff ran, keeping his eyes on the ground for pipevines and roots.

Little brothers being what they are, there was no possibility Bobby Sutton was going to just count to two hundred. At the bubbling center of his fecund ten-year-old mind was the certainty that his brother was scheming against him.

He dropped to his knees to peer around the tree and watch his brother's retreat. Was he being abandoned, as he suspected? His hands settled among the leaves of a woolly pipevine, a bottomland vine with white, fleecy leaves.

His fingers found something else, a texture not of the marsh. He looked down. Almost hidden under the leaves was a patch of coarse blue cloth. He pulled it from the leaves. It was a bag or a pack, and it was heavy. He mouthed the words: "Abercrombie and Fitch." Funny name. Maybe the owners. He unbuckled the leather straps, dipped his hand daringly inside, and pulled out a submachine gun.

He had seen them all. *Yellow Peril, Spy Smasher, Confessions of a Nazi Spy*, and the other Kehoe Theater matinees. Bobby Sutton wobbled as a surge of euphoria passed through him. He had found a machine gun. Thank you, Baby Jesus. He cradled it in his arms like an infant, cherishing it. He was as oblivious to the wild improbability of finding a submachine gun in a North Carolina bog as he was to the tick settling on his sockless ankle.

"Jeff," he called ecstatically. "Come here. Quick."

He ran his hand down the blue metal stock to the short barrel. He unfolded the metal shoulder stock and clicked it into place. He raised the gun to his shoulder to look through the hooded Partridge sight. His father had taught him to shoot at age six, but he'd never held anything as compact and purposeful as this marvel. He pretended to blast the nearest tree. The gun fit him perfectly, like his baseball glove on his hand. It had been made for him, he decided with primitive joy.

Bobby Sutton had found a Schmeisser submachine gun. Two feet long, nine pounds, five hundred rounds a minute, with a muzzle velocity of 1,040 feet a second and an effective range of two hundred yards. Nothing was wasted on the gun. It consisted only of a striated pistol grip, a small housing for the firing mechanism, a short barrel, and a magazine holder. Simple, reliable, and viciously effective.

Jeff had heard the ecstasy in his brother's usually whiny voice. It instantly turned him around. He plunged back through the palmettos.

He skidded to a stop in front of his brother, his mouth agape. "What, what . . . ?"

"Finders keepers, Jeff," Bobby declared. "And I've already named him Mr. Blaster."

"Where did you get that?" the older brother breathed cautiously.

"I found it and it's mine," Bobby replied with irrefutable logic. The law of brothers requires an immediate claim.

"Is it real?"

"You bet. And I found the bullets." Bobby held up a ten-inch bar magazine, holding thirty-two rounds. "Watch this. I'll put the clip in."

It snapped loudly into place. He folded the stock under the

grip, then held the Schmeisser against his hip as he had seen Edward G. Robinson do. He squeezed the trigger.

Nothing happened.

Jeff had escorted his brother to most of those movies. He instructed excitedly, "You've got to pull the bolt back."

Bobby found the lever behind the magazine slot. He pulled it back and released it, chambering the first shell.

"Watch me, Jeff," he cried. He leveled the gun toward a small loblolly pine and pulled the trigger.

The submachine gun roared, bucked in his hands, and sprayed bullets. Azalea and oak leaves trembled from the sound. The trunk ruptured, and the tree twisted and toppled.

"Let me try." Jeff held his hand out and wasn't surprised when Bobby immediately gave him the weapon. Elder-brother worship is seldom understood by either brother.

Jeff aimed the weapon at a rotted stump.

"Now just squeeze real slowly," Bobby lectured importantly.

Bullets tore into the stump. Jeff's ears rang and his hands around the pistol grip tingled. He exclaimed, "I tell you, Bobby, I'm never going to have more fun than this. Never."

"Hey, what's this?" Bobby dropped to his haunches and dug into the bag again. Out came another weapon.

Entirely different, more sinister. It was a rifle, but unlike any of the bird guns or deer rifles they had been raised with. It was in two parts, and Bobby held the stock while Jeff twisted the barrel into its mount. Its stock was very light, almost delicate, but the thick barrel was an inch in diameter. A sniper scope was attached to the barrel. The bolt slid with a precision none of their dad's 30-06s had. The chamber was empty. Jeff pointed it at the ground and brought back the trigger. It moved responsively, as if anticipating his finger. The firing pin clicked quietly.

The strange rifle sobered both boys. Jeff said, "These belonged to the German, you know. He must have hid them here before going into Virgil's Cafe."

Bobby felt his new toys slipping away. "Yeah, I know."

"They never found any guns. These are them."

"Yeah." Bobby scratched his ankle.

"We've got no choice, Bobby. We've got to take them to Sheriff Henley."

"Yeah." Bobby kicked the ground. He looked up at his brother. "You know that stop sign just this side of town, the one with the .22 holes in it?"

"Sure."

"There's more clips in the bag. Let's use another one on the sign. Then we'll give the guns to Sheriff Henley."

Jeff grinned. "Let's go."

A single cloud hovered over Puget Sound, growing smaller under the high sun. Yesterday's south wind had died, and the whitecaps were gone. The blue water was flat and seamless from the island across the sound to the mainland.

Margarete Bayerlein had almost finished her daughter's blouses when the battleship rounded Yeomalt Point and came into view. She lowered the iron to the board and lifted the binoculars from a basket beneath the windowsill. Two years ago her daughter, Mary, had asked her why she looked through her binoculars at only the gray ships and not any of the pretty ones with white sails. Margarete had known the question would someday come. Her lie—that she reported to the U.S. Navy on how many ships passed the point and whether they kept in formation—was feeble and would soon need revision. Try as she might, she still didn't know what her new fabrication would be. She had sworn Mary to secrecy, and the trust between mother and daughter was such that Margarete had not once wondered whether Mary might mention the binoculars to her friends. Mary was outside weeding the Victory garden.

She held the binoculars to her eyes. Battleships always were escorted, even in Puget Sound. A moment later two destroyers also breeched the point.

She stood well inside the room before raising the glasses, avoiding any chance the sun might reflect off the lenses. Through the binoculars the ship's numbers were easily visible. The dreadnought had nine sixteen-inch guns and twenty five-inch guns, and was painted in the new South Sea camouflage configuration. It was the same battleship she had seen arrive four weeks before, a gaping hole amidships and its stern blackened by a fire.

She pulled a loose-leaf notebook from under her knitting and scribbled the date, June 27, 1944, then several marks. Margarete Bayerlein's house was on the eastern slope of Bainbridge Island in Puget Sound, due east of Seattle. All ships departing or arriving at Bremerton, the West Coast's busiest naval base, passed under her house.

She was a nurse on the graveyard shift three nights a week at the naval hospital in Bremerton. And every daylight moment for the past three years she had been on duty at her living-room window or in her yard. She had been told by San Diego not to worry about night movements, as there would be few. Save for ships she might have missed on foggy days, she had recorded every U.S. Navy vessel built or repaired at the Bremerton naval yard in all that time. From a different mailbox each week, she mailed a report to a San Diego address. And on rare occasions she would receive a letter from San Diego, sometimes with instructions, once in a while with a little money.

She arranged another blouse on the board. Her iron hung in the air, caught by her familiar surge of melancholy. Her late twenties had been spent here, behind this window. A recluse, and now her daughter was growing old enough to realize it and ask her about it. Lately she had begun to stare at the mirror over the bathroom sink, wondering if her youth and beauty would last the war.

And she was beautiful. Her brown hair was streaked with sorrel and copper wisps that danced under the window light. Her green eyes were slightly canted, intelligent and playful at the same moment. Her prominent cheekbones made her appear haughty. She thought her mouth was a bit too austere, but it would flash an infectious smile at any provocation. Yes, she was beautiful. Her husband had told her so before he died.

Her husband, Georg. She had met him in line in front of the

Augsburger Bakery in Berlin when she was nine years old. Pushing frantically to get into the store before the bread was sold out, an old man had bumped and overturned her hamper, spilling her half-bushel of marks into the wind. Inflation had reached 2,500 percent that month, and her mother had sent her to the bakery with a basketful of money to buy two loaves of bread. The marks scattered between the feet of the shoppers.

Her Berlin neighbors, civil even when desperate, did not rush for her money, and a boy ran after the paper wads to help her collect them. Georg Bayerlein pushed handful after handful of bills back into her hamper. He was laughing and blond and a year older and dazzling in his chivalry, a Goetz von Berlichingen, last of the German knights. She decided on the spot she would someday marry him.

They laughed about it later, that a nine-year-old would swear an oath to herself, and abide by it and work on it for a dozen years. The longings of a girl that age are as transient as they are earnest. Not in Margarete. In school, in church, on Sunday promenades on Unter den Linden, she had held herself out for him. Finally, he liked to say, he had no choice but to ask her for her hand.

She had written to him at his military training post at Bad Tolz, and they were together again when he was assigned to Abwehr intelligence school in the Charlottenburg District in Berlin. Then they were sent to America on forged Swiss passports. Telling her of his espionage was contrary to his orders, but she was his partner in everything, and she often spelled him at the window overlooking Puget Sound. And then he was dead, and all that remained was their daughter and their work. The window and her daughter were remembrances of her husband that she clung to like last hopes. Twin memorials, and as she had been pledged to him, she now was pledged to them. The sad moment passed, and she returned to the blouses.

"Mom," Mary called excitedly from the side yard. "Mom, there's a man coming."

The girl came to the open window. Her eyes were bright with

expectation. Mary's hair was almost pearl-white and was tied in a precise ponytail. She had her father's eyes, blue and taunting. He had called her his little heartbreaker. "He just drove up in a big green car. Is he a friend of yours?"

"Mary, I want you to stay outside," she said urgently. Her eyes automatically found the binoculars. She slipped them and the record beneath the wool in her knitting basket. She took off her apron and anxiously pushed a strand of hair in place.

"Aw, Mom..."

"Do as I tell you." Margarete was rarely stern with her daughter. The girl fled back to the garden before her mother had opened the door.

He was standing on the porch. Tall and rather thin, with wavy brunet hair and pointed features.

"Yes?"

Without introduction he said, "I was given this address." There was a trace of accent carefully avoided.

"There must be some mistake." There was none, and she knew it before her words had ended. Oh God, that crazy order. That paper. Her stomach turned, and she gripped the doorknob to steady herself.

"Angela, Maria."

"I don't know what those names are supposed to mean," she said, suddenly exhausted, her years of double life overwhelming her. She leaned heavily against the door. "You'd better come in." She stood aside to let him through, and asked, *"Sind sie von Lager?"* Are you from the camp?

Still in English, he said, "You have no pass phrase? Nothing?"

"No."

"Did you know I was coming?"

"I was mailed a message and told to get it into the POW camp at Fort Lewis. Unopened. That's all."

He smiled tightly and asked in German, "So you wrapped it around a rock and threw it at a POW logger in the woods?"

"You're here, so it seems to have worked," she said tonelessly. "What do you want?"

His grin fell away. "I want my assignment. Why else would I show up here?"

"Your assignment?" She laughed genuinely. "Let's see. How about mowing my lawn."

He seemed to vanish and appear three inches away from her face, his hands clamped painfully around her arms. His voice was coarse. "I killed a man this morning to hide my escape from that camp. It isn't going to fool them long. I want my instructions. Now."

She had lived too long with the corrosive fear of arrest as a spy to be afraid of this man. She said calmly, "I don't have your orders. I know nothing about them. Or you."

He slowly released her, his face tight with concentration. He moved to the window and stared sightlessly at the distant water. Of course she wouldn't know anything. So far it had all been haphazard, run almost blindly from Berlin. But now that Monck was out, messages could be secured. They were counting on Monck to know that.

He turned to survey the room. It contained a maroon velour sofa, a defeated rag rug, a small bookshelf, and an upright piano. A pile of *House & Garden* magazines rested on an end table near the ironing board. A leather wing chair and an ottoman were in the corner under a reading light. The chair was worn and comfortable, yet filmed with dust.

His gaze found her again. "What's your name?"

"Margarete Bayerlein. I go by Meg."

"Do you have a radio, Meg?"

She nodded toward the bookshelf. "Right there."

"I'll need it. And a pair of pliers and wire cutters. Will you help me?"

"I can't leave my home. I have a . . . a duty here."

"That doesn't matter anymore."

She glanced out the garden window. Mary was working a hoe slowly, her gaze through the window into the house. Margarete said, "I can't help you. It would be too dangerous for my daughter."

"You've already exposed yourself and your daughter by getting the message to me. And now my detection and capture could lead directly back to you."

Was he threatening that if she didn't help him and he were caught, he would tell the American authorities of her role? Her thoughts were not of the prison sentence, but of being separated from her daughter. She shuddered and wrapped herself in her arms. The man's face was as cold as a carving. His voice was carefully modulated, as if produced by a machine. His stance was that of an animal: slightly bent legs and hands held a little away from his body. He seemed ready to leap. There would be no compassion from him. He would certainly inform the Americans.

And then what of Mary? The war had already taken its toll on her. The day after Pearl Harbor the mother of one of Mary's school friends—perhaps one of Margarete's co-workers at the hospital—had told her girl that Mary's parents were German immigrants and didn't even speak English correctly. The news spread across the schoolyard. The shoving and hitting had lasted only a few days, but the taunting had never ended. Mary had never heard the word "kraut" before the United States entered the war. Now she wore it like a piece of clothing. But Mary was from the same mold as her father. Smart and stubborn and buoyant. Even so, Margarete thought that often much of her Mary's remarkable resilience and spirit were generated to help her mother weather the loss of Georg. At times she was stronger than Margarete.

Her daughter was the price she would pay if she didn't help this stranger. A terrifying thought. She looked at him again and asked, "I'm going to tell my girl that you're a friend of her father's and are just visiting us for a while. I'll tell her you're a naturalized American, just like I am."

"Your husband?"

"He's dead. What do you need from me?"

"First, a tool box. Do you have one?"

She did not have all the equipment he wanted, even after he

tore apart her Motorola and the doorbell. They spent much of
that afternoon driving around Bremerton in her car. She purchased a broken shortwave receiving set at a used-appliance dealer.
Then they both entered a hobby shop on Burnside, and while
she asked about buying a balsa airplane model as a gift, Monck
slipped a Morse sender from a shelf into his jacket pocket. He
tested his English at an electrical-supply shop on Callow Street,
where he bought a spool of bell wire. He used simple phrases,
avoiding tongue-gnarling peculiarities of the language. He didn't
raise an eyebrow on the clerk.

When they drove by the shipyard, her implacable grief rushed
at her. For the first time since her husband's death she was not
on station above the sound when she should have been. Her
absence from the window seemed to weaken a bond between
them, one she had nurtured by her faithful duty. The stammer
of a rivet gun high on a new destroyer's superstructure covered
her little groan.

At a hardware store downtown, she bought a soldering gun.
Then they parked a block from KBRE's broadcast station on
Sixth Street. Monck was gone fifteen minutes. When he returned
he was carrying a frequency meter she didn't think he had paid
for.

They stopped at the post office in Winslow, Bainbridge Island's
one-horse town. She tugged a bulky envelope from her box. It
had a San Diego postmark and was addressed to her. Inside was
a second envelope with "Angela Maria" in block letters on it.
Monck waited until they were back in the car to open it. Inside
were three thousand dollars in ten-dollar bills and booklets of
gas ration coupons.

He spent the rest of the afternoon bent over the kitchen table,
working with the radio parts. The girl watched him for fully an
hour before she approached.

"What are you doing to our radio?" she asked in a small
voice.

Startled, Monck looked up. He had not heard her approach.
"I'm fixing it."

"It wasn't broken." She pulled at her hair. "It sure looks broken now, though."

Monck was soldering bell wire to a metal plate below a coil. He instantly forgot Mary.

She persisted. "I always listen to *Your Hit Parade* about now. Frank Sinatra is my favorite."

Monck held a vacuum tube to the light, then plugged it into its socket.

"How come your hands are so beat up? You look like you fall off a bike a lot."

Monck used a yardstick to measure two identical lengths of wire. "I work in the woods. You get a lot of cuts and scratches out there."

"Why?"

"There's lots of sharp things. Snags, saw teeth, nails."

"What about that scar on your chin?"

"A blackberry bush reached out and grabbed my face."

"My mom's a nurse. She can take care of the scratches. It's too late for the scar, though." Mary slid into the chair opposite the German. She lowered her voice confidentially. "You're the first man to visit since Dad died. I worry about Mom sometimes, with no man in the house."

Humor softened Monck's eyes as he glanced at Meg Bayerlein, who was cleaning the dishes after the meatloaf meal. "Why is that?"

"Well, you know."

"I'm afraid I don't."

Her mother had heard every word. "That's enough, Mary. It's time for your homework."

The girl looked penetratingly at the visitor. "Yes, you do know." She moved along the seat and stood. She bent to his ear. "You wrecked our radio. So you owe us."

She skipped through the kitchen door, her tail of glossy hair flying behind her.

Meg dried the dishes with a diligence they did not require.

"Your daughter knows absolutely nothing about life, or absolutely everything."

"It's nothing, I assure you." There was an unmistakable finality in her tone.

He switched the subject. "Do you have a stepladder?"

"In the basement."

"Help me rig the antennas, will you?"

Daylight was failing as he scouted the wooded lot adjacent to the house for two trees with the right alignment. He used a Cheerios boxtop compass, the only one in the house. It worked perfectly, he guessed. There were household lights visible through the trees to the west and north, but there wasn't enough light left for him or her to be visible. She watched for Mary, wondering how she would explain Monck's work. But Mary had disappeared into her room, as if she were deliberately leaving them alone.

He had strung the first antenna from a fir-tree branch to the ground and was climbing the second tree before she asked, "Why two antennas?"

He secured the anchor twine around a limb and dropped the antenna wire to her. "These two wires will make a broadside-array antenna. It'll give us a direction of maximum radiation." He pointed north to the other wire. "Along the plane containing the antennas we'll get a lot more broadcast power. Berlin is on this plane. And, in the other directions, we'll get correspondingly less power. Anybody east of here, say in Seattle, who is trying to triangulate on our signal will have to look a lot harder."

"Why?" She sounded like her daughter, she thought.

"Because in any direction but north and south, the radiation waves tend to cancel each other out. Power gain is enhanced toward Berlin, at the expense of it in all other directions."

"Why did you do all those calculations this afternoon?"

He climbed down the ladder. "Each half-wave antenna must be a precise length, and they have to be an exact distance apart. And the feeder wire has to be an exact length, all to get the radiation waves in phase."

"Have you got it all worked out?"

He attached the feeder wire to the southerly dipole. "We'll see. Do you have a King James Bible?"

So improbable was the request that it took her a moment to comprehend. Then she laughed abruptly. "A Bible? You? I've known you half a day, and I can already tell a Bible is as foreign to you as this country is."

He walked next to her toward the house, pausing every few steps to push the feeder wire into the grass. "I'm going to use it as the basis for a multiple-substitution code. I haven't asked you what you do for the Fatherland, but I assume you report on ship movements. Right?"

She had not spoken of her work since her husband died. She was incapable of doing so now. She dipped her chin, almost imperceptibly.

"Do you use a code?"

She still could not utter the incriminating words.

He looked down at her hair, in the half-light the color of burnished mahogany. Her scent, a German mingling of highland flowers and black earth, prompted in him distant memories. He quickly bent again, hiding the wire under the grass. He brushed his hands together. "Whoever is giving me orders isn't going to send them undisguised over the radio waves, not with the Americans having numerous Signal Corps units doing nothing but listening for such transmissions. I'm only guessing Berlin will try to contact me with a shortwave. And I can only guess at their code."

"Guess? Aren't codes supposed to make guessing impossible?"

He opened the side door of the house for her. "Mine will be a good guess, and I suspect they'll have anticipated it. I was assigned codes in Africa. They'll have discovered that by talking with my radioman or commander. They'll also assume I'll use the last code I was given."

"Do you remember it?" she asked, lifting the Bible from a bookshelf next to the wing chair.

Without answering, Monck returned to the kitchen booth. The

table was covered with his hybrid shortwave. It was little more than the backless Motorola, a flat board with additional tubes, wiring, and coils, a Morse sender, and a pair of earphones. The shortwave receiver was wired to the Motorola. Feeder wire led from the radio along the kitchen floor to the side door.

He said, "Today is Tuesday, the second day of the week."

"Tuesday is the third day of the week," she corrected him.

"Not according to Genesis. Sunday was the day of rest, the seventh day. So Tuesday is the second day. I turn to Exodus, the second book of the Bible. Today is the twenty-seventh day of the month, from which I'll subtract six, as this month, June, is the sixth month of the year. So I'll be using the twenty-first book of Exodus." He flipped through several pages. "'Now these are the judgments which thou shalt set before them.' It'll take me a while to number each word. Perhaps five hundred words."

Her face brightened with understanding. "And you'll simply broadcast a series of numbers, each indicating a different word of the text."

Monck nodded, his eyes following the pencil. "There are five letters in my last name. So every fifth number I broadcast will be a null. A meaningless fake."

He made connections on the board and wired the Motorola, following a diagram drawn that afternoon. He reminded her of her daughter, with his ability to focus effortlessly on the task in front of him, completely immersed in his work to the exclusion of all else.

She was sure he hadn't even noticed that she had remained in the booth opposite him, staring. But unexpectedly he asked, "What did your husband die of?"

She winced. "He went fishing. A storm came up. The Coast Guard found his body on a beach two days later. Three years ago."

"He was the first to watch the ships?"

"I just continued after he died." She paused, inexpressibly sad. "We didn't miss a ship between us. Not a one, except maybe the day I went to his funeral."

87

"Why was he working for Germany?"

Her eyebrows rose, and then she realized she hadn't told him. "He was a German, of course. As am I. Berliners. We came over here in '36, ostensibly to visit relatives. We never went back."

"And you weren't deported after the war started?"

"No, nothing like that." Her eyes wandered from him as she thought back. "San Diego began altering our backgrounds. One day we received voter registration cards. And, sure enough, when we failed to report that month as aliens, U.S. Immigration never came to check on us. We had somehow become American citizens. The same thing with my job. One day I received a packet from San Diego, full of letters of recommendation from employers I didn't know anything about. A week later I received in the mail a degree in nursing from Oregon State University. I easily obtained a nursing job at the base."

"Are you a nurse?"

"Yes, Berlin Technical University."

"But your co-workers think you were born and raised in this country?"

She shook her head. "I can't fully overcome my accent. But they think I've been here since I was a schoolgirl."

He pushed a battery into the frequency meter. "Have you ever met your San Diego contact?"

"No. He sends a little money now and then, and once in a while a message of encouragement or instructions. I've no idea how he forwards my information."

Monck reached under the table to plug in the radio. The tubes began to glow a dim orange. "I'm going outside. In a few minutes, press the key and release a few times. That'll be enough."

He stepped out, carrying the meter. She waited, then did as instructed. The sender clicked sharply.

He returned quickly to the booth, then brought out a slip of paper from his shirt pocket and spread it on the table in front of him. It contained a series of numbers which from her distance across the table looked like sinister runes. He placed the earphones on his head and stared for a few minutes at the wristwatch he had borrowed from her. She might have been invisible.

Monck abruptly lowered the watch and tapped out a brief message. No more than twenty pulses. He waited a full minute and repeated it. His face clouded. "Nothing."

"Are you sure they're listening?"

"I'm sure," he barked. His lips curled back with tension. "They know I would build a radio. They must know."

"Try it again."

"Only on the hour. Only twice."

"Do you have the right frequency?"

"My African frequency. I don't know any other. Berlin would..."

His hand suddenly dropped to the pencil on the table. He jotted a series of dashes, taking almost a minute. He finally pulled the headset off his ears. He grinned widely, which seemed to test his scar. "They had the right frequency. They've studied me carefully."

She busied herself with a *Life* magazine while he transcribed the message, his eyes shifting with the beat of a metronome between the Bible and note pad. He worked with a bookkeeper's concentration, ignoring her and her daughter, who was reading aloud in the front room.

When he lowered the pencil and looked up, she expected another grin of victory, but his face was ashen, the color of one long dead. His lips parted, but he said nothing, as if distrusting his voice. The vein above his temple throbbed. And his eyes. Something in those hazel eyes had gone to sleep.

8

THE ODOR OF FORMALDEHYDE wrapped around John Wren, encircling him like cold fingers and pulling him into the room. The chill of the floor tile seeped into his bones, and he anticipated a shiver by tightening his stomach. He squinted as a child does during the frightening moments of a movie and approached the dreaded table.

Spread across the stainless-steel examining table, the body was as frightful as the coroner had promised over the phone. Bits and pieces were recognizable as human; several fingers, the crook of an arm, a foot in a boot. Wren averted his eyes, embarrassed for the corpse. It was exposed down to its sinews, stripped of even its humanness.

"Quick, doc," Fred Kinney said as he stooped over the pulp, "you'd better take this guy's pulse. I think he's fading on you."

Kinney was a plainclothes major with Army G2, charged with investigating POW escapes, a job that left him with a lot of spare time. He wore the flattop of an Army lifer. His tapioca face was grained with tiny adipose pods, and his nose was mapped with burst capillaries, as if he had just gulped down several boilermakers. His fingers had been stained walnut from years of Pall

Malls. Kinney's idea of humor was a belch in church. Tattooed on his left calf was a cartoon of a red rooster with a noose around its neck. Kinney had won many a beer betting his cock hung below his knees.

"If you gentlemen will gather around, we'll get on with this." Dr. Ben Guinn looped the apron strings behind his back and tied them across his ample belly. Guinn looked like a country doctor, with kindly basset-hound eyes, a toss of white hair forever hanging across his forehead, and a comfortable double chin. Not enough people died of unusual circumstances in Tacoma and the rest of Pierce County to require a full-time coroner, so Guinn doubled as an obstetrician. By the time he had delivered, spanked, and placed the babies in their mothers' arms, the women were too overjoyed to notice the smell of preservative that clung to their infants.

Wren and Kinney spaced themselves around the corpse. At the end of the table nearest what Wren guessed had been the body's head was a bucket for fluids. A blood gutter ringed the table. At Guinn's right was an implement tray on which were an oscillating bone saw, bone cutters, scissors, hemostats, forceps, and scalpels. Wren imagined that the Star Chamber had looked somewhat like this.

Because paper and pencil would have become bloodied quickly, behind the doctor was a chalkboard for noting his observations. Guinn reached above the body to switch on a surgery light mounted on a universal joint. He tilted the light so that it focused on the left side of the mound.

As Guinn stretched rubber gloves over his hands, he said, "I expected to see G2 visit my autopsy room after I called them, Mr. Wren. But it surprises me that the Secret Service would make an appearance. Can I ask why?"

"I can't comment, Doctor. Maybe someday I'll be able to let you know."

The coroner would never know that a sniper's rifle found in a North Carolina swamp had sent a bolt of fear through the Secret Service. The weapons were examined that night by the

Service's Arms Office in Washington, D.C. The Schmeisser proved to be a stock weapon and told them nothing of the German's mission. But the sniper's rifle was an original, perhaps one of a kind, and expensive. A German *Landser*'s personal weapon was typically the robust Mauser Karabiner 98K, which fired a 7.92mm bullet, usually bruising the soldier's shoulder. It was an unrefined rifle, manufactured cheaply by the millions. The rifle found in the swamp was nothing of the sort.

Its barrel was neither German Krupp nor Terlingen steel, but was from a tiny Norwegian foundry in Drammen, which produced specially refined metal for knives and hunting rifles. Measured with a micrometer, the barrel was found to have tolerances of a fraction of a thousandth of an inch, much more stringent than on production weapons. The barrel had a quarter-inch wider radius than any German production gun, reducing flex and vibration, and adding inertia when the bullet passed through it, making it steadier. When the halves were screwed together like a pool cue, the barrel's length was thirty-nine inches, much longer than standard rifles and carbines.

The Arms Office investigators could find none of the Mauser, Walther, or Haenel design signatures on the rifle, such as a straight bolt or the straight-grip military stock. Rather, the rifle's stock was carved in an unusual configuration, with a pistol grip, elevated cheekpiece, and thumbhole. The Swiss buttplate was adjustable. The scope was a 2.5-magnification Leica and the bullets were dumdums. The investigators concluded the rifle had been made specifically for the German who had died in the North Carolina bog.

Such a rifle could have only one purpose, the killing of someone who was impossible to get close to.

Within twenty minutes of receiving the Arms Office's report, the White House Secret Service Detail had wired every field office in the country. Anything with even the slightest German connection would now be fully investigated by the Secret Service, leaving nothing to exclusive FBI or G2 jurisdiction, even the accidental death of a POW in Washington State. So John Wren had come to visit the Pierce County coroner.

Guinn used forceps to pick up what looked like gristle. "Normally I wouldn't have bothered with an autopsy in a case like this. It's as plain as day that this poor soul was reduced to spaghetti and meatballs by the log. I figure about forty pounds of him are still stuck in the log's bark. But the law of the state of Washington requires an autopsy, so I did some poking around."

Wren was surprised at how quickly he disassociated the corpse from anything human and tragic. He bent over the table, peering at the part the doctor had singled out. He guessed it had been an arm. He marveled at how complicated it was.

Then even his untrained eye found an object startlingly out of place in the mix of flesh and crumpled skeleton. A metal plate was bolted to a portion of bone.

"I see you've already found the reason I called the Army. Some time ago this man suffered a both-bone forearm fracture. The radius and ulna were snapped, I'd guess five to eight years ago. Each bone was repaired during surgery with a metal plate attached along the bone over the fracture. The plate is permanent and allows the bone to knit itself back together."

Using the forceps and a gloved hand, the coroner lifted the ulna to eye level. "Take a close look at the screws holding the metal plate to the bone."

Kinney said, "Looks like normal carpenter's screws."

"Right. The orthopedic surgeons call them cruciate-head screws. They're installed with a surgical instrument that looks just like a flathead screwdriver."

"So?" Kinney asked, wrinkling his nose against the carrion odor.

"Cruciate-head screws are used almost exclusively by American surgeons."

Wren's head came up. "An American surgeon repaired the fracture?"

Guinn smiled, dispensing his knowledge in measured portions, as if it were a prescription. "That's right. European surgeons use a hexagonal-head screw, requiring a tool much like an Allen wrench."

"You're saying this man is an American?" The temperature in the autopsy room seemed to drop.

"Or maybe a Canadian. Not a German."

Kinney sputtered, "But goddammit to hell, Doctor, I talked to this man's buckers today, and I read his papers. His name was Josef Schiller, captured in Africa and brought to Fort Lewis about a year ago. He was a goddam kraut foot soldier."

Kinney's perfect record of no escapes at the Fort Lewis camp was under attack by a corpse and a coroner. His eyes searched the room as he cast about for an explanation. "Maybe Schiller visited the United States before the war and broke his arm here."

Guinn put on his delivery-room smile. "A remote possibility. But once I discovered the American screw, I took this autopsy a bit more seriously. And I found something else." He lifted a glass jar from the instrument table and handed it to Wren.

The agent held the jar to the light. "It's a piece of metal."

"More precisely, it is a barb from a barbed wire," Guinn said, sorting from the mound a length of backbone. "Note that the barb is rusty and appears rather old."

"How do you know it's a barb?" Wren asked, still staring through the glass at the bit of metal.

Guinn shrugged. "I was raised on a dairy farm near Olympia. I've strung miles of wire in my time."

"What's it got to do with the body?" Kinney asked impatiently.

"I found it in the body," the doctor replied, holding the string of bones in both hands. "This is the cervical vertebrae, the neck bones. The barb was lodged in the third vertebra down from the skull. It was rammed in there with great force."

"A war wound," Kinney protested. "A piece of shrapnel healed over."

"Impossible. The shard is rusty, indicating the body hasn't had time to work on it, to clean it. And if it had been there for any amount of time, calcium would have been deposited around where it entered the bone."

Wren's voice was fogged. "This man was strangled with a make-do garrote, and the body was planted under the log so it would be trampled into an unrecognizable mass."

The doctor nodded wisely. "Your German prisoner wants you fellows to think this is him on the table. But it isn't. The POW is long gone."

Fifteen minutes later, John Wren's telex squeezed Mike O'Brien's chest in a vice of fear. First the North Carolina sniper's rifle, and now a German soldier in an elaborate and risky escape from a POW camp. The supervising agent of the White House Secret Service Detail knew the two circumstances a continent apart must be unrelated. But with the president as his charge, even coincidences became ominous.

The next day, Thursday, June 29, the president was traveling to Hyde Park on his train, POTUS. According to a formula concocted by a Princeton mathematician at the behest of the Service, the president was twenty-two times more vulnerable when on the road than when in the White House.

O'Brien had just approached the president in his study about canceling the Hyde Park trip. Roosevelt had placed his hand over the phone just long enough to rebuff O'Brien for what Roosevelt called, not unkindly, an asinine suggestion.

The president's protection circle was known as the bubble. When he traveled, ten Secret Service agents advanced the trip, and another fifteen made up the bubble around him. With Wren's wire on his desk in the tiny office on the White House's ground floor, O'Brien now triggered the Yellow Bubble, the first of a series of stronger responses to increasingly threatening situations.

An elaborate POW escape on the West Coast. A German's sniper rifle on the East Coast. Coincidences, surely. But O'Brien didn't believe in coincidences. He lifted the phone to call in additional agents.

* * *

The interrogation entered its third hour. John Wren and Fred Kinney sat at a table in the POW camp's craft room. In front of them were the *Soldbuch*, the AFW 3000 form, and the rest of the meager file on a POW named Josef Schiller, an antiaircraft gun loader captured in Africa. A rubber stamp and ink pad were on the table next to the documents.

Tom Garvin leaned against the door to the parade yard. On his left and right were two American guards, their helmets low over their eyes and their rifles at parade rest. Against the walls were brick-and-board shelves containing the tools and material for woodcraft, leathercraft, painting, and drawing.

"Ask him again," Wren said dully.

The POW camp administration in the United States was critically short of Americans fluent in the German language. The ratio in some camps was one German-speaking guard for every two thousand men. The other guards used Milwaukee Deutsch, a combination of gesturing and shoving. Kinney claimed that he owed his last two promotions to his fluent high German, learned from his father, an immigrant from Hamburg.

"So you didn't see Schiller slip from the log, Private Prahl?" the G2 agent asked in German.

Prahl's face seemed guileless. "No, sir."

"Why was he on the log in the first place?"

"I don't know, sir." The sweat of tension rolled into Prahl's eyes. His eyelids fluttered. "Perhaps checking the choker."

"But wasn't that your job?"

"Yes, sir."

"Then why was Schiller up there?"

"I don't know, sir."

Every time Kinney paused to translate the circular answers for Wren, the German's lower lip began to tremble. With his thick neck, clamped mouth, and uncaring eyes, Wren looked dangerously like the German propaganda posters' version of an American soldier, often depicted carrying a baby spitted on his bayonet.

Wren rubbed the back of his neck. "We've questioned this prisoner, his fellow bucker, six others who were in the woods that day, and the camp commander. So far, we've learned nothing."

"Just like I said we would," Kinney contributed with satisfaction.

"We don't have time to screw around anymore." He turned to Garvin. "Let's turn them over."

Puzzled and frightened, Prahl cocked his head when Kinney translated Wren's instructions. Turn them over?

Garvin pursed his lips, glanced sorrowfully at the POW, and asked, "You sure, John?"

"They've given us no choice. Let's hand them over."

Kinney provided a running translation of the conversation. Prahl shrunk in his chair as if trying to disappear.

"Bring the other POWs in, but allow the German compound commander to return to his quarters."

The guards moved smartly through the craft shop's back door into the building annex, then returned with the seven other POWs, who shuffled, stared at their bootlaces, and wet their lips in response to the guards' repeated "*Schnell, schnell,*" the one German word the American soldiers had bothered to learn. Because of the escape, the POWs had not been sent to the logging show that morning. They wore their frayed infantry uniforms, stripped of all badges of rank and unit insignias by guards, who sold them as souvenirs.

"I doubt these POWs have ever been beaten by American guards," Wren said gloomily, pausing for Kinney to render it into German. "It's against Army regulations and our sense of fair play. So they think nothing will happen if they continue to lie about Schiller's escape."

Wren stood stiffly and gathered Prahl's papers into the manila folder. "Well, they're right. Nothing will happen, at least not in this camp, not in the United States." Wren lifted the rubber stamp from the table, pressed it firmly into the ink pad, and loudly stamped Prahl's file.

With every movement reflecting his resignation, Wren approached Prahl, who was still sitting in the straight-back chair, his hands tightly gripping the armrests. The line of POWs behind the chair came to ragged attention as Wren neared.

As if a glance would have confessed complicity, the last prisoner in line, Ulrich Schwerin, carefully avoided staring at his friend in the chair. The whine of a truck in low gear sidling up to the building was ignored.

The Secret Service agent held out the file to Prahl. On it in vivid red were stamped the letters "NR."

Wren let the Germans' eyes settle fully on the letters before he said grimly, *"Nach Russland."*

To Russia.

An order from Wren to line up the POWs in front of a firing squad would not have been more terrifying. The Fort Lewis POWs—comfortable with their fish soups, pigs' knuckles, and even an occasional beer with dinner, with their three blankets and wood stoves, with craft lessons and the camp movie theater— had heard horrifying rumors of the fate of Wehrmacht soldiers captured by the Red Army. Starving to death was the most merciful end to a stay in a Siberian POW camp, where rats and boot tongues were standard fare, where brutality was sanctioned, and where the newly arrived German prisoners worked dawn to dusk digging mass graves for prisoners who had arrived a few weeks before.

"Nach Russland?" Prahl croaked. His eyes rolled back in his head and he swayed in the chair. Wren grabbed his shoulder to prevent him from falling.

The craft room's front door burst open, and three Soviet soldiers stormed into the room. They were enormous and moved toward Prahl with the purpose of angry bears. Their wool *ushanki* with the earflaps tied overhead and the red stars made their heads appear unnaturally large and fearsome. The coat collars hung almost to the breastbones, and the black leather waist belts did nothing to contour the bulky coats. Their shapeless pants were tucked into arctic boots. Carried barrel-down on their backs in the peculiar Russian fashion were PPSh submachine guns, with the drum magazines prodding the soldiers' backs.

The Russians were moving too fast for him to make out their faces, but as he backed away from the prisoner's chair, Wren had the impression of craggy peasant features, missing teeth, and even the odor of borscht.

The first soldier swung the submachine gun off his back as he charged Prahl. Unlike most such weapons, the PPSh has a heavy wood stock, designed to double as a club. The Russian chopped the gun at the German's chest.

The sound was of an ax hitting bark. The blow launched Prahl out of his chair, which toppled after him. He frantically covered his face, expecting another blow. The soldiers swarmed over him.

"Vstavai, nemets," the club wielder barked. Stand up, deaf-mute. The sobriquet was the universal name Russians used for Germans, dating from czarist times when German traders who could not speak the mother tongue were considered deaf.

The second Russian leveled his PPSh at the line of POWs, who, pale to a man, backed against the craft-room wall and raised their hands. The other two soldiers grabbed Prahl by the collar and roughly hauled him to his feet. The Russians propped him up between them.

The club wielder growled, *"Iditye snami."* You're coming with us. His meaty hand closed around Prahl's hair. He jerked the German's head back and with a bouncer's rush propelled him to the door.

"Nicht Russland," Prahl cried. *"Nicht Russland. Ich betteln..."*

Visible through the open door was a Soviet transport truck, perhaps a GAZ-AA, grimy and tired, with the red star on the door splattered with mud. The Russians disappeared toward the rear of the truck. The sound of Prahl landing on the cargo bed was followed by Russian curses and the jangle of shackles.

A moment passed, with Wren standing dispassionately to one side and the remaining POWs rigid with dread behind the submachine guns. Then the Russian charged again through the craft-room door. He snared Ulrich Schwerin's neck and buckled him over, intent on throwing him across the floor toward the truck.

"*Bitte... bitte...*" Schwerin shrieked. He twisted his head out of the Russian's grip to implore Wren. "*Bitte...*"

Wren raised a hand, and the Russian instantly released his grip. The agent said in a bored voice. "It's too late for that other fellow. But maybe you'd like to talk a little more about Schiller's escape."

Even before Kinney had begun the translation, Schwerin was nodding so vigorously his chin bounced off his chest. He snatched the watch cap from his head. He squeezed his knees together to keep them from trembling, but they merely shook in unison. He clicked his eyes left and right. The giant Russian was standing directly behind him, out of view, but close enough to breathe on Schwerin's neck. The German shivered as if the breath were a Siberian wind.

"Fred, tell the other POWs to wait in their barracks."

When they had filed out—taking little more than three seconds—Wren nodded to the Soviet soldiers. Without a word, they slung their weapons over their backs and left the room. The trunk cranked into life and pulled away from the building. Prahl's despairing moan sounded clearly over the engine.

"Sit down, Private Schwerin," Wren ordered, returning to the table while Kinney translated. "We have a few questions we don't think you answered quite fully before."

The interrogation lasted another twenty minutes. When Wren knew everything the POW saw, heard, and suspected that day, he dismissed him. Schwerin's eyes teared with gratitude as he scrambled out the craft-room door.

Next Wren and Kinney again questioned Generalmajor Detlef Becker, the senior POW officer, who loudly scoffed at the possibility that genuine Red Army soldiers had dragged away a prisoner. Nevertheless, he was fearful for his men. Becker told all he knew of the incident and seemed relieved as he left the craft room for his hut.

"We didn't learn much," Wren said as they crossed the compound to Colonel Derrick's office. Thousands of pairs of fearful eyes followed them.

"Do you believe the prisoners?" Garvin asked.

"All of it. The rock with the envelope tied around it, the body under the log, the whole story. And I think that's all anyone in this camp knows. Schiller wouldn't let them learn more. He's a loner."

"He's goddam dangerous, and he's loose," Kinney added darkly.

Garvin glanced nervously over his shoulder. He doubted there were this many krauts in Germany. Thousands, all motionless, all staring at them as they walked to the entrance. The gate guard tower loomed ahead. Garvin laughed to settle his nerves. "Nice touch with the Russian soldiers, Fred."

Kinney chuckled. "I've used that trick three or four times before. Never more than once at a camp. And you have to be quick, before the POWs can figure out that what they're seeing is impossible. Machine-gun-toting Russian soldiers in the middle of the U.S., for Christ's sake."

"Does the act always work?" Garvin asked as they passed through the link gate. American guards closed it behind them. They turned along a gravel road toward the POW-camp head-quarters.

"It's never failed yet. I can usually get one of them to piss in his pants as he's being dragged to the truck. The prisoners we carry away are trucked to the nearest POW camp. By tonight, Prahl will be interned in central Oregon."

Kinney and Garvin left for Tacoma to brief the Pierce County sheriff. Wren sat at Colonel Lewis Derrick's desk in his office thirty yards from the fence. He spread the documents out in front of him and flipped on the tulip-bulb lamp on the desk.

He held up Schiller's photo, taken on admission to the Fort Lewis camp. He had studied it before the questioning. It had changed somehow since then. The white scar still ran from his lip halfway to his chin. His dark hair was still tightly waved and cropped. But now the German stared back at him with an arrogant cast to his eyes and a mocking lift at the corner of his mouth Wren hadn't seen before. The man's face transmitted a challenge. Wren loosened his tie and picked up the phone.

At six o'clock that evening, thirty-four hours after the escape, Wren drove to Fort Lewis's Signal Corps HQ to telex another alarming message to White House Supervising Agent Mike O'Brien. "Schiller" was an alias. The prisoner's admission photograph didn't match the *Soldbuch* description. The *Soldbuch's* box labeled "Identifying Marks" was blank. Yet the photo clearly showed a scar below the man's lip. Maybe he had gashed his face in Africa, after the photo was taken, but Wren doubted it. The man looked comfortable with the scar, as if it had accompanied him for a long time.

Admission Form FL listed the escapee's height at six feet one, yet the height of the soldier who had originally owned the *Soldbuch* was 177 centimeters, five feet ten.

When asked about these obvious disparities, Colonel Derrick explained that his camp often admitted three or four hundred POWs a day. He had just one German-speaker on the entire staff and wouldn't be surprised if many of the POWs didn't match their *Soldbuecher*. He just didn't have the resources for a thorough screening job.

The wire to O'Brien contained other evidence. According to the AFW 3000 form, the man who called himself Schiller was captured by the British army's Twenty-third Armored Brigade near Al-Khums. Yet the *Soldbuch's* original owner was a member of the Wehrmacht's Thirty-seventh Antiaircraft Battalion. With a call to the Army Records Office at the new Pentagon building in Washington, Wren quickly learned that virtually the entire Thirty-seventh had been captured a month before the escapee was caught. Wren concluded the escaped prisoner had picked the *Soldbuch* off a body or had purchased it on the Arab black market.

Wren stood near the silent telex receiver, waiting for O'Brien's reply. He knew it wouldn't take long, not a message from the highly strung Irishman who hovered near the president like a watchful pit bull and who believed the secret of protection was aggressiveness.

Fifteen minutes later, O'Brien's return message sputtered out of the machine. It agreed with Wren that the escapee's photograph must be immediately telephotoed to the commanders of each of the 350 POW camps in the United States. Major General William B. Smith, head of the Army Detainee System, whom O'Brien had contacted during those fifteen minutes, personally guaranteed that all 400,000 German prisoners in the United States would be asked within twenty-four hours if they recognized the prisoner.

The wire further said that by nine o'clock in the morning Wren was to have contacted all local police authorities, the Coast Guard, and the Fort Lewis Military Police.

Wren was ordered to seal off Seattle and Tacoma.

9

THE FISHERMAN'S BUICK HAD A MIND of its own, hurling down State 10 a few miles east of Seattle. Eight cylinders and almost four hundred cubic inches. Monck had never driven anything like it. The speedometer was calibrated to 120 miles an hour, and judging from the surging engine, he didn't think it was just a typical American boast.

Again and again he eased back on the accelerator, unwilling to test the threadbare tires by letting the Buick have its reins. But the sudden danger in Seattle had caught him off guard, and now he needed distance.

Last night, he had attempted to leave Seattle on the Chicago-bound *West Coast Hiawatha*. He had been thirty feet from the King Street Station ticket counter when he saw the three policemen standing near rental lockers scrutinizing everyone who purchased a ticket. One of them repeatedly glanced at an enlarged photo, undoubtedly a copy of Monck's POW photograph. The German had quickly lowered his head and turned back to the street.

They were looking for him. Somehow, just a day after his

escape, the Americans had discovered his artifice.

He had returned to Bainbridge Island on the evening ferry and had slept on Meg's living-room sofa. The next morning, now two full days after his escape, he drove the circuitous route, using the west-channel ferry, across the Tacoma Narrows Bridge, and through the Maple Valley to join the state highway east of Seattle, avoiding roadblocks the Americans had erected on routes leaving the city.

Monck had decided to drive only as far as Spokane, then board a train to points east. He turned off at Issaquah, a logging town fifteen miles east of Seattle on the road to Snoqualmie Pass. He narrowed his eyes against the morning light streaming over the Cascades as he guided the Buick to the gas pumps of a Union Oil station.

"Buddy's Union," the sign hanging above the door of the office read. Monck switched off the engine, honked the horn, and peered into the office for an attendant.

On the station's window were two blue stars on a white flag. Meg had explained they were service flags, with one star for each son or daughter in the service. On the door to the office was a sign reminding patrons that anyone owning more than five tires was supposed to turn the extras in. Buddy was a patriot.

The garage bay was vacant. A Penzoil rack near the garage door was empty. Stripped of its tires, a dilapidated Model T rested on blocks to the right of the garage. Weeds had grown to the running boards. The forest ended just behind the garage. Wild blackberries climbed to the roof, as if reclaiming the building for the wilderness.

Monck honked again.

"Hold your horses," came from the outhouse just visible between two fir trees behind the station. After a moment, the crescent door opened and the gas jockey emerged, still fighting the buttons on his overalls.

Hands deep in the overalls pockets, he walked toward the Buick with an insolent pace. With rationing, servile gas jockeys were a thing of the past. The attendant paused in front of the

Buick to put on an expression of indecision. An out-of-state plate. He didn't even have to be polite. He ambled to the driver's side window.

"What'll you have, pal?"

"Ten gallons, please." Well rehearsed, devoid of accent.

"I ain't pumping a drop until you hand over the coupons."

"Of course." Monck pulled a number of C coupons—the same letter as on the window sticker—from an envelope and passed them to the attendant.

"And around here you pay in advance." He put his face at window level and stared at Monck. The attendant's eyes were set close, just at the edges of his nose, and were incapable of anything but a leer. His skin was pale, even for a Northwesterner, and he was missing his lower front teeth. Tendrils of matted black hair protruded from his Union Oil cap. "Five fifty, pal."

Monck hadn't seen a posted gasoline price, and he guessed the attendant was charging what he thought the traffic would bear. He handed over the money.

"Sorry about the delay," the attendant said, the sneer suddenly gone. "My old lady served chili last night, and that stuff goes through me like shit through a goose. Spent most of the time since then on the crapper. I'll ring this up and be back in a minute."

Americans were the most ebullient people he had ever met, and quixotic in their moods. Yet the gas attendant's sudden sociability alerted Monck. As the attendant walked back to his office, the German started the Buick's engine. He followed him closely through the windows, watching his hands, waiting for him to pick up a telephone or reach for a weapon. But the attendant deposited the bills in the cash register, then folded up some paperwork and jammed it into his pocket. He slammed the cash drawer shut and started back to the gas pumps.

Had Monck known anything about Dean Harp, he would have watched him more closely. The paleness the German had noticed was Walla Walla white, the color all prisoners fade to after a tour in the state prison there. Harp had been seventeen when he threw a lighted gasoline-soaked rag into the Issaquah High School annex. That was the fire for which he was caught, but at various times before that he had put a match to Al Edland's barn, the deputy sheriff's Hupmobile, and the Lutheran minister's turpentine-drenched Siamese cat, which remained the funniest thing he had ever seen, bar none.

Five years hard time at the Walls had indeed taught Dean Harp a lesson. The only things he lit these days were his Old Golds, he told his parole-board officer every week. Buddy Jones had hired him because Jones's sons were off fighting the Axis, as was every other young man in Issaquah, except Harp, who was happily exempt because of his felony record.

Harp lifted the nozzle off the pump and twisted off the Buick's gas cap. He whistled tonelessly as Monck glanced at a road map.

"These goddam old pumps are slow, I'll guarantee you that." Harp tapped the Buick's fender to his own whistled tune, then reached to the top of the pump for a clean rag. "Let me get your windows."

"Don't bother. I'm in a hurry."

"No problem at all."

Harp moved along the car, wiping the side windows as he pumped gasoline onto the top of the Buick. He walked gingerly, avoiding the puddle of fuel he had poured onto the asphalt, which was flowing under the car. His whistling and chatter covered the splashing.

Just as the gasoline spilled from the cab roof onto the front window and as Monck inhaled his first potent breath of gasoline fumes, Dean Harp dropped the nozzle, pulled the copy of the *Seattle Post-Intelligencer* from his pocket, and held it up to Monck.

"Look familiar, sauerkraut?" Harp asked in a mockingly sweet voice.

Under a banner headline, "German Escapes Ft. Lewis POW Camp," was a three-column picture of Monck.

Monck pounced on the gas pedal and released the clutch. The ponderous Buick began rolling forward, gamely trying to get away from the pumps. But with the carburetor open wide, the engine coughed and the car stalled, still over the growing pond of gas.

Harp's hands moved as if rehearsed, plucking the box of sulfur matches from his overall pocket and striking a match against the box. Smiling gleefully, he tossed the hissing flame onto the car.

Fire leaped across the Buick's top and cascaded down the rear window. A blazing yellow shroud descended the sides of the car to the asphalt, igniting the puddle of gasoline, which flashed orange, then echoed skyward, enclosing the car in a cocoon of flame. Roiling black smoke rose into the air.

The Buick's roof hung over the driver's window, and it saved Monck by forcing the cataract of fire away from the opening. He could see nothing but flickering orange sheets. Fighting a panic that slowed his every move, Monck stamped on the starter and feathered the pedal. The engine roared. The Buick lurched out of the ignited pool.

Monck spun the steering wheel. The car veered away from the pumps toward the street, fire billowing from its body. The flames sucked air from the cab, and breathing felt as if he were inhaling a red poker. Droplets of gasoline splashed onto his arm and popped into flame. He swatted at them.

A front tire blew, and the steering wheel twisted out of his hands. He fought it, tugging the car around, back toward the state highway. Wind brushed back the flames from the windshield. He glimpsed the gas pumps, with the attendant standing well back, his mouth open with laughter.

Monck muscled the steering wheel to the left. The car careened to the side of the road opposite Buddy's Union. Trailing tentacles of flame, the Buick bounced along the shoulder, then into the high grass, tipping toward the roadside ditch. The wheels lost their purchase, and the Buick pitched toward the stagnant bottom of the trench. The car rolled onto its side and skidded along the muck in the ditch for ten yards before stopping.

On the driver's side the fire died with a sibilant whisper as mud layered over it, but flames continued to eat the other side and the hood and trunk. The gasoline tank exploded with a dull thump that ruptured the compartment wall. The cab filled with a flurry of flames. Heat shattered the windshield.

Shrieking with delight, Dean Harp skipped across the road toward the blazing Buick. Air above the car shimmered and mixed with strands of inky smoke. The blackening Buick crawled with fire.

His creation. A work of art. This sure as hell beat the Siamese cat. And the POW's photo in the paper had given him a license. A Nazi funeral pyre. He'd be a hero. He'd petition the governor for a pardon. No more parole board.

Harp approached the car from behind, expecting to see the German's charred remains pasted against a window, the mouth frozen open during a last agonized scream. The gas attendant walked boldly into the ditch, unafraid of the fire still licking the Buick. His boots kicked through the bunch grass, and he slapped aside the taller tufts.

He came close enough to the sedan to singe his eyebrows. He peered through the flames into the car window. There was no body.

Harp's malicious grin fell from his face. A flare of fear burst in his stomach. He stumbled back, away from dying flames.

With the startling suddenness of a ring-necked pheasant, Kurt Monck sprang from the mud and thick grass on the bottom of the ditch. Harp did not even have time to reflexively raise an arm. Monck's garrote—this one carefully crafted from a wire plucked from Margarete Bayerlein's piano and a broomstick—snapped around the attendant's neck. Harp's eyes bulged, and his fingers clawed at the wire. Monck drew it tight.

But not too tight, not enough to kill.

The German backstepped up the ditch to the road shoulder. Harp's eyes bulged from their sockets, and his mouth fished open. The wire cut off a scream. Pain and terror washed away any will to resist being pulled up the trench.

Monck tugged him across the road, with Harp bending and weaving and staggering, his hands feebly scratching at the garrote, no longer visible on the surface of his skin. When they reached the second pump, the German kicked Harp's legs out from under him and let him topple to the asphalt. Monck rolled him onto his back.

With one hand still cinching the garrote, the German lifted the gas nozzle from its hook. He flipped the pump switch.

He jammed the steel spout through Harp's lips, breaking off his upper teeth. Harp's contorted face slackened at the horrific realization. He tried to rise, but Monck rammed the nozzle farther down the attendant's throat. He squeezed the grip.

Gasoline streamed into Harp's mouth, then bubbled back. A spume of gasoline and blood swirled around the nozzle, overflowed Harp's mouth, then coursed down his cheeks to the asphalt. The German put his weight to the nozzle, forcing it deeper until the handle guard cut into Harp's lip. The attendant's arms swatted ineffectually against his attacker.

Monck pumped gas until Harp's belly began to swell. He unwrapped the garrote and dug into the attendant's shirt pocket for the box of matches. He spilled them on Harp's chest, then scraped one on the asphalt. It crackled to life. The German jerked the nozzle from Harp's throat and dropped the match into it.

A geyser of fire shot from the mouth. Harp spasmodically twisted his head, and the fire spewed along the driveway. A human flamethrower. Harp's belly detonated. Fire and flaming shreds of gore blew into the air, splotching the pump and driveway. The flames lapped and popped, and after several seconds Harp's arms stopped their useless beating.

Monck brushed a shred of tissue from his pant leg. He pushed the garrote into his shirt sleeve, then walked by the body toward the state highway. Fire still worked on Harp's entrails.

Monck said sardonically, *"Lassen Sie sich das eine Lehre sein."*

Let that be a lesson to you.

He arrived again at Margarete Beyerlein's home on Bainbridge Island the following morning. He had hitchhiked several times on rural roads, carefully watching the drivers' reactions when they slowed to pick him up, and he had walked more than sixty miles, much of it cross-country to avoid roadblocks.

When she opened her door, he began bluntly, "I can't make it alone. I want you to go with me."

She stared at him a moment. Her husband's clothes fit him perfectly, even the shoes, which were muddy to the laces. The left arm of his shirt had suffered several burn holes.

"What happened?"

"I make mistakes, mistakes an American never would. I had no idea a newspaper would print a story about a POW escape, picture and all."

"That isn't done at home?"

He gently touched a dime-size lesion on his forearm. "The Reich doesn't want citizens knowing prisoners can walk away from its jails. What government does, except this crazy one? It never occurred to me that almost every person in the area would know my face."

She led him into the house. He wearily lowered himself onto the couch and pulled off his shoes and socks. Both feet were blistered on the balls and large toes. Meg brought him a pan of water, tincture of iodine, and adhesive bandages.

"I made other errors. I bought several sausage links at a store in Tacoma, but not before giving the clerk the wrong ration coupons. She looked at me as if I were a foreigner. And now I'm a celebrity, staring out from every newsstand in the state, maybe in the nation. I have to cross this country, and I can't make it without your help."

She shook her head in vexation. "You just march back to my door and expect my daughter and me to accompany you on some chase. It's not supposed to matter to us." She slowly ran a hand down her arm, as if kneading out a bruise. "No, we're not going with you. I don't care what you say."

His eyes searched hers out. His face was set in stone. "You do care what I say. You care as much as you've ever cared about anything. You are going to accompany me."

Her face lengthened as she sifted through his words. "What are you saying?"

"I think we understand each other. Except for one thing. Your daughter can't join us. It'd be too risky."

So improbable were his words that she involuntarily followed him from one preposterous demand to the next. "Mary?" she asked, as if she had other daughters. "That's just impossible. She's never been without me. I can't leave her."

"Do you know anyone she can stay with for two weeks?"

She peered astigmatically at him, as if divining her future. Monck dabbed at his feet with the iodine, seeming not to care about her responses. Only then did his words fully settle on her. This man wanted to separate her from Mary. The realization was so startling and frightening that she sank to the ottoman in front of her husband's leather chair, the first time she had sat on it since his death. It was the place where great and small family decisions had been made, the three of them together. She had been unable to return to this sacred place after the drowning. Now that she had, it offered her nothing but the sight of the POW. She said weakly, "I can't leave her."

Monck looked up. He smiled, as if with understanding. "I'm afraid that's been settled. I asked if you know anyone she can stay with for a while."

The surge of anger lifted her to her feet. Her mouth pulled back, and her hands balled into fists. With a huge effort, she checked herself. Her turn would come. The only thing that was settled was that she would never leave Mary. She said with a strained voice, "No, there's no one around here she could stay with."

"A letter to your San Diego contact will be all it takes. I've already telephoned the bus line about Saturday departures. To-morrow we'll put her on the bus. Your contact will be waiting for her."

Fear for her daughter rendered her mute. He was so . . . clerical in his disposition of her family. He spoke in dust-dry tones disassociated from the damage of his words. He pulled his socks back on.

Monck said, "You'll send him a message to the same address

you send your shipping reports. You'll put her on the bus. Thirty-six hours later he'll meet her at the terminal in San Diego."

"I've never met him. I don't know who he is. I can't just give her..."

"He's reliable, and he's on our side. That's all you need to know."

His finality was as evident as the garrote he pulled from his sleeve. It slithered free like a reptile from a log. "Now all I need is a way for you and me to leave this town. I passed four road-blocks getting here. The train and bus stations are crowded with police. The only flights out are military. And I don't think I can walk all the way east."

He folded the garrote. He held it up to the light, examining the wire wraps around the handles. Some of the wire glistened with an oily burgundy crust. Monck ran the wire between his thumb and forefinger, restoring the steely tint. He put the garrote away, then wiped his thumb on his sock. She locked her arms in front of her, but could not stop her trembling.

At noon the next day, they were standing in the line to board the Greyhound. Margarete and her daughter were so close they communicated intuitively, and the currents coursing to her from Mary's tightly gripped hands were all of sadness.

"Don't worry, Mom," the girl said. "I'll be back before you know it."

"Yes, yes..." Margarete's voice was tiny. She was embarrassed that her daughter had to compensate for her.

"Tacoma, Olympia, Centralia, Kelso, Portland, and points south, boarding from gate two." The PA system's metallic drone filled the small waiting area. "Last call."

They walked from the building to the boarding area. Meg passed the cardboard suitcase to the driver, who slid it into the bus's undercarriage. Mary sniffled, but wouldn't let herself cry. They joined the line to board. Standing near the back door of the bus were two Bremerton policemen. They stared at everyone getting on board.

Margarete glanced quickly over her shoulder. Kurt Monck was in the window of the tavern across from the Greyhound terminal. She could just make out his face; it was almost hidden by the sun's reflection off the glass. He nodded, encouraging her. Her anger rose again.

"Mary, I want you to listen to me. You know that we bought a ticket to San Diego. And we went across the street to show it to Mr. Monck like he told us to. He thinks I'm putting you on the bus for California. But I'm not."

The line shuffled them toward the bus door. The girl looked up at her mother. "What do you mean, Mom?"

She leaned closer to Mary. "Monck is a dangerous man, honey. He is trying to hurt some people. And going along with him will hurt both of us."

"You said he was a friend of Daddy's."

"I couldn't tell you the truth then, Mary. Monck is no friend of anybody here. He wants to ruin all the work your daddy and I have done. He wants to take it all away. And he wants to take you away from me." She looked again at Monck. He had stepped farther back into the tavern, perhaps seeing one of the policemen who were patrolling the terminal. "Mary, this bus's first stop is in Gorst, the little town five miles south of here along Sinclair Inlet."

"I've been there, Mom. During a school outing to the Christmas-tree farm."

"You get off the bus there and wait for me."

"I'm not going to San Diego?" she cried with relief.

Margarete stepped in front of her to block her smile from Monck's view.

"No. I'll be there to pick you up as soon as I can."

Mary looked around her mother at the tavern. Monck was still in the window. The driver took the ticket of the couple in front of Mary.

"Mom, why don't you call the police? They'll help."

Margarete bent low to her daughter and said urgently, "Honey, I can't call the police. Not now, not ever. You'll just have to trust me on this, will you? Get off the bus at the first stop, and I'll meet you there."

"I don't know what you mean. . . ."

Margarete's voice was sharp. "Trust me, Mary. I'll try to explain later."

The girl nodded tentatively, her eyes reflecting her bewilderment. She gave the ticket to the driver. He tore off a portion and gave the rest back to her.

Mary grabbed her mother around the neck and kissed her cheek. The girl pulled herself away and disappeared into the bus.

She had resolved to lose Monck the first chance she got. It came sooner than she had hoped. The bus pulled away from the terminal and was lost quickly in the cloud of its own diesel exhaust. She walked along the sidewalk toward her car, parked in front of a shoe store two blocks west of the terminal.

She knew the POW had left the tavern and was walking behind her. He caught up with her half a block from the car, and they walked along the sidewalk. He looked quickly over his shoulder. There were no policemen or shore patrolmen in sight.

He said, "I'm sorry about this. There just wasn't another way."

His ability to manufacture a sincere tone was remarkable. She decided to go along with it. "I'm sorry too. More than you can know."

She lifted her key ring to find the car key, and the answer came to her. The suddenness of the solution made her hand shake. The keys rattled against each other. She would simply leave him in Bremerton. Right then. What would he be able to do? He would be adrift. She didn't have time to think it through. She pushed the key into the door and turned it. Monck stepped off the curb to walk to the passenger-side door.

Margarete slipped onto the seat behind the steering wheel and with a quick movement reached across to lock the passenger door. As the POW's hand gripped the door handle, she jabbed the key into the ignition and rolled the engine over.

Monck leaned over to peer into the cab. The window seemed to magnify his lean features as they registered first puzzlement, then a virulent understanding. He jerked on the door handle twice, then started to bring his fist back to ram it through the window.

He didn't get the chance. Margarete released the clutch and stepped on the accelerator. The car shot away from him. He ran alongside and with a speed that astonished her moved ahead of the car, then turned to hold his hands out to stop her. Both a command and a plea.

She pushed the gas pedal to the floor. The big Dodge lunged at him. For an instant she saw fright in his face, and she felt a savage joy. He jumped aside, and the car's enormous fenders brushed his clothing.

As she turned onto Burnside, she glanced at him through the back window. He was walking back to the sidewalk, brushing his hands together as if to rid them of something. She thought he was smiling, but the distance was increasing, and she couldn't be sure.

The bus was ten minutes ahead of her. She drove over the hill behind the downtown area, then descended to Callow Street and turned south toward Sinclair Inlet. She passed more of the naval yard. The superstructure of a damaged aircraft carrier rose behind the repair buildings.

Her shaking had increased, and she gripped the steering wheel tightly. Monck would probably return to Bainbridge Island and wait for them. She had no idea where she and Mary would go. That hadn't entered her sudden calculation. All she wanted was her daughter.

She drove south along Sinclair Inlet, passing the row of quickly fabricated homes on her left, which clung precariously to the hillside and were full of wives waiting for their sailors to return. On her left were the mud flats of low tide, smelling of sulfur and salt brine. She honked angrily at a slow truck in front of her. It obligingly pulled onto the shoulder, and she rushed by.

Gorst is the six-building town at the southern tip of the inlet.

The bus stopped there to take on passengers coming north from Mason County. Margarete slowed near a wrecking yard. A block south was a police roadblock, and a half-dozen cars and trucks were waiting to be searched. She saw the Greyhound at a corner of the Standard station's lot. Two sailors and an elderly woman were waiting to board. The driver was pushing duffel bags into the baggage compartment. She stopped the Dodge near the garage's service bay, got out, and walked toward the bus.

She couldn't see Mary. She quickened her pace, looking left and right. Her girl should have been standing near the bus, waiting for her. Mary should have seen her car. Margarete's chest tightened with fear.

She rushed up to the driver. "Did a blond girl, eleven years old, just get off the bus?"

He looked up. "The one with the ticket all the way to California? Sure did. That's her over there." He pointed to the grocery store next to the service station.

Kurt Monck stood along the side of the store, near a fifty-five-gallon drum that fed fuel oil into the building. He wore a felt hat low over his eyes, and he hid his jaw behind a hand, as if he were thoughtfully rubbing his chin. He held Mary tightly by hand. The girl's face was glistening with tears. When she attempted to run to her mother, Monck increased the pressure on her hand and hauled her back to him. She grimaced with pain, but didn't cry out.

Desperately trying not to sob, Margarete covered her mouth with a shaking hand. She walked unsteadily toward the grocery. When she was within a few yards, Monck released the girl, and she ran into her mother's arms.

Margarete stroked her daughter's hair and whispered soothing words. When Monck stepped toward them, she looked at him, intending to accuse him of cruelty to them both. Instead, all she could say was a ragged, "How . . . ?"

Monck scanned the roadway for police cars, then said, "Before I was sent behind the British lines, I was taught to bypass ignition systems in trucks and scout cars, in case I needed transportation in the desert." He almost smiled. "I can do it very quickly. The car I appropriated passed you near the shipyard gate. That's it over there." He looked toward a black Ford coupe.

He knelt between Margarete and Mary. His words were solemn. "I apparently didn't make myself clear back at the terminal. Listen to me, Mary, because I mean every word I say. If you ever want to see your mother again, you'll get back on that bus, and you'll stay on it all the way to San Diego. If you talk to anyone, if you tell the bus driver about me, or if you don't arrive in San Diego, your mother will just disappear. Forever. Is that clear?"

She fearfully embraced her mother.

Monck tore the girl from her mother's arms and spun her toward him. "I asked you if that was clear."

The girl's face was wild with fear, but she nodded quickly.

Monck stood and said, "And you." He took Margarete's arm in his hand and squeezed to the point of pain. "You'll start doing what I say. I have no doubt of it now."

Margarete shivered. Her mind was racing, searching for a way out. But it could not find anything other than the POW's terrible threat.

She unwrapped the girl's arms and said in a small voice, "Come on, Mary. I'll walk you to the bus."

They walked to the Greyhound leaning into each other. They said goodbye again and again, and Margarete promised they would be together soon. Her daughter asked no questions, and Margarete knew the girl didn't believe her.

At the bus's door, Margarete wiped the girl's damp cheeks with her hand, then kissed her goodbye. She tried to smile, but there was nothing left.

The girl whispered, "I'll wait for you, Mom," and stepped into the bus.

Margarete waited until the bus pulled onto the road and began its journey to Tacoma and the Southwest. She turned back to Monck. He was blurred by the moisture in her eyes. As they walked to the Dodge, she asked, "The sooner you get done with your work, the sooner I'm rid of you, is that right?"

He opened the passenger door. "That's right."

She got into the car. She heard herself say, "I know how to get out."

He smiled indulgently. "Both of us?"

"East?"

He nodded.

"I can have us as far as Chicago by Monday morning."

"Two days from now?" He raised an eyebrow skeptically.

"Yes." Her eyes burned into him. "But that's as far as I go. If I get you to Chicago, away from everyone who's looking for you, you'll let me go and have San Diego send my daughter back. Is that a deal?"

"Sounds fair to me."

She tried to read his tone. It was neutral, without a trace of intrigue or compassion or understanding or anything else. He was utterly without a thought for her, and she had no choice.

Margarete Bayerlein held the scalpel between them, allowing it to catch the morning light pouring in the window overlooking the sound. She moved the blade toward Monck's bare chest.

One inch separated the scalpel from the man who had thrown her into turmoil, the man who had torn her daughter out of her arms. It would be so simple to sink the blade into his neck. He might never again be so vulnerable. Her anguish would be over in a moment.

But, of course, it wouldn't be. Her daughter was a guarantee of her performance. San Diego would do with Mary as Monck or his German control ordered. Monck had her daughter as a priceless ransom, and all that was left for Margarete was her terrible rage.

Her impulse to abandon reason and lunge at his neck was almost uncontrollable. His unguarded artery was an instant away from the sharp steel. Up and in. She had absolutely no doubt she could do it. Her wrath would guide the scalpel deeply into him. It rushed over her again. The steel moved toward his neck.

"What are you doing?" he demanded, arresting her wild act. He sat on the edge of the sofa, his shirt across his lap. The purple scar of an old wound was above his left nipple. On the sofa next to him was a serving tray. "Where's the painkiller?"

"I have none." She brought the steel to a hair's width from his sternum, then let it touch the skin. She pressed lightly, and a bead of blood grew along the blade.

Monck grabbed her hand. "You managed to find a scalpel at the hospital. Why no anesthetic?"

Her voice matched the blade. "Shall we go ahead, or will you stay in Seattle forever?"

After an instant of uncharacteristic indecision, he released her hand. Meg placed a finger on the blunt edge of the blade to exert pressure. The glistening steel sank into his chest, and a thin line of opened skin began trailing behind the blade as it leisurely began sliding down his sternum. The pain pulled back Monck's mouth.

She said, "It's been eighteen hours since I put Mary on the bus. I worked a swing shift at the hospital after I left the Greyhound station. There wasn't a moment during the shift that I wasn't thinking about her."

Monck wet his lips. His voice was hoarse and unsteady. "You were apparently thinking of her to the exclusion of searching for novocaine or ethyl chloride or some other local anesthetic."

"You are very good at giving orders and threatening me. You somehow think that telling me to deliver my daughter to an address in California is nothing to be concerned about. You order me to travel across the country with you, disregarding my life here. And I have no doubt you'll carry out your threats if I don't obey you."

The scalpel moved lower, opening a red rift in his chest. His face was carefully impassive, but a line of sweat had formed on his upper lip. His eyes followed the blade with absolute attention.

"So let me tell you a few things." She leaned on the scalpel, and it inched slowly down his chest. "You were the talk of my shift last night. One of the nurses cut your photo out of Friday's *Bremerton Sun* and tacked it to the bulletin board. Another said her Boy Scout troop was looking for you along the Pleasant Valley Road. And another nurse is married to a Bremerton policeman, who was called in for the weekend to man a roadblock."

Her voice was just above a whisper. "Every man, woman, and child in the Northwest is looking for you. Your face is more familiar to them today than President Roosevelt's. Four days have already passed since you escaped from the logging camp, and you'll never get out of the Pacific Northwest if you don't follow my plan."

Blood trailed down his chest onto his shirt. Monck's eyes were rigidly fixed on the scalpel, but they slipped out of focus as he blinked rapidly.

"Last night I borrowed the master key from the nurses' station and entered Dr. Abram's office. From his file cabinet I pulled all the forms we'll need. The base-hospital discharge, the priority lift transfer, the Great Lakes Naval Station Hospital routing slip, the medical personnel escort form, the bedside charts. I've filled them all out, right down to reasonable facsimiles of Dr. Abram's signature. They'll be expecting us at the field."

"Easy, easy . . . " Monck breathed through clenched jaws.

"With those forms we won't have any trouble passing you off as a sailor wounded in the Marianas fighting, where most of the boys coming to the hospital this week were injured. And because Great Lakes is the main hospital for prolonged chest-wound recoveries, your transfer will make some sense. The same forms will show you've burned your nose and jaw. Bandages will hide your face."

Drops of sweat rolled over Monck's eyebrows. He was breathing like a runner. "Easy . . ."

"During the flight and at every stop en route, a physician or a nurse will lift your dressing to examine the surgical incision for infection and stress on the sutures. So we can't completely fake the operation. An incision, even this shallow one, is needed."

Monck's lower lip trembled. He had bunched a corner of the cushion in each hand, and the entire sofa shook with his effort not to cry out.

The incision was a quarter inch deep and three inches long and growing. "Putting my daughter on the bus was the most painful thing I've done since I identified my husband's body. I couldn't make anybody pay for the heartbreak at the morgue. But today is different."

The blade crawled lower, approaching the base of the breastbone. Monck swallowed a low groan.

"I could easily have stolen a vial of novocaine and a syringe from the hospital, and could have deadened your chest." Meg pulled the scalpel from his flesh. The wound was as long as an ax blade, and was open and angry. She dabbed at it with an alcohol-soaked swab, which instantly turned red.

She lifted a needle from the tray. A vein of 4-0 silk thread floated behind it. As calm as if she were knitting, Meg pricked the flap of skin at the base of the incision, pushed it through the opposite flap, and pulled the needle through. She tugged on the thread, closing a small part of the cleft in Monck's chest.

Monck tottered on the sofa. His mouth was open, and he was heedless of the saliva running from its corner. His face had faded to a ghastly white, and the sun blotches on his forehead stood out like melanomas.

"Yes, I could have saved you this suffering by bringing novocaine. But you were so casual when you dispensed pain to Mary and me yesterday. So this is my way of returning what you deal out so easily."

She inserted the last suture, then tied the thread off with the axle knot she had seen Dr. Abram perform so many times. She clipped the thread with scissors from her sewing basket.

She again dabbed the wound with the antiseptic swab, then applied the chest compress. "There. I wish this made us even."

The Bremerton Naval Yard airstrip was ten miles south of the shipyard. Meg drove a Navy ambulance, fraudulently requisitioned with a form from the nurses' station on the fracture ward. She had to stop at the Gorst roadblock. The shore patrolman didn't ask why a nurse, rather than a corpsman, was driving a Navy ambulance. He glanced into the rear of the truck and shook his head sympathetically at the heavily bandaged sailor. He waved her on.

She parked in a line of other ambulances behind a hangar that had been converted to a loading station. Corpsmen were opening the truck's rear doors almost before it rolled to a stop. They carefully carried the litter into the hangar, where they lowered it to a row of eight other stretchers.

All the injured wore massive chest or stomach dressings. Several were connected to saline bottles that hovered on rods above their heads. One sailor also had a cast from toe to hip. Only Meg's charge had apparently also suffered a facial wound, as white tape crossed the bridge of his nose, his upper lip, and his jaw.

The rumble of a DC-3's engines turning over filled the hangar. A WAVE nurse wearing ensign's bars patrolled the line of wounded, glancing at charts and taking pulses. Meg joined three other nurses assigned to the flight. Two were WAVEs, and the other was a civilian, wearing a white hospital uniform like Margarete's. She introduced herself and thanked them for the cup of coffee.

The loading began. The nurses walked alongside their patients, talking reassuringly. Margarete knew she was being ungenerous, but she felt she needed reassurance more than the wounded sailors. Last night, while Monck slept soundly despite his chest wound, she had worked her last shift at the hospital, where she had time to unravel the full scope of her plight. There was little likelihood the American authorities would not uncover her role in the POW's plan. Not showing up for her shift tonight might be enough to alert them. Or the missing hospital forms. Or perhaps someone might have seen him with her at the post office or driving in Bremerton. Or discovered the radio. The American authorities would find her house, then dig into her background. She and Mary would never be able to return to the island. Their lives there were shattered. Monck had seen to that. She looked down at him, comfortable on the stretcher. He smiled around the bandages, adding to her bitterness.

The wounded sailors were laid like dominoes inside the DC-3's cabin. The transport officer reviewed their papers, stamped that day's date—July 2—and added his signature to all the forms, then took the triplicate copies. Margarete and the other nurses strapped themselves into jump seats. A corpsman closed the hatch, and the engines accelerated to a throaty roar. She looked again at Monck, who was on a stretcher on the center aisle. He was still grinning at her.

Twenty miles to the west at the Seattle city hall, John Wren had just convinced Police Chief Paul Schlay to release another fifty policemen to the roadblock assignment, and was crossing Fourth Avenue to his car. The Secret Service agent paid no attention to the DC-3 passing overhead on an easterly course at four thousand feet.

Part two
THE RACE EAST

10

LARRY LEFFLER WAS THE KING OF Chicago process servers, and the hour he was spending in the fourth-floor men's room of the Liberty Building in Chicago would prove it again.

He stood in front of the sink, appearing to comb his hair. He was too tall for the mirror and bent forward to frame his face. Leffler was so thin he seemed rickety, and his old suit jacket hung from his bony shoulders without touching any meat. Wireless spectacles made his eyes appear watery and confused, and his thin face had the dimensions of a greyhound's, narrow and slight when seen from the front, but full of long, bony protuberances when viewed at an angle. Nothing in his face told of the singular determination and ingenuity required by Leffler's profession. Leffler had stalked his target for two days. And now Martin Hardy would soon walk into the trap.

No one likes being sued. And no one can be sued unless the summons and complaint are served by being placed in the hand. Not put on the doorstep or in the mailbox, but actually touched by the defendant. Getting that hand on the papers can be a tricky and dangerous business. Two of Leffler's fingers were permanently bent out of true, courtesy of a slamming door, and he wore a pucker of brown skin on his right thigh where a defendant had once thanked him for a summons with a .22 bullet.

Process dodgers called forth Leffler's art. His favorite ruse was used when a defendant's home displayed a service flag. Dressed as an Army captain, Leffler would approach the house looking sorrowful and carrying his legal papers tenderly in both hands. Expecting the worst from the European front or the Pacific theater, the parents tremblingly took the papers from Leffler and tearfully began reading them. They were often so relieved they were only being sued they hugged him.

Or, once Leffler had waited two hours on a fire escape near an open window. At the exact instant the woman reached for another potato to peel, he threw the wadded summons and complaint into the bowl. She touched it, and that was enough.

He was an artist, really. Unappreciated by those who were duped into witnessing his work, but an artist nevertheless. He was squinting into the mirror, trying to see his knobby face as one of an artist, when the restroom door opened again. Leffler automatically stepped to the wall stall, but recognized his quarry, Martin Hardy. Florid face around red-rimmed eyes. Leffler veered to the stall nearest the door, and Hardy, without a glance at the process server, walked into the wall stall.

Hardy was a vice-president of the insurance company. Were one to believe his wife's complaint for divorce, he was also a lecher of unprecedented sexual appetities.

Leffler heard the toilet-paper spool spin. Then another whirl of the spool was followed with a grating breath, then an unthrottled scream: "You son of a bitch!"

The summons and complaint had been deftly rolled in with the toilet paper. For Hardy's lawyer's sake, Leffler could only hope Hardy hadn't wiped his ass before seeing them. Hardy slammed his fist into the stall wall, then struggled with the latch. "I'll kill you, you bastard."

The stall door flew open, and Hardy tried to rush the process server, who was leisurely putting his comb into his back pocket.

Hardy's pants were still around his ankles, and only by grabbing at the swinging door did he prevent himself from toppling. In a spasm of frustration, he threw the legal papers into the air and, still off balance, tried to clutch at his pants. He fell heavily back onto the toilet.

"I will now swear in court that you were served today, Monday, July 3, Mr. Hardy," Leffler announced. "Your wife's lawsuit is under way, and you're due in court in fourteen days."

Leffler appreciated clever invective, and he credited Hardy with originality and a certain rhythm as his curses interspersed with the jangle of his belt buckle. But he had heard it all before, and he had forgotten Hardy before he stepped off the El near Wrigley Field and walked to his home.

For a long while after moving to Holmes Street, Leffler had had difficulty distinguishing his house from the dozen others on the street slapped together by the shoddy builder who had paid his architect for only one design. To prevent duped and angry defendants from finding him, Leffler had installed an engraved wood sign on the screen door that said "The Johnsons." With this small lie, his house adequately carried his mark.

But this afternoon there was another difference, something that caught at the edge of his mind, where it rested a moment before nudging him again. An added texture. He stopped on the sidewalk and stared at the plain wood structure.

The bathroom window was misted.

He stepped back, thinking it was a trick of the reflected sun. But there was water vapor on the window, and when he walked closer he saw tracks of drops down the glass. Someone was taking a bath in his house.

For an alarming instant, Leffler thought his ex-wife had moved back. Impossible, as she lived in Los Angeles and thoroughly loathed him. Anything was better than that possibility, so he moved with some confidence to the rear of the building. He crouched as he passed under the window.

The back door was unlocked, and he slowly pushed it open. He gritted his teeth at its grating squeak. On his toes, Leffler crossed his kitchen to the short hallway. Sounds of leisurely splashing covered his footfalls. The bathroom door was cracked, and he tilted his head to align his eyes.

He could see only swatches of skin through the narrow slit. A glistening arm moved in and out of his vision. A sponge ran down a long leg. Entranced, he prodded the door open.

Leffler stopped breathing. A woman sat in his bathtub, with her back to him.

For a moment, he had the peculiar sensation that he was trespassing in someone else's house. But there were his Ipana Toothpaste and Packer's Tar Soap on the sink, just as he'd left them. She had taken his bathrobe off the hook behind the door, folded it, and placed it within arm's reach atop a corner of the sink.

She lifted a sponge from the water and brought it up to her shoulder. Very slowly, she squeezed soap bubbles onto her back, where they trickled down along her spine to the water. Her copper-brown hair was tied above her head, and several damp strands played down her neck.

Leffler could not see her face, only the sweep of her chin, where soap foam had gathered. She gently swept up the bubbles with the back of her hand and returned them to the pool. With the grace of absolute privacy, she brought her leg up to draw the sponge along the inside of her thigh to the curve of her knee. She lingered high on her leg, gently kneading the sponge into the satin-white skin.

It seemed she was lost in a reverie and was caressing rather than cleaning. The sponge floated away, and her hand lightly traced her thigh along the waterline, then crossed to her stomach. She lifted her eyes, as if intent on a vision on the wall, and brought her hand up to cup a breast. Thin ribbons of water fell from her fingers as she massaged it against herself.

Leffler stood transfixed, the scented mist rising from the hot water enveloping him. There was an ineffable sweetness in this shared moment, of which she knew nothing. He felt himself stirring.

She must have felt it, too, as she suddenly spun toward him, her eyes wide, water splashing. Her breast was still in hand, instantly transformed from sensuous to comical. Large and pointing and inappropriate.

As if touched by it, Leffler stumbled back. In his embarrassment and confusion, the familiar hallway seemed dark and alien. A shadow suddenly loomed. Blurred hands spun him by the shoulders and threw him at the wall. His head bounced against the plaster. Anticipating a blow, Leffler squeezed his eyes shut and brought his hands up to protect himself. Rough hands ran up and down his body, jabbing under his arms and along his waistline, searching. Whatever stood in front of him smelled of antiseptic and old blood. Leffler braved a glance.

The man's thin smile was like the glint of a half-concealed knife. He hovered close, as if daring Leffler to move. Leffler clung to the hall wall, so frightened he did not hear the bathroom door slam.

The intruder asked, "Are you Leffler?"

The process server nodded dumbly.

"I don't suppose you were expecting me either."

That he had not been killed outright offered some hope. His voice quavered. "I don't have much. A couple dollars in my wallet. Nothing in the house."

Monck stepped away and said in disgust, "No, you weren't waiting for me."

The man wasn't a burglar. He promptly dismissed Leffler. The trespasser walked into the small living room. Leffler came down from his toes. The intruder was compact, as tight as a wire. Yet his footfalls made no sound as he moved, as if he were a shadow. With his drawn face and raised cheekbones, he looked as if he would always be hungry. He reminded Leffler of the wolves at the Lincoln Park Zoo, caged and pacing, but always scheming and always dangerous.

"Who are you?" Leffler asked tentatively.

Monck lifted a patterned cup from a bookshelf next to the fireplace. He might have seen Leffler start, because just as he was returning it, he held the glass up to the front window's light.

The bookshelf contained half a dozen other glass pieces of curious shapes and shades, looking at first glance like the ornate colored plates and goblets given by the millions to moviegoers in the 1930s. Five other pieces were on the mantel over the fireplace.

Monck absently tossed the cup from one hand to another and said, "I was sent to this address."

Leffler's eyes flew open, not at Monck's words, but at his casual treatment of the glass. The process server lunged two steps forward, then checked himself when Monck's flinty stare found him. Leffler settled for holding up his hand like a traffic cop and whispering, "Careful with that, please." The hand shook.

The German looked at the glass again, studying it as if for the first time. "What is this?"

"It's a drinking glass . . . from Europe," Leffler replied disingenuously.

More precisely, it was a goblet with an upper rim of paper-thin clear glass called *cristallo*, which sat atop an opaque bowl decorated with white trailings and rings made of *lattimo*, or milk glass. The goblet's stem and folded foot were also laid over with the white, opalescent milk glass in precise, waving lines. The exquisite goblet had been made over three hundred years ago on Murano, the small island near Venice where the glass-guild workers had been prisoners of their talent, forbidden on pain of death from leaving the island or even talking with visitors, lest the Venetians lose their glass-art secrets to the hated Genoese. Nine months ago, Leffler had paid twelve hundred dollars for the piece, and with sources of antique Venetian glass cut off by the war, the goblet was appreciating daily.

"Ah, a drinking glass from Europe," Monck echoed dryly, stepping into the kitchen. In the refrigerator he found a bottle of Pabst beer and pried the cap off with an opener attached under the shelf. Leffler drank Pabst Blue Ribbon because the brewery sponsored Ben Bernie, "The O-O-O-Old Maestro," who always signed off his radio program with "Au revoir, a fond cheerio, a bit of a tweet-tweet, God bless you, and pleas-s-sant dre-ams."

Monck returned to the living room and held the goblet to the light again before pouring beer into it. He swallowed, lowered himself onto the sofa. He placed the goblet heavily onto the only edge of the table not hidden by copies of the *Chicago Daily Tribune*. Leffler gasped when the goblet's fragile stand rattled sharply against the wood.

Monck surveyed the room. "Your collection of these glasses is the only decent thing in this house."

They added the only sparkle to an otherwise drab living room, devoid of the touches of family life or even much of a single life. Rented furniture carelessly placed, a defeated rug, a month of old newspapers on a tea table. On the pile of papers were a tin of colorless margarine, a tube of yellow vegetable dye, and a box of Ritz Crackers, last night's dinner. It took too much home-making skill to mix the dye into the tin all at once, so Leffler had used a finger to mix dabs of the color into the translucent margarine while it was on the cracker. The war's shortages and Leffler's bachelorhood combined to give the room a genteel shabbiness.

The intruder said, "These glasses must be valuable."

Leffler leaned against a wall and hid his nervousness behind a shrug, but his eyes did not leave the imperiled goblet. His other pieces were just as distinctive and just as precious.

"Why do you keep them in your house?" Monck asked, taking another sip and placing the goblet down again with even more force. Leffler flinched. The threat was clear. What had this man said about being sent to his house?

The process server cleared his throat. "This place was broken into once, last year. The burglars took ten dollars I had on my bedstead, and left all the glass. They must have thought it was that cheap stuff you win at country fairs by throwing pennies onto plates and cups."

"But it isn't the cheap stuff. How do you afford it?"

"You said you were sent here. By whom?"

Monck sipped, then rattled the goblet again against the wood. The *cristallo* rang, but did not crack. The finely wrought stem might not withstand another such blow. Leffler said hastily, "I moonlight. I serve legal papers for a company during the day, then at nights and on weekends I do the same for the Navy's Office of Procurements."

All true, but it was a preposterous explanation for the wealth in the room, and Leffler was frantically formulating a lie when the woman walked in. She was wearing a red jumper dress he recognized as his ex-wife's. Her hair was wet, and she patted it with one of his threadbare towels as she sat in the cane chair next to the fireplace. Her face was still damp and looked pale and undefended.

She smiled without warmth and said quietly, "We had a long overnight flight. I didn't bring much with me, so I had to borrow one of your wife's dresses. I hope she won't mind."

They both had accents. Faint vowel shifts, and his inflection seemed to fade in and out, as if he had to remind himself to cleanse his words. German? They couldn't be. . . . He arrested his thoughts and replied, "My wife is long gone, out to California with some dentist who deserved her."

"Well, it was a bit presumptuous of me . . ."

Leffler shook his head indifferently and rattled on, hoping to divert the intruder's attention from his goblet. "She divorced me, but I slipped the Cook County judge a hundred bucks, and in the settlement order he didn't even give her her clothes. No makeup, no underwear, nothing. You look a lot better in it than she did, anyway." He paused, giving his goblet the smallest glance. With her in the room, he ventured, "Now, if you'd just tell me who you are."

The intruder lifted the Venetian glass again. "Two jobs still don't explain your collection." Monck stared at Leffler with cold surmise. "Perhaps the wireless transmitter upstairs does, the one under the floor in your bedroom closet."

Breaking the goblet's stem would not have had more effect on Leffler. The words punched deeply into his stomach, blowing the air from him and softening his legs. He swayed as the room swam out of focus. He caught himself with a half-step and worked hard to bring his gaze back to the intruder. He managed a foolish "What did you say?"

"You have a Graber shortwave transmitter upstairs, linked to a colinear antenna that runs out your bedroom window, then along the gutter pipe. What looks like a one-time pad is sitting on top of the radio. There are also several slips of decoding graph paper." Monck tasted the beer again. "I trust all this isn't a surprise."

Leffler leaned heavily against the wall, tilting a small framed print that said in old English script "Do Right and Fear No Man." He inhaled sharply. "Who sent you?"

"The same people you communicate with."

The intruder was baiting him. "I . . . I don't know . . ."

"The same people whose money allows you to buy your glass."

Margarete put an end to Monck's game. "This man's name is Monck, and I am Margarete Bayerlein. Berlin sent us to your house because it is safe, and we'll have time to catch our breaths."

"Berlin?" Leffler muttered. "Oh, Christ."

"They probably weren't able to contact you in advance to expect us," she said sympathetically, seeming to have forgiven Leffler's ogling. "It was the same for me."

"Berlin," Leffler repeated emptily. He hesitated, then could look only at the woman when he said, "That's not good enough."

Monck answered, "We don't have any idea who is controlling us. The Abwehr. The Sicherheitsdienst. The Foreign Armies Office. Maybe even the Gestapo. But we know that our controller, whoever he is, has priority over all these groups. And that means he has priority over you."

Monck rose from the davenport to hand Leffler one of the sheets of ciphers he had decoded on Bainbridge Island. Leffler took the paper, but his eyes were stitched to the goblet, and his hand moved toward it. The German carefully kept the *cristallo* out of his reach.

Leffler clenched his jaw against begging the man, then squinted at the paper through his thick lenses. His address appeared below a row of numbers.

Monck had returned to his seat. He drained the beer. "There's your address, pulled from the airwaves. Tell me what you do for the homeland."

Leffler straightened at the question. He still had no idea who these people were. Even though his radio had been found, he would not incriminate himself further. It was all a trap. "I don't know what you are talking about."

The goblet's rim snapped under pressure from Monck's thumb. The lacy fragment fluttered to his lap. The brittle sound sucked air from Leffler's lungs. His eyes grew wildly, and his overfeatured face blanched to the color of dough. He squealed an unintelligible protest. But perhaps the same instincts that made Leffler a renowned hunter arrested his quick motion toward Monck. The man on his couch radiated a scarcely controlled violence. He would not be toyed with.

Margarete Bayerlein said quickly, "That isn't necessary. We..."

Monck's eyes broke off her sentence. She sat back in her seat, stiff with embarrassment and anger.

The German ignored the drop of blood that squeezed from his thumb as he repositioned it against the goblet. He said casually, "I am going to work right through your collection until all that remains is a pile of glass chips." He broke off another shard of the goblet's rim, then another. Slivers of glass broke his skin, and his thumb smeared with blood. "My guess is that you love this glass like life itself. So eventually you will talk to me. It will be interesting to see how expensive you'll make our little talk."

Leffler held up his hands despairingly. "Don't... please don't." His voice was ragged with loss. "What is it you want?"

Monck's features transformed themselves, charm instantly displacing threat. "We need your help. I was ordered to travel east, and was given your address. I assumed you were part of a Chicago cell and had a radio. It didn't take me long to find it."

"What have you been ordered to do?"

Monck smiled indulgently. "You know I can't tell you that. But it's for the common good."

"Shit on that common good," Leffler said acidly. "I'm in it for the money."

Disapproval turned down the corners of Margarete's mouth. She asked, "What do you use the shortwave for?"

"As I said, I've got two jobs. During the day I serve legal papers for a company downtown. After hours a couple times a week I do the same for the Navy, for their Great Lakes Naval Station. Say a company has contracted with the Navy to provide a weapon or a vessel component, something like that. If they're late in delivery, the Navy immediately starts working on them. Threatens them with a delinquency notice, which I deliver. If that doesn't work, they sue, and I also serve those papers."

"And what are you reporting on the shortwave?" Monck asked as he gently placed the remnants of the goblet on the table.

"I find out a lot about Navy plans just from the delinquency notices and sometimes talking to the contractors," Leffler boasted. "When I give them the papers, they whine and complain that the Navy doesn't treat them right. Impossible deadlines. Low prices. I listen carefully. And I let them think I'm on their side. It doesn't take much more than that to get them talking about their projects."

Monck shuffled a newspaper on the table and looked uninterested.

Leffler hurried on defensively. "You might not think that's much. But I was able to relay the fact that the Navy was having a hell of a time with its twenty-one-inch torpedo on its Fletcher-class destroyers. The Office of Procurements kept sending the manufacturer of its guidance systems—a plant in Skokie—delinquency notices. Finally I asked one of the draftsmen there what the trouble was. He said the Navy kept making changes in the torpedo's steering mechanism, and the company just couldn't keep up with the design changes and the short deadlines. I radioed that the Navy must be having reliability problems with their Fletcher-class torpedoes. I got a bonus for the report."

"How did you get started at this?" Margarete asked. She rubbed her arms as if cold, even though the sunset warmed the house.

Leffler looked away from her, embarrassed. He breathed deeply. "I was suckered."

"How so?"

He hesitated, then cleared his throat. "Well, you might as well know how your people work. Back early in the war, I used to go to a joint down in the Loop called Lip's Lower Level. Lot of servicemen, lot of girls. One night I let myself be picked up by a young lady. She was a pretty good actress, letting me think I was doing all the talking, all the convincing. After a couple of drinks, we left Lip's and ended up at her apartment. One thing led to another. When I left her place a couple hours later, I was arrested by the Chicago police and charged with statutory rape. Booked, arraigned, the whole bit. Turned out the girl was fourteen years old. I was facing five to ten at Joliet."

Leffler pulled at his earlobe. "I made bail, and the next day I was approached by a man while I was leaving my house. He said he was a lawyer, and that he could help me out. He said if I'd let him take a look at the papers I served every day for a month, he'd clear up the charges."

"And he did," Margarete said.

"It was unbelievable. I never heard from the police or the prosecutors again. The charge against me just vanished. And at the end of the month, the lawyer said he'd pay me two hundred bucks a week if I'd continue to stop by with the papers. I knew by then I'd been trapped, but I couldn't very well turn myself in. And then I started liking the money. I've hit them for a couple raises since then."

"Why all the antique glass?" she asked, running her eyes from treasure to treasure on the shelves.

"The war has put me in a bind. I make a lot of money, but I can't spend it, what with shortages and rationing. I can't even dump the money in a bank account, because transactions over three hundred dollars are reported to the FBI."

"Why?"

"To prevent black-market operations. So I've got to do something with the funds. This glass is the answer. I can always sell

them after the war to get my money back." His covert glances
at his collection indicated he would never be able to part with
the Venetian goblets and bottles. The finely wrought art had
become a part of him.

"You aren't German?" she asked warily.

"If I had lower brows and were dumber, I'd be German."
Maybe bravura worked. "I'm an American. I told you, I do it
for the cash. I didn't even know who I worked for for months.
Then, with the money coming in and risks increasing, I was
asked if I'd code and radio my reports directly. I said sure, if the
money was right. It was."

Distaste pursed Margarete's mouth. Monck wiped blood from
his thumb on his sock. He looked at his thumb narrowly, as if
pondering blame for the slight wound. He said, "The Foreign
Armies Office must pay you well for you to afford all the glass.
And you really haven't worked that hard. Your collection has
come rather easily."

Leffler said nothing. Fear for his precious collection soured
his mouth.

"It's time you earned your salary. I'm going to need your help
for several days. I'll need someone who knows Chicago."

They wanted him for something other than his radio. Over
the years he had gained a confidence. Low risk, high reward. A
comforting routine helps even in a dangerous profession, and his
work for an anonymous paymaster in Europe to whom he reported was little more than routine. Now, with this German
shrouded in an elemental power sitting across from him, a chasm
of danger was opening for Leffler. He ran his bony hand under
his nose. His hand was trembling, and he quickly lowered it.
"My help? What could I possibly do?"

"You've already begun." Monck smiled, pulling tight the scar
below his lip. "I used your shortwave to make contact with
Berlin. I've already..."

Leffler asked sharply, "When did you use it?"

"Noon, Chicago time, the prearranged time for my signal.
Something wrong?"

"No, nothing." Leffler moved to the chair opposite the woman. He sat heavily and tried not to look at his destroyed goblet. "I've been warned by my controller to vary my broadcast times. At my discretion, as he seems to always be there. He thinks the enemy may be listening and trying to locate me." Leffler laughed without feeling. "That's his term. The enemy. I've been broadcasting randomly, and less than once a week, never establishing a pattern. My last broadcast was eleven days ago, so yours today couldn't have been predictable."

"Better than that," Margarete Bayerlein said in a tired voice. Monck's eyebrow raised, as if he were surprised by her contribution. She went on, "It's certain our control and your control, Mr. Leffler, have coordinated. Under no circumstances would they have given us a time to broadcast that put you in jeopardy."

Leffler nodded. He asked, "What is it you want me to do?"

His shoulders slumped when the German pulled a list from his pocket.

Only when confronted with the president's direct order did J. Edgar Hoover later cooperate with the Secret Service investigation of that day. Even so, the inquiry met fractious resistance, fueled by long-standing jealousies between the Service and the Federal Bureau of Investigation. And Hoover, who for twenty years had excelled at reaping credit and ducking blame, was ill disposed toward having his organization scrutinized, especially with a "hot football like this baby waiting to hang someone," as he is reported to have said.

But investigate they finally did, and the Secret Service found that on the day of Kurt Monck's Chicago broadcast, Monday, July 3, 1944, FBI Special Agent Ross Howard had been stationed at the intersection of Lake Shore Drive and Belmont Avenue, about a mile southeast of Wrigley Field. In front of him on a tripod was an RCA Victor multiple-band radio direction finder, which Howard described to curious passersby as "new-fangled electronic survey equipment." Three miles east-by-northeast, at the corner of Addison and Kedzie streets, was posted Jerome

McAdams, also manning a direction finder. The aerials of both RCAs were aimed at Wrigley Field.

The technology was not new, but had only recently been adopted by the FBI. For several years an arc of land bases from Newfoundland to the Bahamas had utilized directional antennas to locate German submarines far out in the Atlantic. The net, known as Huffduff (H-F D-F, from high-frequency direction-finding), picked up German U-boats' radio transmissions and radioed their locations to waiting American and British destroyers. The German U-boat commanders made it easy for the trackers, as they had been ordered by Admiral Karl Doenitz to pour information about enemy sightings and sinkings and weather by radio to his headquarters. Huffduff quickly broke the German stranglehold on Atlantic shipping.

The equipment manned by Howard and McAdams on the Chicago street corners was less powerful than the Huffduff stations, but that was about the only difference. Above each black, square box of radio tubes was a circular antennae mounted on a ball joint. The loop was swiveled until the radio received the strongest signal, registered on a needle meter.

Try as they might, the Secret Service never adequately determined why the FBI was monitoring the north Chicago neighborhood that particular day, although they did trace the route of the information the Bureau had acted on. Four months before, the Detroit station of the Radio Intelligence Division of the Federal Communications Commission, whose normal duty was to locate unlicensed commercial broadcasters, had intercepted an unusual, seemingly coded shortwave broadcast. It quickly alerted the Office of Naval Communications in Washington, D.C. Their radio-direction-finding department, known as OP-20-G (and never shortened to anything less tongue-twisting), alerted the Huffduff network. Amazingly, and thanks to dozens of rehearsals, all this took place within ninety seconds, and the Huffduff stations actually pinpointed the last few seconds of the same mysterious broadcast. North Chicago, they reported, but could be no more accurate.

Special Agents Howard and McAdams were stationed in the neighborhood and heard a similar broadcast seven days later. By drawing intersecting lines across a city map, the agents narrowed their search to the uptown area. Then the hidden station failed to broadcast a week later, and the agents were reduced to guesses.

Like most FBI agents, Howard and McAdams were hunch players. The Chicago office did not have the manpower to put radio direction finders on the street full-time, so Howard and McAdams worked their machines whenever they found time. They began listening a day before and a day after the regular weekly dates, guessing the broadcaster was deliberately mixing his schedule. Still nothing. Then on rainy days, figuring radioing is something done indoors. Then the first Saturday of a Cubs homestand. Nothing.

They weren't going to admit to the Secret Service investigators that sheer luck was the reason they were monitoring the north-side neighborhood that day. And it was nothing but luck, as Howard's Packard had been in the garage having its clutch replaced, and the mechanic did not have the car ready on time. So Howard had asked McAdams if he would kill some time with him monitoring the neighborhood that evening until the car was ready.

Both agents heard the shortwave signal that day. On the lake shore at Belmont, Howard adjusted his loop to the strongest signal. The Morse chatter was coming from the northwest. With rising excitement, he drew the line on his map, through Wrigley Field, through the intersection of Lincoln and Montrose avenues, across Foster.

Jerome McAdams also pinpointed the radio clacking. From his street corner, he drew his pencil east on his map, straight down Addison toward Wrigley Field.

Moments later, they juxtaposed their maps. Their lines crossed each other just south of Wrigley Field. Because of radio reflection off buildings, their crosshairs could not be absolutely accurate. But when Howard and McAdams drove through the area an hour later in the repaired Packard, they knew that the sender lived in one of six or seven houses near the intersection of Paisley and Clear streets.

The Secret Service report noted that within thirty minutes, a round-the-clock watch had been established on the neighborhood by FBI agents posing as deliverymen, plumbers, and vagrants. All were told to carefully note arrivals and departures from the houses and to discreetly look for an antenna. Thomas Thornton, special agent in charge of the Chicago FBI office, decreed that if the antenna was not found within two days, all seven homes would be searched, and everyone in all the houses arrested if need be. There would be no more coded messages sent from his town, he assured Hoover.

The Secret Service report showed that a Mr. Lawrence Leffler's house was one of the seven.

11

TWO YEARS IN THE LABRADOR WILDER-
ness would unhinge almost anyone. Eight months
of winter a year, endless black nights, the ceaseless howl of the
wind, broiling clouds of angry mosquitoes, and the utter re-
moteness of the place worked on a mind, prying it from reality
and floating it free. Canadians thought all Labradoreans a bit
daft, and in fact, no visitor to that wild land remained untouched.

Gordon Potts was no exception, but he was, he knew, quite
resourceful and would be able to fight off the Labrador daffiness.
If he kept busy. And Potts was consummately skillful at occu-
pying himself.

Potts was senior radio operator at the U.S. Office of Naval
Communications, Labrador Section. He was a lieutenant (j.g.),
and Potts had added senior to his title when, a year ago, he
arrived at the Quonset hut atop Beadle Mountain and found he
was the only person assigned there. The station was in the Mealy
Mountains east of a tiny settlement called Goose Bay and south
of Lake Melville in the continent's far northeast.

In that year Potts had not once left the mountain, depending
on monthly deliveries of supplies from an RCAF supply driver

from Quebec who could not or would not speak with him. He had been assured in radio conversations with the D.C. office that his request for a transfer would be duly considered. Until that glorious day, he would keep busy.

The Beadle Mountain station was a radio intercept unit, one of a dozen tin-and-sandbag huts strung across northern Canada. The Quonset hut was partly buried below ground, and much of the rest of it was covered with stones and sandbags, insurance against the wind. Next to the hut, the antenna rose two hundred feet into the sky and was secured by twenty aircraft-cable guy-lines which splayed out to the ground like a vast web. An out-house—crescent on the door and all—stood halfway between the hut and the aerial. During winter, the well-worn path to the outhouse was the coldest thirty feet in post-Pleistocene history, Potts believed. The radio outpost had made a negligible inroad against the stark wilderness, and from any distance, the hut and antenna, the small generator shack, and even Potts's distinctive snow sculptures were lost among the brittle trees and jagged rocks of the mountain.

Radio signals above 1,600 kilohertz—the short waves, which reflect off the ionosphere one or more times and therefore can be received long distances from the transmitter—aimed at Germany from the central United States were picked up by Potts's station. Most activity was in the early evening Newfoundland time, which was in the dead of night in Germany, when signal interference on sensitive receivers there was less. At these times, all eight of Potts's wire recorders were on, covering the shortwave spectrum. And at these times, Potts sat next to his bank of receivers, listening for the unexpected broadcast, a Labatt's beer his only company in exile.

It was the other times, the hours and hours a day, which ground away at him. He had always been a loner, but he had never before edged away from his perfunctory sanity. He was even beginning to look demented, with his buried eyes, gleaming head, which had lost most of its hair within six months after he was posted to the mountain, and tangled beard, which he had vowed not to cut off until he received a new assignment.

That might never come, Potts knew. He had made it once, to the cryptanalysis section in Washington, D.C. The post had been the culmination of a twenty-year obsession with codes, which began when he was twelve years old and visited New York's Trinity Church on Broadway at Wall Street. He came across the tombstone of James Leeson, who died September 28, 1794. Etched in the stone under the name was an inscription in cipher. A coded message. Potts was immediately ensnared by the mystery, and after a month's work in the public library with a pad and pencil, he discovered the code was a pigpen cipher dating back several hundred years. The inscription read "Remember Death."

Despite his knowledge of codes learned in the ensuing twenty years, Potts's first assignment after joining the Navy the day after Pearl Harbor was in the Navy's Censorship Office, where he pulled from envelopes all international chess games and cross-word puzzles (both of which could contain coded messages), childish handwriting seemingly from a youngster to a grand-parent (which might in fact be a disguised map), all newspaper clippings (which might have certain letters dotted with invisible ink, thereby forming a message), and lovers' X's and O's (which might also be a code). Dozens of other items were clipped out or removed, and followed with a brisk "Opened by Censor" stamped across the envelope.

After a year reading other people's mail, he was promoted into OP-20-G, and in light of the dedication and hard work required to get there, his self-inflicted downfall was all the more bitter. After a particularly nasty exchange between Potts and his su-perior, Commander William Petes, Potts suggested in writing on the envelope of a routine plaintext message he forwarded to Petes that Petes engage in an outrageously obscene act that Petes might, with extreme agility, perform on himself. He wrote it in invisible ink—urine to be precise, long used in the spy trade—thinking the joke was on Petes, who would never know what he was actually holding in his hands as he took the plaintext from the envelope.

But the joke was on Potts, and it was a cruel one, because the envelope, now scrap, was forwarded to the stripping laboratory a floor above, where students in a steganography class did a number of tests on waste paper, as if there were secret messages hidden on the paper. Instead of trying the spectrum-wide developers being used that day by other students, one chief yeoman, completely by coincidence and simply for practice, held the envelope over his bunsen burner, lightly charring it and bringing out Potts's spindly, damning words. The message and particularly its ink incensed Petes, who that night banished Potts to Labrador.

Potts fought the absolute isolation. In his world of incessant wind and amplified static, he grasped at the insignificant and the curious to ease him through the smothering boredom.

For five weeks it had been the perfect shuffle. On this July day, between occasionally fiddling with his shortwave receivers and swatting deerflies the size of twenty-five-cent pieces, Potts shuffled and resorted a new deck of playing cards again and again. His object was to shuffle the new deck so the cards fell in exactly alternating sequence. After hundreds of hours of practice, he could do it frequently now. His ultimate goal was to shuffle them perfectly eight consecutive times, thereby reforming the deck into its original order. Only three men in history had been able to do so. Potts would not quit until he became the fourth.

Before that it had been ice sculpture. Most days that winter had found him wrapped in layers of wool and goose down patting together mounds of snow, carving them with a shovel, then wetting them with buckets of water until the sculpture hardened into glittering ice. Only this month had his work begun to soften under the distant midday sun. Near the antenna was a double-life-size sculpture of Washington crossing the Delaware. Behind the outhouse was Ahab at the bow of his hunting dinghy harpooning Moby Dick. The whale was to scale, and it had taken Potts weeks to gather the snow. Near Moby Dick's tail was an outsize, naked Anne Boleyn, with the three breasts and twelve fingers Potts had once read she had possessed.

All pointless tasks Potts elevated to ritual. At work with a pencil or knife or hoe or deck of cards, he could blink twice and two or three days would disappear forever, time he had not spent in the Mealy Mountain wilderness.

Potts shuffled and sorted, shuffled and sorted, until a purposeful clicking snared his attention. He lowered the cards and turned his head toward his number-two shortwave receiver, a Gonset 400. He stood from the three-leg milking stool he had received after requesting a rocking chair from the Quartermaster General and reached to turn up the Gonset's volume.

The stool, a workbench below the radio equipment, a cot, and a bridge table were the only creature comforts in the hut. The floor was made of old railroad ties, making the room perpetually smell of creosote. He glanced at the Edison recorder wired to the Gonset. The Morselike signal continued, and a sound meter indicated the Edison was registering the broadcast.

Normally he forwarded the recordings to the Office of Naval Communications without interpretation or comment. He would punch an intercepted message onto a teletype tape, dial a number on the teletypewriter exchange, then feed the tape into a mechanical transmitter that consumed the message at sixty words per minute.

Potts's signal would reappear on a page printer in Room 1649 of the OP-20-G, the cryptologic organization in the Navy Department Building on Constitution Avenue in Washington, D.C. The printer was positioned beside the desk of the watch officer, who waited until the intercept had been printed in an original and a carbon copy on yellow and pink paper. Then dozens of young codebreakers would work on the cipher, hunched over row after row of desks, looking like medieval clerical transcribers, except for the slide rules and rolled-up sleeves.

The very qualifications that landed Potts the job at OP-20-G —his facility with ciphers—dictated the only timekilling obsession that had lasted the entire year, code crunching.

Many of the clandestine shortwave broadcasts from the States were done from one-time pads. The sender and receiver had identical paper pads, with each sheet of paper or foil on the pad having a different coding sequence. After each message, the code was torn from the pad and burned, leaving a new code sequence on the next sheet. The codes were virtually impossible to break because each new message established a new pattern.

The message clicking through Potts's amplifier had a different cadence. It was registering on the signal meter at the same strength as the broadcast eleven days ago. But this was not the same fist or code. Perhaps it was a random drop or a multiple substitution or a straddling checkerboard. In any case, Potts knew he had something new to work on, something to divert him from the perfect shuffle.

He scribbled down the dots and dashes. The message was lengthy, more grist for the mill. A series of numbers in standard Morse. And it wasn't a spurt transmission, made by tape-recording the message, then radioing it at high speed. Potts had the spurt equipment, but most spurt senders used the Blank machines (Potts's label for the Enigma, a name he did not know) and the older Siemens machines, which weren't available to Potts in exile. So this was an old-style signal, something he could work on. Perhaps a multiple substitution, used earlier in the war. Potts smiled through his beard, revealing uneven teeth. These took time, and he possessed huge dollops of that. The broadcast ended a moment later with a long series of dits, as did virtually all shortwave Morse broadcasts the world over.

His German had been another project, his first on the mountain. From not knowing a word in German to being able to read fluently had taken him just three months, ten hours a day, seven days a week, using the Signal Corps's scratchy recordings and tattered lesson books. He had since graduated to Hamann and von Gerder and other *Sturm und Drang* writers. His German was still bumpy at times, he knew. The new language should have earned him a transfer off Beadle Mountain. It hadn't yet.

Potts had worked on eight multiple-substitution codes before this one. He had cracked one of them, which, to his great chagrin, turned out to be a request by an unknown broadcaster for an unusual sausage recipe, one of the fifteen hundred kinds of sausage made in Germany. OP-20-G determined that a Central American V-man had been given a sending time and had nothing to send, so he had asked for the recipe. No transfer here, either.

He brought several books down from the shelf above the receivers. From his reading on the German people, he had decided that almost every household in Germany had each of several books: The Luther Bible, Brehm's *Animal Life*, translations of Shakespeare's plays (Germans loved the poet almost as much as the English), and, of course, *Mein Kampf*. A sender of a multiple-substitution code would use a widely available volume, one obtainable in countries with only a few expatriates. That way, an agent could travel without carrying a volume that gave away his nationality, and yet be certain of finding the volume on arrival. He also had books frequently owned in North America: a King James Bible, the 1944 *Old Farmers Almanac*, and the *Red Cross First Aid Manual* (which was the second most widely distributed publication in the United States, due to the fear of imminent Luftwaffe bombing).

Potts would forward the recording of the signal to the smart boys down in D.C. later that evening. But he wanted a few hours' head start.

He began with the most widely owned book in North America, the King James Bible, with Genesis. The message's first number was seventeen. He counted seventeen words into the text, to the word "and." The next number was twelve. Twelve words after "and" was the word "the." After a series of numbers he had a nonsensical phrase: "and, the, the, God, at, of, God, then." He continued until the first thirty numbers had been correlated with words from Genesis. Nowhere in the string of words did several form a recognizable phrase. He tore off the top sheet of his pad and pushed the paper to the top of the desk. He would return to it later, dropping a word or two in pattern here and there, trying to compensate for nulls.

Potts now began with the second chapter in the Bible. If

nothing was there, he would search the third. All the way through the Old Testament, then the New Testament. Then to the Luther edition. It might take weeks. Or months.

But he had the time. And the fervid determination. Moby Dick, looming next to the Quonset hut, could testify to that.

Margarete Bayerlein sat in Larry Leffler's kitchen writing her daughter. This was her second letter of the day to Mary. They would both be sent to the San Diego address. Monck had told her not to mention their Chicago address, in case the San Diego controller had been captured and his mail was being read by the FBI. This would mean Mary was also in the hands of the American authorities or, worse, lost and alone. She pushed those thoughts away.

She wrote only briefly about Kurt Monck, never mentioning his name, calling him "our visitor." She spoke in terms Mary would appreciate, about how his accent was thicker than hers and how he was a sourpuss because he didn't smile much.

But she omitted her other observations about the man who forced her to come to Chicago, and she lowered her pen as they again ran through her mind. Kurt Monck was a mixture of decency and pitilessness, and she had not figured out how to react to him. Other than his iron resolve to reach his goal, he was never consistent. His personality flickered between the avuncular and the predatory. And his very being always demanded a response.

When he was near, scents were amplified and her vision grew more acute, as if she had regressed to an animal existence, alert to the slightest shift in her surroundings. He emitted a penetrating current, muddying her thoughts and addling her memory.

She was not the only one who felt it. Twice she had seen dogs come within twenty feet of him, then turn tail and run. An umbrella of stillness surrounded him. Birds were silent. Children hushed. The leaves stopped brushing together. When he moved on, they all started up again.

Her response would be caution. He demanded her presence

for a while longer in Chicago. But she would try to stay only at the fringe of his awareness. She would do as ordered, nothing more. Perhaps he was like a tiger, who can see its prey only when it moves. She would be still in Chicago, and he would simply forget her.

"I'm afraid you're going to have to add a postscript to your letter."

Monck's sudden words made her jump in her chair. In his utterly silent way, he had wafted into the kitchen and was standing behind her, reading the letter over her shoulder.

She nervously lowered her pen. He moved to the chair opposite her. She asked, "What postscript?" But she already knew. She could see it in the tight lines of his face, the rigid will.

"I know we had a deal. Only to Chicago." His eyes were unblinking, and they stitched her to the back of her chair. "I'm going to have to change that."

He spoke for another minute, telling her why she was needed. His accent, his unfamiliarity with the customs, his need for a partner in some of his plans. She had heard it before. She quelled her anger. She was too exhausted for it, and he had shown it was futile. But his words were heard across an enormous chasm of despair.

When he left the kitchen, she closed her eyes for several moments, holding back her fear and anguish. Then, with a trembling hand, she ended her letter to Mary, telling her it would be a little longer before she came to get her. She wrote that maybe "our visitor" would pass through their lives and leave them unmoved and unscarred. And then, she finished, they would be together again.

12

HER HOUSE SMELLED OF PERFUME AND cold smoke and abandonment. Wren stood in the back of the room, her bedroom, slowly examining the feminine effects on her dresser. He treated her possessions gingerly, not wanting to disarrange her life, respecting her order of things.

A tortoiseshell comb with several chestnut strands of hair on its teeth, bobby pins neatly pushed into a pile, a tiny spray bottle of perfume, and not much else. A red lisle cotton blouse was folded to one side of the dresser, as if she had changed her mind about taking it. Wren ran his fingers over the blouse, fighting a surge of memory. He lifted the blouse to his nose. Duz or Ivory or something, but it was his wife's scent.

He returned the blouse to the dresser. A moment passed before he could take his hand away. Wren had never met Margarete Bayerlein, who owned the home. He had not even seen a photograph of her. Yet each turn he had made in her house reminded him of his wife. Not that their possessions were so similar. But Wren's defense against sorrow had been to try to rid his life of everything that reminded him of Linda. Not to think of her was

easier than enduring a jolt of grief each time his eyes settled on
something of hers.

He found himself in the mirror above Margarete Bayerlein's
dresser. His mouth was compressed to a narrow line, which made
his large jaw appear even more square. His slate-gray eyes seemed
stoical, not reflecting the turmoil this room was causing him.

He could occasionally think of Linda now and not come to an
abrupt, shuddering halt in whatever he was doing, as if a hand
had seized his neck and yanked him upright. That had taken
months of denying her. Before moving to Seattle he had crated
everything of hers—clothes, soap, college annuals, jewelry,
everything—and shipped it to a Mayflower warehouse in Seattle.
He was still paying a small monthly fee to keep it away from
him.

So complete was his attempted removal of the scars that his
modest house in Seattle was without any homey touches. He
had not put anything on the walls. Most of the dishes were still
in the box they had been shipped in. The furniture remained as
the moving people had left it. He had not hung curtains in any
of the rooms. The prior owner's rose garden—once a source of
pride in the neighborhood—was forgotten and overgrown. He
had avoided the least bit of domestication, knowing order and
comfort in his new house would remind him of her.

Wren had refused to think through the reasons for his slow,
almost grudging handling of his grief. He might have found
himself childish. But the memory of those years with Linda—
they seemed like a few sunny days—and the maddening irrationality of her death could not be handled normally. He was
afraid to deal with the memories, so he pushed them away in a
mechanical fashion. Not a day passed that he did not make some
adjustment to exclude them. It wasn't working.

And in the event of a crisis, he kept one small framed photograph of Linda in the lower right drawer of his desk.

Margarete Bayerlein's home had surrounded him with all those
things he had tried to forget. The soft touches and the faint
scents. While the Seattle police detectives dissected the rest of

her house, his investigation of her bedroom was inhibited by his past.

Slowly, like a man wading upstream, he moved to her closet. It was almost full, with only a few hangers empty. The clothes were well-worn, prewar fashions. There were also three white nurse uniforms. He was relieved to discover that, judging from her clothes and the three pairs of shoes on the shelf above the rack, Margarete Bayerlein was slightly larger than his wife had been. Almost everyone had ration points for one or two new dresses a year. She must have taken hers with her. On the floor of the closet were a suitcase and a steamer trunk. Between them was a space the size of a second suitcase.

On a shelf above the hanger bar was a book of some sort. He brought it down. It was a photo album, with no dust on it, despite having been stored in an out-of-the-way location. He opened it to a middle page. A young man and woman stared at him from a photo. Both wore large smiles as they leaned into each other, their arms around each other's shoulders. The photo showed an exuberance that gripped Wren. The other photos on the page were the same. A man and woman celebrating their love, laughing and holding each other.

The woman in the photos must be Margarete Bayerlein. She was robust, and her health and happiness shone in the snapshots like a bright light. From the black-and-white photos, he guessed her hair was a chocolate brown. Her face was square, not quite feminine, but certainly handsome, even a bit vulnerable. He wished he knew the color of her eyes.

He turned a page. More of the same. The couple sitting in a park near a river. Margarete and the man sipping beer in a city plaza. The two of them rowing a small boat with three swans escorting them. Holding each other again, this time on the steps of a library or other large public building. Above their heads, a clock with its Roman numerals was about to reach three o'clock.

In many of the photographs the man was in a uniform. It was black and well cut. German, most probably, although there was not a swastika anywhere, nor a sidearm. And he certainly didn't

have the severe, haughty expression seen in so many Nazi propaganda photographs. His engaging smile offset the severity of
the uniform. His eyes were set at humorous angles, and his
brown hair in most of the photographs was in slight disarray.
She had just run her fingers through it, Wren supposed. That
must have been one of her affectionate rituals, messing up his
hair an instant before a snapshot was taken.

Wren's jaws were locked rigidly together and were aching.
Why should this woman, who looked nothing like Linda, remind
him of her? Why should he be covetous of this soldier's time
with Margarete Bayerlein, and of their happiness?

With an act of will so enervating that his head dropped onto
his chest, he pushed such thoughts out of his mind. He would
forward the photo album to Washington, where OSS specialists
would construct an intricate analysis of Margarete Bayerlein and
the soldier's lives from the photos. He put the album in an apple
crate in the center of the floor to be loaded into the car.

Near the shoes on the floor was a hatbox with "Mainbocher,
Paris, New York" printed on it. He opened it, expecting a red
beret or a turban—hats and other accessories were in wide use
as wardrobe extenders—and instead found a small packet of
letters wrapped in twine. They bore German stamps and post-
marks, and were addressed to Oberleutnant Georg Bayerlein,
Bad Tolz, Bavaria. They were dated 1935, yet still smelled of
perfume. Wren heard footsteps in the hall, and he impulsively
pushed the envelopes into his jacket pocket.

Garvin's red hair seemed to light up the room. He said, "I've
searched the little girl's room. Nothing there. A clearly American
little girl, ten or eleven years old. She has magazine photos of
some horses on the wall above her bedstead and a small American
flag hanging from the top of her mirror. I'd have trouble distinguishing her room from any other little girl's."

Garvin removed his suit coat. His shirt was gray with sweat,
and it clung to his back. He said, "The dicks found the cause of
the smoke odor. Take a look."

Wren followed Garvin into the kitchen, then to the breakfast nook. The scent was stronger. Garvin said, "He did some soldering here, looks like. There's a small burn on the tablecloth, which probably isn't a cigarette burn because we can't find any evidence anyone smoked here. It's pretty clearly a burn from a soldering iron. And if that isn't enough," Garvin continued, kneeling near the table, "a couple of drops of alloy are on the floor here. Maybe lead or tin. The cops are going to scrape them up and run them to the lab, but I wanted you to have a look first."

"What was he soldering?" Wren asked. "A radio or a weapon of some sort?"

"A radio, most probably. Take a look in here."

Garvin led him into the living room to a bookshelf near the sofa. Standing there was a fireplug of a police detective, short and thick, with his badge pinned to his belt. His eyes were those of a bulldog's, drooping but ferocious. Annoyance crossed his face as Wren and Garvin approached.

He did not wait for an introduction. "Why don't you hot-shot federal boys let me know what's going on here?" he asked in a gravelly voice. "I heard you went out to Issaquah to snoop around after we traced that burned-out car to the murdered fisherman."

Garvin said jovially, "John Wren, this is Detective Sergeant Bud Bledsoe."

"Yeah, great," Bledsoe said without extending his hand. He lifted his hat to run a sleeve across his forehead. "How'd you find the woman's house?"

"A milk-truck driver returning to Winslow saw a man in her yard," Wren answered.

"He saw the POW's face as he was driving by?"

"Didn't see anything but a quick glimpse of a man. But the driver says he's been traveling by this house for several years and has seen the woman and her girl many times out in their yard, but never before saw a man. So he figured the man he saw might be the POW."

"That's it? He called you based on that flimsy reasoning?"

"With the German on the front page, people around here are

looking for anything strange. Looks like the milkman was right."

Bledsoe's dark eyes rhythmically switched from Wren to Garvin and back, looking for a trace of cooperation. "Now, you federal people don't know crime scenes, so occasionally you call me and my people over from Seattle. The call usually comes from Army G2 or the Shore Patrol. But suddenly my boss, Chief Schlay, and the other police chiefs around Puget Sound get requests from Washington, D.C., to inform the Seattle Secret Service office of all crimes committed in the area. So what's the Secret Service got to do with the POW, or anything else around here? I don't suppose..."

He interrupted himself to yell at a young detective kneeling by the fireplace. "Owens, for good bloody Christ, there's no sense using the tongs on the fireplace ashes. You're not going to find prints on them. Just get them into the sack."

Other detectives crowded the room, one in shirt sleeves dusting a candle holder on the mantel for prints, another taking photos, and another standing next to Bledsoe fingering through each book on the second shelf. Wren begrudged their intrusion into Margarete Bayerlein's house.

Bledsoe turned back to Wren and Garvin. "Why don't you save me some guessing and come out with it? Why the Secret Service?"

"I'm sorry, Sergeant," Wren said. "If I could, I would."

Bledsoe's voice rose. "Shit oh dear, I'm not the enemy. I'm a Great War veteran and have twenty years on the force here."

Wren shook his head apologetically. "Why don't you show me what you've found?"

"Bureaucrats," he said sharply, invoking the West's strongest curse. The populist tradition was still alive here. "Goddam bureaucrats."

He pulled a flashlight from his back pocket and lowered himself to his haunches. He held the light at an angle low to the top shelf of the bookshelf. The detective said, "She was a good housekeeper, but not a great housekeeper. I guess she dusted maybe two weeks before the radio was taken off this shelf."

"What radio?" Garvin asked, bending low over the shelf.

Bledsoe glowered at the agent. "There isn't a house in this country what doesn't have a radio. Do you see one here? No. But there was one. Look close, and you can see its outline in the light dust."

He slowly ran a finger across the shelf, then held it up to his eyes. "When investigating a crime, once in a while you've got to get a little dirty. You just can't sit in an office, which I'd be tempted to do, if I was paid as much as you guys." Bledsoe allowed himself a caustic smirk, lest Wren and Garvin miss his point. "Seeing how the doors and windows were all shut in this house, and that no one has been doing any housework to kick up the dirt, there's five or six days' worth of dust on the spot where this radio once was. So someone removed a radio from this shelf a day or two after your man escaped from Fort Lewis."

"He rigged a two-way?" Wren asked.

Bledsoe nodded. "And he put it together out in the kitchen."

Wren said, "That fits in with what I've found."

The detective's eyebrows rose.

"I asked Chief Denmen of the Bremerton Police to do some checking there and in Winslow and Poulsbo, and as far south as Shelton. They sent a squadron of men out. Last Tuesday a man matching the escapee's description was seen at a hobby shop on Burnside Street. The owner says a Morse key is missing. A day later, a radio station there reported that a frequency meter had been stolen."

"He was out getting parts for his radio," Bledsoe concluded. If he was impressed with the Secret Service agent's initiative, he did not show it. "And he sure as hell didn't have it with him when he rolled the flaming Buick into the ditch."

He stood to step around Wren. "Hey, Owens, and you, Coffee and Chalmers, drop what you're doing and search the yard and neighborhood. You're looking for a radio that looks like it's been tampered with. Look in garbage cans, compost piles, dumps..."

Wren interrupted, "Tool sheds, barns, roadside ditches..."

"They get the picture," Bledsoe cut in. "Take a couple of the uniforms with you." Bledsoe had surrounded the house with beat cops, as if expecting it to be stormed. "Don't come back until you find it."

Wren called after them, "And don't touch any knobs on the radio. Maybe we can discover his frequency."

The telephone on the end table rang. Bledsoe lifted it and said, "Yeah?" He immediately pulled a pad from his shirt pocket and began making notes. After a moment he said, "That's it? Nothing else? I don't want to have to come down to the lab and go through the goddam thing with my tweezers, Murray. And, believe me, you don't want me down there either." He paused to lift a handkerchief from his back pocket and run it under his nose. "All right, I believe you. Thanks, Murray."

He turned to the agents and stabbed a short finger at Garvin and asked, "How old are you?"

Garvin's eyebrows climbed. "Twenty-eight. Why?"

"Christ, you look twelve." Before the agent could react to the barb, Bledsoe summarized his notes. "The fisherman's Buick was checked out by the lab over in Seattle. Not much. A few bits of skin, probably the driver's, were stuck to the steering wheel, where he grabbed it while his hand was on fire. Not enough to get a blood type from. There were some ration coupons thrown around in the car. No leads from that. No suitcase, no clothes. The inside driver's door handle was bent to the frame, where he had lunged at it getting the door open. The car had been hotwired and had a couple feet of wire hanging below the dash." Bledsoe returned the pad to his pocket. "That's it."

Wren wanted the detective's opinion on whether the POW could have had a rifle with him, in the trunk or on the rear floorboards. He said cautiously, "I saw that car in Issaquah before it was put on the truck and taken to your lab. I don't think Schiller could have had time to grab anything out of the car before he got out. He made it by seconds."

Bledsoe nodded. "I agree. He was traveling light. And I also don't understand how the woman and her kid got out. The car must have been a ball of flame."

The phone jangled again. The detective listened for a moment. "Thanks, Doc," he said and lowered the phone. His look at Wren was a weapon. "You boys have something hot, and you're not telling us small-timers, isn't that right?"

"What'd the coroner just say?" Wren asked, staring right back at the squat cop.

"Dean Harp died of burns or of drowning in the gasoline in his throat, the coroner can't be sure which. But under the burns on his neck were severe line abrasions, dug into the windpipe." Bledsoe waited a moment, as if accusing the agents. "The gas jockey was also strangled with a thin piece of wire or rope. Probably wire, as the coroner said he couldn't find traces of twine." There was a hint of pleading in the detective's voice. "We got an escaped POW who builds a two-way radio and is running around with a garrote. Why don't you fellows let me in on the rest of it? Who is this guy?"

Tired of the confrontation, Wren avoided Bledsoe's spiteful eyes by staring blankly at the upright piano. A certainty about that instrument suddenly made him inhale. He said quickly, "Tom, you once said you played the piano."

"What?" Bledsoe bellowed. "For Christ sake, will you stick to the subject and . . ."

"Sure, some."

"Play every key on her piano. Listen for a blank."

Garvin smiled malevolently at the detective, happy to be an irritant. He crossed the room, pulled out the piano bench, and sat down. He began at the bass keys, stroking one after another, his head cocked toward the instrument. The white keys, then the black. The instrument was well tuned, even Wren could hear that. Margarete Bayerlein played the piano. German or American songs? he wondered. He was disappointed when every key sounded.

Garvin's face opened with understanding. "You're looking for his weapon."

"Yeah, but it's not from the piano."

"Not so fast, John." Garvin began again, this time sustaining each key, listening more carefully. "You probably thought that there was only one wire per key. Not so. On the bass notes, there are two, and on the treble, three." His hands moved slowly up the keyboard. The sound filled the living room. He grinned. "I've got it." He pressed C an octave above middle C. "Hear it? That metallic, wavering noise is a beat frequency. There's something wrong with the note."

Garvin stood to open the piano lid. The name "Clarendon" was stamped into the metal harp. He played the note again, watching for the felt hammer. "There it is," he said, delighted with himself. "There should be three wires under the hammer, one to each post. If you don't have all three, the note sounds tinny. But one string here is missing. The POW unscrewed the top and bottom posts and took the piano wire out."

"And that explains the broom without the handle in her garbage can," Wren said, running his hand through his thick hair. "He needed handles for the garrote."

Wren turned to the sound of laughter through the front door. The detectives were returning, and Owens carried a Motorola radio—at least that was Wren's first guess, as the front had been removed. The detective had wrapped handkerchiefs around his hands in an attempt to preserve possible fingerprints. Dangling by wires from the radio were a Morse sender and an additional socket board. As they stepped into the room, Chalmers held up his hand, around which he had wrapped a long length of wire. The antenna.

Owens, a burly, black-haired detective with a face so flat he looked as if he slept on it, said, "Found it down the hill in back of the house, almost lost in the blackberry vines. I wouldn't have seen it except that the sun glinted off the metal of the tubes."

Wren did not know enough about transmitters and receivers to learn anything from the radio. George Johnson, of the Service's scientific office, was due in Seattle that afternoon. He would dismantle the radio until there was nothing left larger than a postage stamp.

A uniformed cop ushered an elderly woman into the living

room. She moved arthritically, avoiding a hundred sharp pains. Her face was wrinkled with age and knowledge, and was set with newfound importance. An official escort. More attention than she'd had in a decade. Her dress was from another era, resembling the green, choking foliage pattern so common to wallpapers.

The officer introduced her, "Mr. Wren, this is Ellen Stoltze. She says she..."

She waved her hand in front of the policeman's mouth. "Shush, you. I'll tell him." She puffed with pride. "I saw him. Make no mistake about that. He was as close to me as you are, a short truck seat away."

"Who did you see?" Wren said, knowing the old lady's answer. She might be as old as fire, but she wouldn't miss much.

"That escaped German soldier. The one whose photo was in the newspaper. Last Thursday, my husband Ben and I were driving our pickup back from the wholesaler, had delivered a couple dozen flats of strawberries. We were heading back to our farm near Gig Harbor, and this nice-looking young fellow walking along the road stuck out his thumb. We obliged him."

"Where had you and Ben been? What town?"

"Tacoma, at the produce siding there."

"Tacoma?" Wren asked, bending lower to her, as if to read her lips. "You mean he was traveling from east to west?"

"I've driven that road a thousand times. It's east to west, all right."

"And you're sure it was last Thursday?"

"Old doesn't mean crazy, sonny," she said sharply. "Yes, last Thursday."

"And he was traveling alone?"

"By himself. Nice-looking fellow, if you like them beat up a bit. He had a scar under his lip, I saw clear as day. And after he got into the truck—sat right next to me, three of us in the cab—the truck smelled like burned meat. I sniffed around a might and saw he had some burns on his arm and fingers. Not bad, but they looked sore. Red and seeping. He said he was handling some coal oil carelessly. Made sense to me."

"Ma'am, are you sure his wounds weren't that bad?" Wren asked. He had found blood-soaked bandages and swabs in the trash can, along with the broom. He had assumed—rather, hoped—the POW was badly injured. "Could he have been really hurt and have been hiding it?"

She squinted her eyes in thought. "Maybe, but I don't think so. He acted healthy to me."

"Did he say anything else?" Tom Garvin asked. "Anything at all?"

"He smiled his thanks when we dropped him off in Gig Harbor, and didn't say a thing else. Quiet type, I figured. And that's okay by me. My Ben's quiet. He can go three days and not say more than 'Pass them wheatcakes' a couple of times."

To rid his words of accusation, Wren asked in a kind tone, "Ma'am if you gave him a ride last Thursday, why didn't you tell the police until today, Monday?"

"I only saw the newspaper with his picture on it today," she said aggressively, not wanting her bravery diminished. "It was in the pile of other papers we was using to line the berry flats. The picture just leaped out at me, what with me having been sitting right next to him four days before."

Her information meant that the POW had been in Margarete Bayerlein's home twice. Once to get the Buick and a second time after the Issaquah incident. It also explained the miracle of the woman and her daughter getting out of the flaming car safely: they hadn't been in it.

Wren thanked the old woman, and she was taken back to the squad car. He said to Garvin, "He's still around, might even be on the island."

"I spent much of the morning checking on the perimeter," Garvin said. "The roads in a forty-mile radius have been shut off completely since Thursday morning, and thanks to Mrs. Stoltze we now know he was still inside the circle on Thursday. So he's got to still be inside."

Although the man they were searching for was a mystery to

Detective Bledsoe, the Secret Service agent's authority was not. John Wren was in control of over one hundred police officers from five cities and four hundred soldiers from Fort Lewis. He had even heard him give orders to Seattle Police Chief Schlay. It was time to defer to the man. Bledsoe asked, "What do we do now?"

"We start looking in earnest. We maintain the perimeter cordon, and we begin a house-to-house search. We'll start with Bainbridge Island. Every room of every house."

"And then we'll search every house in Bremerton, then in Tacoma and Seattle?" Bledsoe asked incredulously. "That's crazy."

"I'll entertain a better idea, Sergeant. But you don't have one."

Automobile brakes squealed. A moment later Fred Kinney ran into the room. Sweat glistened through his flattop, and his veined, potato-size nose seemed red enough to burst. "I caught the four-ten ferry, just to check up on you guys. I called headquarters from the Winslow terminal to see if General Smith's men had found anything. We're in luck."

The fifty-foot run from the car across the lawn into Margarete Bayerlein's house had winded Kinney. He gulped air a moment. Anxiety gripped Wren. He wanted to grab the G2 man's tie and shake the information from him.

"General Smith's order paid off," Kinney said between breaths. "The camp interrogations have been going on all across the country. It took a lot longer than we thought, but we found him."

Detective Bledsoe crowded into the circle. "Who is he?"

"A soldier in the North Africa campaign, a captain. He was with the Twenty-first Sapper Corps, a bunch of mine layers under a Major General Karl Beulowius. Quite a few soldiers of the Twenty-first were captured by the British in January 1943 at the Homs line, near Tripoli, Libya. They're now interned at a POW camp near Phoenix."

Kinney paused to wipe his upper lip. "A lot of the POWs recognized him. Told quite a few stories, too. He's kind of a legend with them. Some of them whooped like crazy, figuring he was alive, or we wouldn't be showing his photo around."

"What's his name?" Wren asked.

"The man known as Schiller at the Fort Lewis camp is actually Captain Kurt Monck."

Monck. A peculiar, sinister name, Wren thought. Finally knowing the name weighed heavily on him, a reminder of the sluggish pace of the investigation. Days of work, and he had only a name. "You'd better tell us about him."

"You're not going to like any of it," Kinney said darkly, lowering himself into the leather wing chair. "This Monck is very, very clever, and he's meaner than a cornered snake."

13

TERRIER MADE HIS SIXTH LOOP OF THE White House, walking leisurely west along Pennsylvania Avenue, then south on 17th Street toward the Ellipse. Only when he was behind the Victory Monument, out of sight of the building and the tourist rabble, did he pause to make a few notes.

His first guess had been correct. The soldiers manning the antiaircraft guns on the White House roof were mannequins. They had been frozen for the entire two hours he had watched them. He could not tell whether the guns were real, but he suspected they were made of balsa. The White House roof in all probability would not support the guns, as his research indicated the roof supports had last been replaced in 1814 when the building was restored after being burned by British General Robert Ross and his troops. But the heavy-caliber machine guns on the east and west terraces were not decoys. Two soldiers were posted at each nest. He scribbled his conclusions onto the pad, praising himself with a large exclamation point at the end of the sentence. He continued walking.

When his contact in New York had given him the code name

Terrier back in 1938, Otto Stroop had been insulted. He had expected something more forceful; Shark, Bear, even Wolf. Then he discovered that terriers were originally bred in England as ratters. Bettors placed the dog into a pit filled with rats, with wagers riding on how many rodents the dog could kill in two minutes. After the New York contact disappeared in 1940— caught in an FBI dragnet, Stroop assumed—Stroop proudly reported as Terrier to the San Diego dropback address.

It suited him. He was a ratter, biting into piles of economic statistics, shaking the life out of them until they were understandable, and propelling them to the front lines. He had believed these preposterous martial analogies were as close as he would ever get to the war action, until the shortwave message five days ago.

Run a security reconnaissance on the White House, it had ordered. He had little idea what such a reconnaissance entailed. But he had thrown himself into it. And he was convinced his analysis was accurate. Berlin would not like his conclusion.

Stroop even looked like a terrier. His goatee was brushed forward and was gray with random brown tufts. His chin was pointed and his nose bent at an awkward angle. He liked to tell anyone interested that it was a football injury, but in fact he had been born with a skewed nose. Years of pipe-smoking had darkened his teeth, but he thought them distinguished and wore brown ties to match. Always bow ties, with plaid vests. They were his trademark in the economics department at Georgetown University.

He and his mother had emigrated from poverty-stricken Munich in 1920, three years after his father had died for Germany at the Second Battle of the Marne. His grandfather had died for Germany in 1884 in a tribal uprising in the German colony in South West Africa. His great-grandfather had died for Germany in the Austro-Prussian War in 1866.

The Terrier was too intelligent to die for Germany, but he found it profitable to work for his homeland. After a Washington Bund meeting in the spring of 1938, during which Joseph

Goebbels's latest propaganda speech had been read and lustily applauded, Stroop was approached by the Bund's treasurer, who had worked for the National Socialist Party since the early 1930s and claimed a personal acquaintance with Hitler. Owing no particular allegiance to the United States, Stroop quickly agreed to provide business information—gathered and analyzed—to the Reich Economics Ministry. For a hundred dollars a week, with a bonus for any report over five pages. After a year of careful reports (many of which were simply condensations of the material from the *Wall Street Journal*) mailed to the New York address, he was honored by being given a shortwave radio. Stroop was instructed on its use and a code, and told to listen to 20.5 megahertz every Wednesday at seven in the morning.

Prior to five days ago, he had never heard his code name on the air and had never received a radioed message. This was his first, and he was determined to earn a bonus.

Stroop walked along the iron fence separating the White House grounds from E Street. It was a warm, humid day, and he removed his tweed jacket, even if it made him look more like the slack-jawed gawkers from Iowa and Nebraska who were roaming in front of the building. There were more of them today, the day before Independence Day, than usual. Maybe they thought it was their patriotic duty.

Before the war, an American flag always flew above the White House when the president was in residence. For security reasons, the flag was now always flying. But there were other ways to tell if the president was in. During Stroop's first day walking his route, eight limousines arrived and departed from the porte-cochere on the north side. He thought he had recognized Roosevelt's adviser and crony Harry Hopkins walking into the building through the high Ionic columns. He certainly had seen Treasury Secretary Henry Morgenthau, who, to Stroop's fury, was publicly proposing to turn Germany into an agricultural country after the war. And he had glimpsed Secretary of State Cordell Hull passing through the gate in a Lincoln limousine. A flurry of activity, it seemed.

Since last Thursday, however, the White House had been quiet. No limousines, except for Secretary of the Navy James Forrestal, who was turned away at the gate, apparently unaware the president and his closest advisers were no longer in residence.

No telling where they were. Wartime secrecy, largely voluntary on the part of the press, was absolute. Roosevelt's statements were released from the White House irrespective of where the president was, letting the public believe he spent most of his time there. In fact, Stroop knew from reading newspaper and magazine stories from before the war that Roosevelt frequently journeyed to his family estate in New York and his retreat in Georgia. No reason the war would change his travels. Perhaps Berlin had also ordered reconnaissances of these places.

Stroop leaned against the pedestal of the statue of General Sherman. The Terrier's survey was complete. There were always eighteen uniformed policemen on duty; six at or near the east gate, four at the north entrance, and the remainder walking the grounds in irregularly timed patrols, one of which always featured a German shepherd on a leash. Additionally, three or four plainclothesmen, probably Secret Service agents, seemed to be stationed just inside the north portico, as they frequently stepped outside for a smoke and a survey of the grounds. A green Dodge sedan continuously circled the White House, with two men in the front seat, neither looking like a tourist. And another plainclothesman wearing binoculars around his neck was always in a second-story window of the Treasury Building due east of the White House.

There were others, undoubtedly, hidden here and there. Stroop hadn't seen any automatic weapons or bazookas, but they would also be there. There were rumors of an escape route, a recently dug tunnel under East Executive Avenue between the White House and the Treasury Building. If it in fact existed, it would be as heavily guarded as the front door.

He had also received drawings of the White House's interior, found in the public library, and dating from the building's last refurbishing in the early 1900s. They were a public-relations

ruse, Stroop had concluded, as there were no bathrooms or closets shown on the plans. There would also be a number of deadly
surprises planted there recently by the Secret Service, also not
shown on the old plans. Small rooms with armed agents posted
twenty-four hours a day. Automatic steel doors, foot-pressure
alarms, listening devices. All the latest electronic technology, all
secret.

Terrier had no idea why he had been ordered to survey the
White House. Probably to determine if a German agent could
get inside. At least, that idea made his work seem vital. But his
control in Berlin would not appreciate his conclusion. Not at all.

Stroop walked toward Constitution Avenue across the Ellipse.
He shaded his eyes against the sun. With only limited knowledge
of the White House's security after his extensive search, and with
that knowledge all negative, he had concluded the building was
impregnable. No one would get inside the White House unin-
vited.

"Do you believe him?" Theodor Paeffgen asked, spreading the
decoded message across his desk with his palms as if spreading
bread dough. The office in the warehouse was always cold, and
the colonel was wearing his suit jacket.

SS Major Carstenn nodded, little more than a tremble of his
modest chin.

"Why?"

"Terrier has always been dependable, even resourceful, in his
analysis. I'm sure he exhausted all sources before he radioed us."

"Nothing is impregnable," Paeffgen said, blowing air over his
hands. The wiring in the warehouse had been strung hastily,
and the green banker's lamp on his desk flickered continually,
adding to the chilly atmosphere of the building. Berlin's early-
morning warmth had not seeped into the interior office.

"You're correct, if you have sufficient knowledge about the
target," Carstenn replied. "Here we don't. Terrier is usually
exhaustive. Tediously so. He loves research like most men love
a woman. But this time he gave us only surface data, and little

of that. We can assume there simply is no further information. Trying to send Monck into the White House with only what we know would be like issuing him a blindfold."

Paeffgen leaned back in his chair. "I agree. Two months ago I had dinner with Major Hans Resfeld of the Leibstandardte Adolf Hitler, which guards the Fuehrer. A bottle of Russian vodka into the meal, he boozily described the protection that surrounds Hitler when he is in residence here or at the Wolf's Lair. It is meticulous and quite ferocious. We can only assume the Americans are as thorough."

"So our first impression was right?"

Paeffgen nodded. "Major Resfeld also told me a person is most vulnerable when traveling, when those protecting him are out of their routine. Monck will have to intercept the target while he is away from the White House." Paeffgen leaned over his desk. "Let's hear what Fala found."

The intelligence clerks working in the warehouse complained they were being treated like dogs, with some justification, as they were putting in sixteen-hour shifts. After discovering that Roosevelt was always accompanied by an overbearing Scottish terrier named Fala, the clerks had adopted the name as their own.

The clerks were organized in the same manner as they had been in the search for Monck. They were arrayed along the long tables under bulbs hung from the high ceiling. At the end of each table was a section chief, usually an RSHA lieutenant, who acted as a sifter of the information gleaned by the clerks. The lieutenants' reports were forwarded to Major Carstenn.

Virtually all the information on Roosevelt was gained from public sources. On the first day, only German material was available, such as Julius Streicher's *Der Stuermer*, so vitriolic in its hatred for everything non-Aryan that even the National Socialist Party members among the clerks found it embarrassing. In the newspaper were such items as Roosevelt's penchant for small boys and a graphic analysis of his surgery to remove a third testicle. Both patently absurd. Streicher lived his fantasies through his malicious stories. But the articles were cut out of the magazine with razors and eventually found their way to Carstenn's desk, where in disgust he wadded and tossed them into the trash bin.

Soon better information arrived at the RSHA warehouse. From Berlin's universities and libraries and from the pouches of agents in the *Kriegsorganisationen* came legitimate articles on Roosevelt. The clerks were amazed at how much an American president would let his countrymen know about him. *Collier's* magazine noted that Roosevelt had a gold tooth that he unscrewed and put into his pocket when not in public. *Time* magazine reported the president could will himself to sleep, which prompted one intelligence clerk to add in pencil to the article that that must be a blessing, what with a wife who resembled a water buffalo. The *Saturday Evening Post* tattled that Roosevelt played poker, particularly seven-card stud, a game the German clerks had never heard of. The prudish *Chicago Daily Tribune* reported that Roosevelt enjoyed making a "Haitian libation," learned on a visit to the Caribbean when he was Assistant Navy Secretary, and which required dark rum, orange juice, brown sugar, and egg white poured into a frosted cocktail shaker. Various newspapers discussed his rumored ailments: coronary thrombosis, a nervous breakdown, a brain hemorrhage, an aneurysm of the aorta, and a malignant skin cancer. And on and on.

The German intelligence agents were puzzled by the American people, who demanded that their leader be trivialized, and by the American press, which fed their appetites for useless, diverting information. The most intimate details of the president's life appeared to be the subject of dinner conversation. In Germany, the leaders were lionized, were made larger than life. What was known about Hitler's personal life? He loved children. And that was enough, most Germans agreed. A gold tooth Roosevelt put into his pocket? A writer of anything along those lines about the Fuehrer would have been shipped to the eastern front by popular acclaim.

Carstenn spread a file across his lap. "All together, Fala read enough material on Roosevelt to fill a Phaenomen truck. In fact, that's what it was hauled away in. Amid the effluvia of personal details, a surprising amount of knowledge was gleaned about his travel patterns."

Paeffgen interrupted, "Why don't you take your uniform cap off, Major?"

"Sir?"

"Your cap. The light is reflecting off the patent-leather rim and is in my eyes."

Carstenn quickly removed the cap, unsure whether the colonel was jesting. The cap was always worn in the presence of a superior officer. Not to do so was almost *Beamtenbeleidigung*, the offense of insulting an officer on duty. But Paeffgen was notoriously casual about dress regulations. He was known to be independent, even irreverent.

To compensate for the sudden informality, Carstenn deepened his voice. "The most striking thing we learned is that on his own Roosevelt is quite immobile."

Paeffgen's questioning right eyebrow rose.

The major continued, "At first, Fala assigned the rare stories about Roosevelt's crippling illness, poliomyelitis, to the same rubbish category as the reports of his other ailments. Then Lieutenant Branden noticed that no recent photograph of the president showed him walking. He is always sitting, or sometimes standing behind a podium or desk that hides his legs."

Carstenn placed a dozen enlarged photographs on the desk in front of the colonel. "The last three of those photographs have never been seen by the American public. After our blanket request for information, they were forwarded by the Finnish ambassador, who took them himself. They show two bodyguards, probably American Secret Service agents, helping Roosevelt into his car."

"Who is the black man?"

"Roosevelt's valet, a retired Navy noncommissioned officer named Arthur Prettyman. We've got about forty photos of him, and they've been analyzed by the dress people. We don't think he wears a weapon under his coat."

"But the others do, these fellows assisting Roosevelt?"

"Certainly. And this one here..." Carstenn leaned over the desk to point to a black-haired agent with a thick, drooping mustache. "We can't be certain, but we think he always carries a stockless submachine gun hung under his right arm. Maybe a British Sten gun. The bumps in his coat, seen in at least thirty-five photos of him, conform to such a weapon. Anyway, if Roosevelt ever could transfer himself from his wheelchair to an automobile seat, he can't now. A bodyguard is straining to lift him in many of these photos."

Paeffgen arranged the photographs on his desk, as if a new sequence would reveal more about the man. "How does Roosevelt stand up, say, to give a speech?"

"He wears leg braces, and they have to be snapped into place. This photo shows one of his guards kneeling to unlock the braces, so the president can be lowered into his wheelchair."

"I had no idea he couldn't walk."

"Most Americans don't know it, either. Or they choose not to think about it."

"It means he can't run, can't escape on his own," Paeffgen said quietly, a tinge of shame coloring his words. He cleared his throat. "The very last obstacle to this type of operation—the target's ability to flee—has been eliminated for us." He pensively ran a hand through his blond hair. "What else do you have?"

"The president's trips inside Washington, D.C., are very limited. He never dines out. He is a fisherman, but we don't have any knowledge about him fishing in the last few years. He loves baseball, and occasionally attends a game at Griffith Stadium. He is also a bird-watcher."

"What? A bird-watcher?"

"He and his bodyguards sometimes travel to one of several places near Washington, D.C., to watch birds. With binoculars. In his wheelchair."

Paeffgen had never heard of such a thing. "Why?"

"I don't know why one watches birds, Colonel," Carstenn answered defensively. "I'll attempt to find out." He ventured ahead with his report. "When not in Washington, Roosevelt is almost certainly at one of three other locations: at his family home in New York, at a retreat called Shangri-La in the Catoctin Mountains in the state of Maryland, and at his retreat in Warm Springs, Georgia. His schedule is never announced in advance, and, in fact, most of the time the public never learns of his journeys."

"How does he travel?"

"Almost exclusively by train," Carstenn answered. "He will journey several thousand miles by train, and almost never flies."

"Why? Superstitious?"

"When he was Assistant Secretary of the Navy, he took his maiden flight. It was in a U.S. Navy seaplane near his summer home at Campobello Island, off the Maine coast. It apparently terrified him, because he has mentioned that flight several times during interviews. It appears that to this day he is afraid of flying and will only do so on long overseas journeys, as he did when he met with Churchill at Casablanca in January of last year."

"So he almost always travels by rail?"

Carstenn laid out more photographs. "The president's train is called POTUS, which is short for President of the United States. The train usually has nine or ten cars in it, pulled by two Southern 1400 Series locomotives, steam engines. You can see they are enormous. Behind the engines are a Baltimore and Ohio auto car..."

"Baltimore and Ohio?" Paeffgen asked, holding the photo to the light.

"It's the name of a railroad company. Roosevelt's armored Ford automobile is transported inside it. Next is a Southern baggage car, then usually two Pullman sleeping cars, these long ones. Next comes a radio car, and our analysts have examined the aerials on top of it. They think Roosevelt is capable of connecting with the public telephone system from the moving train."

Paeffgen pursed his lips. He knew that nothing of the sort existed in the Reich.

"Next is a lounge car, another Pullman, named the Hillcrest Club."

"Why do they name railroad cars?"

Carstenn said, "Who knows? They're Americans."

A perfectly acceptable explanation. The colonel motioned for Carstenn to continue.

"Next is another sleeping car, a six-compartment Pullman. Then a Southern Railway dining car. You can see its number here, 3155. Then a seven-compartment lounge car, named the Conneaut. Finally, the last car is the president's, another long, green Pullman."

"I don't see any name on it?"

"We checked the small registration numbers you can see on the forward end. It was christened the Ferdinand Magellan, but the Secret Service painted it over, probably because they didn't want anyone to know which car the president was in." Carstenn smiled ruefully. "Now it's the only Pullman car in the country without a name on its side. Fairly obvious. And Roosevelt always, always travels in the last car. There's a club of sorts in the United States, composed of people who as a hobby check off on a list all the Pullman cars they see, sighting them by the cars' names. They are called car knockers. When one of them sights the president's car, it is acceptable to list 'one blank Pullman.'"

Paeffgen wearily shook his head. "I assume it's armored."

Another photograph. "We've had Messerschmitt engineers examine these photographs showing Roosevelt grinning through the windows of the Ferdinand Magellan. From their measures of the windows' refractions, they think the glass is three inches thick. Bulletproof against anything up to a Panzerfaust. Nothing else can be discovered about the Ferdinand Magellan, except that the rear platform has an elevator built into it, to allow him to board and exit the car."

Paeffgen leaned back in his chair. His eyes were slits, narrowed by his concentration. "But all this doesn't get us very far, Friedrich. Not until we find out when Roosevelt will be on the train, and its route."

"We're still working on it, as you know. However, we have come up with something." The major paused for emphasis. "I don't know how Terrier discovered this, but he reports that not once in all his years in the White House has President Roosevelt begun a journey on a Friday. He always begins his weekend trips late on a Thursday night."

Paeffgen chewed on his lower lip. "Now this time it must be superstition."

"Probably. Couldn't be any other reason. Terrier also radioed that Roosevelt prefers the Baltimore and Ohio Railroad to all others. He will travel quite a distance out of his way to use their tracks."

"Any idea why?"

"None. And I don't know how he got the information. There's one last item we know about his travels. Our engineers believe two Southern 1400 engines under full steam could pull those nine or ten cars at close to a hundred sixty kilometers an hour. Yet when the president is aboard, it never exceeds forty kilometers an hour. That's very slow."

"And, of course, you have some speculation why."

Carstenn hoped that somewhere in the wry tone was a compliment on his efficiency. "That stumped us for a while. Our engineers uncharacteristically gave up on it. Then we came up with the answer."

"'We,' meaning you." This time his boss's voice clearly carried praise.

"Well, I brought the problem to Dr. Joachim Raeder, who is attached to RSHA as Kaltenbrunner's personal physician."

"The latest status symbol. A chauffeur doesn't seem to be enough these days."

Carstenn was never comfortable with the colonel's lapses into unorthodoxy. High-ranking officers were cashiered for less. The major's eyes cast around the room, as if looking for microphones in the walls. But even in an organization known for treachery, his trust in Paeffgen was implicit. He would never jeopardize the operation, or themselves.

The major said, "Well, Raeder believes a long, jolting train ride would be excruciating for someone in leg braces like those Roosevelt wears, with their hinges and buckles. In an interview we found in a 1938 magazine, the president said he orders the train to travel slowly because he likes the scenery. But I think Dr. Raeder's conclusion is accurate."

The office door opened abruptly, and Paeffgen's young secretary hurried in, huffing loudly and glancing over her shoulder. A man in a brown suit followed her closely. His gabardine jacket was sweat-drenched to the buttons and was rumpled like wadding. His black shoes had a purple stain along the sides, and a corner of a pocket was torn from the jacket. He was breathing heavily and weakly dabbed at his face with a white handkerchief.

"I'm sorry, Colonel Paeffgen," the secretary said, rolling her eyes with exasperation. "I told him you were busy, but he pushed by me."

"Dr. Paeffgen, I am Colonel Heinz Freissner," the man said, extending his damp hand. Freissner was a wispy, timorous-appearing man. His eyes were moist and restless, and his chin seemed soft and impermanent. His perfectly oval head seemed insignificant under his hat.

Paeffgen hesitated before standing and shaking Freissner's hand. Carstenn jumped from his chair and could close his mouth only with an effort.

"I am with the Geheime..."

Paeffgen's voice was tight with disapproval. "I know who you are, Colonel. Why have you come here?"

"Orders. Believe me, I wouldn't otherwise, ah, interrupt..."

"Orders from whom?"

"I spoke with Reichsfuehrer Himmler moments ago. He asked me if I realized my duty tour was ending in two weeks. I, of course, said I did, and he..." Freissner wiped his brow with the handkerchief. "I have never before spoken personally with the Reichsfuehrer. I must tell you... ah... he..."

Paeffgen cut in, "He frightens you, like everyone else. Go on, Colonel."

"Yes, 'frightens' is the word. He ordered me to immediately escort you to my office. A 'tour' is the word he used."

"A tour of your operation in the Prinz Albrechtstrasse building?"

"I'm afraid so, yes." Freissner's voice was grating.

Major Carstenn had never before heard Paeffgen's voice quaver. He heard it now. "Why, Colonel Freissner?"

Freissner studied the warehouse floor. "The Reichsfuehrer is searching for my . . . ah . . . replacement. Himmler is considering transferring you to my position."

Paeffgen blew on his hands. His eyes were shaded, and Carstenn knew his superior was struggling to suppress his fear. Paeffgen said with a controlled voice, just above a whisper, "We're extremely busy, Colonel. Can it wait?"

"I'm sorry, Dr. Paeffgen. Himmler insisted that you be shown my offices today. It will be in both our best interests if we obey the Reichsfuehrer. Immediately."

"My God," Carstenn said tensely, "do you suppose . . . ?"

Paeffgen raised a hand to stop the major, then asked the question for him. "I will be returning to this office, will I not, Colonel Freissner?"

"Yes, yes, of course. A tour is . . . ah . . . all I have been ordered to give you."

Paeffgen rose stiffly from his chair. "Then let's get on with it."

Freissner's driver looked more the part. With their trenchcoats worn even on warm days, their rubber-soled shoes, their swaggering, and their knowing eyes, Gestapo agents broadcast their omnipotence.

The Daimler swerved around bomb pocks along the Kurfuerstendamm. With each sharp turn, Paeffgen's arm pressed against the manacles hanging unused from a bolt in the car door. The sidewalks swarmed with Berliners, gay and lively, the July sun having brightened faces made haggard by seven consecutive nights of Allied bombing. With vendors selling the first oranges the city had seen in a year, and with bright red, white, and black party banners flying from balconies, the street retained some of its prewar cheerfulness. The gutted buildings and the rubble could be ignored.

A few moments later the car turned onto Prinz Albrechtstrasse and approached the high, arched door of the block-long gothic building that housed the Geheime Staatspolizei. They passed a Gestapo agent, leaning against the gray stone, appearing idle and bored. It was rare to see one loiter.

Following Paeffgen's eyes, Freissner volunteered quickly, "I had to post him there on the sidewalk, as there's a ventilation grate there down to the basement. Children were spending far too much time with their ears to the metal."

The Daimler stopped in front of the main entrance. An SS sentry wearing a coal-scuttle helmet and double lightning bolts on a black lapel opened the door for Freissner. His salute was returned with an "Ah... thank you, Private."

Freissner gripped Paeffgen's elbow as he emerged from the car. "I didn't want this job, you must understand. In fact, a week ago I wrote Kaltenbrunner asking for clarification in writing of the fact that I... ah... protested this assignment."

Paeffgen straightened himself. "What good do you think that'll do?"

"A document? Proof in writing that the cellar was not my idea? A lot of good, believe me," Freissner answered with conviction. "The Americans and English examine evidence, Colonel. The legal mind is part of their ... ah ... peculiar makeup." Another sentry pulled open the double doors for them. "Not that I'm a defeatist, mind you. I simply think the record should be clear."

Paeffgen followed the little man down the stone stairs into the cellar, leaving the sunlight, and, for so many prisoners, all hope, behind. Guards hastily pulled open an iron gate. Its grating echoed in the long hallway, answered by a groan from somewhere. The corridor was lit dimly by a few bulbs irregularly spaced, but the hall remained so dark that its end was lost in distant darkness. Doors lined both sides of the passage. In each door was a sliding panel covering a view hole. In front of two doors were desks at which Gestapo agents were stationed, each with earphones over his head, connected to an amplifier, with wires running into the doorframe. The hallway was chilly, but tracks of sweat streamed down Paeffgen's back.

"This is my office," Freissner said as he waved a hand at an open door without pausing. "But more interesting is the medical room, here. One of my innovations, really. Another thing which I will have documented, even from statements signed by the accounts, is the . . . ah . . . humaneness of the questioning. In many instances, drugs are used, sodium thiopental or amobarbitol."

The room was brightly lit and painted clinical white. On the walls were enamel-and-glass medicine cabinets. A tray of hypodermic needles and rolls of surgical tubing sat on a metal table in the middle of the room. On a counter were a sphygmograph, a box of finger splints, and packets of rubber gloves.

"You see, Dr. Paeffgen, much of the discomfort can be avoided by someone who is innovative, as I have been, if I may be so . . . ah . . . immodest. I'm sure that's why the Reichsfuehrer is considering you for this post. Running the RSHA North American Section, you have gained a reputation for problem-solving." Freissner's voice had gained the singsong quality of a museum guide.

He led Paeffgen down the hall. One of the agents half rose from his seat, expecting Freissner to wave him back down, which the colonel did. "Did you know I was chief accountant at the Sicherheitsdienst before coming here? I was an auditor, really. I call prisoners under my charge my accounts. And I brought an accountant's thoroughness to this operation. I have received a citation from Kaltenbrunner himself."

Paeffgen's mouth felt full of cotton. He managed, "Evidence for the prosecution?"

"I have destroyed it already," Fleissner replied with no evidence he understood the sarcasm. "But I did earn it, believe me. Let me show you one of my recent successes."

Thirty minutes later, the tour was over. His stomach churning, Paeffgen halted at the steps and waited for the gate to open. He felt as if he had been in the cellar a week. He was as cold as if he were in a Ukrainian winter.

Freissner had insisted on escorting him out. He said, "Some of this is more . . . ah . . . bothersome than most duty for the Reich, I must admit, Colonel. But there are certain rewards. The men, for example. Never have I worked with a more dedicated group of people."

Paeffgen halted at the steps and waited for the gate to open. He turned to Freissner and demanded, "How long until the decision on my transfer is final?"

"Two weeks, I believe. At least, that is what the Reichsfuehrer indicated."

Paeffgen charged up the stairs, and a woman's scream chased him out of the building. Himmler's threat was clear, and terrifying. Unless Kurt Monck succeeded in crossing America and intercepting the target, Paeffgen would be transferred to the Prinz Albrechtstrasse horror chamber. Paeffgen stepped into the Berlin sun, which lifted his spirits like a pardon. Two weeks.

14

TOM GARVIN LED THE YOUNG WO-
man into the room and was startled when Wren
waved him away. The boss never worked solo on an investigation.
Garvin covered his surprise by glancing at the girl, then bawdily
winking at Wren. He backed out of the office and closed the
door.

"Miss Anderson, thank you for coming in," Wren said, dredg-
ing up a smile for the girl, who seemed frightened. "I'm sorry
to have you come down on Independence Day. Please sit down.
May I call you Mary?"

She said nothing.

"I know the dean didn't tell you why I wanted to speak with
you, because I didn't tell the old goat."

This apparently was not as humorous as Wren had hoped, as
she still sat woodenly, gazing at him with incomprehension. She
was twenty years old, but with a child's face, with innocent
brown eyes and a ruddy tint to her cheeks. Her lips had the
perfect peaks of a Gibson girl's, and her seal-brown hair fell in
large waves to her shoulders. She wore the half-sleeve blue jumper
dress that was almost a uniform among college women. Showing

at the neck was a bright silver blouse, whose color reflected onto her long neck, making it as graceful as a grebe's.

"The dean said you were a Secret Service agent," she said, her voice a ghost of a whisper. "I'm not even sure what that is."

"We're like other law-enforcement agencies. We look for people who have broken the law." Wren tried another grin. "The person we want speaks German, and that's how you can help us."

"Is it the prisoner of war who escaped from the Fort Lewis camp?"

Wren nodded. "You speak German, and I have some letters that I'd like you to translate for me."

"Written by the POW?"

"By a woman he's traveling with. I'm hoping the letters might give me a clue to where they're hiding. Perhaps she mentions relatives in the United States, or a part of America they heard is nice and might settle there, that sort of thing."

That was part of it. Only vaguely had Wren admitted to himself a desperate need to know this woman. Her photographs, her small possessions, her home, and these scented letters were more contact with a woman than he had allowed himself since that terrible day. She was anonymous. He would never know Margarete Bayerlein, except perhaps to testify at a trial, so he could explore her without betraying Linda's memory. A memory he let shackle him. A memory he worked to suppress, but could not be unfaithful to. Margarete Bayerlein's letters might allow him a little of the warmth he had been missing.

The coed was saying something. "... but I'm not German. All I know is what I've learned in my classes."

"The dean says you speak fluently. Why don't you try one?" Wren pulled the first of a dozen onionskin letters out of its flimsy envelope as delicately as his thick fingers would allow. The letters had been written before Margarete and Georg Bayerlein and their two-year-old daughter had come to the United States. Half the envelopes had a Bad Tolz address and a Berlin return. The others

were answering letters. Both Margarete Bayerlein and her husband had saved them. The first was dated June 4, 1935. Wren
unfolded the letter and glanced at the flowing handwriting. A
few of the letters were unrecognizable, looking like double *S*'s.
Some vowels had two dots above them. He passed the letter
across the desk to her.

She glanced at the first paragraph. "I think I can do this." Her
voice was stronger. "Should I read it all?"

"Every word."

"'My dearest Georg. I saw you off at the Zoo Station only
two hours ago, yet I must write this letter right now.'" Mary
paused. "Or I guess that could be 'immediately.' Anyway, 'Your
departure has left a rock...'" She smiled and looked up at Wren.
"Let's make that 'stone,' which is more romantic than 'rock.' 'Your
departure has left a stone where my heart was. I write this,
having returned to our bed where only a short time ago you held
me in your arms and...'"

Mary abruptly stopped, and her gentle face caught fire, the
violent blush racing from neck to hairline in an instant. Her
charming mouth fell open, and her astonished gaze rose to Wren,
then dropped back quickly to the letter, then jerked to the wall.
She held the letter away from her as one might soiled tissue
paper.

Wren frowned with concern. "Something wrong, Mary?"

"I can't read this. It's ... too romantic."

Wren leaned forward across the desk. "Too romantic? What
does that mean?"

She cast her eyes around helplessly.

Understanding crossed the agent's face. "I see." He rubbed
his jaw with his knuckles. "I didn't mean to embarrass you, Mary.
The dean said he spoke a little German. Maybe he can come
down to the office."

"Italian and Portuguese and Spanish are his languages. His
German is terrible. He doesn't understand the colloquial."

Angry at another dead end, Wren stared out his window. Seattle's Federal Building was a gift of Franklin Delano

Roosevelt. It overlooked Elliott Bay, the city's portion of Puget Sound, which the other Roosevelt had called "the world's most beautiful inland sea." A Foss tug, identifiable by its green stack, was nudging a freighter into Pier 59. The sun sprinkled the water with dashes of color which rippled along the tug's wake. Kurt Monck is out there, perhaps gazing at the same water, Wren thought. The sun's reflection taunted him.

He said, "The POW is going to try to kill someone, and you and I need to stop him. There may be hints in these letters to his companion's location now."

"I can go on with the letter, Mr. Wren. I know it's important." She continued bravely. "'... where only a short time ago you held me in your arms and kissed my neck and my ... my breasts. My nipples still feel the caress of your lips.'"

Mary's skin again burned. She held the letter higher to block Wren's view of her face. "'The magic of your mouth has left me shaking,' or I suppose 'trembling' is better. 'How my damp nipples longed for you when your lips slid down to my stomach and lingered there. Then even lower, to the warmth that has always been yours.'"

She looked at Wren. "I don't understand what he is doing here."

Wren's face remained impassive, but Mary must have seen wisdom in it, for she gasped, "Oh, my God! Do you mean he's going to ... How can he?" Her lovely face screwed up. "That is so icky."

"Well, maybe I'd better find someone else ..."

"No," she said emphatically. "We all must do our part in the war effort. And if this is mine, so be it." She was a martyr, her jaw set, her eyes ablaze with righteous indignation, her shoulders back. "'Your marvelous tongue. How it played and played within the folds of me ...'"

There was more, much more. Each letter began with a torrid love scene, longingly remembered and vividly detailed. Mary read with singular dispassion, but Wren found himself perspiring and shifting uncomfortably on the hard seat. Only when the bursts of prosaic passion had been spent did the missives begin the news of their one-year-old daughter, and continue with gossip which might contain evidence of her hiding place in the United States.

There was something. The letter dated August 12, 1935, mentioned her sister in Kentucky, who had gone to the United States with her husband five years before. Lilli was her name, but there was no mention of her married name or where in Kentucky she lived. The sister had sent her father a bottle of a "strange spirit" called bourbon.

The letters contained other glimpses of Margarete Bayerlein. She had returned to her parents' apartment in Berlin while her husband was training at Bad Tolz. She played the piano, and she filled lonely hours with Chopin and Bach. She thrilled to the German writer on the American West, Karl May. She and her girlfriends were experimenting with a sugar-coated puff pastry, a French dessert suddenly the rage in Berlin. Her schooling at Berlin Technical was going well, and she had passed her catheterization exam, "thanks to my familiarity with your sweet thing." Much older than she had been twenty minutes ago, Mary Anderson did not even blush at that one.

In the last letter, Georg described Margarete as *ewig-weibliche*, a phrase Mary recognized from Goethe and translated as "ever-womanly." "Well," she sniffed virtuously, "this Margarete is certainly that."

Garvin rushed into the office without knocking. His red and freckled face was creased with perturbation. "John, line two, from Washington. It's a response to our interceptor request."

Garvin ran to the next office to lift the extension phone.

Wren took the receiver off its cradle. "This is John Wren."

"Admiral Franklin McWhorter here. We have something for you."

McWhorter was in charge of 20th Division of OPNAV, the Office of the Chief of Naval Operations, the Navy's headquarters

establishment. The 20th Division was the Office of Naval Communications. Under him was the G Section, the Communication
Security Section, OP-20-G.

McWhorter asked, "Is the line secure at your end?"

Wren reached for the base of the phone and dialed 1. A click
was heard. A placebo. He didn't have time for Navy security
games. He replied, "It is now."

"Good man," the admiral said. The line was filled with static,
and even the admiral's booming voice faded in and out. "I have
on an extension phone Lieutenant Richard Morris, a transmission
security analyst in our department. He will be giving you some
of the details."

"Good afternoon, Mr. Wren," another voice said.

The admiral cut off any response from Wren. "You requested
any unexplained and unusual radio broadcasts from the Seattle
area. We've got what you want. And let me say first that before
I decided to give you this information on our radio equipment,
I ran a security check on you, even though your boss, Chief
Wilson, said you were okay. You passed."

For Mary's benefit, Wren looked at the ceiling in an exaggerated way and replied, "I'm relieved."

"Now, on to more pressing matters. We've got your man on
a wire recording, picked up by one of our receiving stations only
a couple of miles from the house on Bainbridge Island where
you think he did his broadcasting."

"You have an intercept unit there?" Wren asked.

"Right on Bainbridge. It's a large antenna complex most is-
landers don't know anything about. One week ago today the
Bainbridge unit operator almost had his headphones blown off—
those are his words—by a transmission emanating from right
nearby. It was loud and crystal-clear, and it kicked on his automatic recorder immediately. We've been studying it for a week,
but had no idea of its connection to a Secret Service investigation
until your Chief Wilson spoke with me. Interestingly, we think
the message was made with broadside-array antennas, as the

signal wasn't picked up anywhere other than at the Bainbridge Island station, which is three miles on the Berlin side of this Miss Bayerlein's house."

"What does that mean?"

"In words you can understand, it means your man knows radios."

Wren leaned back on the chair's two legs, covered the phone's speaker, and said to Mary, "The man I'm talking to is a pompous ass. You wouldn't like him anywhere near as much as you like me."

Mary smiled widely.

Wren asked into the phone, "Was the message in code?"

"Yes. In a damn good one."

"So you haven't broken it?"

"Don't expect miracles, Wren," Admiral McWhorter answered condescendingly. "We're working on it. But that's not the real reason I called." McWhorter paused for emphasis. "The man you're looking for is no longer in the Seattle area. He is in Chicago."

Wren's chair slammed down. "Chicago? That can't be. We have him bottled up here."

The admiral's laugh was from his belly. "You've got nobody bottled up there. He's in Chicago, probably laughing at you just like I am here in Washington. You'd better explain it to our Mr. Wren, Lieutenant."

Wren flushed from frustration and anger. Chicago? It couldn't be. Kurt Monck couldn't have broken his circle.

"Mr. Wren," said the weaker voice, "I specialize in what we call transmission analysis. I look for similarities in sending patterns, so we know if an enemy sender is traveling. I do it by looking for a sender's distinctive signature. Your man's Morse is diagnostic."

"What does that mean?" Wren demanded.

"It means that his pattern of sending tells me a lot about him, and it can't be confused with anyone else's pattern. For example, your man varies speeds considerably from number to number.

That tells me that he is more comfortable with certain numbers, and therefore is either new at Morse or is rusty at it. And your man has a distinctive pause between the numbers five and eight. I slowed the recording way down and timed the gaps between his fives and eights. It's always the same amount of time. He also puts a long gap after a seven, as if he has to think back to see if he got the numbers confused. All combined, these traits are as distinctive as a fingerprint."

"So how do you conclude he is in Chicago?"

The admiral resumed charge. "Yesterday a signal interceptor in Labrador picked up a broadcast. He got the wire recording of it and played it back over the telephone here. Morris got right on it and figured out quickly that the man had the same signature as the Bainbridge Island sender."

"Why do you know he is in Chicago?" Wren persisted.

"Although the Labrador station was the only one to get a recording, six other sub-spotter units in Canada and on our East Coast heard it. They immediately triangulated it to the Chicago area. That's as close as they could pinpoint it, what with all the other static coming from the area."

"That's a big city, Admiral."

"You haven't heard all of it. I spoke with Mr. Hoover a few moments ago. His agents have been trying to track a signal source on the north side there for some time. By complete coincidence, they had portable radio direction finders in the field when your man broadcast. His FBI boys also got a fix on it. They've got the location narrowed down to a handful of houses near Wrigley Field."

Wren came out of his seat. He was exultant. They'd found Kurt Monck. "Lieutenant Morris, you deserve a promotion."

"I'd rather have Pacific duty." There was yearning in the words.

"Admiral," Wren went on, "in terms you understand, this man is a loose cannon. It is essential those messages be decoded as soon as possible."

"As I said . . ."

Wren hung up on him. He swept around the desk and gripped

the girl's arm. "Mary, you're wonderful. Don't let those letters get to you."

He and Garvin met in the hallway. "I'll call Chief Wilson. They'll put a lookout on those houses and nab Monck the first time they see him."

"You and I are headed for Chicago?"

Wren smiled hugely. "I only hope they don't arrest him until we get there. I want to see his face when we nail him."

15

PETTY OFFICER OTIS WHITE'S RIGHT hand had always been his breadwinner, first at the Ford plant in Detroit, where it had affixed 964,520 passenger-side window wipers, and then in the Procurement Office at the Great Lakes Naval Station, where it had rubber-stamped over two million purchase orders and receipts.

White was comforted by repetition, and he loved his job. His right forearm was fully two inches larger in diameter than his left, and with his pipe and narrow eyes, he was inevitably called Popeye by his mates.

His duty station was in the Procurements Building, at a heavy oak desk in front of a window. The building was a brick rectangle with a small office near the street and an enormous warehouse behind. The depository was the distribution point for supplies for all Navy personnel at the largest Navy training station in the country.

White stamped the morning's receipts to the whistled tune of "Is You Is or Is You Ain't My Baby." Into his rollicking fifty-second verse, his arm stopped midway on a downward stroke at the sound of a car door slamming. He looked up.

A woman in civilian clothes, slumping to the ground. She had been crossing the street and had just been struck by a car. A green Chrysler was speeding away, hadn't even stopped. The sound must have been her body ricocheting off the car's fender, not a car door.

"Chief," White called as he launched himself out of his chair. "Better get out here quick."

White sprinted through the office door into the street. She lay on her back in huddled shapelessness, with one leg cocked under her and her neck twisted painfully against the curb. Her eyes were open but glazed and unseeing.

"Ah hell, no," White said miserably as he knelt over her. He put his ear near her lips. A very shallow breath. Her face was as pale as summer whites. He grabbed her wrist for a pulse. It took him a moment to find it, but it was surprisingly strong. Maybe she wasn't dying. "Can you hear me, miss?"

Chief Petty Officer Ray Dierdorf rushed out of the office, his square black glasses bouncing on the bridge of his nose and his belly swaying over his crossed-anchors belt. "What happened? Christ, look at her. Is she alive?"

"Yeah. She's hurt bad, though." White looked up, expecting orders.

"Don't move her. No telling what's broken or ruptured." Dierdorf anxiously sucked his lower lip. The top two buttons of her blouse were open, and he resisted glancing at the lace of her bra. The injured deserved special consideration. Her brown hair was sprayed against the concrete. Even as she lay there battered and disarranged, she was a fine looker. "How'd it happen, Popeye?"

"I don't know. I looked up just as she hit. I've never seen anything like it. She was thrown down and splatted against the street, like a lifeboat dropped from the davits."

A sentry had been patrolling the exterior of the building. He turned the corner, then came running. He was a bony shore patrolman with a band around his arm and a .45

government-issue on his hip. As he ran, he held his helmet on
with a hand.

"Don't move her," he yelled as he approached. He knelt over
the woman and performed the same tests White had done. "She's
alive."

"I know that, for Christ sake," the chief said. "We've got to..."

"Call the base hospital," the shore patrolman cut in. "They'll
get an ambulance here pronto."

Popeye White ran back into the office. The shore patrolman
surveyed the injured woman. A tapered, frail nose, but large,
forceful eyes. Quite stunning. But she was so pale. And her skin
was pasty.

The woman groaned, and her head turned to one side. Her
eyelids rose and fell slowly, as if the simple act required all her
remaining strength. She moaned again.

"Easy there, girl," the chief said soothingly. He fanned her
face with his handkerchief. "We've got help coming. You'll be
all right."

"Does she have any ID?" the patrolman asked.

Dierdorf glanced around the street. "No purse. I don't see
anything. We won't even have relatives to notify."

White returned, sweating from the short run and his fear for
the woman. "They're coming. Couple minutes, they said. Them
and some SP investigators."

White checked her pulse again, then looked up and down the
street, which was lined with warehouses and administration
buildings. He said urgently, "Dammit it to hell, I wish that
ambulance would get here."

The shore patrolman suddenly turned to a ripple that seemed
to come from the office. It was an indistinct sound, over almost
before it began. It was another crease in an already incredible
day. White and Dierdorf also heard it, and they followed the
patrolman's gaze. None of them saw the woman's quick, fearful
look at the building.

The shore patrolman was a gangly youth whose polite face

hid a suspicious mind. The sound was that extra straw of un-
accountable detail. He drew his service revolver and entered the
office.

Four minutes passed before the Shore Patrol arrived at the
Procurements Building to investigate the hit-and-run, and ten
minutes later, after discovery of the warehouse's smashed rear
door and the semiconscious sentry, they turned it over to the
FBI.

The Bureau's report answered only a few questions. Shortly
after the sentry had entered the building, an olive-green 1937
Chrysler—Petty Officer White swore to the make and year—
had approached from the north, and while the sailors looked on
dumbfounded, the young woman had simply risen to her feet
and climbed into the backseat. Neither thought to look at the
two men in the front seat for later identification. Both men saw
the Chrysler's badly crumpled rear fender.

The semiconscious sentry was found sprawled between a
row of storage shelves. When he could talk, he said he had
been walking to the rear door of the warehouse when a wire
or a rope had been dropped over his head by someone who
had approached from his rear. The sentry hadn't heard anyone,
and the garrote appeared out of nowhere. An instant later, as
he felt his windpipe beginning to collapse, another man ran at
him yelling, "Don't do that, there's no need," and hit the sentry
on the head with a goose-necked table lamp, one of two hundred
stockpiled in the warehouse. The sentry didn't remember his
fall to the floor.

The FBI asked the sentry about it again and again, but he
stuck to his story. The garrote came from behind. The second
man, the one who rushed down the aisle in front of the sentry,
apparently wanted to save the sentry's life by knocking him
out, proving to the garroter there was no need to kill the guard.

A straightened crowbar was found near the double doors at
the rear of the warehouse. It had apparently failed to spring open
the doors, so the trespassers had resorted to plowing into them

with the Chrysler. They used the back of the car as their ram, protecting the radiator and engine. It suggested they were in a hurry, anxious to obtain whatever they were looking for before an ambulance arrived for the woman lying in the street.

The FBI asked that weapons, explosives, and other items that might be used by saboteurs be immediately inventoried. It took a crew of Navy clerks only an hour.

And when White and Dierdorf identified the decoy woman from a photo, the FBI notified the Secret Service's Chicago office.

16

A PASSERBY WOULD HAVE SAID THE neighborhood this July 5 was as it had been every other day that summer. Sally Robertson circled the block pushing her firstborn in a stroller. The twelve-year-old Bushnell twins were at it again, playing catch and mercilessly accusing each other of having a crush on Susy Quin. Separated by a picket fence, an Irish terrier and a dachshund were gaily barking at each other. The mailman delivered an antique-glass auction notice to Larry Leffler's house. Several blocks away at Wrigley Field, the Cubs had just crawled out of the cellar to the rarefied heights of seventh place by beating the Boston Braves in an Independence Day doubleheader, 7–1 and 4–2. All was normal and well.

In truth, little was normal. Today the mailman was a Secret Service agent who was on his twelfth trip up and down the block. Passing Leffler's house for the twentieth time, the yellow school bus with Skokie Lutheran Bible Camp painted on its side contained eight FBI agents, hunched down on their seats. The occupants in the homes on all three sides of Leffler's house had been quietly taken away and replaced with Chicago policemen carrying Thompson submachine guns.

In front of the house, John Wren and Tom Garvin wore telephone linemen's uniforms, with tool belts, hardhats, and overalls. They stood near a panel truck commandeered from the telephone company. Inside were two more Secret Service agents. Wren had not climbed the pole, but every once in a while he would stare up it. The agent held what looked like a lineman's portable telephone, but was actually a two-way radio with which he was overseeing the operation. Wren needed a shave, and his eyes were lined. It had been a bumpy overnight flight from Seattle.

They were beginning the fourth hour of the wait for Larry Leffler. And for the German killer, Kurt Monck.

Garvin nudged his boss, indicating down the street. "What's this? Another phone-company truck?"

Wren swore under his breath. They had ordered the phone company to stay clear of the area. The pickup pulled to a stop behind the panel truck.

Wren and Garvin were astonished to see Secret Service Chief Frank Wilson emerge from the pickup. He, too, was wearing a repairman's uniform. He smiled briefly as he walked toward his men. Wilson's square head was topped with a trace of brown hair, carefully combed back. He wore rimless spectacles under slanted eyebrows that gave him a stern appearance. His mouth was wide and always compressed. His prominent jaw was dotted with a peculiarly wide dimple. Wilson had not been handsome one day in his life.

"Hello, John, Tom." His mouth lengthened, but showed no teeth. "I hear you followed a POW east." Wilson always did this, pretended to know little about an operation, when in fact he knew more than the agents running it. "Is he in there?"

"No movement since we've been here, sir. I'm beginning to think the house is empty."

Wilson looked around, his hands in the baggy pockets. He

looked as uncomfortable in the overalls as a coal miner in a cummerbund. Wren wasn't surprised to see the tie beneath the overall bib.

"I've been reading your reports, John. Following them with some interest, actually. So has Henry the Morgue." Wilson's tongue pushed out his cheek, as if he were fishing for a raspberry seed stuck between his teeth.

So Wren had gotten their attention. Chief Wilson's superior, Secretary of the Treasury Henry Morgenthau, usually took little interest in Secret Service activity. Wren asked, "Is Mike O'Brien tightening things up?"

"As well as he can. I swear the president purposely makes things difficult for us. You know how FDR is."

Wren could not help himself. "I used to know how he was."

"And now you have lots of salmon and totem poles out in the Northwest, and an Arizona sheriff isn't around to ask questions about your last vacation. Life is a series of trade-offs, John." Wilson ventured a small smile. "And I see that your cherubic partner refuses to age like the rest of us. Just keeps getting younger and redder."

Garvin indeed did get more red at Wilson's words. He turned away on the pretext of watching the house, then walked toward the front of the truck.

Wilson was a field chief, seldom content to stay in Washington when the action was elsewhere. He said, "Henry the Morgue is asking questions. He thinks you're overreacting to coincidences. He says your conclusion that a POW is traveling across the country to kill the president is unwarranted."

"There ought to be a law against cronies gaining high political office," Wren said evenly.

"That crony is my boss, and I do what he tells me." Wilson scratched his chin. "Morgenthau has refused to allow me to transfer more men to the Chicago office. The president is making a campaign stop here on his way to the Coast for the convention, and Morgenthau doesn't want it to appear as if Roosevelt is under siege."

Wilson smiled briefly. "The Secretary even asked for your file. Said he wanted to know who the hell you are."

"I hope you cleaned it up a little."

"I did. Took me a while, though."

Wilson looked over his shoulder, as if making sure Morgenthau was not in hearing distance. He said, "Like you, John, I believe few things are entirely coincidental. The North Carolina German and the Northwest POW are somehow connected. And someone is going to a lot of trouble to free the POW and move him east."

"It's all speculation, of course. A hunch."

"You're a good hunch player," Wilson said. "I told Morgenthau that, but he has his own concerns. Our service is charged to fear the worst. And this Kurt Monck seems like the worst possible case." Wilson nodded pleasantly to Mrs. Robertson, who was returning home with the stroller, unaware her neighborhood had become an armed camp. "I also spoke with the president."

"Let me guess. He refuses to alter his schedule."

"Precisely. He said, and I quote, 'It would ill behoove the leader of the free world to cower because a POW escaped his confinement at the other end of the continent.'"

"Monck is no longer in Washington State. He's right here in Chicago."

"So it would appear. I spoke with Hoover this morning. He said you had it narrowed down to a couple of houses. But you're focusing on this one right here. What'd you find?"

Wren pulled a clipboard from the back of the panel truck. On it was a photograph, highly magnified and grainy. It showed the upper corner of a window, close enough to see paint flakes on the putty. He said, "We used a Leica 70-millimeter with a high-speed automatic film-transport mechanism powered by a battery, taken out of the belly of a recon P-51. We put it into an RCA radio delivery box, and Garvin and I walked it all over the neighborhood this morning, like we were making deliveries. Took about six hundred shots of the seven houses that were suspect, all in an hour. They were developed and analyzed by Jim Jacobson and his FBI crew this morning downtown. They found it right away."

Wilson bent closer to the clipboard. "I don't see it."

Wren pointed. "The small wire here, running through the hole in the lower right windowpane." He flipped to the next photograph. "Here you see a wood rain gutter, and you can also see the wire running along it, then down another gutter to the ground. It's an antenna."

"Could he be just an amateur radio operator?"

"Why would he hide the antenna, then?"

Wilson nodded. "Sounds like the FBI is cooperating, for a change. Maybe my little talk with J. Edgar had some effect."

The chief rose to his toes and settled back down, taking a long breath. "I've got some more news about Kurt Monck, all of it bad."

A dilapidated Ford wandered down the street. The driver might have hurried had he known he was in the sights of at least ten weapons.

"I haven't heard anything good about him yet," Wren said.

"General Smith of the Detainee System has had his men continue the interviews. He's learned a lot about Monck, not only from the soldiers in Monck's Twenty-first Sapper Corps interned near Phoenix, but also from POWs who knew him at the Baron von Weyrauch Cadet School in Hamburg and at Wehrmacht Engineers School near Potsdam. They've talked to his cadet bunkmates, one of his professors, and his subordinates in Africa. Quite a few POWs claim to know him, but when questioned more closely, they only wanted to appear to have rubbed shoulders with him."

Wilson glanced at Larry Leffler's house. "We've found six other credible stories of his missions, all from the time before Monck went underground behind Montgomery's lines. And then there are a dozen or so apocryphal tales told with relish by the POWs, big explosions credited to Monck simply because by then all mysterious explosions were given to Monck."

Two boys whisked down the sidewalk on scooters made from old roller skates, two-by-fours, and apple crates. The skate wheels made enough noise on the cement that Wilson had to wait for them to pass. He continued, "I've put everything else we've gotten from the POWs in a memo you'll get shortly, John."

An old pickup passed them, a rusting Model A with "Vern's Vegetables" on its side. Chief Wilson nodded to the driver, a Secret Service agent.

Garvin returned from the front of the truck. "Chief, you're wanted on the truck radio."

While Wilson attended to the call, Garvin said, "On a radio-telephone linkup, I got ahold of the Four Horsemen Process Serving Company, where Leffler works. He's not due in today. And he sure hasn't shown his face here. Think we spooked him and Monck?"

"No chance. They'll show. The woman, too."

A moment later, Wilson hurried back. Behind the spectacles, his eyes seemed deeper, and his mouth was a pressed line. "The bad news keeps coming, John. Two hours ago, two men and a woman hit a storage warehouse at the Great Lakes Naval Training Center north of here. The lady they used as a diversion matched Margarete Bayerlein's photo."

"What do you mean, they hit it?"

After Wilson summarized the raid, Wren asked, "Is the woman all right?"

Garvin glanced at Wren.

Wilson answered, "Not a scratch on any of them. The car had been reported stolen that morning. The owner isn't going to like seeing what's left of it."

"What'd they get?" Wren asked.

Wilson looked at both of them in turn. "The Navy just completed an inventory. RDX plastic explosive. Four packages of it. And blasting caps."

Garvin whistled.

"Now let me tell you gentlemen something." Wilson reverted

to his office tone, distant and formal. "I'll admit that your first reports were met with a little skepticism in Washington. Not from Mike O'Brien at the White House, but from me. A POW escape in Washington State didn't interest me much. Now I'm convinced this Kurt Monck must be stopped. He's still six hundred miles from the White House. And that's as close as he is to get. Understood?"

Both agents nodded.

The Secret Service chief walked back to the pickup without another word.

Garvin waited until the truck had driven away before he said, "I don't know who I'm afraid of most, Kurt Monck or Chief Wilson."

"That's a hard choice, I must admit." Wren ran a hand over his large jaw. "If Leffler comes back and Monck isn't with him, we go in anyway. We can't wait any longer to find out where the German is. One way or another, Leffler will tell us."

Larry Leffler had reason to feel good. He had survived another encounter with the mad German. He laughed as he parked his Dodge a block from his house. He used to park it in front of his home, but one night an unhappy defendant smashed all the windows out. He started down the sidewalk to his house.

Yes, feeling good, damn good. The audacity of the German. Stealing a car, faking an accident, storming a Navy warehouse, never giving up. He had never seen anything like it. Monck didn't have a nerve in his entire body. And, Leffler congratulated himself, neither had he, what with stopping the German from strangling that shore patrolman.

Leffler waved to the Bushnell twins. He had been scared shitless the entire time, he admitted to himself. But looking back, it was as if he had been drunk, loco with the action and tension. Monck ordered, he obeyed. And, miracle of miracles, it had all worked out. Leffler patted the wad of bills in his pants pocket. The kraut had given him five hundred dollars, out of the blue. He just coolly passed him the bills. Said, "Good work."

And did Leffler ever have a laugh. A few minutes after the three of them had transferred back into Leffler's Dodge, the German announced that he had a plan to steal some weapons, a shotgun and a pistol. He said he had thought about the plan a long time and was certain it would work.

Leffler had the exquisite pleasure of asking, "Why don't you just stop at a sporting-goods store and buy them?"

The kraut had been dumbfounded, although he tried to hide it. Just buy them? Finally Monck had asked what kind of strange country this was, when a person walking off the street into a store could buy firearms. Leffler had almost wet his pants laughing. Margarete chuckled along, and finally the kraut started laughing, too. Not a bad fellow, actually, for all his craziness.

Leffler kicked a beer bottle out of his yard, then climbed to his porch for his mail. A glass catalogue. Maybe he'd someday find a replacement for the piece Monck had destroyed. While he fingered through his keys, he frowned at the telephone repairmen across the street. They were like a Cook County road crew, a lot of standing around, almighty little work.

Leffler unlocked his door and walked into his living room. The place still smelled of the veal and scalloped potatoes she had cooked last night. Quite a switch from his normal tuna and raisins, mixed together and eaten out of the can. He immediately found the new ten-dollar bill he kept on the lamp table near the sofa. Because it was there, he did not need to inventory his Venetian glass. A burglar would have taken the money. He pulled the five hundred dollars out of his pocket and put it under a roll of twine in an empty cold-cream jar he kept in the table drawer. He closed the drawer. His legacy from the Depression was that he didn't trust banks.

Leffler started toward the bathroom.

The room flashed white, a blinding, disorienting noncolor that sliced into his eyes. At the same instant, a thunderous, brain-cracking clap chased everything from his head. A blast of air knocked him off his feet.

The eruption was over in that same second. His eyes squeezed shut with fear, Leffler tested his fingers, then his legs. He felt his carpet beneath him. He was alive. Disoriented, his nose full of cordite, his eyebrows singed, but alive.

He opened his eyes. Two inches from his pupil, the business end of a .45 looked as large as the mouth of a railroad tunnel.

"Get up," barked the man behind the pistol.

Confused and coughing, Leffler hesitated a second. One second too long. The pistol man filled his hand with Leffler's hair and swept Leffler up to his feet as if Leffler weighed but a few pounds.

"Take it easy . . . easy," Leffler sputtered. He felt dizzy. The man had not released his hair, and it felt as if he were being scalped. His head cleared enough for him to look around the room. Amazingly after such an explosion, his glass collection was intact. But his front door had been splintered, blown inward, leaving just a ragged outline of it around its frame. A pane from one of the side windows was also broken. On the floor near the window was a smoldering canister of some sort, maybe the noise-maker.

The man holding him was thick in all directions; a huge chest, biceps that pressed against the fabric of his overalls, and a square head with small rosette ears. He looked like a prizefighter. Leffler glanced at the company logo on the man's overalls and said, "I swear to God, I mailed my last telephone payment four days ago."

The living room suddenly filled with weapons-carrying men who just as quickly drained into other rooms, rattling his glass. Leffler heard them pound up and down the stairs. Doors were thrown open and orders were shouted. More men rushed through the front door, some with submachine guns. It looked like a Movietone News film clip from the front.

"You're under arrest," the big man said, releasing Leffler just as a red-haired fellow brought the process server's arms around to snap handcuffs on him.

"What for?" Leffler asked, batting his eyes. The concussion had induced spurts of double vision. The pistol looked twice as ominous.

"We'll see in a moment."

They were searching every room, Leffler could tell. He heard drawers opening and closing, and his medicine cabinet squeaking. His bed rolled across the floor. Downstairs they were pushing around some of the boxes he stored old things in. Someone clicked on his bedside radio a moment. In the living room, one of the men opened the table drawer, then lifted the cold-cream jar, only to look quickly at the household papers under it. He put the jar back unopened. Leffler heard his dresser upstairs being pushed around. He was sunk.

The men drifted back from the other rooms, gathering around the big man and Leffler. He had uneasy recollections of a few of them from the federal courthouse, where Leffler would occasionally go to testify that a defendant had been served. They looked recently bathed and primly dressed. All of them were cut from the same cloth. FBI agents, of course. Yes, Leffler was truly sunk.

The other men returning to the room were not cookie-cutter duplicates of each other, like the G-men. Their sizes varied, as did their clothing. Some were in telephone repairmen's uniforms. Others had work jackets on. A few wore suits, but, unlike the FBI agents, these men looked as if they had earned them, not as if they had been issued them. And these fellows had the unsettling habit of never letting their eyes rest. They scrutinized everything: Leffler's eyes, the FBI agents' hands, the big man's gun, the windows, the precious glass, everything. Leffler had no idea who they were.

Several uniformed Chicago cops joined the group. One of them picked up an eighteenth-century Venetian beaker on which was painted a scene of the birth of Christ. The dolt scratched the paint with a thumbnail as he would a beer-bottle label.

"Hey, you," Leffler yelled. "Knock it off with the glass."

The cop looked at the pistol-carrying man, who nodded, and the cop replaced the beaker on the shelf. So the big man ran the show.

Leffler's voice caused one of the FBI agents to peer more closely at the process server. Then he stepped closer, and his eyes grew smaller as he gazed at Leffler. The agent was slightly rotund, and his jaw had lost its definition. He had a brown shadow of beard that made his face seem smeared, yet his puffed jaw and cheeks also had pink razor burns, where he had shaved as close as he could without taking a layer of skin. FBI grooming rules. He had already shouldered his weapon, but his hands balled into fists as he stared at Leffler.

He said finally, "Remember me, pal?"

Leffler's eyes came around. He blinked behind the spectacles. The room still was hazy from the concussion grenade. "Can't say I do."

The FBI agent edged closer. His head came down like a bull ready to charge. "Sure you do. I'm Roger Foster. You served me some legal papers about a year ago."

"You're one of a thousand." Leffler admired the intrepidity of his own words. "I'm not paid to remember every defendant's face."

The FBI agent's voice was guttural. "One day I got a call from my daughter's grade school. A man identifying himself as the assistant principal told me my little girl had lost a couple of front teeth in a playground scuffle, and that I'd better come running. I did just that. And when I got to the school, the assistant principal met me at the door and handed me some forms. Know what they were?"

Leffler sucked in his cheeks. "I could probably guess."

"They were a summons and complaint from my wife's lawyer. She was suing me for divorce. You're the shithead who was pretending to be the assistant principal."

Foster must have been a lineman in college, because he barged across the eighteen inches to Leffler and raised his arms as if he were blocking for a rusher. His fingers were open and aimed at the process server's weedy neck.

Moving even faster, the pistol carrier stepped around Leffler and blocked the agent. He effortlessly threw him across the room, and the agent stumbled backward over the tea table and toppled onto the davenport. He scrambled to his feet and glowered at his colleagues. He must have had a reputation, as none of them even started a smile.

Another FBI agent descended the stairs. Leffler had the stupid urge to tell him his pants were too short, that he looked as if he were going wading, but as the agent came down, he saw he was carrying the pads. "Look at these. One-time pads."

A delighted grin on his face, the agent flipped through a pad. "I didn't find any potassium. Leffler must be getting sloppy."

The pad was a thick square sheet of alternating green and black paper. Green for enciphering and black for deciphering. The paper was made of cellulose nitrate, used for film in the early years of the movie industry, which was highly flammable when potassium permanganate was thrown onto it. The resulting fire was a virtual explosion, destroying the pad without leaving a latent image.

"No radio?"

"No. But the antenna looks like it was torn off a shortwave."

Grins spread across the room like streetlights blinking on at dusk. There were a few handshakes.

The big man said in a kind voice, "I've got the answer to your question."

Leffler stared at him blankly. "What question?"

"What you're being arrested for." The man slipped the .45 under his overalls. "It's treason."

They entered the second hour of questioning. Larry Leffler sat in an armless wood chair. They had allowed him to remove his jacket, but he was still perspiring profusely, and drops of sweat trailed down his arms and dropped onto the floor with a plinking that was unnaturally loud in the cavernous room.

He didn't know where he was, as they had blindfolded him in the car. Somewhere west of the Loop, he thought. From his quick looks into the dark corners of the room, he knew it was no federal or county government building, as he had been in them all. This was more of a warehouse. He could see splinters of light in walls that were far away.

Leffler knew they were trying to frighten and confuse him. The concussion blast, the pistol in his face, the dozens of policemen, the blindfold, the interrogation. They hadn't allowed him to get his bearings. He had not been able to ask questions. A bright light hung directly over him, and its heat on his forehead was as oppressive as a mustard plaster. He could see the interrogator only when he shaded his eyes with a hand.

The fellow asking him questions was the big man with the pistol, who had introduced himself as John Wren, a Secret Service agent. That explained who all those other armed men in his home had been. Leffler didn't think he had ever seen a Secret Service agent before. They looked tougher than the G-men. Especially this one, who appeared as hard as a city alderman. There were others in the room. Leffler didn't know how many. Only occasionally did they wander into the nimbus of the overhead light, and then he could only make out their feet.

"I'm going to ask you again," Wren said, his voice bored. "Why did the German come to you?"

Leffler matched the agent's tedious tone. "I'm not going to answer any questions until I talk to my lawyer."

"When did he and the woman arrive at your house?"

"Don't I have the right to a phone call?"

"Did he tell you how he escaped the Seattle area?"

Leffler shook his head and sighed loudly. The one-time pads were on the table near the Secret Service agent. It spoke of the inevitability of Leffler's future. He must have known it since the moment he first saw the German. Nothing the kraut touched remained orderly. He had an unearthly power of dissolution, the ability to cause disarray. If Monck ever walked into a cathedral, its stones would begin to shift against the mortar and cracks would appear in the stained glass.

So it had been with Leffler's life. With the one-time pad discovered, it was all gone now: Leffler's home, his glass collection, his freedom, maybe his life. His fate was as clear as fine *cristallo*. Hopelessness gave him courage. This John Wren's questions meant nothing to him.

"You're not listening to me," the agent said gravely, bringing Leffler back to the questioning. "I've just given you a choice."

Leffler brought his hand up to block the light. The agent was fierce, make no mistake about that. His curly hair was short and looked like a helmet, and his teeth, revealed in an expression that could have been a grin or a snarl, were small and regular, resembling a radiator grille. Muscles sculpted the skin on his neck.

"I'm sorry," Leffler answered. "I didn't hear you."

The Secret Service agent pushed back his chair. "I've asked my last question. I want to know where the German is right now. Either you talk to me, or we go on with it."

"Listen, goddammit, I'm here on a treason charge. What else can you do to me?" Leffler laughed defiantly. "I'm not telling you a thing. Not a goddam word."

Leffler sensed motion toward him on the periphery of the light. He guffawed. "And you feds aren't the Chicago cops. You never beat the crap out of anyone to make them talk. I've been around the courthouse long enough to know that."

Wren said in a diminished tone, "No, we never do."

Rough hands seized Leffler and yanked him from the floor. The room was suddenly colder. They carried him toward a wall. He could see light seeping under a door. Leffler looked wildly about him. Too dark to see much. The agent named Wren was following them, leafing through a notebook.

The door opened, and the process server was transported into a bright chamber. Leffler hooded his eyes against the light. As they adjusted, he could make out a desk sitting on an elevated platform, with a United States flag on one side and an Illinois flag on the other. On the floor in front of the lectern was a rail that crossed the room, and near it were two tables. Several rows of pews were arrayed across the rest of the room. Sitting at the bench was a white-haired man wearing a black robe. Leffler had been escorted into a courtroom.

Two black-suited men, apparently prosecutors, sat at the table on the left. Another fellow sat behind the table on the right, scribbling rapidly onto a yellow legal pad. They all turned to watch as the process server was guided down the aisle between the pews to the bar.

One of the prosecutors rose to intone, "United States versus Lawrence Leffler."

The judge had sunken black eyes and brows that crossed his forehead as if drawn there with a T-square. He said with a formal tone, "Will the defendant approach the bench."

"Defendant?" Leffler cried. "I haven't even seen a lawyer yet." As an afterthought, he added, "Your honor."

The judge read from a piece of paper he held in front of him. "Mr. Leffler, you've been charged with treason. How do you plead?"

"You honor, how can I be arraigned? I haven't been allowed to see counsel."

The judge looked up. "Under the Emergency High Treason Act, arraignments have been dispensed with. This is your trial, Mr. Leffler."

The process server was aghast. He had to work his tongue to generate saliva before he could speak. "Your honor, I've never heard of such a law."

Now it was the judge's turn to be bored. "Let me read from the act's preface: 'Trials for treason will occur *in camera*, and as rapidly as possible. The court will try the case sitting without a jury. Only by these measures will the Axis enemy be prevented from learning the extent their intelligence networks have been penetrated or defeated.'"

"This is crazy," Leffler yelled, turning on his heels to bolt for the door. John Wren had been standing behind him, and he picked Leffler up and replanted him as easily as if he had been an errant child.

"Young man," the judge said, "another outburst like that, and I'll gag you and strap you to a chair." He looked at the prosecutors. "Will the government begin."

The trial lasted seven minutes. The wire antenna and the one-time pad were offered as evidence. Leffler's court-appointed lawyer did little more than plead for mercy. There was none.

The judge concluded bleakly, "Lawrence Leffler, I find you guilty of treason and sentence you to death by hanging. Sentence to be carried out immediately."

Leffler had been silenced, not by the judge's threat of gagging, but by the shock of the proceeding. His bravado had drained from him like blood. The trial was over before he could clear his head. He was a condemned man.

Again he spun and tried for the door. The same arms pulled him off his feet again. He was hauled back through the courtroom doors into the darkened cavern. The agents hurried, as if anxious to end this day, their footsteps echoing off the far walls and sounding like the rush of a whitewater stream.

A dim light was ahead, an aura against the back wall that was cut in half by a beam just below the high ceiling. As they stepped closer and around a puddle on the cement floor, Leffler saw the rope loop hanging from the center of the crossbeam. It was a noose.

A wooden frame supported a platform under the crossbeam. Leffler's legs gave out. The agents had him by the armpits, and they did not break step. A priest stepped from the shadows under the gallows and began muttering a prayer.

"My God," Leffler gasped as he was dragged up the stairs. As he approached the beam, the noose seemed to grow to fit him. The red-haired Secret Service agent again secured Leffler's arms behind him. Several hands pushed him to the center of the platform. The boards creaked as his weight settled on the hinges of the trapdoor. The agents' heads were below him in the darkness, and they all stared up at Leffler, as if they were a choir waiting for their cue.

"Look, maybe I..." Leffler squawked. Terror constricted his chest, squeezing off his words. He swallowed air. "The German ...maybe I could..."

A black cloth dropped over his head. Leffler screamed. The noose came next, chafing the bridge of his nose as it was lowered. The half-inch-thick rope with thirteen loops above the slip knot was cinched tightly, making him fight for air.

The process server shrieked again, piercing the priest's drone. He fought against the handcuffs on his wrists. The trapdoor hinges creaked.

From the floor below, the judge said magisterially, "Let the sentence be carried out."

A second, the longest in Leffler's life, passed. Then the earth opened below him and he fell into the chasm. He rushed down an infinite space. At the faraway edge of his consciousness, Leffler heard his neck snap, like the tearing of a bundle of twigs. His head was wrenched back as the noose reached its full length. And Leffler hung.

Only for an instant. A ripping sound came from the beam. Leffler fell again and landed softly, spinning to his side and hitting face first on a coarse fabric.

He lay there, inhaling in huge gasps, sucking the hood in and blowing it out. He risked turning his neck. It worked. No pain. He tried wiggling his toes. They also worked. A cold button pushed against his chin. He was lying on a mattress.

His mind seemed not to work. He was baffled and terror-stricken. He could not make sense of the next words.

"Who did that?" John Wren asked sharply. "The rope was supposed to be completely unattached. Who tacked a couple of strands of the rope onto the beam so he'd feel a jerk?"

Special Agent Roger Foster answered venomously, "I wanted the bastard to feel a tug, just like I did when he told me my little girl had been injured."

Leffler missed the next words between them. There might have been a blow. A moment later Leffler's hood was lifted.

John Wren said, "I've made a deal with the prosecutors. I can guarantee you a maximum of three years for your radio broadcasts. No more. Now, either you talk to me about Kurt Monck, or this time we tie the other end of rope to the beam, and we walk you back up the scaffold."

Leffler sat up. His neck stung where the rope had bitten into the skin. He coughed. "Yes. I..." His neck seemed to have collapsed around his vocal cords. He tried again with a ragged voice. "Monck. Yes, I know where you'll be able to find him."

17

THE TELEPHONE RANG IN MIKE
O'Brien's office, bringing him away from Friday's
visitors schedule. Charles de Gaulle was arriving to confer with
the president tomorrow, July 7. Roosevelt thought de Gaulle
was a pompous pest and called him Joan of Arc, and had asked
O'Brien to interrupt the meeting thirty minutes after it began
with some fake emergency that would call the president away.
Some things about O'Brien's job were great fun.

The telephone rang. Draped over the phone was a list of those
in the United States who had been released from insane asylums
during the past month. He pushed it aside. "O'Brien," he said
loudly into the phone, as if he could frighten away bad news.

It didn't work. His mouth pulled back with concern. "When
does he want the car, Grace? . . . Goddammit, we just can't operate with twenty-minute warnings. I'm going to tell him that. . . ."

Grace Tully, the peremptory secretary whom many viewed
as Roosevelt's general manager, said something over the phone
to defuse the agent. O'Brien laughed. "Yeah, you're right. I'm
not going to tell the president anything. Any idea where he wants
to go? . . . No, he doesn't tell me either, but I've got a pretty good

guess. All right, the car'll be there. Thanks, Grace."

O'Brien punched a button on the phone. "Pancho, the president is going for a drive. Pick me up and we'll visit the garage first."

He pressed another button. "This is O'Brien. I want Rock Creek Park cleared . . . Yes, you heard me. . . . I know we haven't done that in the past. Just do it."

O'Brien pulled a map from a desk drawer, then held the phone with his chin while he unfolded it. "From Wise Road south to Porter Street. All entrances blocked, all walkers cleared out of there. Search any parked cars, but not, and I repeat, not her Cadillac limousine. Don't even go near that. He always enters the park on Military Road, then ranges south." He gave instructions for another minute.

The agent ran a hand over his forehead, debating with himself. There was no question in O'Brien's mind about the woman. But Roosevelt opening his car door near another automobile that hadn't been searched was not prudent. Perhaps the White House security chief would have tolerated it before Kurt Monck's escape. Monck, who was in Chicago. But they had thought he was in Seattle, and he had simply evaporated, to reappear in Illinois like some sort of Houdini. And according to John Wren's latest report, they didn't know where the hell the German was. Certainly he couldn't have journeyed to D.C. by now. Still . . .

O'Brien ordered, "I want a marksman in that clump of trees near where she parks. Tell him to cover her door. If it isn't her who emerges from the car, he's to stop instantly whoever else it is. . . . Yes, that's what I mean by stop. And, Mark, the president's car will enter the park in about thirty-five minutes. That's how long you've got."

O'Brien put the phone down before he could hear any protest about impossibility. It would be done, just as the Secret Service always did it, irrespective of impossibility.

Max Smythe appeared at the door. He had taken to waxing the corners of his mustache and turning them up. The agents had a pool going on how long Chief Wilson would allow it.

O'Brien's bet was on tomorrow at 12:23 P.M., which was three minutes after the chief was due back from Chicago. O'Brien walked with Smythe along the basement corridor.

With a mean smile, Smythe said, "I heard Wren broke that process server."

"I don't want to hear anything about it." O'Brien knew all there was to know about the mock courtroom and the gallows, of course. He had flinched at Wren's method.

"I think Wren missed his calling and his century. He should have been a bounty hunter in the old West." Smythe laughed, very quietly, appropriate for the august building, even if they were in the basement. "You know how he is, boss." Smythe nodded at his own words, encouraging a seconding of his judgment.

"Yes, I know how he is."

"If I knew John Wren was chasing me, I'd be scared shitless. I almost feel sorry for the German."

O'Brien finally joined Smythe with a grin. "Yeah. As tough as Kurt Monck is, and we're beginning to learn he's plenty tough, I almost feel sorry for him."

They exited the White House from the north portico, where a car was waiting for them. A few minutes later they arrived at the Service garage, four blocks from the White House. A metal gate slid inward, and they entered the one-story building and rolled along the parking garage to the south wall. They passed two other Secret Service automobiles, armored Packards. Between them was the door to the toilet, on which was a poster showing cartoons of Hitler, Mussolini, and Hirohito over the caption "Come on in, brother. Take it easy. Every minute you loaf here helps us plenty."

Three Secret Service agents were waiting for them, leaning against the limousine. One of the agents had a German shepherd on a leash. The dog pulled in his tongue and rose to his feet, perhaps recognizing O'Brien as his master's boss. Sitting on a nearby car's running board was one of the mechanics, wearing grimy overalls, his hands clasped in front of him. Only he did not come to attention when O'Brien and Smythe got out of the car.

One of the agents, a twenty-year veteran named Lloyd Wood, said in a friendly tone, "Checking our time again, Mike?"

"The president will be at the north portico in fifteen minutes." He brought up his watch. "Let's get going."

The agents knew the search like a fire drill. They began at the trunk, checking every space in the car larger than a golf ball. The automobile was an armored dark-green Ford, weighing 7,500 pounds. Ever since Edsel Ford had given a huge gift to the Warm Springs Foundation, Roosevelt had insisted on Fords. The automobile company rented the car to the Secret Service for ten dollars a week. Because of the armor plating and bulletproof windows, the Ford's interior was slightly smaller than that of a production model, but it could still comfortably seat seven. The body and glass of the car could withstand a direct spray of bullets from a .30 caliber machine gun, and the reinforced top could repel a hand grenade dropped from a height of 250 feet.

The agents moved from the trunk to the cab, first removing the backseat to search the compartment between it and the trunk. Metal oxygen bottles there were designed to flood the cab with air should the car encounter gas of some sort. They tested the windows. In 1939 the King of England came within a hairbreadth of fainting from the heat because these windows were locked. Roosevelt had since insisted on being able to roll them down, but O'Brien didn't like it. The agents searched methodically, with synchronized movements designed by O'Brien and Ford engineers to allow a thorough search in a short time.

O'Brien waited, occasionally checking his clock. The mechanic rose to his feet to reach for a rag resting on the lubrication rack. He idly wiped his hands. His name was George Bell, a retired Navy PT boat mechanic. Bell had a long, rubbery face, incapable of holding an expression for more than a few seconds. He was as thin as a bed slat and looked lost in his overalls.

O'Brien had never determined whether being able to open the

219

closets of almost everyone he had contact with was a benefit or a burden. In George Bell's closet was his compulsive card playing. He frequently busted out with his entire paycheck on the line.

The agents were now under the hood, quickly removing the manifold cover, held in place by specially designed butterfly nuts. Eight minutes after it had begun, their search was completed. Now the agent with the dog circled the car. Not an inch escaped the shepherd's nose. Then, without an order, the dog entered the cab. It had been trained for TNT, dynamite, nitrocellulose, nitroglycerin, picric acid, cyclonite, and old-fashioned gunpowder. The dog emerged from the cab reluctantly, knowing there'd be no biscuit today, as he'd found no explosives.

"It's clean," Wood said.

O'Brien and Smythe rode in the Ford back to the White House. They entered the east gate just as John Mays, the White House butler, walked out onto the porch, which meant the president was less than two minutes from the door. The president was always thirty minutes late for everything, except these visits. The big Ford followed the paved driveway to the portico. O'Brien and Smythe climbed out, instinctively scanning the fences, the roofs of neighboring buildings, and the trees.

President Roosevelt appeared at the door, his wide smile in place and his black Bakelite cigarette holder at its impish angle. Roosevelt, who all his years in the White House had exuded optimism and confidence, had these past few months occasionally allowed himself to surrender to lassitude. He often appeared tired, even distraught. But these clandestine visits with the woman were miraculous restoratives.

Six agents blocked access angles to the president and moved with the wheelchair, while O'Brien and Smythe waited at the armored Ford. A Secret Service automobile was at the gate, and another pulled up behind the Ford.

O'Brien knew the president had spent much of the morning reading clemency appeals from federal prisoners, a job he did regularly and diligently. He would grant a pardon in an unusual case, but never for narcotics violators. He hated them. He called doing paperwork "hanging out the laundry."

The president was wearing a blue pinstripe suit and a red tie. His face had regained some of the ruddiness it had lost recently. He was sixty-two years old and had been in the wheelchair for twenty-three years. Yet today nothing about him seemed withered or inanimate. He broadcast a huge amount of energy and gaiety with the powerful movements of his head and his strong gestures. He rolled toward the Ford.

Again, and as always, O'Brien was struck with the simplest of all feelings. He loved President Roosevelt. Just like a hundred million other Americans, perhaps. But, goddammit, he loved this man. The surge of emotion always surprised him.

O'Brien knew more about Roosevelt than any other man alive, he suspected. Who else knew that Roosevelt always slept with the window open? Not Eleanor, certainly, as their rooms and their hearts were a good walk apart. Who else knew that his favorite newspaper was, surprisingly, the *Washington Star*, no booster of the New Deal? Or that he loved leggy musicals? Or that Eleanor habitually read his mail? Or that he used tongs to reach things on his desk? Or that he called the cocktail hour "the children's hour" and that his martinis had become drier and drier over the years? Or that anyone who used the loathed phrase "kill two birds with one stone" would automatically have the request denied? Or that the only complaint this brave man ever voiced aloud was that he was never alone? And who else knew of the drain Winston Churchill's visits caused him? Roosevelt was a morning man, and Churchill a devotee of the wee hours. The president simply could not stand to miss the late-hour conversations—"thrilling," he called them—between Churchill and Harry Hopkins. Roosevelt would be groggy all the next day.

Arthur Prettymen helped the president with the wheelchair. Roosevelt signaled him, and he bent to the president's ear. They exchanged whispers, and Roosevelt's nostrils flared like a racehorse's as he laughed. Roosevelt had a remarkable laugh, a patrician belly laugh, if there was such a thing. He laughed hard and often. O'Brien had only seen Roosevelt angry twice, once when Josef Stalin, at a dinner with Churchill and Roosevelt at Tehran, drank a toast to the summary execution of fifty thousand German officers after the war, and another time when, aboard a Navy ship, the President's dog, Fala, who was wandering on deck, had a small lock of hair clipped from its side by a sailor who wanted a souvenir. Other sailors also wanted something to remember the president's visit. By the time the Scottie got back to FDR, it was shorn to its skin.

Here came the little monster now, darting out into the north portico and barking once to announce its arrival. Roosevelt held up the procession to the car long enough to gather up the dog and give it several pats.

Secret Service agents called the dog the Informer. The Scottie was an endless problem for them. O'Brien could sneak the president's ten-car train into a town without anyone knowing it, until Fala demanded a walk at the station. God help anyone who refused the dog. Every schoolchild in America recognized the Scottie, and quickly the entire town would know Roosevelt was there.

Roosevelt lowered the dog, then wheeled the chair so that his back was to the car. He sniffed loudly; his chronic sinus problem. O'Brien put his hands under the president's arms to lift him, and Roosevelt reached back to grip each side of the car door. The president surged out of O'Brien's arms and onto the jump seat, a tremendous burst of energy. He brought his hands back once more and pulled himself into the rear of the car. So practiced was the maneuver that he could do it in front of a stadium full of people, and those thousands would never suspect his paralysis.

Only after he was in the car did Roosevelt say cheerfully, "Good morning, Mike."

"Morning, sir."

"I don't suppose we could dispense with the trailing car today, could we? A little privacy?"

It was an intricate relationship indeed in which O'Brien could pull rank on the President of the United States. Both understood it. "I'm sorry, sir."

Roosevelt shook his head with resignation, then grinned. "You'd follow me into the toilet, if you could. Admit it."

"You haven't seen me there?"

Roosevelt laughed heartily. O'Brien closed the door and waved the Secret Service driver on. Under the seat behind the driver's feet was a Thompson submachine gun.

The convoy of three automobiles passed through the east gate and turned north. It skirted Lafayette Square and started north on 16th Street. A Secret Service sweeper car had minutes before driven along 16th, and another car was a block ahead, both of which FDR was unaware. They passed Scott Circle, then Meridian Hill Park.

O'Brien and Smythe rode in the trailing car. There was no motorcycle escort, so the entourage stopped at a number of intersections, moments when O'Brien's breath came quickly. A short while later the cars turned onto Military Road, then entered Rock Creek Park. Policemen at the barricades waved the president and the Secret Service through.

They drove for another minute, then began to slow as they approached a blue Cadillac limousine parked on the right-hand side of the park road. O'Brien looked into the trees, right up the barrel of a rifle, hidden to all but trained eyes.

The president's Ford pulled abreast of the limousine, and the doors to both cars opened. O'Brien fingered his Smith and Wesson.

Lucy Mercer Rutherfurd slipped from her car onto the seat beside the president as gracefully as a cloud crossing the moon. The doors closed, Roosevelt slid the window up between them and the chauffeur, and the parade began again.

"Pancho, give them forty yards," O'Brien said.

"That's real generous of you, boss," Smythe replied, allowing the president's car to pull a little ahead.

O'Brien saw Roosevelt look out the rear window and smile his thanks. His and Lucy Mercer Rutherfurd's heads leaned together.

They drove slowly for an hour, visiting every corner of Rock Creek Park. O'Brien had an urge to urinate the entire time. Then the cars stopped again at her limousine, and she left him, as she would always do. When the president's car pulled away from the Cadillac, O'Brien could feel his sadness.

The utter sorrow of the man. The Secret Service agent wanted to weep for the most powerful person in the world.

18

A N AMERICAN BOMB HAD DESTROYED
a substation in the Tempelhof District, so the
meeting in the warehouse office was lit by kerosene storm lan-
terns that cast long shadows on the walls.

Berlin radio was reporting that morning, July 6, that power
would be resumed by nightfall, but this same station was also
announcing that Wehrmacht troops were gaining against the enemy on the Cotentin Peninsula in northwest France. Colonel
Paeffgen knew the U.S. Ninth Division had utterly wiped out
the German army on the Cotentin a week before.

General Rauff gestured expansively. "So it seems that if the
White House cannot be breached, then Monck must find the
target out of the White House."

Von Schlieffen said caustically, "Your reputation for grasping
the unavoidable is truly well earned, General Rauff." He looked
at Friedrich Carstenn, perhaps unwilling to attempt his lordly
stare on Paeffgen. "The question is, how do we know when and
where Roosevelt will be out of the White House?"

Paeffgen answered, "I doubt there is a document on Franklin

Roosevelt in the Greater Reich that has not been examined by Fala."

Rauff chuckled, his belly rippling under the uniform. "Fala. I love that. If Roosevelt only knew."

Rauff was wearing parade dress and had stopped at the meeting en route to another stop on the interminable social round demanded of the Luftwaffe General Staff. His uniform was called the Luftwaffe Waffenrock, consisting of cinder-gray tunic over a blue-gray shirt and black tie. Gold braid hung from Rauff's right shoulder to his lapel. On the left side of the tunic was a gaudy array of medals. The general looked as if he had been dipped and rolled in them. Von Schlieffen had once termed Rauff's medals "flatulent honorariums."

"We are not sure where President Roosevelt is today," Paeffgen said, "but he always holds his news conferences on Tuesday mornings and Friday afternoons. He is scheduled to hold one tomorrow, Friday afternoon, in Washington, D.C."

Paeffgen blew on his hands, then jammed them into his suit pockets. It was July, but he was always cold. "We know nothing of Roosevelt's schedule until July 20, two weeks from today. That is when he will speak to the Democratic Convention in San Diego, where he will accept the nomination for his fourth term as president."

"He has to be nominated?" Rauff asked. "A sitting president?"

Paeffgen nodded to Friedrich Carstenn, who explained patiently, "Even an incumbent president must be nominated by his party, for his party's ticket. For Roosevelt it will be routine, but under no circumstances will he miss the convention. He will give an acceptance speech that evening." Compared with Rauff's lively dress uniform, Carstenn's black SS tunic, breeches, and knee-length riding boots looked foreboding.

"Which means," continued Paeffgen, "that Roosevelt must travel to San Diego, three thousand miles west of Washington. As you know, he very rarely flies, so we believe he will take POTUS, his train." Paeffgen rose from his chair to point at an enlarged calendar of the month, July 1944, hanging on the wall behind him. He pointed at Thursday, July 20. "If he must be in California on this day, he will need to leave no later than the previous weekend. The train will take at least that long, particularly at the slow speeds it travels."

The colonel moved his hand up the calendar. "And because Roosevelt never leaves for a trip on Friday, we believe he will leave the White House the prior Thursday, July 13, in the evening. One week from today."

Rauff whistled. "You're right, Paeffgen. Roosevelt will undoubtedly board his train that very day."

Von Schlieffen grinned, a razor's edge, the only praise he ever dispensed.

Paeffgen pulled down the calendar. Underneath was a map. "We have new information about the train. Before the war, Roosevelt always left Washington from Union Station, a large train depot a mile from the White House. He no longer does. Now he boards at a little-used siding at the Bureau of Engraving." He pointed to the building five blocks south of the White House. "The spur is normally used for loading currency. It's not much closer to the White House than the station, but it's far more private and secure."

Carstenn added, "One American president was assassinated at a railroad station. The American Secret Service has apparently taken the lesson to heart."

"How do you know about this siding, Colonel?" the count asked.

"Major Carstenn will pass you the only two recent photographs we could find of Roosevelt boarding a train in Washington. You can see portions of a building in the background. We have obtained, courtesy of General Rauff here, photographs of every government building in Washington, ordered by Reichsmarschall Goering in 1939 to plan the eventual bombing of Washington."

Von Schlieffen laughed loudly, uncharacteristically. Rauff purpled.

Paeffgen went on, "These photographs match those we have of the Bureau of Engraving. Terrier reports the train, except for the engines, is housed at the bureau's siding. The engines are here, at the Virginia Avenue yard."

He returned to the long table and passed around several more photographs. "We are quickly learning about the precautions taken when Roosevelt travels on POTUS. These magazine and newspaper photographs of Roosevelt also show in the background, circled here, a young Secret Service agent who can be found only when Roosevelt is traveling away from Washington. The agent was recognized by one of the Fala group as Wilbur Gottschalk, a competitor for the Americans in the hundred-meter swim at our Berlin Olympics. We have concluded Gottschalk is assigned to travel with Roosevelt because he is a strong swimmer."

Carstenn helped with the next set of photos. "We have two photographs of this mechanism carried by a Secret Service agent."

Rauff held the photograph up. "Looks like a rope-and-rung ladder, rolled up."

"Exactly. And note the brawny agent Gottschalk carrying it. He obviously is assigned to carry the crippled president bodily away from any danger. He will never be far from Roosevelt on the train. There are usually twenty or so other agents traveling with him. They are identified on the list in front of you by facial description and photograph, as we don't know most of their names."

"Who is their commander?" von Schlieffen asked.

"The first name on the list, an Irish-American named Michael O'Brien, chief of the White House Detail. We haven't been able to discover anything about him."

"Anything more on Roosevelt's railroad car, the Ferdinand Magellan?" Rauff asked.

"Nothing, except that in a U.S. steel-industry trade journal called *American Steel* we found an article saying the Ferdinand Magellan was armored in Cincinnati, Ohio, at the River Iron Works."

"Captain Monck is an explosives expert," von Schlieffen said. "How would the Americans handle something like that?"

Major Carstenn dug in his briefcase, then pulled out a photograph clipped from a *Washington Post*. He passed it to the count. "This is the Secret Service's bomb carrier. We believe it was built by the U.S. Navy from designs provided by the New York City Police Department. The bomb compartment on the back of this Ford truck is about the size of an oil truck's tank. We've had the photograph analyzed by the RLB." The Reichsluftschutzbund, the German Air-Raid Protection Association, which defused Allied time-delay bombs and duds.

Carstenn skimmed their report again before continuing, "When confronted with a bomb, the Secret Service will probably dip it into oil to gum up the mechanism, then put it into this truck. The RLB says the truck's container is made of interwoven one-inch cable, weighs three tons, and can withstand an explosion of fifty sticks of dynamite."

"Does Roosevelt travel with it?" Rauff asked.

"We don't think so. But when he visits large cities, their police bomb-disposal trucks are usually nearby."

The colonel spread several new sheets in front of him. "Almost a year ago we received this document from our embassy in Buenos Aires. They paid a large amount of money for it, but I understand it originally came from a Washington garbage can. It is a Secret Service document entitled 'Presidential Travel Defense Plan.' It outlines four steps in an emergency when Roosevelt is on the POTUS, and was drawn up in case of a Luftwaffe air attack."

Rauff glanced menacingly at the count, who this time spared the general his grating laugh.

"We believe the Secret Service will use this plan or a similar one in the event of any danger, not just air attack. First, the Secret Service agents on the train will be notified of the danger on a frequency-modulation radio from Mitchell Field or from the Secret Service district through which the president is traveling. Second, the train will be stopped on the nearest siding or the nearest safe point on the track. Third, the armored automobile will be unloaded from the train. Finally, the president will be taken secretly to the safety of an isolated farmhouse or urban home, far distant from any military or industrial objectives."

Von Schlieffen challenged, "Of course, you have distilled something from that list that might be good news for Kurt Monck."

Paeffgen was surprised by von Schlieffen's statement. The count was a quick study. "Yes. Nothing in the plan calls for the Secret Service to strike back at the cause of the danger. Major Carstenn and I have discussed this in detail with Major Resfeld. Whereas his men of the Leibstandarte are ordered to protect the Fuehrer, they are also to immediately strike back at the source of the danger."

"And the Secret Service does not return fire?" General Rauff asked.

"We can't be sure. They surround the president and get him away from the danger, and we think they leave the offensive action to others."

"Are you saying Kurt Monck has a chance to escape?"

"If he is clever enough to get close, he may be clever enough to get away." Paeffgen gathered the documents and said perfunctorily, "But we do not have the time or the resources to plan for Monck's escape."

The secretary entered the office, carrying a long yellow sheet of paper that trailed down to her knees. She passed the sheet to Paeffgen, then glanced at von Schlieffen on her way out. The count's reputation as a gallant was widespread and hard-earned. She exaggerated her walk as she left the room.

Paeffgen worked his lower lip as he read the message. His face darkened. He leaned back in his chair. "We have just decoded Terrier's latest message, an unscheduled broadcast. He reports that as of noon Washington time yesterday, security was redoubled at the White House." Paeffgen glanced again at the paper. "There are now forty-five Secret Service agents and uniformed police patrolling the grounds, twice the previous number. Four new machine-gun posts have been added near the fences, on the compass points. And an M8 armored car is now stationed at the north door to the building."

"The Americans have found out about Monck's mission," Rauff said in a resigned voice, rubbing a temple with a sausagelike finger. "And they know he is getting closer to Washington."

"Why else would they suddenly refortify the White House?" von Schlieffen agreed testily.

"How could the Americans have figured it out?" Rauff demanded. "Even if they discovered the POW escape, the purpose of the escape should have eluded them."

Paeffgen bitterly stared at his pencil, rolling it slowly. All eyes were on him. He shifted in his chair as if bracing against the possibility of the Prinz Albrechtstrasse assignment.

After a moment he exhaled slowly and said, "We haven't lost yet. The train is our target, not the White House. We'll radio all this information to Chicago. Believe me, gentlemen, they aren't going to stop Captain Monck."

He caught her staring over his shoulder. She was surprised when he said, "Sit down. I'll show you what I'm doing."

Margarete pulled a wood folding chair up to the table. They had abandoned the damaged Chrysler and left Leffler in Chicago. Monck had told her it was too risky to broadcast again from Leffler's house. Monck had promptly produced another automobile, this one taken from a hospital parking lot.

They had driven north and rented a cottage at Diamond Lake. In the middle of the third sparse year for summer renters, the owner of the string of ramshackle one-room cottages on the muddy end of the lake thirty-five miles from the Loop was glad to take their money, even, as he explained importantly, if reservations were usually required. The cabin contained a table, the chairs, a bunk bed with ragged mattresses, and a wood stove. The water pump and the outhouse were out back.

Monck grinned for her. She was amused at how he could personalize a smile, as if it had her name on it. He was as focused with his charm as he had been with the plan to obtain the explosives. She was also startled at how affecting it was.

He had been working on her, she knew. His improbable politeness, his reassurances, and once in a while an unconvincing attempt at levity. He was trying to change their relationship from something other than that of kidnapper and hostage. She had resolved never, not for one minute, to forget the pain he had caused both her and her daughter. Since Mary had boarded the bus, Monck had not again threatened that harm might come to her. And although the girl was never far from her thoughts, Margarete could tell that Monck was slowly making her think like an accomplice, not a victim.

Not so slowly, in fact. The diversion in front of the Navy warehouse had been her idea. Monck had wondered aloud how to get into the warehouse, and she had found herself contributing, amazed at herself even as she outlined her plan. Now, a day later, she still had no idea why she had helped him.

As she sat next to him, she reminded herself she was still a hostage. Thinking of Mary would do it. She and her daughter were still at his mercy. She was satisfied when her anger returned.

Monck was in front of the Graber shortwave, a green box with rows of dials and knobs. The radio emitted an irritating high-pitched electronic whine. He had rigged the antenna a few minutes ago. It hung from an apple tree. In front of the Graber was the Bible.

Monck looked at his watch, as he had been doing repeatedly · for fifteen minutes. He said quietly, "The Graber is set at 14,550 kilocycles. I'll use my call sign, *AAD*. Listen for it now."

He tapped out a series of dits and dahs on the key. "Now I'm going to send a series of *V*s so Berlin can tune exactly to my signal."

"How do you know it's Berlin?" she asked, watching him as he repeated *dit dit dit dah* several times. They were speaking German.

Again the smile. "Come to think of it, I don't. Might be an *Abwehrstelle* in Hamburg, or who knows. Our intelligence service is a confused mess." He lifted his hand from the sender to adjust the frequency control. The other hand held the headset to his ears.

He said, "They've locked onto me and are sending a series of return *V*s. There, that's as good as I'll hear them. I'm going to send the letters *KA*"—Monck did it as he spoke—"which means my message is to begin. They'll reply with *GA*. . . . There it is, which means 'Go ahead.'"

Monck tapped rapidly, staring at the paper in front of the shortwave. A few seconds later, he said, "Now I send *AR*, which means my message has ended." The sender clicked several times.

"What did you say?"

"I just gave them my name, Angela Maria. And now I take their message. Here, listen." He twisted one of the earphones toward her. She leaned forward, their faces inches apart. It was closer than she had been to him since he had grabbed her in anger in her Bainbridge Island home that first day.

For fifteen minutes his hand raced across the paper. The letters were in groups of five, each group sent twice to check for accuracy. He filled four pages before sending *RRR*, meaning he had copied and received, then *AR*, meaning the broadcast was over.

He put the headset onto the table, and they both leaned back against their chairs. There was a palpable shifting of moods in the room.

His question brought her forward again. "Do you still think of yourself as my captive?"

"I'd be with my daughter were it otherwise."

She had believed him incapable of tenderness. But he took her hand. "I know how much Mary means to you, and I'm sorry."

His eyes were a fathomless brown. She wondered at all those eyes had seen in Africa and the prisoner-of-war camp. The hardship and cruelty. But there was a gentleness in them she had never seen before.

He said, "You think I haven't given a thought to you these past days. That isn't true. I know I've robbed you of everything important."

She wanted to respond to him, to answer with kindness. But she knew her growing need for his understanding, even his affection, was due to strain and fatigue. She had a sudden dependence on Monck that was alien to her. For food, for the roof over her head, for conversation, and for comfort. In all the time since Georg's death, she had not allowed herself to be helpless. Georg had been her strength, and since his drowning her strength was an act of will, rationed as needed from an unknown reservoir. She needed it now.

She said, "Yes, you robbed me." She stood stiffly, but his hand remained around hers.

"I know what you are guarding against," Monck said, searching her eyes. "You are suddenly without your familiar handrails, and you are afraid to fall. You think you are more vulnerable here on the road, so you are on constant watch. In the Afrika Korps, we called it a watch-in-three. Always on duty."

"Afraid to fall?" Her anger flared. "Of all the brazen. . . . " She laughed sharply. "I've been expecting a come-on, but nothing so subtle, nothing that depended on logic or insight."

She laughed again, a victorious and angry sound. "I was girding myself against deadly charm and maybe force. Your intuition caught me off guard." She sat down again, still smiling broadly. "You know, I'll admit, you had me going."

Monck joined her with a smile. She thought it calculating.

He said, "Tell me how I had you going. I'll try again, maybe when you're more tired and your defenses are down."

"This little pass fits you," she said, still fixed on his eyes. How long could he hold this tender expression? "I've seen how you operate on this mission, and I imagine it was the same in your Africa tour and your POW camp escape. You move quickly, exploiting the unprotected points. You have an infallible sense for weakness. And you thought you saw one in me."

His smile faded. "That must be it." His tone was of deference. Or might there have been a touch of melancholy? He turned to his transcription and pad. And he reverted to form. She was instantly forgotten.

Or so she thought. Just as she was about to rise again from

the chair, he said, "I'm not quite as heartless as you'd like to believe."

"Give up, will you?"

"In the last message I radioed Berlin, I asked about your daughter."

"You did?" Margarete fell back into the chair. She stared at the dots and dashes on his papers. They looked like chicken scratchings. Anticipation ballooned in her. She cried, "Do you know if they have her?"

"I haven't had time to decode it. Too busy fending off a psychological analysis."

She didn't hear his dry words. "Please! Hurry!"

He tried his smile again and turned to the work. His hands went back and forth between the Morse message and the Bible. The lengthy message would not be hurried, because when the Bible did not contain the precise word, it had to be spelled out, using the first letter of the word. He paused several times, digesting the decoded message, and she could feel him planning with the new information. She wanted to prod him, but held herself back.

Finally he lowered his pencil. "What's 'Johnny Comes Marching Home Again'?"

She leaped at him, grabbing his arms. "That's her new song on the piano. My San Diego contact must have a piano." Her spirits flew. "Tell me, what does it say?"

Monck picked up the transcription slowly, playfully withholding the news for a moment. "Let me quote. 'Mary fine. Too much "Johnny Comes Marching Home Again." '"

"That's all?"

"That's all."

She inhaled slowly, tasting the message, turning it over, relishing it. "Oh, God, what wonderful news." Her grip on his arms softened, and she pulled away. Then her hand returned to his biceps. A very short caress.

"Thank you, Kurt. Thank you."

19

JOHN WREN HUNCHED BEHIND THE steering wheel, his eyes on the door of the hardware-and-sporting-goods store a block north.

Monck had chosen well. Larry Leffler was to purchase the weapons and meet him and Margarete Bayerlein in front of the store. The area around the store on the Skokie highway north of Chicago offered little cover. The store was surrounded by vacant lots, except for the butcher shop sharing a common wall on the north side, and a gas station next to that. The road's shoulders were spotted with maple and white birch. Next to Wren was a pasture with a barbed-wire fence keeping a small herd of Guernseys from roaming. The neighborhood at the edge of town had recently been farmland, but now there were several new homes and businesses along the road.

The store was a one-story white stucco building with large display windows and a swinging door. On a lean-to placard near the door was a poster that read "Back the Attack, Be a WAAC." A hand-drawn sign in a window told customers there were no cigarettes that day, a new spot shortage that had much of America growling.

There were almost forty Secret Service and FBI agents within two blocks of the store, and Wren couldn't see one of them. The hardware-store clerks, the butcher, and the gas-station attendants were all agents. The barn to Wren's right was full of them. The car in the gravel parking lot next to the hardware store had an agent on the back floor. Several were in the roadside ditch fifty yards north of the store, wearing camouflage green and covered with reeds and grass. Others were in automobiles along the shoulder. The road shimmered with July heat.

Wren saw a slight motion on the hardware store's roof. A blaze of red hair glimpsed above the false front. He picked up the car radio. "Get down, Garvin."

Garvin's voice was tinny over the two-way. "I can't see the street from behind here."

"Don't worry. I'll cue you." Wren heard the tension in his own voice. "Just keep that red hair down. It's as obvious as a baboon's butt."

Wren looked at his watch. Ten minutes. The key was in the ignition and his .45 was on the seat next to him. He wet his lips.

A dusty blue car pulled into the driveway of a home behind him. A fellow in a gray business suit emerged from the car and walked toward Wren. He carried a briefcase and moved nervously. He was a frail, bookish man, uncomfortable with walking. When he glanced skyward, his jaw opened and he almost sprinted to Wren's car.

The man twice looked over his shoulder—a twitching motion resembling a tic—before pulling open the car door and slipping into the car seat next to Wren. He launched into an apology. "I'm not a field man, you know. They tried me a few times, figuring I'd be inconspicuous, but I couldn't handle it. And I just jumped two feet off the ground when I saw your man in the tree."

In a canvas blind twenty feet up a maple tree near Wren's Ford was a Secret Service agent named Lefty Jones, a legend in the Secret Service. Jones had been an Idaho big-game guide before he joined the American Expeditionary Force in the Great

War. He first saw action at Château-Thierry, where on his first day he killed eight Germans with the Winchester Lee rifle he brought into the Army with him. Asked by Wren to be the lead rifleman in the operation, he had shrugged and said, "What's another one?" No one knew why he was called Lefty, as he was right-handed. Jones had a hand-talkie, a SCR-536, on his belt with a wire to an earphone. He was to take the first shot at Kurt Monck. The only shot, Wren hoped.

"I'm John Wren," the agent said to the OSS analyst.

"Harold Purdue." He had a wet handshake. His face was leprous white, and everything on it was too small. His eyes, nose, and mouth had all been somehow reduced. It made him seem nippy, like a lap dog. Purdue pulled out a pack of Lucky Strikes in their new red pack—Lucky Strike Green Has Gone to War—and set a match to one of them. He drew on the cigarette greedily, noisily, like a child sucking the last drops of a milkshake through a straw. The car filled with smoke.

"I appreciate your quick work on the photos. What'd you find?"

Purdue withdrew a stack of white paper from his attaché case. On each sheet was pinned a photograph. They were from Margarete Bayerlein's album.

"Quite a bit, actually." His voice had a tremor, and he constantly glanced out the Ford's window toward the store. "Usually we don't get this much to work with. Sometimes just a photo taken from the nose of a dive-bomber or by an agent from under her coat as he walks. This was quite a treat. I feel like I know this girl."

So did Wren. He looked at his watch again.

"First, the body. Margarete Bayerlein is five feet eight inches tall and weighs approximately one hundred and twenty pounds. Because she never wore revealing clothing, we can only guess at her measurements. Suffice it to say, they are quite generous. She reached puberty rather late, at about age fifteen. Then she made up for it in a big way, if you know what I mean." He tried to laugh lecherously.

Purdue plunged ahead. "Although all the photographs are black and white, we concluded she has dark-brown hair, which for a brief period in the late '30s she hennaed."

"What color are her eyes?"

"Don't know. We can tell they aren't dark brown. They could be blue or light green, maybe even gray."

Not knowing her eye color bothered Wren.

"Also, sometime during her childhood she broke her ankle badly. A trimalleolar fracture of the right ankle."

Purdue waited for Wren's question. Finally the agent obliged, "How do you know that?"

"Her right ankle is slightly larger than her left. Not much at all, but using a caliper the difference can be detected in several photos."

"Does she limp?" Wren asked, hoping not.

"No. The FBI examined her shoes found in her Bainbridge Island house. No evidence of uneven wear."

The OSS analyst shuffled the photos. "We know she was raised in Berlin. There are a number of photographs here taken of her as a child and as a teenager at the Berlin zoo, and one at the Brandenburg Gate. We believe she had a stern, doctrinaire upbringing. Her father was an anti-Semite and a member of the party."

"How can you tell?"

"Here, this photograph of him in a parlor chair. On the mantel to his right is a copy of Arthur Dinler's classic Jew-hating novel *Sins Against the Blood*. Plus, on the lapel of his suit in several photos, you can see this circular gold medal. It's the coveted Golden Honor Badge, indicating the wearer was one of the first hundred thousand members of the National Socialist Party. Hitler wears only three medals, and this is one of them."

"What did her father do for a living?"

"We don't know." Purdue coughed, ending in a long sputter, and he immediately filled his lungs with smoke again. "None of the four photographs of him show him in a uniform. Based on photos of his home, he made a comfortable living, though. Because there are no callouses on his hands and the skin on his neck and hands isn't darkened by sun, we figure he worked indoors."

"Is Margarete Bayerlein a member of the party?" Wren asked.

"Not that we can tell. No photos of her in a League of German Girls uniform. No swastikas or portraits of the Fuehrer in her Berlin home, either. She did have a photo of Glenn Miller pinned above her bed in Berlin." Purdue chuckled. "I'll bet her lack of political conviction drove her father crazy. Germans view children as recruits, and she wouldn't be recruited."

Wren put the radio microphone to his mouth. "Barnes, stay where I assigned you. Don't get any closer." Two agents had been posted a hundred yards north of the store. They had been creeping closer in their car along the road, hoping to get the first look and maybe the first shot at Kurt Monck.

"Margarete Bayerlein is right-handed, as this photo of her writing in a diary shows. Until about her fifteenth birthday she chewed the nail on her left index finger. Always had it gnawed to the quick. She quit about the time she started following fashion."

Another pause. Wren fed him, "How'd you find that out?"

"Well, this photo shows her eyebrows overplucked, even for one following Paris fashion in the early 1930s, as she was doing. This photo shows a copy of *Vogue* on her bedroom desk. Her fingernail is fine in this one."

Purdue paused to look out the window into the tree. "That man up there frightens me."

"He frightens everybody."

A pedestrian approached the stores from the north. Wren's hand went to the microphone. But it was a teenager carrying a fishing rod. The boy entered the hardware store.

Purdue blew smoke, then went on. "Now we get more conjectural when we try to distill her personality from the photos. This one is the most revealing." He gave Wren a studio photograph of the family, showing the parents and three children. "Her mother and father are sitting rigidly, their mouths composed carefully, their expressions stern. A brother and a sister, aged about six and eight, are also reserved, their hands carefully placed in front of them, their necks stiff. These people look like they're in front of a firing squad, not a camera. But not our Margarete."

Our Margarete. She had been nationalized.

"Look at her, standing a little apart from her family, her hand on her hip, wearing a saucy smile and a scarf she purchased by mail from the Maison Worth in London. She had the fun in this family, that's easy to see."

Purdue lit another Lucky from the butt of the old one. "She had some spirit, you see. Look at this picture, taken at a picnic about 1926 when she was twelve. All the boys are playing tug-of-war with the rope, pulling mightily. All the girls are standing in the back, watching, hands over their mouths as they giggle. Except for Margarete." He pointed at the photograph. "Here she is, third person from the end of the rope, pulling as hard as any of the boys."

Wren studied the photo. Her wild grin and fierce expression lit up the picture.

"And look at this one," the analyst said. "She's in a rented ten-foot sailboat on the Grosser Wannsee in southeast Berlin. There are six other sailboats in the photo, and she's the only girl at any of the helms." He gurgled again as he drew in the smoke. "What we've concluded is that she's got some cheek."

A Dodge coupe drove past Wren, then pulled into the store's gravel parking lot. Larry Leffler climbed out of the car. He walked toward the door, looking once very quickly over his shoulder at John Wren. He rubbed his chafed neck as he entered the store.

Wren said into the microphone. "That's Leffler, right on time. Get ready." He put it back on its mount. "Anything else?"

"One other item leaps from the photos in her album, and that is the duration of her relationship with the boy who would be her husband. His name is Georg. It's truly remarkable, as he begins showing up in photos when she is ten or eleven. In this

241

snapshot, taken when she was about thirteen, she's holding his hand, and Georg is making a big production out of trying to pull away."

Wren glanced at the photo. The worship in Margarete Bayerlein's eyes irritated Wren.

"They had a lot of fun together. Look at this one, taken in front of the Reichstag. She's sixteen or so. Georg is holding up a notebook paper that has LMA printed on it in pencil, and she's trying to wrestle it away from him. LMA is the German abbreviation for 'Kiss my ass.'"

Purdue coughed a laugh and said, "I like my girls with spunk, don't you?"

"You bet."

Leffler reappeared through the hardware-store door, carrying two cardboard boxes. Inside the short one, Wren knew, was a Colt New Service .38 Special. Monck had told Leffler to purchase a pistol, anything larger than a .22. He hadn't said whether he wanted a single- or double-action, a revolver or magazine load, and he had not specified a brand. It indicated to Wren that the German knew nothing about pistols, or that they weren't important to his plan. Inside the longer box was a Stevens Model 311 12-gauge shotgun. Were Monck to check the boxes before Lefty Jones got a clear shot, Leffler would swear he had forgotten the ammunition for both weapons.

Even at Wren's distance, Leffler looked agitated. His protruding Adam's apple jerked up and down, and he rapidly shifted on his feet.

Purdue hadn't noticed Leffler, or the taxi that passed them. "There are a couple of other small things we found out, and . . ."

The cab stopped in front of the store. A woman opened the passenger-side rear door and reached for the packages. Leffler hesitated, casting the smallest of glances at Wren, then passed her the boxes.

Wren couldn't see her face, as the cab was facing away from him, but he knew the woman must be Margarete Bayerlein.

He wanted to study her movements. Maybe she would look out the taxi's back window, and he would see her face. Instead, he grabbed the mike. "Monck isn't in the cab. Hold your fire, Lefty. Tom, stay down."

Goddammit, he said sorely to himself. Then into the microphone, "It's the woman. Monck sent her instead of coming himself to pick up Leffler."

One of the agents, Wren couldn't tell whom, asked, "Could he have suspected the stakeout?"

"I don't know. We'll follow them with a three-way tail. Adams and McLaughlin, fall in after me. I'll trail the cab for three or four blocks, then turn off. One of you take over at that point. We'll rotate every couple of blocks. The cab will take us to Monck."

Another agent said over the radio, "Chicago cabbies drive with the pedal to the metal. Don't let him get too far ahead."

Margarete Bayerlein slid over, and Leffler hesitated once again, then climbed into the cab beside her. The cabbie wore a porkpie hat at a rakish angle. He put his arm out the window to signal the cab was pulling into traffic.

The taxi was a prewar Chevrolet sedan originally yellow but now dappled by rust from hard Chicago winters. Even the rooftop antenna to its dispatch radio was bent and old. The taxi traveled only forty yards before turning west on a dirt road. The sedan threw up a dust cloud, which ended abruptly a block later as it gained a paved street on its way back to Chicago.

"Shouldn't you let me out?" Harold Purdue asked, grabbing for the door handle.

The Ford was already rocketing forward. It sprayed gravel as it skidded to a stop in front of the store. Tom Garvin ran through the store doors and threw himself into the backseat.

"Let me out," Purdue pleaded, again too late, as Wren wheeled the car onto the Skokie highway. Two other Secert Service automobiles approached from the north, ready to follow. Wren turned into the dirt road in time to see the taxi disappear behind a house as it turned another corner, heading west again.

Garvin was panting from his scramble down from the roof. "Is she trying to lose us?"

Wren put the car up and back through the gears, then turned the tight corner west. The photographs spilled out of Purdue's lap. The taxi was a quarter-mile ahead. Wren gave its location and direction into the mircophone, then added to Garvin, "It's not picking up speed. Maybe she doesn't suspect anything."

As they entered Skokie, traffic increased. They were in a residential neighborhood. One-story houses with tiny lawns. More businesses. Wren knew that by now four Secret Service vehicles and at least that many FBI cars were tuned to his frequency and were all shadowing the taxi, some paralleling it on side streets, others several blocks ahead of it, anticipating Margarete Bayerlein's journey.

Barnes's voice came over the radio. "Wren, I'm boxed in three cars behind you."

"That's all right. I've got her."

Suddenly he didn't have her. The cab had sped up, taken a right turn on Oakton, and by the time Wren made the turn, the taxi had disappeared.

Wren punched the accelerator. He and Garvin peered north and south down side streets. They slowed, thinking they saw a yellow fender disappearing around a hedge. Wren backed the Ford up, then chased down the block. Another turn revealed the yellow car, a canary-yellow Studebaker driven by a young lady being taught to drive by her father, who was gripping the seatback so hard his knuckles were white.

Wren wrenched the microphone off the dashboard. "I've lost the taxi. Anybody on it?"

Nothing but static.

His voice was charged. "Somebody's got to be on her tail."

Again nothing but crackle from the speaker. A car with two FBI agents pulled up behind them. Wren turned to look over his shoulder. Anger and frustration tightened his neck. He said into the mike, "You back there, you were on this side street. Didn't you see the cab?"

"Didn't see a thing, Secret Service man," came over the radio. The FBI driver raised his hands, palms up, a magician showing he had nothing up his sleeves. Then he said, "Looks like you blew it."

Garvin grabbed the mike. "You overeducated FBI assholes."

Harold Purdue offered, "I found nothing in the photographs that said she was sneaky."

Wren fumed. He raced the engine. His words were leaden. "Dammit, Tom, was there an alley in the middle of the block, or some turn we didn't see?"

Garvin started a condolatory answer, but the radio broke in. "I've found the cab. Just north of Oakton on Ferris." It was Barnes.

"Keep your distance," Wren ordered into the microphone. "We'll close in only when we're sure where the German is."

He released the clutch, and the Ford sped forward. Wren had to ask directions, and Barnes replied. They turned onto Ferris and parked in front of Barnes's car. The street was lined with well-tended homes and mature trees. The yellow taxi was sixty yards ahead, stopped next to a hydrant. Wren craned his head forward over the steering wheel, as if a few inches would bring the cab closer.

There was only one person in the cab. Leffler, in the backseat. The cabbie and Margarete Bayerlein were gone.

Wren said into the radio, "Watch for her on foot." He wanted to add that she might be walking with the cabdriver, but that didn't make sense.

He was torn between waiting them out or rushing to the cab to find out from Leffler where the woman had gone. He had grabbed his pistol and was running toward the cab before he had consciously decided.

He neared the taxi. Leffler's head was slumped forward and twisted left at a peculiar angle, as if he were looking at the cabbie's license on the seatback. Wren slowed, the tentacles of defeat ensnaring his legs. He knew what he would find.

Larry Leffler's shirt was covered with blood from the crease around the neck where the garrote was buried. The wire was knotted in front, because Monck hadn't had the time to hold it as Leffler went from unconscious to dead. Leffler's limp tongue hung almost to the tip of his sharp chin. His eyes were open wide and seemed to mirror bafflement.

Wren opened the taxi's door. The front panel of the cab's dispatch radio had been pulled off, and from two of the radio's wires hung a spool-size medal box, a variable frequency adjuster. From the taxi's speaker Wren heard: "This is McLaughlin. Have you heard from Wren?" And Barnes's reply: "Yeah, he's just ahead of me. He's found Leffler. It doesn't look good."

The porkpie hat lay on the front seat.

At the hardware store, Wren's eyes had been locked on Margarete Bayerlein. He hadn't looked twice at the taxi driver. The cabbie had been Kurt Monck.

Part three
THE HUNT SOUTH

20

SHE HELD OUT HER THUMB, UNSURE of the protocol. She wiggled it. Too enticing. She held it rigid, pointed to the sun. A passing truck threw up a cloud of dust, and she could feel it coat her like face powder. The afternoon's heat rose from the roadway, and the vehicles materialized out of a flickering mirage to bear down on her. Because of gas rationing, there were few automobiles on the road, and most of them would be on short trips. She gestured only to flatbed trucks.

Margarete Bayerlein was on the state highway just south of Gary, Indiana. She had walked across the bridge over Turkey Creek before trying to hitchhike. Her pasteboard suitcase contained only one dress and a scarf, yet it seemed to be pulling her arm from the socket. She was tired to death, but she held her thumb higher.

The rumble of a Reo Speedwagon jumped to a whine as the driver downshifted. The air horn bleated twice, and Margarete stepped farther back on the road's shoulder. The orange six-wheeler drifted onto the road bank and slowed, its exhaust-pipe cap rattling. On the flatbed behind the cab was a row of olive

Sherman tank turrets, buckled to the bed by a web of chains and come-alongs. A wave of grasshoppers leaped to avoid the Reo's wheels, looking like water split by a boat's prow.

A scarlet sign on the cab door read "Whitey's Freight Line, Louisville." The truck ground to a stop, and the door swung open. "I'm heading south, far as Louisville," the driver called.

Margarete pushed her suitcase onto the seat, grabbed the side window mount, stepped onto the running board, then slid into the cab. The driver swept a lunch pail, a roll of Copenhagen, and a clipboard out of her way.

"I appreciate your stopping," she said with care, avoiding her accent. She looked at the driver. This must be Whitey, as his hair was yellow-white, the color of an old dog's teeth.

He brought the stick back and released the clutch before he said, "Name's Whitey McKay."

She nodded, wondering at the crumpling sound coming from the floor as she moved her feet. Years of dirt from others' feet, she supposed. Her side of the dashboard had bits of brown crust stuck to it.

McKay was squeezed in behind the steering wheel. He must have been six-three; his knees rose to the wheel. His sleeves were rolled to his elbow, and he had the largest wrists Margarete had ever seen, as big around as signposts, and not any hair on them, as if he shaved his arms. His pug nose had an inverted angle, straight down from his forehead, then jutting out at the last chance. He wore a white shirt with the buttons missing. A small fan in a wire cage was clipped to the window frame between the visors. He turned it on and adjusted it so that its draft cooled her face. She smiled her thanks.

"What's your name, girlie?"

"Meg. I'm going about as far south as you are." She shifted her feet along the crunchy substance, then dared, "What's that on the floor?"

Whitey McKay chuckled shortly. "Sorry about that. I dip snoose. In the winter on these central-states runs, it gets too blasted cold to roll down a window every three minutes to spit.

I've got pretty good aim, so I just launch it over there. I'll get around to sweeping up one of these days."

Pretty good aim, except for the scabs of tobacco clinging to the dash. Since last winter. Margarete wanted to crawl out of her skin. Instead, she laughed uproariously.

McKay glanced at her, appreciating her understanding. But she was laughing at herself, cringing at dried chewing tobacco, when for the past week and a half she had been consorting with Kurt Monck.

Much of that time he was not with her, although it seemed his presence lingered long after he disappeared on one of his errands. She never knew where he went. Yesterday he had returned to Diamond Lake with a bag filled with hair, or at least so it had seemed before he sorted it out. At a novelty store he had purchased several glue-on mustaches and two beards, and fake eyebrows that looked like caterpillars. He also had several wigs, good-quality from the look of them. From another bag he withdrew bottles and sticks of theatrical makeup. Once he disappeared for an hour and came back only with two pairs of spectacles, one made of gold wire and another of the new tortoiseshell. She had tried them both, and the glasses didn't have a correction in them.

After another trip he returned with a pair of needle-nose pliers and a role of telephone wire. And on another errand he procured a ring of skeleton keys and a small box of dentist's steel probes. He said he might have to use them as lock picks.

Monck reminded her of Heinzie, her childhood cat in Berlin. She never saw the violence the cat inflicted on the neighborhood's mice and birds, but many times the cat came into the house licking gore from its paws and whiskers. One day she found Heinzie's trophy room, under the back steps, full of tiny bones that looked like whisks from an old broom.

Monck said he had killed someone at the POW camp. And he had come back from his first attempt to leave Seattle with burn holes and drops of blood on his shirt. And she prayed today hadn't been another kill. It couldn't have been.

McKay interrupted her thoughts. "Here we go with some Burma Shavers. 'Within this Vale.'" He waited for the next red-on-white sign. "'Of Toil and Sin.'" He grinned widely, anticipating the punch line. "'Your Head Grows Bald.'" Another wait. "'But Not Your Chin.'" McKay laughed fully. "I love those poems. Shakespeare's got nothing on them." The sponsor's name flashed passed.

The notion that the scratchy, infrequent voices on the cab radio were policemen stalking them hadn't occurred to her. After they picked up Larry Leffler, Monck took those violent turns, braked hard, and ordered her into the car parked in front of them—another one he had hot-wired—leaving him and Leffler behind in the cab. Seconds later Monck joined her. She had waved at Leffler over her shoulder as Monck and she drove away.

Monck and Leffler had been alone only a few seconds. Surely not enough time for Monck...

She didn't want to examine it further. Whitey McKay was chattering away, something about his son's swing resembling the Babe's. She had no idea who the Babe was. She retreated into herself, letting the Indiana countryside slip by.

Her increasing malaise since leaving her window over Puget Sound frightened her. For all those years she had assumed her motivation was love for the home country and a sense of duty to Georg's work. And she still longed for her husband, and Mary. But stripped of the routine of the window, she realized she owed Germany nothing. Increasingly distant memories of her Berlin neighborhood were her only contact with the Fatherland. She had no fondness for the National Socialists and didn't understand the nationwide cult of worship surrounding the Fuehrer. How could she feel those things, separated from Berlin by half a world? Reading the *Bremerton Sun* didn't exactly whip her into a German nationalistic fervor as the *Berliner Tageblatt* might.

She was out of touch. She had no idea what her old Berlin friends were dreaming of and working for. They were being bombed daily. For a while not sharing that dreadful experience with her countrymen had distressed her. Now not at all. What romance was there in sitting under a horde of B-17s as they opened their bomb-bay doors? Yet Berliners seemed anxious for it. They were obsessed with the hardened mask—its mouth turned up in a skull's rictus—that hid reality. A German is a person who never tells a lie unless he believes it. The war was a lie. It was lost. Yet it went on.

She frowned. Germans. She was thinking of them as foreigners.

She was still a German, she supposed. But her daughter? Now they were separated not only by half a continent, but by a nationality. Mary was as American as Shirley Temple. Recently, she had begun to correct her mother's pronunciation. "Pucker up, Mommy, like a whistle, then blow. And you'll be able to say your 'w's like everyone else." Margarete laughed then, and again when Mary stuffed two towels under her sweater and outrageously imitated her mother: "Vot do ve do vit de vorms in de garten?" Margarete had grabbed Mary and pretended to spank her, and they ended up on the floor, holding each other and rocking with laughter.

Why did that seem so long ago? It had been just two weeks, and it was before Kurt Monck and all the irrationality he had brought into her life. Why had she gone along with him? Fear for her daughter and herself. Why was she now helping him? Fear might be some of it, but it alone wasn't an adequate answer. Out of a sense of duty? Away from her Bainbridge Island window she was unsure she had any duty. Because Georg would have wanted her to? Her husband had been a realist, not an obsessed adventurer. Why, then? A long while passed, Whitey McKay talking all the while, and she still didn't have her answer.

The truck had begun to rattle. Margarete couldn't remember when the driver had stopped talking. She looked at him. Whitey McKay's face was set in a fierce expression, one at odds with his talkative streak. She glanced at the speedometer. The Reo was barreling down the road at seventy miles an hour. Its fenders shook loudly in the wind, and the engine bellowed. The stick shift vibrated like a tuning fork.

"I've got to hand it to those boys," Whitey McKay yelled over the motor. "If they've got the truck dispatchers covered, they must have everybody notified—trains, buses, out at the airport, maybe even the lake terminals, the works."

She wondered at his words and grabbed her seat cushion with both hands. "Don't you think you should slow down? This old truck. . . ."

McKay interrupted, "This old truck is doing exactly what I'm telling it to." The speedometer notched up. "Take a look at the clipboard."

She obliged. The first sheet on the board was a bill of lading. "Just dig down there another one."

She lifted the first sheet. On the next, under the Federal Bureau of Investigation's logo, were two photographs, one of Kurt Monck, and another of her. The caption read "Escaped POW and Accomplice."

Margarete sagged against the door and closed her eyes. She wasn't frightened. She had lost the ability to be afraid days ago. She was simply resigned. A captive in a highballing Reo Speedwagon in the middle of Indiana. It made as much sense as any of it.

Whitey McKay said over the roar of the engine, "While you were lifting your suitcase into the truck, I just took a quick look-see into my overhead mirror. Usually I can't see anything out of it, because cargo blocks the back window. Not this time, not hauling tank turrets. I saw your boyfriend climb on. He moves fast, I'll hand that to him, but not so fast as a body can't see him. That's always been the trouble with you bastard Nazis. You can't move fast enough."

McKay spat out the window, perhaps for the hundredth time this trip. The gob arched fiercely and raced back to the turrets. "We're approaching Lafayette, and just this side of it my friend Lud Fellows sits on his Harley Davidson behind a Standard Oil sign waiting for speeders. He's a cop, you see. He'll pull me over, sure as we're sitting here."

Moments later they rushed by the billboard, which read "Standard Oil at War" and showed a misty-eyed young boy saluting a formation of P-38s flying overhead.

The undulating wail of a siren brought a grin to McKay. "Old Lud's as predictable as a clock. I paid over a hundred bucks to the city of Lafayette before I learned that lesson."

The Reo slowed. Margarete saw the motorcycle in the side mirror, weaving back and forth in the lane in some sort of victory dance. A white-helmeted head bobbed above the Harley's windscreen. The truck bellowed as Whitey McKay downshifted. He pulled onto the shoulder.

Margarete swung the suitcase off the seat and threw it at Whitey's head, intent on dazing him and leaping out of the rig to yell a warning to Monck. McKay's piston-size arm easily deflected it, and it fell to the floor behind the stick shift. He said without rancor, "I expected no less from you sneaky bastards. Trying to KO me with the suitcase is the same kind of thing you did to Poland."

Gravel sounded under the tires, and McKay hauled back on the emergency brake. He pulled a tire iron from beside his seat. "We gypos call this a convincer. Now you just sit here while me and Lud take care of your German boyfriend."

He pushed open his door and jumped from the running board. He ran, shouting at the trooper to get out his pistol.

Then she heard nothing more. She waited a moment, expecting a shot or the sound of the crowbar on flesh, at least some German or English curses. Again, her utter absence of fear surprised her. She didn't know if it was due to an abandonment of caring or, worse, to a complete trust in Kurt Monck. The rolling song of a meadowlark filled the cab.

She pushed a hand through her hair, took a long breath, and opened the door. She walked along the flatbed, past rows of turrets. Indiana summer heat swaddled her.

She knew what she would find. Sure enough, there Kurt Monck was, wearing a blond mustache and wig, standing between the truck and the overturned Harley, offhandedly surveying his work. The motorcycle's rear wheel was spinning as its engine idled. The trooper was kneeling motionless near the V-cylinders, his face on the gravel, his arms around his head. He groaned painfully.

Whitey McKay was sprawled on his back, his nose splayed toward an ear and gushing blood.

Was she so inured to Monck's violence that her only thought was that the high sun made his blond wig look white? Wading in and out of consciousness, McKay slowly lifted a knee. His jaw slackened.

"I hope it was this son of a bitch who was spitting tobacco, not you," Monck said. She couldn't tell if he was smiling under the mustache.

His white shirt was streaked brown, and speckles covered the back of his neck and his arms. She laughed insanely, not caring about Monck or the trooper or McKay or herself.

"Help me get them into the brush." The German rolled the patrolman onto his back, then pulled him by the arms across a culvert into the undergrowth. They disappeared in the brush. A meadowlark squawked at them, then burst from the ground, its yellow-and-black breast flashing in the sun.

She sat on the Reo's fender. Her eyes filled. If she could just walk away...

Monck emerged from the scrub. He ignored her, dragging the trucker into the brush, between the American linden and black gum trees. He moved quickly, his strength easy and flowing. The brush rustled. He jumped again over onto the shoulder and righted the motorcycle. He lifted a leg over it, studied the gear lever for a moment, then popped it into first. The Harley bounced across the culvert, its balloon tires churning the soft earth, following the trail of the trucker and the policeman.

Not a vehicle passed them. A tear streamed down Margarete Bayerlein's face. When had this journey been set in its irrevocable course? She only wanted her daughter. She...

The horror of a new thought sucked air from her lungs. A certainty lodged in her like a dagger. A sureness of death, imminent and nearby. She stood, trying to peer through the canoe birch and underbrush.

A resolve, a redeeming determination, filled her. Stepping on the trailer hitch, she searched between the turrets. She stepped up to the bed and across several lengths of chain. The turrets looked like enormous turtles.

Margarete found Monck's shotgun and his pack. She didn't know how to crack the breach to see if shells were in the chamber. But what good would an unloaded gun be to the German? She jumped from the flatbed, then stepped across the ditch and high-stepped over twigs that plucked at her skirt. She pushed through the brush. The bunchgrass under her feet had been brushed flat by Monck's work.

Thirty yards into the scrub she found a clearing. The motorcycle was upright on its stand, but the officer and McKay were still down. The trooper tried to rise, but he collapsed again, clutching his face. Monck wrapped a length of wire around McKay's neck. His face was impartial. He might have been polishing his shoes.

She brought the Stevens up. "You did that to Larry, didn't you?"

He ignored her, bringing the strands across each other behind the trucker's neck. McKay's head twisted forward, and his eyes opened. They stared without seeing as he struggled to bring himself to the surface.

The shotgun pealed, and the Harley Davidson's gas tank ripped open. Rivulets of gasoline fell onto the hot pistons and flamed, the fire lunging back up to the tank. The explosion was almost silent, sounding like a cough, but it sprayed gasoline onto the rest of the cycle. Fire ran along its frame, then quickly died.

"You drop him, or I'll do that to you."

This time Monck paid attention. He stared at her with cold surmise, then released his grip. McKay was still breathing. He moaned.

"These two know where we're going. We can't let them talk to Wren."

"Who's Wren?" she asked over the side-by-side's barrel.

"That's the name we heard over the cab radio." He stood slowly, the wire dangling innocently from his hand. "He's the one chasing us. He coordinated the hardware-store trap. And he must be the one who figured out my escape from the POW camp, who found out we were in Chicago, and who turned Leffler."

"I don't care about him. Or about you." She hoped her voice carried her threat. "If you don't come away from those two fellows, I'm going to kill you, and not think once about it afterward."

Monck looked at both his victims, as if deciding whether they were worth challenging the woman's will. Finally he said in a muted tone, "Your eyes were alive in that cottage, talking about your daughter. They're dead now. I've no doubt you'd gut-shoot me."

The garrote disappeared in his shirt. He let McKay slump to the ground, where he rolled onto his side and groaned. Monck found a pair of handcuffs on the patrolman's belt, and he secured him to the trunk of a small birch tree. He unlaced McKay's boots and used the leather thongs to tie him to another tree.

Margarete followed Monck out of the brush, the Stevens at his back. For the next fifty miles in the Reo she rode with the shotgun across her lap pointed at his midriff.

The sun through the windshield and the swaying truck eventually made her doze. When she awoke, the bird gun was on the floor beneath her feet, and Monck was still driving. He smiled gently at her, as if events in the underbrush were forgotten.

21

THE SCRATCHING AT THE DOOR BROKE
Gordon Potts's concentration. He pushed himself
away from the bench and rubbed his eyes. He had last emerged
from his cogitative trance three hours before, when the sun was
still high in the Labrador sky. Now dusk was enveloping the
mountain range, and Potts's best friends and his mortal enemies
were at his Quonset hut door.

He gathered his notes, about twenty pages, and added them
to the shelf. Next to his *Langenscheidt's English Taschenwoerter-
buecher* there were eight inches of notepaper all generated by
Potts in his five-day flurry.

He stood slowly, knowing the scratching would only get louder.
He stretched mightily, then cracked his knuckles. The scraping
at the door intensified.

"Goddam this place," Potts muttered. He stared bleakly at the
coded message on the bench, dimly lit by a bare bulb. A page
of numbers. He hadn't cracked it. Last he heard, neither had
anyone at OP-20-G.

Wouldn't it astonish that bastard Commander Petes and his
smug superior Admiral McWorter if he could beat them to the

code? That single thought had kept him at the bench twenty hours a day since Monday.

He stepped across the Quonset hut to the wooden cooler, dug into the side of the tin building, and pulled out a paper-wrapped wad of hamburger. Unwrapping the meat, Potts sniffed tentatively. Still good. His provisioner, the mute RCAF supply driver, delivered sixty pounds of ground round to Potts each visit, a snafu Potts had never bothered to correct. He once tried to trade the meat for a screen door, with no luck. His bones ached from hours on the stool. The scratching urged him on.

"Will you hold your horses?" he yelled. He pulled the meat into fist-size chunks.

He had given up on Monday's intercepted message. He couldn't connect it to an intelligible phrase. He had pushed the encoded text away in disgust. All that work for nothing. He just couldn't begin again, not on the same ciphers.

But a message by the same fist had been sent from Washington State on June 27, six days before the second broadcast. Potts had radioed a request to his friend Lieutenant Ray Edwards at Station S on Bainbridge Island to spurt-rebroadcast the tape on a little-used frequency. Potts had re-recorded the spurt signal and slowed it by a tape transfer, and for two days now he had been working on the sender's first message, and on the Berlin response to the message, also taped and forwarded by Edwards.

All in violation of regulations. But what could they do to Potts? Banish him to a more remote wilderness? There weren't any. Potts was discouraged. It was already Saturday, July 8. The messages were getting cold.

Potts walked to the front of the hut with the hamburger balls. He braced himself, then opened the door. A mass of churning fur spilled in, encasing his legs and almost toppling him. The raccoons mewed and snarled and hissed and climbed over each other to get closer to the meat. Like a man struggling through a snowdrift, Potts waded through the door. Only when he started throwing the hamburger did the raccoons abandon him to chase the meat. He tossed the balls toward Moby Dick, now nothing but a dripping stump of dirty snow.

When the mountain of meat was first mistakenly delivered, he had fed some of it to a raccoon with a gimp leg. The animal must have invited his cousins, because now each day more than eighty of them appeared at the Quonset hut.

Between each toss of meat, he slapped at his enemies, who hunted him each dusk. Enraged horseflies and mosquitoes swept in at him, wing-on-wing strafing runs. Even during the summer months, Potts slept under two blankets and wore thick wool gloves. Despite the precautions, every morning he awoke with some new part of him swollen. The flies attacked without provocation, and their bites left purple scars. The mosquitoes were villainous kamikazes.

Potts tossed the last of the meat and hastily retreated, slamming the door behind him. From under his bunk he pulled a flit gun and quickly filled the hut with a choking cloud of DDT. It would only stun the bastards, he knew. These rapacious carnivores had mutated beyond vulnerability to pesticides. The flies, mosquitoes, and boredom were his personal Axis.

Potts coughed his way through the cloying mist to the bench. He paused to gather his strength for renewed combat with the ciphers and stared contemptuously at his library. He had them all: the rare pamphlet by Major General Joseph O. Mauborgne on the British field cipher called Playfair, the Signal Corps's *Contributions of the Crytographic Bureaus in the World War*, Bentley's *Complete Phrase Code*, *the Acme Code and Supplement*, and *New Standard Half Word Code*, and a half-dozen others, all outdated. He even had a Hebern cipher machine in a box under the bench. A fragile antique, but fun to play with.

All useless for a multiple-substitution code. He sighed loudly and leaned over the bench, pulling a clean sheet of paper and the Bible toward him.

Lieutenant Potts would be unable to tell the Secret Service whether ten minutes or an hour then passed. But the key finally came to him, not in an instant of serendipity, but as a result of hoeing the long row.

The first run on each chapter of the Bible had produced nothing but a few puzzling fragments of sentences. He had compensated for nulls of two or six letters, the most common, and still had nothing. Then Potts had begun that morning playing with the calendar, a long-used encoding device. He had three calendar numbers, twenty-seven, two, and six.

The message had been sent on the twenty-seventh day of June, so he had started at the twenty-seventh book, Daniel, then added two books, to Joel, for the date of the week, and added six more, to Habakkuk, for the month. Potts had never even heard of Habakkuk. He counted into the verse the prescribed number from the code and found the word "did." But counting further according to the code's numbers produced nonsense, even when he experimented with nulls.

He next tried twenty-seven plus two, to Joel again, but this time he counted six verses further, rather than six books further. Another nonsensical result. He tried scores of other variations. All the while, he kept a record of the meaningless amalgams.

He felt like a safecracker, endlessly spinning the dial, waiting for the right combination.

After the identification and tuning signals, the message began with the letters, 7, 8, 316, 128, 339, 345, and 411. With Potts looking at the twenty-seventh verse minus six verses of the second book, Exodus, the numbers corresponded with "Thou shalt slay door father mother death rise."

"Slay" pricked his interest. He played with it further.

An out-of-sequence number, 128, usually meant there was a change in format. Potts dropped the indicator word "door," then tried the most common change, from words to letters, and usually to the first letter of the word. That left "Thou shalt slay F M D R." He eliminated each word as a null, and when he crossed out the fifth cipher, the *M*, he heard the tumblers click into place.

Even in Potts's crabbed handwriting, the plaintext sizzled on the paper.

The lieutenant stood to pace the small room, letting the electricity of his discovery work its way through his body. Breathing deeply to savor his victory, he lifted the telephone receiver.

The Navy had paid thousands to string a telephone line to the remote hut on Beadle Mountain because phone lines were far more secure than airwaves.

"This is the Labrador monitor post," Potts yelled into the static. "Get me Commander Petes...I don't care if he is off watch. Telephone his home. Tell Ironpants he'll regret it if he doesn't take my call."

22

WREN AND GARVIN MARCHED DOWN the dark marble hallway, echoes of their footfalls urging them on. At eleven on a Sunday morning, few employees were in the Treasury Building. Through several open office doors, the agents glimpsed the White House, relucent in the morning light, across East Executive Avenue.

A plainclothes guard stood beside double oak doors ahead of them.

"I'm going to hate this," Wren said.

"There are times I'm truly happy you're agent-in-charge, not me." Garvin straightened his tie. "The abuse we're about to witness in the conference room might not trickle down to my level, not when they've got you there."

"Thanks, pal." A brave front. Sweat was flowing down Wren's back, chilling him each time the damp shirt touched his skin.

"Have you ever met Secretary Morgenthau before?"

"He nodded at me a couple of times when I was on the White House Detail. I wouldn't call him a bosom buddy."

"Who all is going to be there?" Garvin asked, showing the guard his silver star.

"Only Secretary Morgenthau and Chief Wilson, as far as I know."

The guard led them through the massive doors into a sparse reception area. Above the receptionist's desk was the Treasury Department's hand-carved seal, the size of a garbage-can lid. The guard pulled open the inner door and with a wide gesture ushered them inside.

"Ah, goddammit," Wren said under his breath, surveying the room.

All eyes turned to the Secret Service agents. Secretary Henry Morgenthau, Jr., a dark mole of a man lost in an oversized brown suit, was at the head of the massive conference table. Behind him was a court reporter, her hands on a transcription machine mounted on a short tripod. She wore the new look, a tailored suit, with a jacket with sharp lapels, a single center button, and shoulders so padded she reminded Wren of a fullback.

Flanking the Treasury Secretary were Chief Wilson and Mike O'Brien. Next to O'Brien were two Navy officers, an admiral and a commodore. Sitting distinctly apart from the others was J. Edgar Hoover, glowering at Wren with his bunched face. In a chair against the wall was an FBI agent, branded by his crew cut and suit glistening with age. He had a pen poised over a yellow legal pad.

Across from Hoover was a two-star general Wren guessed was William B. Smith, head of the POW camp system. A newspaper on the table near him was headlined "RAF Bombers Pound Caen."

A few of the conference room's windows were still barricaded with sandbags, and on the wall was a poster entitled "What to Do in an Air Raid." On a stand under the poster were two OCD helmets. There should also have been several whistles on pegs, but early in the war someone had noticed that the whistles bore the legend "Made in Japan" and had removed them.

Still staring at Wren, the FBI director said gruffly, "Let's start by getting your story of the Chicago mess out in the open."

His fingers laced in front of him, Chief Wilson said, "Mr.

Secretary, see how easily J. Edgar sets the tone of the meeting.
It's a joy to watch, really." Hoover loathed being called J. Edgar,
and Wilson knew it.

Hoover turned angrily to the Secret Service chief and thrust
a finger at him. "If you'd given us the job in the first place, this
German maniac wouldn't have gotten out of Seattle. Read your
organization's charter. Your men are bulletproof vests, that's all.
You're not bounty hunters."

Morgenthau raised his palms. His smile failed. "Let's maintain
a little order, please. Have a seat, gentlemen." The Secretary
pulled a Parker 51 from his suit pocket, although there was no
paper in front of him. "Mr. Wren, you've heard of OP-20-G's
decoded message?"

"I haven't even heard of OP-20-G."

The Secretary introduced Admiral McWhorter and Commander Petes. McWhorter's smile was professionally charming.
His smoky eyes were unlined, and his teeth were precisely even,
giving his mouth a feminine quality. His face was delicate, but
not weak.

Petes had a miser's face, with bright, avaricious eyes and a
pinched mouth. The black hair growing from his ears looked
harvestable. Both officers were in summer whites.

The admiral said, "A lieutenant at our Labrador monitor post
decoded Berlin's first message to Kurt Monck."

Morgenthau asked, "Why is someone so valuable up in Labrador and not here? Your office is always complaining you don't
have enough good men."

A red flush spread across Petes's face like paint rolled onto a
wall. McWhorter saved him a reply. "We've corrected that over-
sight. He'll be at our Washington offices by nightfall. In any
event, the message is an order to murder President Roosevelt."

Wren laughed harshly. "For Christ's sake, we've known of Kurt
Monck's mission almost from the day of his escape. I haven't
been chasing him for the fun of it."

It was Hoover's turn to laugh, more a snarl. "It sure looks like
it's been for the fun of it. You're sitting with your thumb up

your butt in Chicago, and he and that woman are hijacking a truck in Indiana. The driver frees himself and has to find another state trooper to free the motorcycle trooper, who'd been hand-cuffed to a tree. Then the truck was found abandoned in the middle of Indiana at four o'clock yesterday. And your German and his accomplice could be anyplace. Thumb up your butt to the wrist, I'd say."

Tom Garvin sprang from his chair so fast it toppled behind him. Wren quickly put a hand on his arm, but the agent jabbed the air in Hoover's direction. "Listen, you, if it weren't for Wren guessing the plan, Monck'd still be out there completely unde-tected. We almost had him, we came close, and that's better than anyone else is doing. All this meeting is is a protect-your-ass exercise. You're trying to build a record, showing you tried, in case of disaster. You even brought a secretary to scribble down every word. You're like a hyena, fighting with its ass on the ground so it won't get bit."

Utter calm had apparently settled over Hoover. Only his eyes gave him away. They were fixed on Garvin and looked like bullets in the cylinder of a revolver seen from the business end. Those eyes told Garvin the depth of the hole he had just dug. The agent's mouth closed with a snap.

"Now, now, Tom, sit down," Chief Wilson said soothingly. "We realize you and Agent Wren haven't had any sleep in two days. J. Edgar, I would offer an apology on behalf of the Ser-vice"—he grinned at Garvin—"were it warranted."

It took a moment for Garvin to realize what Wilson had said. Wren glanced at his sidekick, who fumbled with his chair as he righted it and resumed his seat. Wilson always did something like this once in a man's career, and it always worked. Mike O'Brien knew it, and he smiled knowingly at Wren. Garvin gazed with utter reverence and gratitude at the chief. The young agent was now Wilson's man, forever.

Wren asked briskly, "Why were we called to Washington?"

Morgenthau noisily cleared his throat. "Mr. Wren, I must admit to dragging my heels a bit on this matter. It just didn't seem logical that a POW..." The Secretary waved away his apology. "So, it appears you've been correct all along. But it also seems you no longer have the slightest idea where this Kurt Monck is. I thought we would all benefit from a meeting, to orient ourselves."

"You shouldn't have taken us off his tracks."

"What tracks?" Hoover demanded. "You've lost him completely. Admit it."

"We think he went to Kentucky. The woman he is traveling with, Margarete Bayerlein, has a sister who lives there."

"How do you know that?" Hoover asked, drumming his fingers on the table.

"She mentions her sister Lilli in several letters written before the war. No address, no town, just that she moved to Kentucky with her husband in the early '30s. Lilli's married name isn't given, but her maiden name is Jaeger, same as Margarete's. I've contacted Miles Bradley, chief of the Naturalization Service. He's setting up a search of immigration files, looking for any German visa applicant giving Jaeger as her maiden name."

"How long will that take?" General Smith asked. The general had a peculiar yellow complexion, as if from an overdose of antimalaria tablets. He was bald, and a horseshoe of white hair surrounded his scalp. His peaked uniform cap lay on the table next to the newspaper.

Wren gestured restively. "Two or three weeks. Bradley says there's three tons of material to sift through."

"At the rate Monck is apparently moving, that's going to be too late," Morgenthau said somberly. "Admiral, can't you triangulate on him? He broadcasts every few days."

"Monck is only sending a tuning and recognition signal. We usually need thirty seconds of broadcasting to get our direction finders on the beam. The last message the German sent was recorded by us, but it wasn't long enough to fix on."

Hoover asked, "So his controller isn't getting any dope about him?"

"Not over the shortwave," McWhorter answered, his tone one

of infinite patience. "We believe Margarete Bayerlein was a ship spotter. Mr. Wren's people found a makeshift radio near her home. But we think it was made by Monck for just one broadcast. She probably had been reporting by mail to a cell leader somewhere. And now she may be writing or telephoning that same person about Monck's work. There's a dozen ways to get a message out through Mexico or Cuba, but it's slow. So Berlin isn't getting information very readily."

The Secretary said, "I trust your men are working on the other messages received from Berlin."

"The German doesn't use the same substitution enciphering formula twice. We've got the June 27 message broken. It gives him his orders and tells him about Lawrence Leffler's safe house in Chicago. Nothing more. We haven't cracked the July 3 signal. You can be assured we're working on it."

"Margarete Bayerlein had a daughter," Morgenthau said. "Any luck finding her?"

Wilson responded, "Whitey McKay, the driver of the truck, reports the girl isn't traveling with them. We're looking for her on Bainbridge Island and the Bremerton area, thinking her mother hastily dropped her off with a neighbor."

"How'd Monck get the drop on the patrolman and the trucker?" Hoover asked, curiosity softening his face.

"Neither knows. The trooper saw a blur. McKay didn't even see that. Monck broke their noses and their collarbones both on the right side, as if it were some sort of drill."

The FBI director smiled as if he had just sipped some rare and very fine wine. Wren was beginning to think Hoover was as tough as his propaganda said he was.

Wilson added, "The truck driver came to just as the woman threatened Monck with a shotgun. He recognized the woman from our picture, but not the POW. He swears the German had sandy-colored hair, almost blond, and a mustache of the same color. We know Monck's hair is dark brown. McKay can't remember the scar, although he says he was still groggy. So Monck is disguising himself now."

The Secretary asked, "Chief Wilson, what's your next move?"

Hoover suddenly leaned forward and said, "Wait a minute here, Mr. Secretary. Wilson's next move is to run back to the White House and start protecting the president. That, and only that, is the Secret Service's job. As of this minute, I take over the search for Kurt Monck."

Morgenthau had a timid appearance, but he shrank from no one, not when he had the ear of the president. He looked squarely at the FBI director. "Chief Wilson has convinced me that Mr. Wren should continue to lead this operation. You will please provide him with whatever assistance he requires." He ignored Hoover's baleful stare. "Chief?"

"We want to inform the newspapers in Indianapolis and Louisville and Cincinnati that the POW may have reached their cities. That'll put Monck's photograph all over their front pages."

Morgenthau was shaking his head before Frank Wilson finished. "I'm concerned about perceptions. He was on Seattle's front pages, then Chicago's, now Cincinnati and Louisville's. It's not going to take long for the public to realize this POW is aiming for the nation's capital, and to guess what his mission is."

Wren asked impertinently, "What's that got to do with anything?"

"The most powerful man in the world, the leader of this country, is not going to shrink before the threat of an assassin. The president cannot be seen as distracted or concerned in the slightest, not at this stage of the war, and, let me be candid, not just before an election campaign."

Wren drew himself up. "With his photograph plastered all over the Midwest, we can turn every citizen into a hunter. Instead of dozens of pairs of eyes looking for him, we'll have millions."

"Wren is right, Mr. Secretary," Wilson said. "At this point we need all the help we can get. I must insist you allow us to release the story of the German's escape from Chicago to the media."

Morgenthau sucked in his cheeks and stared a moment out the window at the White House. "All right. I'll explain it to the president. Now, what about the White House? Is Monck going to try to get inside it?"

Mike O'Brien answered, his words devoid of the Irish brogue he occasionally played with. "The building is invulnerable. We have men stationed in every room, in every aisle, in every closet, on the elevator, at every window. There are automatic weapons, automatic gates and doors, and four alarm systems. We have doubled and doubled again the perimeter patrols, and have installed several antiaircraft weapons on nearby buildings."

"What's the armament?" General Smith asked.

"Two .50 caliber Browning M2 machine guns on portable stands on the roof above us here and a 37mm MIA2 on a platform carriage on the Commerce Building. And we've got antitank guns pointed at the gates of the White House grounds."

"The president told me he was getting tired of the increased security," Morgenthau said, "but he agreed to cancel most of his meetings and the press conferences between now and his departure."

O'Brien looked at a list in front of him. "Other than Secret Service personnel, nobody is scheduled to enter the White House except you, Mr. Hopkins, the president's physician, two secretaries, his press secretary, and his valet. Speaker Rayburn and Senator Barkley also have appointments that couldn't be canceled. They'll all be searched thoroughly."

"Protesting all the while, I imagine," Morgenthau said. "What about Eleanor and all her hangers-on?"

"We've asked her friends to stay away from the White House until after the convention. Mrs. Roosevelt herself is in Hyde Park."

"You are telling me, then, Mr. O'Brien, that I shouldn't worry about the White House."

"I've done the worrying. It's secure."

"What about the president's train?"

Frank Wilson said, "We are on record as preferring that the president fly to San Diego."

"He flatly refuses. He is leaving the White House this Thurs-

day, four days from now, at ten-thirty in the evening to board
POTUS. Is the train secure?"

"We are also on record as preferring the president take a random route to San Diego," O'Brien said, a shade of resignation
coloring his words. "The fact that Mrs. Roosevelt is at Hyde
Park is known to anyone who reads the datelines on her newspaper columns. It is also common knowledge that she always
accompanies the president to the conventions. Therefore, it
doesn't take much figuring to know that the president will travel
north to New York State to pick her up before heading west.
The route is too predictable."

"The president has friends he wants to see at Hyde Park. And
he simply wants to visit the homestead. The destination can't
be changed."

Mike O'Brien had known all this, but it was his job to lay out
the safest procedures. He lifted several wide sheets of paper from
a satchel and spread them over the table. Morgenthau rose for
a better look.

"The first nine cars of the train are already made up and are
at the Bureau of Engraving. The rear car is the president's, the
Ferdinand Magellan. Just before departure, another nine cars
will be backed down from the Virginia Avenue Station by the
engines, two Southern 1400 steam locomotives. The VIPs and
the pool newsmen will board at Virginia Street."

"How many Secret Service people will be aboard?" Morgenthau asked, lifting the staging sheet.

"Twenty-two, distributed throughout the train, with six in
the Conneaut, the Pullman in front of the president's. There'll
also be a twelve-man crew, eight Navy cooks and waiters, and
three Signal Corps radio operators."

"And who has the president invited to travel with him this
time?"

O'Brien read from a list, "Admiral Leahy; the president's doctor, Vice Admiral McIntire; his aide, Rear Admiral Wilson Brown;
Pa Watson; another physician, Lieutenant Commander Bruenn;

his masseur, Lieutenant Commander George A. Fox; another secretary, Lieutenant William M. Rigdon; his valet, Petty Officer Prettyman; and his dog, Fala. A number of others will be boarding with Mrs. Roosevelt at Hyde Park."

"We know Monck is carrying plastic explosives," Morgenthau asked. "Enough to derail the train?"

Wren answered, "Easily. He also has the knowledge."

"What we hope Monck won't have is the opportunity." O'Brien opened a map and slid it toward the Secretary. "POTUS will travel north on Pennsylvania Railroad tracks. We're going to borrow heavily from local police departments, the Army, and the Bureau. Nowhere between the Bureau of Engraving and Hyde Park will there be a length of track unobserved by police or military personnel. Each guard will be able to see the guards north and south of him."

"All the way?" Morgenthau asked, impressed.

"All the way."

The Secretary thought for a moment. "But won't that alarm everyone on the train?"

Wilson answered, "The more we learn about Kurt Monck, the less we worry about alarming anyone. Our main goal is to stop him, any way we can."

O'Brien continued, "There'll be a squad of soldiers at each bridge the train goes over, as we think that's a natural place for Monck's attack. Army engineers will also continuously search each bridge for explosives." He shuffled a few papers. "A sweeper will travel a half mile ahead of POTUS, and a trailing train will be a mile behind it. The sweeper locomotive will be pushing two empty boxcars ahead of it. If, despite our precautions, Monck is able to place pressure-sensitive explosives on the track, the sweeper will set them off."

"What if he uses a radio detonator instead of a pressure plate?" Hoover asked.

O'Brien answered, "The sweeper train will have on board five broad-band portable radio broadcasters, each emitting pulses over a wide spectrum. We think we've got it covered."

"Is it possible the German's attempt might come from the air?" the Treasury Secretary asked.

"We find nothing in Monck's background indicating he can fly an airplane. However, we request that another car be added to POTUS, a rolling AA-gun wagon that is presently at Bolling Air Force Base. It's a Combination Mount M54, which has a single 37mm gun and two .50 caliber M2s."

Morgenthau laughed abruptly. "The president would have an apoplectic fit. The rail gun would make him look like a South American thirty-day dictator. That's out completely."

"We figured as much," Wilson said. "But a wing of P-51 Mustangs from Bolling Air Force Base will alternate over POTUS, no fewer than two planes at any given time."

"That's fine. Just don't get them too close to the train."

O'Brien said, "At four hundred miles an hour, they don't need to be too close."

John Wren was fascinated. He had always viewed the protection of the president as an all-out, no-holds-barred effort. That's what it seemed at his level. But these men were negotiating, basing the president's safekeeping on factors other than the mere need to stop a bullet or defuse a bomb. Appearances, politics, territories. It seemed tangled and inefficient. He had an immense urge to spring out of his chair and run back to the field. Chief Wilson might have sensed it, because he was staring right at Wren, pinning him to the seat.

Mike O'Brien unrolled a tube of blueprints and placed a pen and his keys on two corners to keep them flat. "These are drawings of the president's Pullman car. The car was built in 1928, and when I first proposed to President Roosevelt that it be armored, he was dead set against it."

"Yes," Morgenthau said amiably, "he told me about that. He said you convinced him by mentioning the Pullman would also be used for future presidents."

O'Brien went on, "You can see from these specifications that the car now has little in common with other Pullmans. All steel was cut off the body by acetylene torches, and the outer shell was replaced with heavy-gauge steel. The undercarriage is a solid six-inch plate of steel. The rear door, the one out to his campaign platform, weighs fifteen hundred pounds. The glass in all windows is three inches thick."

O'Brien pulled the top diagram away and directed Morgenthau's attention to the one below. "The Pullman's four-wheel trucks have been replaced by six-wheelers to hold the extra weight. The doors are self-locking and can only be opened from the inside." He pointed with a finger. "The roof has submarine escape hatches in case it is derailed on a bridge and is submerged. The car weighs 285,000 pounds, so much that unaccustomed engineers trying to get POTUS rolling often think the air brakes are still on."

He moved to another blueprint. "The normal five compartments in the car have been reduced to three, and the president's is the rear one." The same blueprint also showed the interior colors to be subdued green-gray, with green and buff upholstery on the chairs.

Bending low over the diagrams, the Treasury Secretary asked, "How many Secret Service agents will be in the Ferdinand Magellan with the president?"

"Two, sir. Wilbur Gottschalk is one of this country's best swimmers. In case of danger in a river, his job is to hold the president above the water until assistance comes. And Max Smythe will also be with the president."

"Smythe? The fellow with the black mustache and the machine pistol under his jacket?"

"That's him."

Morgenthau dipped his chin approvingly. "Tell me one last thing about the Ferdinand Magellan. If this Monck were to somehow get a bomb with all his plastic explosives close to the Pullman, what damage would result?"

"As I mentioned, he has enough to derail the train. But the armored Pullman is an iron cocoon. Even with all Monck's explosives in one blast, say from the railroad bed or from the side of the car, the Magellan would protect its occupants."

Morgenthau was suddenly irritated. "Then what in hell is the German's plan?"

"We don't know, Mr. Secretary," O'Brien conceded.

Morgenthau turned to John Wren. He pointed at the agent. "Then you stop him before he gets to the train. You got that?"

"Yes, sir."

J. Edgar Hoover said loudly, "Mr. Secretary, that is the FBI's job. I must again request that Wren and the other Secret Service agents be taken off the case."

Morgenthau airily waved away the suggestion. "That's already settled. Good day, gentlemen."

A few minutes later Wren and Garvin entered the restroom. Garvin said, "Louisville, you think?"

"That's where Whitey McKay's truck was heading. That's our best clue at the moment. We've got a Navy plane taking us there in an hour."

J. Edgar Hoover was standing at the far-right urinal. Wren took the far-left one, Garvin next to him.

Hoover asked, "Feeling unsocial today, are we?"

"Not at all," Wren answered easily. "It's just that every time you FBI people get close to anything, you take a photo of it and put it into a file. I don't want to take any chances."

Hoover grinned. His teeth reminded Wren of a Puget Sound ratfish's. "Hey you. Garvin. You got any college?"

Startled, Garvin dried up. "Sure."

The director laughed. "Two years of undergraduate classes in the French horn at Oberlin. You call that college? But I like you. If you ever get tired of the dropout squad, you come and see me. I'll find a place for you."

Hoover shook himself. "Wren, you noticed that I didn't press my point in there. You'll do all right on Monck's trail. It's just too bad cactus doesn't grow around here."

Garvin gasped. He had never asked Wren about the rumored

Arizona incident. Garvin had assumed it was just another Secret Service myth.

A long moment passed before Wren asked, "What do you want, Mr. Hoover?"

Hoover zipped himself up and walked to the sink. "There's a lot of bullshit between the Secret Service and the Bureau. So you might find this surprising, but you and I are on the same side, and I'm going to back you up as far as I can." The director lathered his hands. "I've got my own files on German immigrants into this country, copied from the Immigration Service's. I'll dump as many agents on the job as it needs, and if it's in the file, I'll have Margarete Bayerlein's sister's Kentucky address to you within forty-eight hours. You count on that."

Wren stepped away from the urinal, expecting the hooker.

Hoover went on. "Another thing. McWhorter is right about Monck's using the woman's old contacts to inform Berlin. Slow, but sure. Why don't I flood the telephone switchboards in Indianapolis and Louisville and Cincinnati with my people? They'll be listening to every single long-distance phone call out of those cities. If Monck calls, we'll get it down, and we'll feed you the information immediately."

Wren was nonplussed. He said finally, "You've stepped out of character, Mr. Hoover."

Hoover smiled widely. "Wilson affects me like a boil. Any cooperating I do, I don't do in front of him." He pulled an envelope from his breast pocket. "Here's some photos you might be interested in."

Wren opened the envelope. Inside were photographs of the operation in front of the Skokie store, taken at a great distance with telephoto lenses. The first showed the cab as it was arriving. The cabdriver, Monck, wore his cap over his eyes. Margarete Bayerlein was in the backseat, glancing to her right, toward Larry Leffler. The next photo, taken with a more powerful lens and blown up until it appeared as if a layer of sand had been sprinkled on the print, was of Monck's face. He had pulled down the sun visor to hide himself, but his crooked grin showed clearly. The last photo was of Margarete, a grainy full-face shot showing her pronounced cheekbones and slender nose. She appeared to be staring through the cab's windshield directly at the camera.

"Taken at two hundred yards," Hoover announced proudly. "I've had them analyzed, but they don't show anything you boys don't already know."

Wren ran this thumb across Margarete's face, as if he could wipe away the blurry gray of her eyes. "You FBI gents too poor to use color film?"

Hoover chuckled. "Not even I can requisition that. The only people taking color shots these days are the flyers doing air recon. You can have those photos."

The three men walked out of the bathroom. Hoover stepped toward two aides waiting near the door, then turned back and said, "This Kurt Monck. I've had experience with people like him. Can I give you some advice?"

Wren nodded.

"Put the bullet in his back, and from a great distance, if you have the chance. Don't even let him look at you. It'll be too dangerous."

Wren smiled grimly. "I've already got that figured out."

"I thought as much." Hoover spun on his heels and walked away.

23

THE RUBBLE-STREWN BANK OF THE
Ohio River was an improbable location for a
picnic, but deckhands on the tugs that churned passed Kurt
Monck and Margarete Bayerlein did not give them a second
glance. Lovers enjoying the July sun, they assumed.

So it carefully appeared. Margarete had spread a wool blanket
on the grass bank, avoiding a rusted snarl of wire and a tattered
boot. Two meatloaf sandwiches on paper wrappers and an unopened bottle of wine were on one corner of the blanket. Monck
had asked her to sit next to him, their shoulders touching, giving
the passing crews something to talk about other than the binoculars Monck raised to his eyes or the notepad she jotted on.

In front of them a ten-foot rowboat was moored to the bank
by a rock resting on its bow line. The wood-plank dinghy tugged
gently at the line as the Ohio River near Cincinnati moved leisurely west to the Mississippi. Oars rested across the seats, and
a bamboo fishing rod hung over the stern. "Ace's Boat Rentals"
was painted in red block letters on the forward freeboard.

"Can you see everything?" Margarete asked, narrowing her
eyes as the setting sun flickered off the water.

"Everything I need to." Monck toyed with the binoculars' focus adjustment. He was wearing a black wig and a mustache, and he had darkened his eyebrows. "I'll have exactly a hundred and twenty seconds. A lot of time."

The day's humidity lingered along the Ohio. She turned away from him before unfastening the second button of her blouse, then seeing she was still decent, turned back. She was damp from the heat, and there was no breeze along the river. She had purchased the binoculars and her skirt and slacks in Louisville that morning before leaving for Cincinnati. The blouse was tobacco-brown and made of spun rayon. The pants, worn by American women for the first time during the war, were held together with buttons hidden in back, as most zippers had gone to the front.

That morning Monck had been off on one of his mysterious errands, so she had had time for a shower in their hotel room. She had also visited a beauty parlor for an oil shampoo and a manicure, inexpressible luxuries after three years at her window on Bainbridge Island. Hairpins were unavailable, so the beautician had sewn curls in Margarete's hair with thread. She had felt wonderfully refreshed, until Monck had returned with his grim determination and told her they were leaving Louisville.

That afternoon in the car—this time a DeSoto—she had finally generated the courage to ask what his mission was. He had only shaken his head and smiled, sadly, she thought.

Margarete now asked, "Are you sure this is the only way in?"

Still peering intently into the binoculars, he replied, "This morning I drove around the mill several times. Because it's a war plant, each gate has several military guards. They check photo identification of every worker entering it. Before I saw the newspaper this morning, I thought I could lift an ID and stroll right in. Not now."

"Your POW photograph seems to be following us. You chased the war off the front page of the Louisville newspaper." She inexplicably felt like teasing him. Maybe it was the sun. "It's the scar on your chin, you know. Otherwise, nobody would spot you, as your features are rather plain."

He smiled under the binoculars. "I'm glad you noticed, plain features or not."

"Most women like a distinctive scar on a man. Yours is a bit ragged, though. It looks like permanent drool at the corner of your mouth."

He laughed and looked at her. Perhaps she should have said something more. A moment passed, and he turned back to the river.

"Germany is doomed," he said abruptly. "You know that, don't you, Meg? Look at that mill. Acres of plant. Raw materials go in one end, steel plates come out the other. Not an enemy bomber over it, no heavy artillery pounding at it. No underground saboteurs. There must be thousands of plants like this in America, spitting out war matériel as fast as they can."

"If the Fatherland is lost, why continue your mission?"

Again he looked at her. She expected something heroic or patriotic or sacrificing. Instead, he shrugged and turned back to the glasses.

Across the river was the River Iron Works, a misnamed steel and rolling mill. North of the mill near the riverbank was the storage yard, with cone-shaped mounds of iron ore and limestone. Suspended over the piles, ore bridges carried ore and limestone from the stockpiles to transfer cars for subsequent distribution. A dock extended into the river, where a bulldozer was unloading a barge.

Next to the yard was the melt shop, and because of the summer heat, many of the enormous building's walls had been rolled to one end, allowing air to circulate inside and revealing the works. A maze of cranes, beams, pipes, skips, cables, runners, and ladles filled the building. Flashes of fire blazed from inside the building. The mill's grinding hum carried across the river. A thick cloud of smoke hovered over the plant, obscuring the distant hills.

Monck gave her the binoculars and said, "Those bowl-shaped

vessels are open-hearth furnaces. the bottom of them is first covered with limestone, and then iron ore is added. When it all heats up and the slag is drained off, it's tapped and poured into a ladle. You can see it there." Monck pointed. "That looks like about a fifty-ton ladle, and they're probably doing a hundred tons a heat."

"Is it hot?"

He stared at her, deep clefts on his brow.

She said defensively, "Don't expect me to know anything about it. I've never seen a steel mill before."

"That orange-yellow glow is molten steel, twenty-eight hundred degrees. It's like lava, as hot as the fires of hell." He turned back to the river. "The ladle is being lifted by those overhead cranes you can see in the middle of the building, and is being carried over to the pouring platform."

"And you said you're interested in the molds?"

"On that balcony above the riverbank are the ingot buggies, on rails like a train. Those things that look like empty cannon shells are the molds. They're six feet high, maybe three feet across, and hollow. Each buggy has three ingot molds on it. That worker you see there is pushing the ingot buggy into the building to the ladle. The workman on the pouring platform is called a ladleman and is using a rod to open and close a hole in the bottom of the ladle. Each mold is being filled with molten steel, which is called teeming. Then the molds move along for cooling and stripping."

"Then where to?"

"Well, this plant also has a primary rolling mill and a hot-strip mill. The end result is heavy plate."

She took a bite of her sandwich. "So where do you get your hundred and twenty seconds?"

Monck said, "The ladleman is filling one mold." The interior of the building glowed when the stopper was opened and hot steel poured into the mold. "Now the buggy is moving a few feet to position the next mold, then the next." Monck checked his watch. "Now all three are filled, and the buggy is automatically moving out from under the cradle, and the next one is rolling under it. It's an unvarying routine."

Monck looked at his watch. Another mold was teemed, sparks spraying around the mold's lip and falling to the floor in incandescent arcs. "Once the buggy hook takes over, the pusher turns his back on the molds to go back for another buggy. That's when I can jump out. I'll be in the last mold on my buggy, which means I've got exactly a hundred and twenty seconds between when the buggy pusher turns away and when molten steel is poured into the buggy's last mold."

"Won't the ladleman see you?"

"He's not looking anywhere but at the mold he's filling. And he's got dark glasses on to protect his eyes. He won't have any idea I'm there."

"Do you know where the engineering office is?"

"I saw the headquarters building near the south gate. It'll be in there. Once I'm on the mill floor, I won't be conspicuous. I'm dressed like everyone else there."

"Except for your face, and the scar."

"I'll walk with my chin to the ground." Monck had been timing all the while, and when the fiery liquid dropped into another mold, he glanced at his wristwatch. "A hundred and twenty-two seconds that time."

"I see a lot of other workers in there."

"Grinders, scarfers, the masonry gang, the melter. They won't see me either." He put the binoculars in their case. "I hope you can row."

When she began to fold the blanket, he said, "Leave it. We won't need it."

They climbed the bank, Monck with a hand on her elbow. When her shoe slid on a loose rock, he lifted her like a derrick and dropped her back to firmer ground. Her eyes widened at his strength. He didn't even slow down.

He held the bow. She knew to step over the gunwale to the

center of the rowboat so it would not rock. She took the oars, and he sat in the stern. She was a strong rower, and the shore receded quickly.

She dipped the oars mechanically, leaving a trail of expanding rings in the water behind them. Glancing over her shoulder every few strokes, she angled the bow upstream of the steel mill, compensating for the current. After a while her back and arms began to ache.

At the center of the stream, Monck again began to time the ingots. He mouthed the seconds. "A hundred and twenty-two."

She strained against the stronger current in the middle of the river. A hand slipped off an oar, and she wiped the perspiration from her hand on her slacks. She said, "When you get into the mold, use your watch. Don't rely on a mental count. The noise and the sparks will throw you off."

His eyes found hers. "A safety tip from someone who just held a shotgun on me is doubly appreciated." He grinned. "You're right, Meg. I'll use the watch."

They neared the south shore. Sweat freely coursed down Margarete's face and dripped off her chin. She was breathing heavily. Monck played with the rod and reel, counting again and again.

"The ladle is going back to the hearth for another load. It'll return to the pouring platform in a minute, and they'll start filling molds again."

A crew of six men pushed a long rod through the open-hearth furnace to clean the tapping hole. The liquid metal began to flow again into the ladle. Dusk had darkened the mill, and the molten steel bathed the melt shop in a gold glow that gradually weakened in the labyrinth of beams and cable farther away from the furnace. The flow of hot steel looked like an enormous orange neon tube. The hammering and grinding in the mill enveloped the boaters as they neared the buggy platform on the shore.

"How're you doing?" Monck asked.

"Tired," Margarete said between drafts of air. Her blouse was soaked through. "I'll get away all right, though."

She suddenly brought her gaze from the river and found him staring at her. She looked away quickly, but wondered about Monck's expression, one she hadn't seen before, one without the calculation. She pulled harder on the oars.

The mill loomed above them, its overhanging roof cutting off the darkening sky. Margarete pulled quickly on the left oar to spin the dinghy around. A few reverse strokes brought its stern to the shore. It ground against fist-size steel chunks that had dropped from the buggy platform over the years.

She searched for something to say. "Don't get cooked."

Monck gripped her damp arm, silently wishing them both luck, then jumped onto the shore and climbed the bank. The metal lumps acted like ball bearings, and the German repeatedly slid back toward the water. Finally on hands and knees he made it to one of the platform's support pillars, which was cross-braced to other pillars with diagonal boards. Above him was the buggy platform, made of four-by-fours on which rails had been laid.

Margarete rowed away from the shore. She remembered she was supposed to be fishing, so she slowed her pace. She was so wet with perspiration her feet seemed to be swimming inside her shoes. Her pulse pounded in her neck. The din of the mill was overwhelming and disorienting. She lost Monck for a moment, then spotted him again between the crossed bracings.

Little light remained under the buggy platform. Monck patted the pylon, a lesson learned at a pier in Benghazi, Libya, on a sapper's mission. It had been low tide, and he had cruelly cut his palms on the barnacles. A needless precaution, as this was fresh water. He pulled himself up to the crossed boards, then stood on one leg to reach for the platform. He chinned himself on the water side of the balcony, then kicked his leg so that his heel caught on the balcony ledge. He pulled himself higher, then rolled under the safety rail onto the platform.

He glanced over his shoulder. In the waning light, the river was indigo and vast. Margarete was forty yards from the bank, slowly drifting, the darkness blending her with the river. A tranquil setting, except for the roar of machinery behind him. On the upriver end of the platform, a buggy just returned from the melt shop carried empty molds still shimmering red with heat.

The German stepped onto the buggy that would be next into the mill. He planted his palms on the last mold's uneven rim, made rough by splashed and hardened steel. He levered himself up and raised his leg to the rim.

"Hello," Margarete Bayerlein called over the noise. "Nice night."

Monck's head jerked up. Margarete was looking at the west end of the buggy platform, thirty yards in front of Monck. Her smile was as bright as a boat's beacon. He followed her gaze.

A soldier had walked from the mill out onto the balcony for a smoke. He was wearing olive fatigues, corporal's stripes, and a holster. If he glanced to his right, he would see the German as plainly as a target on the rifle range. But at Margarete's voice, he straightened up and walked over the tracks to the railing.

"Hello yourself. Any luck out there?" He leaned on the rail and dug into a pocket for matches.

Monck swiftly swung both feet over the rim and dropped six feet into the throat of the mold.

A sudden pain in his leg was so ferocious that Monck lurched over, only to smash his head against the side of the mold. It felt as if a firebrand had been pressed against his left leg, searing tissue to the bone. He choked off a scream, but a garbled moan escaped. The pain crawled into his groin, then into his belly, nauseating him. The mold was too tight to reach down to his leg. His shoe filled with blood.

Stuck to the mold's base was a sixteen-inch shard, jutting up like a stalagmite. Pointed like an icepick and made of steel remaining after the mold had last been stripped, it had entered Monck's descending leg at the Achilles tendon, and his weight had driven it up and inside his calf to the spike's full length. Paralleling the shinbone, the point had stopped three inches below his knee.

The closeness of the mold and his swarming unconsciousness merged. Monck sagged against its tight sides. The pain ebbed as he slipped into blackness. With a desperate effort of will, he wrestled his mind back, and the coursing fire crawled up his calf as if he had just skewered himself again. His leg felt as if it were being amputated an inch at a time. Nothing below his knee but unspeakable pain.

Reason emerged only between jolts of agony. Pressed on all sides by the mold, Monck could not bend to feel his leg, nor could he see it or the cause of the torture. When he could not move his left foot, he thought it might be paralyzed, that the wound had severed a nerve. He tried again, and felt a tug and a rip in his calf. Another blast of pain.

Seconds passed before he could think again. He only knew that he was pinned. When he tried to raise his leg off the spike, his knee bumped into the mold. His head lightened, and the first tendrils of shock seeped down into the mold to wrap themselves around him. The mold swayed. His mind was full of cotton. He vaguely knew he might die here. And try as he might, he could not extract from the web of pain the reason he had fallen into the cavern.

When Monck disappeared inside the mold, Margarete Bayerlein had tried to gently brush off the soldier. But he insisted on keeping up his one-sided conversation. He was built like a reed, and he had a southern accent, the first Margarete had ever heard.

Apparently intent on fishing, she let the rowboat drift away from the platform. The guard got the hint, threw his butt into the river, and turned back into the mill.

The buggy pusher, who had a sixteen-year-old's scattering of acne, walked out from the pouring platform. His brown overalls were tattered from catching on jagged lumps of steel stuck to the molds. He laughed defensively when the corporal said the kid ought to get some honey on his stinger to clear up his complexion. The pusher leaned into Monck's buggy, and it rolled along the platform, then turned on the rails into the melt shop.

As night enveloped the plant, the orange glow from the teeming glittered off the river. Margarete rowed upstream, peering into the mill. The pusher was backlit by the radiant metal, reducing him to a silhouette. Monck's buggy collided with the one being filled. The pusher turned away to retrieve the next buggy. Margarete glanced at her watch. Two minutes from that instant.

But the corporal was not part of the calculation. He stood near Monck's ingot, yelling a joke at the ladleman, who laughed, but did not take his eyes from the mold he was filling, the last one on the buggy ahead of Monck's. Margarete felt the breath of fear.

Maybe the corporal was going to tell the Army's entire repertoire of coarse gags, Margarete thought wildly.

The ladleman punched the stopper closed with his rod, then the filled molds rolled toward the stripper on their carriage. Monck's buggy moved forward.

The corporal gestured crudely with a middle finger, which must have been another punch line, as the ladleman chortled again. At Margarete's distance, the laugh was inaudible, and the mill's cacophonous braying filled in for the laugh.

The joke had taken thirty seconds. Sparks billowed from the mold's rim and skidded across the platform, ignored by the ladleman as his gaze followed the molten steel into the first mold on Monck's cart.

The soldier stuffed his hands into his pocket and leaned closer to the shower of steel sparks. A few bounced off his shoes. He hollered again and craned his head back to laugh at his own gag. The ladleman cheerfully waved a hand at him, dismissing him. The soldier walked away from the ladleman toward the stripping station.

Sixty of Monck's seconds had drained away.

Now, now, Margarete silently urged him. She released her oars and stood cautiously in the center of the rocking boat, as if she might help Monck out of the mold.

Something was dreadfully wrong. Margarete slapped her hand over her wristwatch, a futile attempt to stop the passing seconds. The steel pour stopped. The first mold was filled. She could see nothing of Monck in the third mold. Nothing.

And ever so oddly, Margarete felt again the first pangs of widowhood, the wave of shock and anger and suffering. She sank to the boat's floorboards, gasping with sorrow for Monck, or Georg. She didn't know. The current leisurely carried the boat away from the mill.

With the spout now above the second mold on Monck's buggy, the ladleman opened the tap. A river of molten steel gushed into the mold, and sparks sprayed away from the rim.

A hot cinder landed on Monck shoulder, snapping him upright and lifting him out of shock's gentle haze. The pain below his knee was excruciating, yet he looked above him, up through the neck of the mold. A dazzling array of sparks were shooting across its mouth, like a meteor cluster on a clear night. Several cinders bounced into Monck's mold, searing his shirt and clearing his head.

He raised his hands to the lip of the mold and clasped the rim. When he again tried to raise his foot, the pain bit into his leg to the bone. He was still pinned. He clenched his teeth against the pain. And used it. He furiously kicked his spiked leg backward, and the lance snapped at its weakest point, just at his heel.

Monck curled with agony against the mold's side, but refused to release his grip on the lip. Cinders burned tracks across his hands, telling him his end was near. With the shard still in his leg like an extra bone, he frantically pulled himself up the wall of the mold. His head emerged, and he clamped his eyes against the rain of sparks from the next ingot mold. The ladleman, his peripheral vision blocked by protective goggles, didn't look away from his ingot.

The German levered his elbows under him and pushed against the rim. His buttocks slid onto the mouth ledge. As the ladleman hit the stopper of the buggy's second mold with his rod, Monck raised his pierced leg out of the mold, swayed back and forth a moment, and toppled down the side of the mold to the buggy, his good leg sliding out after him.

He bounced hard on the ragged steel nuggets covering the cart's deck. The ingot cart moved three feet forward. Monck crawled off the buggy to the melt shop's floor. His leg hit the cement, and a new wave of raging pain engulfed him.

As fluid steel poured into his mold, Monck lay on the shop floor, panting with agony, his eyes squeezed closed, unaware of the sparks falling on him or the melt shop's tumult or the soldier forty yards from him, repeating his jokes to a grinder.

Seconds before the drifting boat took her out of sight of the ingot platform, Margarete Bayerlein saw Monck rise, stagger at the mold's rim, and drop like a duffel bag to the floor.

Kurt Monck pushed himself off the floor and rolled into a sitting position. He looked at his leg. The shank of the serrated steel dagger protruded an inch from his calf, the blade disappearing up into his calf. The skin near it was shredded, and blood flowed steadily from the tear. He touched the steel pike, intent on pulling it out of his leg. A grenade of pain exploded in his leg. He left it in.

Seeing the wound for the first time oriented him. He wasn't bleeding much, just a little down into his shoe. He would live. He pushed himself along on his seat several feet to a pillar, then used it to gain his feet. The pain was now a steady throb, torturous, but manageable. He patted his wig to ensure it was on straight, then tried weight on the wounded leg. He could feel the spike shift under his skin. With sweat covering his face and eyes damp with pain, Monck limped away from the pouring platform.

He worked his way to the rear of the melt shop and discovered that if he walked on the side of his foot, he could almost eliminate the telltale shuffle. The wound was a drum of agony, dispensing portions of it with each step. Monck heard his teeth grind together over the clamor of the mill.

Unchallenged, he walked past the mold stripper, the soaking pit, and the rolling mill. Rows of steel blooms and billets lined the shop wall like soldiers at attention. He stopped at a row of lockers near the melt-shop door and lifted a white skivvy off a hook. He lifted his pant leg and wrapped it around his calf. It closed off the bleeding. Monck left the rolling mill, stepping out of the way of a forklift.

He walked between buildings, a breeze cooling his wet face. A line of Standard American Scout Cars, 4X4 White M3s, which had just been armored at the plant and were ready for shipment to the ETO, were parked along the south fence. A sentry idly walked his patrol in front of the scout cars. He strolled out of sight.

When he had been trying not to limp, Monck's entire body had been constricted, but now out of view of the workers, he relaxed, favoring his injured leg. A new wash of pain came over him, and he stumbled against a power pole, his jaw trembling.

The German held himself against the pole, searching for reserves of strength. He pushed himself away and began again, limping toward the River Iron Works headquarters. The pain gave time an accordion quality. An hour may have elapsed before he found the office door, or just a few minutes. He pushed through the swinging door.

The lights were still on. On his way out of the building, a quality-control supervisor wearing a tie and a lab coat passed Monck and said, "If you're looking for Mr. Kroger, he's in the coffee room."

Monck walked along the hall, reading the signs on the doors. The hall lights were doused as he reached the stairs. The last of the engineers and managers must have just left the building. He climbed the stairs, one step at a time, his movements brittle. Halfway down the second-floor hallway he found the engineer's office.

Glancing along the hallway, Monck pulled a small pocket knife from his pants pocket. He opened it and jimmied the door. It refused to spring open on his first attempt, but he wedged the blade farther up the narrow gap between the door and the frame, and he felt the bolt slide back into the lock. He opened the door.

The room was dimly illuminated by light from the yard lamps coming through the windows. Elevated drafting boards, tilted at an angle toward their stools, filled the room. Along the north wall was a row of horizontal cabinets. Monck limped to the cabinets and tried to blink away his double vision. His leg felt as if a magnesium flare had been planted beneath the skin.

Pulling open the first cabinet, he leafed through the engineering designs. The German looked for twenty minutes until he found the six sheets he wanted. They were beginning to yellow with age and were smudged at the corners. He rolled them tightly and pushed them down the right leg of his pants.

Returning to the hallway, he found several rags in a janitor's closet. He reentered the office to wipe a few drops of blood from the linoleum floor.

Moments later he threw the rags into a scrap bin and walked through the plant's main gate, in a stream of other swing-shift workers on their way to a mobile canteen across the street. The gate guards remained in their shack, concerned only with those walking into the plant. He held his hand in front of his chin, as if he were about to sneeze. No one looked at his face, nor did anyone see the sprinkling of blood deposited on the road at each step.

Margarete Bayerlein was waiting for him in the DeSoto half a block from the gate. She saw his limp and drove along the street to him. When she leaned across the seat to push open the passenger door, Monck collapsed into the car. He braced his hands on the dashboard, fighting vertigo from the loss of blood. Margarete was urgently asking something he didn't hear over the roar of his pulse in his ears.

He leaned back to pull the sheets from his pant leg.

She kept asking him questions, her voice agitated and concerned. She saw the clotted blood on his pants cuff and gently pulled the pant leg to look at the wound. "Oh, God," she said miserably.

"Help me unroll these," he said weakly.

They pulled the rolls open. They were the armoring blueprints for the Ferdinand Magellan, identical copies of the plans Secret Service Agent Mike O'Brien had shown to the Secretary of the Treasury the day before.

His head lolled against the seatback. His voice was faint. "If I don't die first, it looks like we're on our way."

24

OTTO STROOP STEPPED INTO THE BLUE
Eagle Tavern and wrinkled his nose. The tavern
and its patrons represented everything he had spent his life getting away from. The grime, the broken fingernails, the vulgar
language, the drunken laughs, the odor of dried sweat.

After leaving Bavaria with his mother, Stroop had spent years
in Pittsburgh. From one mill neighborhood to another. The specter of his failing the long climb from the milltown and returning
to those wretched people, German or American, haunted him.
By sheer dint of his intellect, he had managed to flee his background. But this place brought it all back.

He moved gingerly between captain's chairs toward the bar.
The Blue Eagle was full, as he knew it would be. Early in the
war, restaurateurs and tavern owners across the country had
noticed that when the war news was good, their places were full.
When bad, they couldn't sell a drink. And today, July 10, the
news was very good. American forces had just crushed the final
organized resistance on Saipan, and 27,000 Imperial Nipponese
soldiers had become good Japs. In Italy, the U.S. Eighty-eighth
Division had taken Volterra. And the American advance near

St. Lo continued at a fast pace. The men at the Blue Eagle merrily drank to these victories, and to anything else that came to mind.

Stroop signaled the bartender. "A beer, and kindly make sure the glass is clean."

The bartender pointed to a sign behind the bar reading "Be Kind to Our Help. Customers We Can Always Get." The sign was a plea from the owner because labor had been in short supply since Pearl Harbor. The barman drew Stroop's beer and passed it to him. If he thought Stroop was out of place in the Blue Eagle, with his bow tie, vest, and meticulously clipped goatee, he made no remark.

Stroop took the beer without giving thanks. He was in no mood for pleasantries, having spent the entire day at the B&O and Pennsylvania Railroad offices, studying four years of shipping schedules and train logs. He had presented his Georgetown University credentials to the office managers and said he was drafting a paper for the ODT. With pleasure and self-importance, the managers had escorted him to the companies' libraries, assuring him their railroads were doing everything in their power to defeat the Axis. Buffoons.

But he had found the pattern. Brilliance on his part, actually. Berlin would be generous. And there might be more information. He would return again to the railroad companies.

Stroop surveyed the Blue Eagle through cigarette smoke roiled by the overhead fans. Over the bar was a full-color copy of Otto Becker's lithograph showing General Custer's last moments, distributed by Anheuser-Busch to taverns in 1895 and still seen in thousands of them. Under the glass on the bar were several pages of a 1941 *Time* article entitled "How to Tell Your Friends from the Japs." Rows of steins glittered from glass shelves stacked on top of each other on the back bar. A hand-printed sign taped to the bar mirror announced "Whiskey out in Baltimore. Shortage headed this way. Drink up while you can." Another sign was wrapped around a stein on the bar. It read "Tipping is not a city in China." The day's take, two war nickels with the funny feel, were at the bottom of the glass.

Near the back wall of the tavern was a pool table, with deep tracks worn in the linoleum around its base. Two players leaned on their cue sticks, waiting for another to line up his shot. They were playing cutthroat. From the jukebox came Harry James's "Sleepy Lagoon." Undoubtedly more robust fare would also be there, including "Remember Pearl Harbor" and "Johnny Dough-boy Found a Rose in Ireland."

Fifty men sat around small tables covered with pitchers and steins. Two beleaguered waitresses tried to replenish the pitchers. Many patrons drank boilermakers, their shot glasses emptied in one toss. Stroop searched the faces. Their similarity was disheartening. Skin darkened by sun, brown teeth, shaggy haircuts, hands calloused by lifetimes of work. Shaped by the strain of hard labor, these workmen had grown to look alike.

Stroop found his man, sitting alone at a table near the restroom. He crossed the room, his draft held high to avoid spilling.

"Mr. Bell? Remember me?"

Bell looked up from his beer. His eyes grew with fear, and his lips parted as if he were going to say something. Instead, he looked quickly away and seemed to return his full attention to his Budweiser.

Stroop pulled out the chair opposite Bell and sat down. He placed his glass on the table. "It's been a long time, Mr. Bell."

"I told you never to get ahold of me again, Smith." Bell's voice was strained. His features were elongated, and he had heavy pouches under his eyes. His face was an unhealthy white, as if he were recovering from an illness that should have been mortal. His hair was matted, and his fingernails were so blackened with grease they looked painted. His overalls were streaked with brown-green stains, as he had used them as a wipe rag, and one shoulder strap hung loose, almost into his glass.

"May I buy you a beer, Mr. Bell?" Stroop asked, enunciating precisely, his comment on the rabble.

"You can't buy me anything. You already tried that, and I told you to go to hell."

In 1940, a friend had taken George Bell to an America First meeting in Washington. Bell went along because they were serving free beer after the speeches. His name was taken at the door, and several weeks later Otto Stroop had approached him at the Blue Eagle. For three hundred dollars, Bell had agreed to describe the automobiles in the Secret Service garage. It almost seemed harmless. Stroop had met Bell once every month for a year and a half. Each time Bell talked about the limousines, and each time Stroop gave him three hundred dollars.

With all Stroop's probing and testing around Washington, D.C., George Bell, an unimportant auto mechanic who never set foot in the White House, was the closest the German Abwehr ever came to placing someone near the president. And Bell had made it clear that he would never do anything other than talk about the autos.

After Pearl Harbor, Bell had told Stroop to stay away from him. The mechanic liked to think it was newly fired patriotism, but in fact, with the United States's declaration of war, he had realized he was playing a dangerous game. That the man with the goatee might someday return with some demand or threat had haunted him for a while, but the years passed, and Bell had allowed himself to almost forget "Smith."

Stroop signaled a waitress anyway. Bell looked quickly around the tavern, then asked nervously, "What do you want?"

"Money is on my mind," Stroop answered, sipping his beer. "I have too much of it and want to unburden myself of it."

Bell anxiously cleared his throat. "Smith, I told you way back in 1941 that I don't..."

"I have a proposition for you, one I think you'll be very interested in."

Bell intercepted the beer from the waitress before she could place it on the table. He downed half of it in a gulp and wiped his mouth with the back of his hand. It calmed him. "I'm not interested in anything you have to say."

"I've kept up with you, you know." Stroop stared across the

table at him. 'You've badly missed the money you earned from me. After you broke off our relationship, you went into debt and can't seem to get out of it."

Stroop pulled a notepad from his inside vest pocket and reviewed a few figures. "It's my guess you now make sixty dollars a week at the garage, and you lose about a hundred a week at Louis Del Rosa's poker table. I don't know how you make up the difference, but probably by small-time stealing, small-time blackmarketing, or small-time liquor running. Whatever it is, I'm quite sure it is small-time, as that is your nature."

Bell's glass slowly descended to the table. "I never liked you much, and I'm liking you less and less."

"You owe four hundred dollars on your Ford coupe, and you missed the last three payments. A midnight reclaimer has been looking for it for several weeks. You pay sixty dollars a month rent on a place where you share a bathroom, and are a month in arrears. Your landlady has said she'll padlock the door this Saturday if you haven't come up with the cash. And finally, thirty days ago you borrowed three hundred dollars from one Phillip Miller, and Little Phil, as he is known in your circle, is charging twenty percent per week, and after next week he'll start adding one of your knees a week to the interest. Is this all fairly accurate, Mr. Bell?"

Bell tried to return the stare, but had to look away.

"But you are in such desperate straits that if I bought you another beer, you'd sit here and listen to the rest of the facts I've collected about your miserable life since we last met. They're a litany of desperation. You are a squalid Dickens character without the charm."

Stroop put his elbows on the table. "I want you to listen carefully, Mr. Bell, because what I'm offering will never come along again in your life."

Bell finished his beer and loudly rattled his glass on the table. His eyes were slits that opened quickly when Stroop took a manila envelope from his coat pocket and put it near Bell's beer.

"There is a thousand dollars in this envelope."

Forty years of cynicism still encrusted the mechanic's face. His hand ventured toward the envelope, but stopped short of it, as if he expected a booby trap. The fellow in the beard didn't move, so he lifted the envelope and pulled open the flap. Inside were fifties, a lot of them.

"A thousand?"

"That's right, Mr. Bell." Stroop took the envelope from the mechanic. The professor's gaze was penetrating. "And in that miniature mind of yours, you have realized, dimly and with unprecedented effort, the possibility that there is more money where this came from."

Bell laughed caustically. "That's a tidy sum, but if you think I'm going to knock off someone, you've got me mixed up with some gangster." Bell rose from his chair.

Stroop said quickly, "You still work at the White House garage. All you have to do is make one small adjustment on one of the cars there, and you'll get another four thousand."

Bell paused. Encouraged, Stroop went on, "Think of it. Four thousand dollars for two minutes of work."

"No deal. The Secret Service takes care of those cars like they were jewelry or something. I'm not risking anything for you anymore." The mechanic turned to leave.

Stroop's words caught him. "I was hoping I wouldn't have to bring this up, Mr. Bell. But you haven't thought of the other side of the coin. Four years ago, I kept a record in a notebook of every nickel I ever gave you. The same little book also has a full list of the many pieces of information you gave me. If you walk away, I'm going to turn it over to the FBI tomorrow. You'll hang from a gallows."

Bell lowered himself unsteadily into the seat. "You wouldn't do that."

"You have my word on it. You'll be arrested before you even show up for work tomorrow."

Bell glanced desperately at his empty beer glass. He tried to sound brave. "If you think I'll plant something..."

Now it was Stroop's turn to laugh deliberately. "Nothing like that. All I'm talking about is a small adjustment on one of the cars."

"And then what?"

"And then you never hear from me, or anyone else, again. And in one fell swoop, all your money problems are solved."

"What are you up to?"

"You've already guessed I can't tell you that."

George Bell dug in an ear with a finger. "How long do I have to think about it?"

"You just had all the time you're getting. Yes or no, Mr. Bell."

The mechanic stared for a long moment at the professor. "I don't have much of a choice."

Stroop's head lifted, allowing him to assess Bell down his nose. He handed Bell the envelope. "You'll get the rest of it when we meet again. But I'll give you a warning, Mr. Bell. I realize I don't look like much, sitting here. But I have a partner in this venture, who'll be in town shortly. He makes your banker, Little Phil, look like an amateur."

Stroop's next words were said kindly, almost sweetly. "Should you try to bilk him, he'll spread you out over a mile of roadway and leave you for the crows. The gallows would be nothing compared to him."

25

LITTLE HAS CHANGED IN THE VALLEY since the first settlers arrived two hundred years ago. Seen from the mountain south of Allamuchy Township, the north-central New Jersey terrain appears to have handily weathered man's efforts to harvest timber, graze cattle, and grow corn. A pasture can be seen here and there, and a few roofs are noticeable, but the churches, barns, graveyards, roads, and grazing flocks hide below clouds of red oak and birch leaves.

Quakers settled the valley sometime around 1745, and the Methodists came later. But soon large estates controlled the valley. The Ryan, Stuyvesant, and Rutherfurd families soon owned most of the land. The town grew around their holdings, as medieval towns grew around English castles. Most of the townspeople serviced the estates.

In 1882, the Lehigh and Hudson River Railroad laid tracks through Allamuchy, and a census six years later showed there were twenty-eight houses, two stores, two grist mills, a train station, a blacksmith and wheelwright shop, a post office, a hotel, and a creamery.

By the Second War, gas stations had replaced the grist mills, but little else had changed. Looking north from the mountain, the railroad runs along the valley left to right, crossing the Pequest River at Long Bridge, where the trains often stop at the creamery. The folks in New Jersey call a stream a river and a hill a mountain. True to form, Long Bridge is not long, just several car lengths.

A mile east of Long Bridge is the railroad station, where Johnsonburg Road crosses the tracks. The two-room station guards one seldom-used siding. A short way south on Johnsonburg Road, toward the mountain, is Allamuchy, camouflaged by its trees.

Overlooking the town is Tranquility, Lucy Mercer Rutherfurd's estate. Built in 1905 near a large, hushed pond, the mansion has fifty rooms in three stories. Five steep gables face the circular driveway. The brick building would be ponderous were it not for the many white-trimmed windows and the window bays extending from the north and south wings. Third-story French doors exit onto balconies which have views of the placid valley. The massive front door is guarded by cement planters filled with carefully pruned junipers. Attached to the west end of the mansion are the servants' quarters, made of the same brick and slate, yet less significant and partially hidden behind white birch trees.

Sitting behind a bay window in the second-floor den, Lucy Mercer Rutherfurd penned a note on embossed stationery. She used a goose quill, frequently dipping the tip into an ink bottle. She smiled once at a memory, then signed her name. Her hair was pinned in back of her head, but a few curled strands had floated free to accent her neck. Like water in the pond behind the mansion, her eyes changed from blue to gray as a cloud passed in front of the sun outside her window. It was the noon hour, and the alabaster color of her cheeks was tinted with rose, the color of expectation.

She was a part of the room, as sumptuous and as complicated. Her desk was from China. The writing surface was ebony with a village scene inlaid with malachite, coral, and jade. The den walls were papered with silk, decorated with lively hand-painted chrysanthemums. A pair of Classical Revival armchairs were under the bay windows. A rock-crystal chandelier, modified for electric light thirty years before, hung from the ceiling. Filled with freshly cut roses, French Empire urns sat on both sides of the door.

She folded the note, her slender hands working quickly as they put it into an envelope. She glanced at the grandfather clock next to her desk. She reached again for the pen, then put it down. Her fingers tapped the table. She rose to gaze through the window at the valley, at the soft landscape of trees and the hazy hills in the distance. Over the years this view had been her friend and confidant, but today it offered nothing to ease her impatience.

A light knocking came from the den's door. "Mrs. Rutherfurd?"

"Yes, Elaine?"

"The White House is calling, ma'am."

She quickly lifted the telephone receiver from the desk. "Yes, this is she."

Five seconds elapsed, during which she returned to her chair. Her mouth widened into a lovely smile. Her excitement changed her satin voice to that of a little girl. "Hello, Franklin."

Her marvelous grin grew. "Oh, that's wonderful. Tell me when exactly, and I'll have everything ready for you."

She laughed, sounding as if a breeze had brushed the chandelier. A blush of intense emotion suffused her face. "Friday, in the morning? So early again? Franklin, that's wonderful."

"How long? . . . An hour and a half?" Her expression changed. "No, it isn't much time." She brightened again. "But I wasn't expecting you to stop at all, not on your way to the convention. It's just wonderful."

She listened for a moment, then asked, "What about all the people on the train, just sitting there, not knowing what's going on?"

Lucy laughed throatily. "God, you're wicked. I know you're President of the United States, but that doesn't mean you can ignore all those people on POTUS. . . . It does?"

She giggled. "That's terrible. I don't know where you've learned these things. Not from me, certainly. Probably from Stalin, if what you tell me about him is true."

She listened again, then said, "Everybody in the township knew about it last time. This is a tiny place. Even if no one recognized you then, as unlikely as that was, the Secret Service agents who showed up here tipped the townfolks off. The dozen gray-suited, square-jawed police types sitting elbow-to-elbow at Ed Hayden's soda fountain, when old Mrs. Crampton is usually the only person to visit him all day, might have given them a clue."

Another pause. "It doesn't bother me, Franklin. I don't care about that." Her voice saddened. "What are you going to tell . . . Hyde Park? Last time when she asked why your train was on this side of the river, you said the Secret Service didn't want to risk taking the Ferdinand Magellan over the New York Central's Hell Gate Bridge. That didn't sound very convincing. . . . The same thing again?"

She covered her eyes with a hand. "All I care about is seeing you."

She smiled suddenly, then laughed again. "I know Fala doesn't eat horsemeat. I'll tell the kitchen again."

A long, silent moment. "Until Friday. I can't wait." She whispered her special goodbye, just as she had for thirty years. "*Au revoir*, Franklin."

A string of bells tied to the door jingled when Wren and Garvin entered the Ohio Boat Repair and Salvage Company's office in Louisville. The building was on the river shore near a dock where a pushboat and a cabin cruiser were moored.

The office was comfortably nautical, with a handmade model of the U.S. *Constitution* resting on the proprietor's desk and a ship's-wheel clock on the wall. Framed Ohio River navigation charts covered another wall. Windows looked out on the river.

Mounted on a stand near the back door was the company's treasure, a Siebe diving rig, a one-piece canvas-and-rubber suit under a brass breastplate and helmet. The helmet had round windows facing all directions. The glittering brass looked as if the owner polished it daily. Around the suit's waist was a tool belt, and at the bottom of the stand were a pair of lead boots weighing forty pounds. The suit was so carefully placed over the stand that it appeared a man was standing rigidly in the diving suit, patiently waiting to be lowered over the side.

The bells chimed again. Wren turned to an outstretched hand.

"I'm Art Erickson. You must be the Secret Service people I called."

Wren introduced himself and Garvin and, putting away his silver star, asked, "You said the woman was in here about one o'clock?"

"Standing right where you are. Nice-looking girl, too, though I can't say as I took my eyes off her handful of money very long. Paid cash on the barrelhead."

Erickson looked like a diver, with a bellows chest. He had so much hair on his arms it resembled fur, and it grew up under his short-sleeved shirt, uninterrupted up his back to his head. His eyes were the same color as a husky's, luminous gray with black flecks. His five-o'clock shadow was so dark it made his face look oily. Perhaps to offset his hirsute appearance, his black hair was carefully combed and parted.

Tom Garvin asked, "How'd you spot her?"

"I didn't. But the fellow who was driving, who didn't come into the shop, got out of the car for a moment to help her put the suit into the truck. It was him I recognized."

Erickson walked to his desk. He held up the *Louisville Times.* "Over coffee every Monday morning, the crew and I usually chew the fat over the weekend sports. But this morning, all we talked about was this Kurt Monck. Me and my men studied this face, never thinking he'd show up here. My caulker, Dudley Wilbur, said the POW looked tough as nails. Now that I've seen him in the flesh, I'd have to agree."

"How long did you look at his face?" Garvin asked skeptically.

"Two seconds, maybe three. But that's long enough. He was

wearing brown pants and a white shirt, open at the collar. His hair was longer than in the photo. And I clearly saw the white ridge of skin on his chin you can see here in the *Times* photo. You'll be making a big mistake to doubt me."

Wren said, "We don't. It's just that the POW has been wearing disguises until he showed up here."

"Maybe he's getting careless," Erickson offered.

"That's unlikely. Show me what the woman bought."

Erickson stepped across the room to a cabinet near the diving suit. He pulled out a rubberized diving suit. "I don't know if you've seen one of these before. They're new, and I had to buy mine direct from the same company that sells them to the Navy." He held it up to his chest. "It's a wet suit."

"I've seen them before," Wren said, pressing the pliant black material between a thumb and forefinger. "Did she buy the vest and pants?"

"Both pieces. And a face mask and snorkel."

"Any air canisters or a regulator?"

"Nope. And no fins, either."

"Didn't you think it peculiar that a woman would walk into a salvage shop and buy a wet suit?" Garvin asked.

Erickson drew a finger across his upper lip. "Looking back, I suppose I should've. But money doesn't flow freely around here. I was only too happy to make a sale. I didn't think twice about it until the POW climbed out of the car."

"Do you remember the car they were in?"

"Black DeSoto. Kentucky plates, but I didn't get a number."

"And the direction they were heading?" Garvin asked.

"Back to town. At least, that's the way the road out front goes."

"What was the woman wearing?" Wren asked.

"Black pants, just like a man, if you can imagine. And a red blouse. I don't remember anything else."

Wren leaned toward Erickson, as if to hear his thoughts. "What about the color of her eyes?"

"Can't tell you."

Garvin thought he saw his boss deflate.

The agents thanked Erickson, and as they got into their automobile, Garvin said, "First he's got plastic explosives, and now he's got a wet suit. Chief Wilson isn't going to like that combination at all."

Wren shoved the gearshift into first. He had the thousand-yard stare of a weary infantryman. The red-haired agent needled him. "Why don't we call her Orphan Annie?"

"Pardon?"

"In your attempt to reconstruct the lovely but missing Margarete Bayerlein, you've discovered she apparently has no eye color. Just large white circles, like Orphan Annie. It seems to me you're looking pretty hard to fill in those empty eyes."

"Lay off, junior."

Garvin grinned, his pink face alight. "Who're you chasing, anyway?"

Wren answered coldly, "Kurt Monck is going to find that out soon enough."

O'Brien stood quickly when Frank Wilson entered the Secret Service office in the White House basement. O'Brien asked, "You heard, Chief?"

"Helen told me the news when I got back to my desk a couple minutes ago." Wilson ran his hand through his meager hair. "On his trip to Hyde Park and the convention, the president is going to stop in New Jersey Friday? Christ, I can't believe it."

"He called me with the announcement two hours ago. I wish I had the time to speculate about what hold that woman has over the president, to have him stop in Nowhere, New Jersey, now of all times."

Wilson nodded, his mouth tight with concern. "I'll do all our speculating about that relationship, Mike. Which is none at all. I've got an appointment with him in ten minutes. I'll let him know in no uncertain terms what we think of this surprise. And I'm going to request, plead if I need to, that he cancel the detour."

The Secret Service chief moved to the back wall of O'Brien's office, all of three steps. "This is the town of Allamuchy, as I recall."

"Taken from a Navy plane at our request the day before President Roosevelt's last visit there." The enlarged photograph was the size of an office window.

"Tell me what you've arranged there," Wilson ordered.

"A train would normally stop at the station, here." He pointed to the intersection of the Lehigh and Hudson River Railroad and Johnsonburg Road. "But we're going to stop at Long Bridge, where there's nothing but a creamery. We'll offload there, then the president will be driven down Alphano Road toward Allamuchy, about a mile and a half toward town. Instead of going through town, we're going to take him on this farm road, between these two barns, and along the east side of Allamuchy, up the hill to Tranquility."

"Those barns..."

"They'll have our people in them," O'Brien said. "And there won't be a building in Allamuchy that doesn't have one of us inside it. Not a building."

"Where're you getting the men?"

"I started calling the regional offices an hour ago. Chicago, New York, Atlanta. They'll start arriving in Allamuchy this evening."

Wilson nodded approvingly. "What about Mrs. Rutherfurd's home?"

"She's been very cooperative in the past. I spoke with her a few moments ago, and she has no objection to posting agents inside the mansion, and others on the grounds."

The chief drew his hand across the blowup. "There's a hundred places to hide in this photo. Under every tree."

"There'll be more sharpshooters than birds in those trees. Allamuchy is going to be choking with our people."

Wilson continued to stare at the enlargement. "As you know, Wren reported a short while ago that Monck now has a wet suit. Doesn't that fact and his plastic explosives confirm that he has targeted a bridge?"

"As we told Secretary Morgenthau, we've got the bridges covered. But I'm going one step further. I've contacted Rear Admiral David Rohan of the Seabees. Under all bridges over water deep enough to hide a diver, the Seabees are going to detonate several cut-down, waterproofed Mark III grenades three minutes before POTUS arrives. The Susquehanna, Schuylkill, Delaware, anywhere Monck could hide. Not enough blast to damage a bridge, but enough to bring a diver to the surface, dead."

Wilson allowed a smile. "I hadn't thought of that." He again brought his hand up to the photograph. "What about this body of water behind Mrs. Rutherfurd's mansion?"

"That's Allamuchy Pond. It'll get the same treatment."

"Is there any way to get from the pond into the mansion? A water or sewer line?"

O'Brien shook his head. "We searched last time. Nothing at all. And we'll have several people between the pond and her home."

"All right, Mike. If you think of anything else, do it. Don't wait for my approval. Anything new from Wren and Garvin?"

"They're sifting through the fourteen calls they've received claiming sightings of Monck. It seems anybody with a scar on his face is fair game. One helpful Louisville citizen turned in his brother, who has a harelip."

Wilson looked at his wristwatch. "The president is expecting me now." He squared his tie and wet his lips.

"Impress on him that his safety may depend on going right through to Hyde Park, skipping Allamuchy and Mrs. Rutherfurd altogether."

Wilson cleared his throat, an orator preparing for a speech, then left the office, turning toward the stairway.

O'Brien returned to his scheduling. The meeting must have lasted only a few minutes, because the first time he looked up from his work, Frank Wilson was back, leaning against the door-frame for support.

The color had been wrung out of him. "Perhaps you should

have warned me how sensitive a subject Mrs. Rutherfurd is with the president."

"How would I know?" O'Brien protested. "I've never mentioned her name aloud to the president in all the years I've been here. I know my role. He plays the tune and I dance."

"Yes, well, I was certainly dancing up there. In a nutshell, POTUS is going to stop at Allamuchy for an hour and a half on Friday. There will be no changes in that plan. Absolutely none."

26

MONCK LAY ON HIS STOMACH, A PANT leg cut off at the knee. Margarete hovered over him, wondering where to begin. The steel shard looked like a giant leech that had crawled up under the skin of his calf, a monstrous parasite working its way along a vein to Monck's heart.

His eyes were locked open, and sweat poured from his face. They were staying in a cottage motel in Cincinnati, in the white bungalow nearest the street. The room was sparsely furnished, and the thin rug was bunched under Monck's hands. Muscles on his leg stood out like rope wrapped around a fence post. His breath came in irregular gulps.

She held the scalpel she had used on him on Bainbridge Island, and she lowered it to his leg. "The sliver is jagged at the lower end, like a series of fishhooks. It's not going to just pull out."

He released his lower lip. "Sliver?" His voice wavered. "It feels like a roll of barbed wire in there."

"Brace yourself." The blade dipped into the skin. Monck jerked once, then lay still as she opened the leg around the shard to clear tissue away from tiny barbs on the steel's shank.

Through clenched teeth, Monck said, "I asked you not to cut

me again. But here you are once more, knife in hand."

He might have intended his words as levity, but his voice cracked. She gently spread the flesh away from the shard, then gripped the end of it between a thumb and finger. She pulled it firmly, and it slid out of Monck's leg.

"Got it," she said, delighted. She lay it in front of him on the carpet. He stared at it while she cleaned the wound as best she could, probing along the wound canal with a tissue swab soaked in hydrogen peroxide. His leg shivered uncontrollably under the swab, and she had to hold it with an arm to complete the disinfecting. She wrapped the leg in a bandage puttee. To her surprise, Monck immediately rose and walked across the small room to the table, his limp almost imperceptible.

"Does it hurt?" she asked ridiculously, still sitting on the floor.

He lifted a metal file from the table. "I've been hurt worse."

"My," she mocked, "what a very brave thing to say."

After a moment he smiled. "Excruciating pain brings that out in me. My calf is killing me, but I don't have much time to think about it."

"Are we on a schedule?"

Absorbed with the tool, Monck might not have heard her. He lifted the aluminum frying pan she had purchased for him, after looking for a black-market outlet for two hours. Aluminum was no longer in the stores. Monck began scraping the pan, collecting the filings on a newspaper below. He drew the file across the pan with powerful strokes, quickly wearing away the pan's side. A silver cone of aluminum powder grew on the table. Next to the newspaper was a can of chromium oxide, used as a pigment, she had bought that day at a paint store. Also on the table were several bottles of India ink, and a small battery with a homemade switch, the Geronimo blasting caps, and a short length of magnesium ribbon.

She waited in silence, the file's scratching filling the room. She abruptly put her hand on his, stopping the tool. "Why don't you tell me why we're crossing the country? What is your mission?"

He looked at her, then at the far wall of the small room. His face was hard with thought, an expression that told her nothing.

"You must know by now that I'm with you on this. I could have escaped many times. I didn't. How can I help you when you keep me in the dark?"

"I'm going to kill a man," Monck said quietly, making one stroke with the file, as if for finality.

She should have known all along. Perhaps she had. She persisted. "Who? Why?"

He looked directly at her, as if searching for understanding. "The man's name is Klaus Kauffman. He was employed as an engineer in the Luftwaffe Technical Department, and he defected to the British, carrying with him a bombsight called the Korten Four. The British now use copies of it in their Lancasters. The Americans brought him to the States to hide him from retaliation, and he's now living near Washington, D.C."

"And you're going to take his life." It was not a question. Margarete was staring intently at him.

"Kauffman is a traitor. He did incalculable damage to Germany, and he will now pay the price."

Monck resumed his filing, his face impassive.

She should have been horrified, she thought. To kill. The gravest of all offenses. Yet, wasn't that what she had been doing for years? Spying on passing gunboats, sending encoded messages, lying to a daughter. A bit farther from the target, but to the same effect. Why is the woman who makes the bomb on the production line less a warrior than the bombardier? Faced with Monck's revelation, she did not enjoy the pleasure of numbness or outrage. She had been a warrior all along.

The rasp stopped again. "Wren. What would he be like?"

"The man whose name you heard on the taxi radio? How would I know that? Why do you ask?"

"He is chasing us. I'd like to meet him someday. Face to face. At the hardware store where we picked up Leffler, there was a sniper in the tree behind us. Did you see him?"

"Good God, no."

"The sun reflected off his scope, and I saw it in the mirror. Wren wasn't going to wait to ask us any questions. I want you to remember that."

"Then I do know something about Wren. He's a lot like you."

The corners of his mouth turned up. "Maybe."

The filing began again. The mound of aluminum dust grew.

"Do you have a family? A wife, maybe?" Her question was out before she could stop it.

"Are you thinking of your sister? I'm sorry she wasn't in Louisville."

She shook her head. "I wasn't thinking of her at all. She and her husband are in Pascagoula for two months, down in Mississippi. He's a marine engineer working on destroyers."

"Does he work for the Reich?"

"He's as much a Yankee as if he'd been born here. I think he works those eighty-hour weeks for the U.S. Navy to excise his German heritage. I asked about you. Do you have anyone waiting for you?"

He lowered the file and pan. "No one, no."

"Why no wife?"

He pursed his mouth. "I'd like to think it's because I didn't have the time or the chance." He smiled ruefully. "Since '39, I've gone where I've been told, and there weren't many women in those places."

She smiled. "Your parents must be getting anxious about you, getting older and still a bachelor."

"Only my mother and sister are still alive. At least, they were when I heard last."

"Didn't they write to you in the POW camp?"

"They think I died in the African desert."

Her face cleared. "Died? Why? Haven't you written them?"

His gaze seemed to lose focus. "I don't usually believe in premonitions. But when I left Africa, I knew I'd never see Germany again, that I would die in America. So there was no point in telling them I had survived."

"You have no one, then?" she asked.

He closed his eyes briefly. "When I was in Libya, my fellow soldiers thought I had a talent for desert warfare. I had a reputation for being good with the weapons and planning. But what I truly excelled at was being alone."

"How does that help?"

"The desert is easier if you don't need anyone."

"So you don't need kindness or comfort?" she asked, running her hand along her bare arm, as if warming herself. "You're either very strong or are fooling yourself. Either way, I envy you."

She hesitated, breaking off her stare at him. The two weeks with Monck rushed by her, a confusing stream of jarring images. She had been with him constantly, yet she had never been more alone. Her eyes filmed. She said abruptly, "I drew all the strength I could from Mary, but sometimes it wasn't enough. And it isn't enough right now."

Her gaze fell to the floor, and her thoughts were so distant that she was unaware of Monck's approach until his arm was around her shoulder.

He whispered, "I'm not much at offering comfort, but I'd like to try."

She nodded. They sat next to each other on the rug a long while, her face pressed against his neck and her hands on his chest. He gently rocked her.

Margarete would look back and wonder when it began, perhaps when she started drawing her fingernails across the light hair just beneath his collar, a small caress she was unaware of giving, one remembered from better days. Her hand moved to the nape of his neck to gently massage him.

His lips moved against her temple. She could feel his slight breath, then the brush of his mouth against her hair. He slowly brought her against his chest so that her breasts touched him. It had been so long since her nipples firmed for anything but the Northwest chill that they startled her. She arched her back, a slight motion, pressing them on him.

He tentatively kissed her lips, silently asking her. The remembered sensations flooded her as she explored his mouth and passed her hands under his shirt, feeling the taut skin, rediscovering lost stirrings.

Her imagination sculptured Monck, lightening his hair and his eyes, setting his mouth at a new angle, rubbing away the scar on his chin. As he carefully unbuttoned her blouse, she transformed him, one treasured memory at a time. When his hands cupped her breasts, she almost gasped the old name, the name of the man she had loved all her life.

Monck said in a low voice, "Meg, please don't see me as someone else."

Startled at his accuracy, she began to pull away.

He said, "I haven't been with a woman often enough these past years for you to wish me away. Make love to me, not someone else." His voice softened. "Please, Meg."

And she did, letting him lift her to the bed and undress her. He was only the second man in her life to touch her where he did, and to kiss her where he did. And when they became one, it was Kurt Monck, not a memory, who was strong and loving, rocking against her and bursting within her.

An hour later she lay next to him, his thigh warm against hers. She thought he was asleep, as his breathing was deep. Cast through the window, the moon's light reduced the room to shades of gray. She wondered why moonlight always made things seem simple.

She was sure she would follow Monck, even if he had come up with the preposterous lie about a bombsight and an escaped traitor. He must have known she would see through the story, and in telling it was at the same time apologizing for it.

His threat remained. Following him was the only way she would see Mary again. But now there was something else. A rebirth of long-dead emotions. Lying next to him in the moonlight, she knew it was clear. She would stay with him.

Margarete always awoke with a start, going from sleep to full alertness in an instant. She was still on her side, facing the window. The light of early morning made her squeeze her eyes closed for a moment.

She was alone. The night had passed so quickly it seemed that Kurt Monck had simply vanished from the bed. She played her hand over the spot where he had slept, and it was cold. He must have gotten up while it was still dark, and was away on one of his errands he would not tell her about.

She showered, then peeled and ate an orange while she dried her hair with a towel. She tried without success to smooth the wrinkles out of her pants with her hand. She opened the door slowly, looking up and down the street before briskly walking to a newspaper box on the corner. She dropped a nickel into the box and pulled out a copy of Tuesday morning's *Cincinnati Enquirer*.

Monck's photograph was on the front page. They must be publishing it everywhere the American authorities thought he might be. The two-column headline read "POW Still at Large." She had turned back to the building before the second headline brought her to a sudden standstill. "Accomplice's Daughter Found in San Diego."

Margarete felt as if she had been clubbed, and she took a jerking step forward to prevent herself from falling to the asphalt. She mouthed the headline, trying to will it away. The words of the article filled her like a poison, weakening her. The eleven-year-old daughter of the Bainbridge Island, Washington, woman believed to be traveling with the escaped German POW had been found in San Diego after an intensive FBI search. The girl, Mary Bayerlein, had apparently traveled to California on a Greyhound bus, arriving eight days ago. The girl was caught leaving a grocery store on Market Street near the Navy Supply Depot in San Diego. The FBI would not reveal if they knew where or with whom the girl had stayed during the previous eight days. The girl was cooperating with the authorities.

Fighting the exhaustion of hopelessness, Margarete ran back into the building. The newspaper spilled from her hands as she swept her toothbrush and comb from the sink and threw them into the open suitcase at the foot of the bed. She pulled her few clothes from the closet, not bothering to take them off the wood hangers before dropping them into the case.

Running her hands through her hair, then holding her head as if she were in pain, she stared at the open suitcase. Utter panic worked on her, making her breath come in short gulps. She had no idea how she would get to San Diego, or what she would do once there, or how she would find her daughter. She had nothing but the certainty that she had to be with Mary. She folded the suitcase and snapped the locks. She lifted it and turned to the door.

Kurt Monck stood in the doorway, a copy of the *Enquirer* in his hand. He said, "The story is a fake."

Margarete rushed at him, hoping to bowl him out of her way. He easily pushed her back into the room.

"Let me go," she yelled. "Goddam you, let me go." Her words ended in a wail.

He held her by the shoulders. "Meg, listen to me. The newspaper story is a plant. This Wren has put a false story in the newspaper to scare you, hoping you'll run from me, or turn me in."

She pushed again against him, this time halfheartedly. "My girl is in trouble."

"No, she isn't." He brought her against him. Her shoulders trembled as she struggled for control. "Wren is desperate. He wants to split us up. He knows no other way than to strike at you through your daughter."

She breathed deeply, wanting to believe Monck. "How do you know?"

"I'm learning about this Wren. It's what he'd do."

She stepped away from him, fury crossing her face. "In other words, you're just guessing the article is made up. You don't know anything." She moved again toward the door, determination narrowing her mouth.

He held up a hand. "There's a way to check. The U.S. has

several national news services. What are they?"

She looked puzzled. "AP and UPI."

Monck walked to the telephone, lifted it, and held it out to her. "This article, if it's genuine, would certainly have been sent over the wire services. Call the local AP office. Tell them you're a Chicago reporter, and got a garbled bulletin, and want to check the spelling of Bayerlein."

"If he's as sharp as you think he is, Wren would have coordinated with the local AP office."

Monck lowered the telephone. "You're right."

"But he couldn't have notified every paper in the country." She stepped quickly to the phone, as if anxious to validate Monck's reasoning. She asked for a long-distance operator, then asked to be connected to the *Tacoma News Tribune* in Tacoma. In a moment she was speaking with the morning-shift copy editor.

"My name is Carolyn Jones of the *Louisville Times*," she lied smoothly. With effort she could almost eliminate her accent. "I'm working on background for a story on your POW escape at Fort Lewis. I'm running down the facts on the accomplice's daughter being captured. . . ."

The editor cut her off. Margarete's face lit up. "You haven't seen that come over the wire? . . . No? . . . Well, maybe I'm mistaken. . . . Thank you."

She lowered the phone, her smile wide. "The Tacoma newspaper hasn't heard anything about it. You were right. The story is a fake."

He smiled quickly. She wanted to cross the room into his arms, a remembrance and a confirmation of last night, but he walked to his bag at the foot of the bed and said, "We've got a lot to do. Let's get started."

The elephant, a colossal bull with tusks five feet long, lay on its side, its legs jutting rigidly from its body, stiff with death. The shrapnel wound on its flank lay open and angry, and the cloud of flies around it sounded like an engine.

The elephant's name was Fritzie, a twenty-year resident of the

Berlin Zoological Garden. A battle now raged in the city's newspapers whether to add him to the meat ration or to bury him
properly and with honors, perhaps even with an army wound
stripe. Three other elephants huddled together near their house,
glancing toward Fritzie's body, their eyes wide and white. The
wayward British bomb had also killed a giraffe, less beloved and
already reduced to sausage.

At first, Berliners had raged against the bombings. Then
their emotions became ragged and finally dulled by weeks of
attacks by British and American planes. But a generation of
children had fed Fritzie. This one bomb had incensed them
all over again.

Colonel Paeffgen shook his head at the sight. He and Friedrich Carstenn walked along the iron fence, around dozens of
Berliners who had come to say goodbye to the animal. The
onlookers wore expressions of overwhelming sadness. Paeffgen
felt it, too.

He and the major walked away from the zoo house toward
the Tiergarten, Carstenn's hands clasped behind him in unconscious imitation of the colonel. Because the Americans were that
day bombing a refinery on the Oder River east of the city, the
all-clear horn had blown, and thousands of Berliners were spending the warm Tuesday in the park.

The city was dappled with uniforms, and Paeffgen and Carstenn passed a gaudy array: a striking blonde wearing her Luftwaffe Signals Auxiliary uniform with flat silver braid worn as a
chevron, a parade of boys in the black scarfs and white working
uniforms of the Marine-Hitlerjugend, a traffic policeman in his
white linen with gilt buttons, and many others. When several
lederhosen-clad kindergartners smartly saluted Carstenn, he
smiled and touched the rim of his cap.

"We may have been underestimating Terrier all these years,
Friedrich," Carstenn began. "He's done a remarkable job."

"Perhaps he should be sent a bonus."

"Stroop claims he had to pay the mechanic ten thousand
dollars. I suspect he has built a sizable bonus for himself into

that figure, giving the mechanic a smaller amount and threatening to turn him over to the FBI. Even so, it's well earned. We have several safe deposits in Washington, opened several years ago by Teckel from Boston, using Terrier's forged signature. We sent Terrier the keys, but he doesn't know which bank or box they're for. All we have to do is send Terrier the number of one of them, and he'll be able to get into it, using his own signature. Monck may also be needing more money by that time."

Carstenn grinned. "You didn't trust Terrier with knowing the box numbers?"

"I wouldn't trust myself with that much money."

"Terrier doesn't seem to be having trouble with the spurt equipment."

Paeffgen loosened his tie and continued, "We don't know precisely how the British and Americans are doing it, but it's clear they can pinpoint a radio broadcast. Doenitz has finally begun to issue his U-boats the high-speed tape-recording and transmission equipment. As you know, Stroop received his in the mail from San Diego three months ago and now often limits his broadcasts to ten seconds, sometimes having to send at five different times to get his entire message to us."

They found a bench next to a dry drinking fountain. Berlin's water supply had become unpredictable. Carstenn pulled a map from his uniform pocket and unfolded it across his lap.

The colonel asked, "Give me your estimate on the quality of Terrier's information."

"He brings a peculiar passion to this clerical work. I suspect he actually went into the railroad companies' offices and pored over their records like a detective after a criminal. He may have spent days in there. And I have long noticed a self-congratulatory tone to his messages. He's a bit of a braggart when he thinks he's found something important. His latest message was almost insufferable that way."

Paeffgen smiled briefly. "I noticed that, too. I think we should count on him."

"So do I." The major lifted the map. "This shows Roosevelt's route last time he traveled from Washington to his family home in Hyde Park, New York. Terrier says he left Washington June 29 and arrived at Hyde Park eleven hours later. Even if the train traveled no faster than forty kilometers an hour, as we think it does, it shouldn't have taken all that time for the journey."

"That route across New Jersey doesn't look like the shortest way from Washington to Hyde Park."

"It isn't," Carstenn replied. "And it's on tracks owned by a company called the Lehigh and Hudson River Railroad, whereas we know Roosevelt prefers Baltimore and Ohio Railroad tracks, here, which would have been a more direct route. So Roosevelt must have had a deliberate reason to use the Lehigh tracks through central New Jersey."

Paeffgen said, "The Americans keep POTUS's movements secret. How did Stroop identify the president's train?"

"He took great delight in telling us that it was simple deduction. When POTUS moves, virtually all other rail traffic on America's eastern seaboard comes to a halt. He said that during the evening of June 29, 1943, and in the early morning of the following day, no rail cargo or passengers moved at all in eastern Pennsylvania and central New Jersey. An area that lives by rail service suddenly had none. Freight trains pulled onto sidings, passenger trains didn't leave their stations on time. Operations just stopped."

"Except for this one train?"

"That's right," the major answered. "As POTUS moved north, it paralyzed everything around it."

"And what about this little town?"

"Stroop checked and rechecked his discovery, he says. The next day, June 30, POTUS passed Buttzville, New Jersey, at seven fifty-eight in the morning. It passed the next town on the line, Townsbury, twelve minutes later, at eight-ten, and Great Meadows at eight-fifteen. The train was traveling right at forty kilometers an hour. It arrived at the small town called

Allamuchy, New Jersey, at precisely eight-thirty that morning."
The major moved his hand along the map. "And POTUS
passed the next village on the Lehigh and Hudson line, Hunts-
ville, five miles beyond Allamuchy, at fifteen minutes past noon
that day."

"So the train was in Allamuchy four hours?"

"That's what Terrier concludes. He says POTUS did the same
thing three months before. Five and a half hours that time. Terrier
has been back to those railroad offices several times. We received
his latest message with his new discovery this morning. He has
learned that when the railroads are given warnings to stop traffic
in a particular area, they are also told an approximate time when
they can resume operations. For example, for the June 30 stop
in Allamuchy last summer, they were told in advance to halt all
operations in central New Jersey for four hours."

"What about Roosevelt's trip this weekend?"

Carstenn tried to keep his victory grin to a minimum. "The
railroad companies have become accustomed to the professor
from Georgetown. When he finished with their trip logs, he
asked to see their weekly shipping orders, which detail the
schedules for the upcoming days. They happily pointed him to
the records. Terrier reported this morning that all trains in the
Allamuchy area have been ordered to pull onto sidings for an
hour and a half Friday morning."

"Compared to Roosevelt's previous stops, that's a short visit."

"I trust Terrier's research."

"An hour and a half. We'll let Monck know." Paeffgen joined
the major in a smile, then Paeffgen shaded his eyes against the
high sun. A distant rumble came from the east, probably
American bombers on their return run. They would fly well
north of Berlin and its Flak 30s and 40s. The B-17s braved
the AA guns when Berlin was their target, but never on a
retreat to England. "Does Roosevelt have any relatives in Allamuchy?"

"His roots are in Hyde Park. His wife's are also in New York.
We can't find any relatives in the town."

"What about friends, cronies, old fishing pals, that sort of thing?"

"Fala didn't find anything." Carstenn folded the map.

"The president often goes to Warm Springs for a cure. Anything like that in New Jersey?"

"Not that we know of."

Paeffgen said, "I find myself resisting this next question, Friedrich. It seems slanderous. But does Roosevelt have a woman there?"

"Stroop believes so. Two reasons. First, whenever he has stopped at Allamuchy, Eleanor has been at Hyde Park. At least, that's where her syndicated newspaper column says she is. And second, Stroop became puzzled one day when he was watching the White House. Suddenly all activity came to a halt. Nobody arriving, nobody leaving, not even service people. Then, during all this calm, a chauffeured limousine arrived, and a tall woman climbed out of it and walked into the White House. She stayed an hour, during which the freeze on arrivals and departures continued. Only after she left was the usual hectic pace of the place renewed. Stroop got a look at the limousine. It was from New Jersey."

"How would he know that?" the colonel asked. An attractive woman wearing the field-gray walking-out uniform of the SS Auxiliary smiled at him as she passed. He nodded noncommittally.

"The states have different-color license plates."

Paeffgen sorted the information for a moment. "All right. We'll send Monck our estimate that POTUS will stop in Allamuchy Friday morning for an hour and a half. Relying on that fact is a risk, but..."

A shriek interrupted the colonel. The woman who had just smiled at him was pointing at the eastern sky, a look of bewilderment and horror twisting her face. Paeffgen and Carstenn rose from the bench, following her gaze.

An American bomber was coming at them, a B-17 with both port Wright Cyclone engines on fire and trailing plumes of smoke across the sky. The wing behind the engines was scorched black. As it drew near, now at two thousand feet and falling quickly, Paeffgen saw that its rudder and most of its right stabilizer had been blown off. The pilot was trying to fly it with the flaps. The Flying Fortress bore the red-and-yellow markings of the U.S. Eighth Air Force's 487th Bomber Group. From one end of the Tiergarten to the other, heads turned to the crippled bomber.

"He's had it," Carsteen whispered. "He'll never get it down. He can't even lower his landing gear."

"He wouldn't be over Berlin if he had any control over it."

The bomber continued to sink as it passed over the Brandenburg Gate. A crewman tumbled from the waist, followed by another. Attached by static lines, their parachutes billowed immediately. The remaining engines roared as the pilot pulled the yoke back. Sun glinted off the glass nose and the ball turret. To Berliners, the sleek B-17, with its thirteen probing machine guns and its three tons of bombs inside the vast gut, was the stuff of their renewed nightmares, replacing the trolls and witches of their childhood dreams.

The wounded plane screamed over their heads as another crewman jumped. Suddenly the bomber banked sharply, rolling onto its port wing, ropes of oily black smoke twisting after it. At that instant another American threw himself out the waist, but the plane had begun its spiral, and his chute lines snarled in the stabilizer, snapping him around, then carrying him with it like a rag doll behind a running girl. The doomed flier spun wildly, flailing his arms and trying to kick free.

The B-17 was on its back when it crashed into a row of apartment buildings on Hardenberg Strasse near the western end of the park. Fire spilled from the building, then the old structure collapsed completely, filling the street.

When Paeffgen looked back to the park, an American was landing on a grass knoll. The crewman's knees buckled under the weight of his sixty pounds of gear, and he rolled several times before he was able to gather his feet under him. His white parachute swelled in the mild breeze, rolling like a wheel before it deflated. The flier unbuckled himself. He unholstered his .45, dropped it onto the grass, and raised his hands over his head.

He looked pitiable, even ludicrous, standing alone, dressed for the forty-degree-below-zero temperatures at twenty-five thousand feet. He wore a steel-reinforced vest under a fleece-lined flight suit. Over the suit were his Mae West and parachute straps. His leather helmet and goggles were still in place, as was the wool-and-leather mask across his nose and mouth to prevent frostbite as he stood behind the machine gun at the bomber's waist. His oxygen mask was attached by a leather strap to his helmet, and the long rubber oxygen tube hung from that. The tube dangled like an elephant's trunk.

Perhaps it was this similarity, combined with pent-up rage, that prompted a woman to abandon her baby's stroller to charge the American. She cursed him as she ran, removing her shoulder bag to use as a weapon. An elderly pensioner followed her, shouting at the top of his voice, the cane in his hand whipping the air. Their black neckerchiefs flapping behind them, two Hitler Youth also rushed the airman. Others in the Tiergarten began to stream toward the flier, most with hands balled into fists.

The woman arrived first, and flailed her bag at the American. He lowered his hands to cover his face. The cane struck him on the cheek, laying it open. The two boys swung at the waist gunner with roundhouses, and when he fell to his knees, they began to kick him. Another man threw a stone at him. The angry cries grew.

Paeffgen started to run toward the growing crowd. He yelled over his shoulder, "Draw your pistol, Major."

When they reached the mob, the flier was sprawled on the ground, trying to rise, but being repeatedly knocked back to his stomach. Blood streamed from his nose, soaking the mask. The crowd had quickly realized their body blows had little effect against his flak jacket, so they were aiming shoes and boots at his head. The horde wore a single expression, flushed and knotted fury.

Paeffgen rammed into the crowd, shouldering aside men and women, stepping over children. A wild swing caromed off his ear. He pushed aside the two Hitler Youth and bent to the American.

Three quick shots rang across the grass, arresting feet in midswing. The crowd turned as one toward Friedrich Carstenn, who had his Walther in the air.

His voice carried icy authority. "That man is a prisoner of war, and is mine. Back away from him." The feared black uniform with the lightning runes on the collar reinforced the order.

Muttering imprecations, the throng melted away, allowing Paeffgen to help the American to his feet. As soon as he was steady, the flier shrugged off the colonel's arm. He pulled off his soaked mask and spat blood. Wincing from his bruises, he raised his hands again.

Paeffgen said in English. "You look sixteen years old. Are you all the Americans have left to terrorize us with?"

The gunner was trembling violently. He said through a split lip. "Nicholas Scott, Sergeant, United States Army Air Forces, serial number two..." He stopped abruptly. His next sound would have been a sob.

Paeffgen cut in to save him the indignity. "Save it for your interrogation. I don't care who you are." Paeffgen paused to stare fully at the airman. "Unless you're from New Jersey."

"Michigan."

Its siren blaring, a police car rushed across the Tiergarten's lawn toward them. Two municipal policemen spilled out of the back doors before it had stopped. They brusquely thanked Carstenn, who was holstering his pistol, and escorted the sergeant toward the car. A policeman roughly shoved his neck to bend him into the backseat.

As they drove away, the colonel said, "There is a reason I asked you to meet me here today, rather than at headquarters,

Friedrich." He brought an envelope from his suit pocket. "I want you to look at these documents, but I don't want comments from you about them."

The major lifted the envelope flap. He brought out a Swiss passport. His face slackened when he saw his photograph—a full-face shot with him in civilian clothes—next to the name Friedrich Schwartz. The given names of his wife and two sons also appeared on the document, with their last names changed to Schwartz. The passport listed an address in Bern. Deeper in the envelope were five hundred Swiss francs and a note with several Swiss and Italian addresses on it.

"What's all this?" Carstenn asked, his voice tight.

"I have just put my life in your hands, Friedrich. Some would interpret those documents as treasonous. Anybody who can read, in fact."

Paeffgen glanced over his shoulder. "This morning I received a letter from General von Schlieffen advising us to end the operation, as it had little chance to succeed, and saying he was no longer to be consulted about it. I expect a similar message from Rauff shortly. They are distancing themselves from us, probably suspecting what the future holds for Monck's controllers should the mission fail. If Monck doesn't succeed, Himmler will want to rid himself completely of the embarrassing stain of failure."

"I still don't understand..."

Paeffgen waved away the question. "I told you about my visit to the Prinz Albrechtstrasse cellar. At first I thought the transfer to that repugnant duty was the extent of Himmler's threat to me. I have since learned that SS Standartenfuehrer Ernst Eberhardt was notified of his appointment to that position three weeks ago. I can only interpret this to mean that the reprisals that wait for me, and for you, upon failure of this mission will be worse than a transfer to the cellar."

The major blinked. "I can think of only one thing worse."

"Precisely, Friedrich. As you know, the Gestapo makes most of its important arrests after midnight. I have asked my neighbor,

Hanna Schmidt, to telephone you immediately should I be taken away one night. You and your family may have enough warning to flee Berlin. And if you get as far as Switzerland, those documents will see you through."

"What about you, Colonel?"

"I have my own plans. It's best you not know of them."

"I don't know what to say...."

"Don't say anything." Paeffgen smiled at his friend. "Particularly to anyone at headquarters."

"We may succeed, Colonel."

"It will be a grisly thing to celebrate, but with Kurt Monck working for us, I'm counting on it."

27

THE TELEPHONE RANG, AND JOHN
Wren lifted it wearily. The desk sergeant said,
"Wren, there's another Kurt Monck here for you. Interested?"

Wren sat behind the desk in a detective's office on the second
floor of the Louisville police station. Tom Garvin leaned against
a wall, his tie loose, sleeves rolled up, and eyes closed. Wren
said flatly, "The last one you sent up was sixteen years old and
tried to pass off acne pox as the German's scar. Can you do better
this time?"

"Afraid not."

"Then send him home."

"It's a her. About seventy years old, I'd say. Five feet tall by
four feet wide. Says she's been to Europe once. But she doesn't
look entirely unlike the photograph in the paper. Same eyes."

"Send her home, Sergeant," Wren ordered, "and spare me the
rest of the cranks." He lowered the phone and muttered, "Goddam this mess."

Garvin nodded at the accurate summary of their day's work.
It was Tuesday evening, two days before President Roosevelt
was scheduled to leave Washington.

"I've let him slip away, Tom," Wren said, leaning back in the chair. "We were closing in, and now we don't have a clue, not even a hunch."

"It's my bet he's in Louisville."

"Along with the other twenty-three Kurt Moncks?" Wren asked acridly. "His ability to simply disappear is unearthly. One minute he creates havoc—at a gas station near Seattle, then at a naval base in Illinois, then on a road in Indiana—and the next minute he's gone. People just can't do that."

The phone rang again. Wren grimaced before lifting it. The voice on the other end of the line was distorted by long-distance static. "Wren? This is Hoover."

Wren's chair came down. "Yes, sir. Do you have anything?"

Hoover laughed, a sound that weaved in and out of the interference. "You still at work? It's after ten o'clock at night."

"I'm still at it. Very busy, too."

"Like hell," Hoover said. "But I've got no time for idle conversation, as pleasant as that would be. It pays to keep files, Wren. I set up a production line here. Hardly let my boys go out for a leak. Drove them hard."

Wren rose half out of his chair to slip into his jacket. "What do you have, Mr. Hoover?"

"I'd say I've scratched your back here, wouldn't you, Wren?"

"If you've got an address, you have. Otherwise, you're wasting my time, and I'll get back to working with what I've got."

Another grating laugh. "What you and Carrot Top have out there in Louisville is a flat zero. I know that better than you do. Get your hand out of your pocket and write this down." Hoover gave an address on Eleanor Avenue, five miles east of Churchill Downs and the same distance south of the river. "That's where this Lilli Jaeger Sperrle and her husband live."

"Got it." Wren grinned fiercely, then took a jab at the director. "Thanks, J. Edgar."

"The last fellow who called me that went from FBI agent to marine in three days, and is now on a troop ship headed for Saipan."

"I'll let you know what we find."

"Remember my warning about him, Wren."

"Got that, too."

Twenty minutes later, Secret Service agents and Louisville policemen had cast a net over the neighborhood, blocking every street and stationing themselves in side and back yards, all out of sight of anyone in the Sperrle house.

Wren and Garvin moved behind the homes across the street, stepping over fences and around Victory gardens, brightly lit by a slice of high moon. Wren carried a leather satchel. They ducked under an empty clothesline and walked along a brick path to the back door of the house across from the Sperrles's. Wren knocked against the screen frame.

After a moment, the door to the kitchen opened. The woman's mouth dropped, and she tried to push the door closed. Wren stopped it with his hand and held up his star. "Ma'am, we're Secret Service agents. May we have a moment of your time?"

She held her blue terry-cloth bathrobe closed at the neck. She might have been twenty-five years old. She was striking, at least five feet ten, and buxom, which not even the dowdy terry cloth could hide. Her eyes were wide and blue, and her nose was a perfectly turned chip.

"Secret Service? What do you want with me?"

"Nothing at all, ma'am, other than to use your living-room window for a short while. We're running a surveillance on the house cross the street."

"The Sperrles's house?" She licked her full lips with the news. "They're from Germany originally, aren't they? Have they done something wrong?"

"Nothing of the sort. May we come in?"

"Well, I was on my way to bed. . . . Sure, if you need to."

She stepped aside for them. "My name is Vera Monroe." She smiled tentatively, showing teeth as even and white as piano keys. She led them from the kitchen.

The living room was small and patched. Like most other American women, Vera was an artist at making do. Antimacassars covered worn spots on a sofa and a chair. Badly in need of a new speaker cone, a box radio filled the room with the crackling, yet still sorrowful dialogue of *Pepper Young's Family*, followed by a commercial featuring a foghorn voice calling, "Beeee-Oooooh." Leaning against a wall was a Victory bicycle, with its wicker basket over the undersize front wheel. On an end table was a framed photograph of an Army Air Forces flier, inscribed, "Your loving husband, Steve."

Garvin switched off the lights in the room, then opened the curtains of the picture window. The house across the street was dark and appeared to have curtains drawn across all front windows. It was a red brick home with an enclosed porch, white shutters, and rain gutters. Someone had been taking care of the house, as the grass was clipped and green.

"Mrs. Monroe," Wren said, lowering the satchel to the floor, "have you seen anybody coming or going from the Sperrle house in the past few days?"

"Just this afternoon a fellow came by. That's his car just to the right out there. I knew it wasn't Willy Sperrle returning, because he drives a Dodge."

"Who'd you think it was?" Garvin asked.

"I didn't give it much thought."

Wren gave her a photograph, and she walked into the kitchen to look at it.

She said, "I didn't get much of a look at his face, so I can't tell if that was him."

"And you haven't seen him leave?"

She shook her head. "But there's a back door to the place. And it's been dark awhile. I might have missed him."

She joined them at the window. She put her nose almost on the glass. "I can see some light in there, seeping out through one edge of the curtain."

Wren said, "I don't see it."

"In the window right next to the front door. The house has been completely black before tonight."

"Let's go, Tom." Wren lifted the satchel.

Garvin thanked Vera Monroe. She let them out the front door, then the porch door. As they crossed the street, Wren glanced left and right. Police cars barred the road at both ends of the block. Through the darkness, they saw marksmen over their scopes. Lefty Jones was one of them.

They moved quickly, using several trees and the parked automobile as cover. As they approached the Sperrles's front door, crouching along the hedge that lined the front of the house, they drew their handguns. They stepped up two steps to the porch, under an empty trellis that rose to the porch roof. On the door window was a V-Home Certificate, earned by conserving food, salvaging essential materials, and buying war bonds. A curtain blocked the view through the window.

They stood on each side of the door. Wren felt himself tightening, and he pressed the pistol against his belt for a moment to stop its shaking. The government-issue Colt weighed two and a half pounds, and one shot from it could stop a horse midstride. It had a mind of its own, and Wren felt it was ready to go through the door. He wasn't sure he was. Garvin preferred his lighter Smith & Wesson Model 20, which he held alongside his ear.

He whispered, "You went in first at Leffler's. It's my turn."

Wren pulled a bolt breaker from the bag. The charge looked like a midget version of the German Stielhandgranate 39, the potato masher. On the grenade body was a gob of adhesive putty. Wren pulled off the protective wrapper and stuck the breaker to the door below the bolt. Squeezed up against the doorframe, Garvin nodded. Wren held the breaker firmly against the door and yanked the pull cord. He stepped away and pressed himself against the wood siding and silently counted to five.

The explosion lit Eleanor Avenue like a flashbulb. Splinters and bits of bolt blew away from the door. The sound was a muted crack, like a car door slamming.

Garvin spun onto the porch, dug his feet into the floor, and threw himself shoulder first through the door.

The young agent might have seen the spring gun an instant before his death, its malevolent double barrels staring at him like the vacant black eyes of a specter. Secret Service analysts would later conclude that Kurt Monck had geared the twine connecting the door to the triggers so that the first person through the door would have an instant to gaze upon the Stevens. A terrible trice of comprehension, like the fraction of a second between barking a shin and feeling the pain.

The shotgun was propped on a chair and held in place by stacks of books leaning against its stock.

For an instant Wren thought the second explosion was somehow the bolt breaker's echo. Then he recoiled as a sharp pain bit into his cheek and tongue. It was forgotten when Garvin drunkenly backstepped and fell down the stairs onto his back.

Little was left of his throat, and his head flopped to one side at a grotesque angle, like that of a fallen puppet.

Wren burst through the door, firing at the shotgun, then at a shadow, then at a mirror above the mantel. An instant later, the sounds of the shots still crashing through the house, he knew it had been a spring gun, and that there was no chance Monck was still in the house.

The grief would come later. Wren felt nothing but a vast expanse of shock. His friend was hardly recognizable, sprawled in the bony formlessness of death, a black pool expanding beneath him. Lefty Jones sprinted by Wren into the house, holding his rifle like an infantryman.

Wren knelt near the body. He could not say goodbye, as this wasn't Tom Garvin. It was a jest, one of Garvin's pranks.

Addled by the sight, Wren said, "Come on, get up, Tom."

There was no movement, of course. Another Secret Service agent and several Louisville plainclothesmen ran by.

"No, I know you can't. I'll take care of the rest of it. Don't you worry.' His words were slurred around the blood and flaps of tissue in his mouth.

Wren rose, absently putting his pistol into the shoulder holster. He was only vaguely aware he was injured. A piece of shot had ricocheted off Garvin, punctured Wren's cheek on the left side of his face, and embedded itself in his tongue. He heard peculiar sucking sounds as he inhaled, and his tongue felt double its normal size, but an emotional paralysis blocked the pain.

He walked down Eleanor Avenue forty yards, then numbly leaned into the broad trunk of a maple tree, his eyes closed and his large chin trembling. He would remain there until Lefty Jones helped him back to the car.

Part four

THE TRACKS NORTH

28

GORDON POTTS HUNCHED OVER HIS
new desk in Room 1649 of the Navy Department
building on Constitution Avenue, the home of OP-20-G. He
wished he were still in Labrador's remote mountains.

Not that he minded the change in his appearance: clean-shaven,
polished shoes, and creased uniform pants. Shining brightly on
his sleeves were the stripes of his new rank, first lieutenant. But
no one had told him about the pressure of the job.

He looked up from his calculations briefly, very briefly, to
survey the crowd around his desk. It had grown again, and they
hovered over him in a circle, as if they thought it would make
him work harder.

Petes, of course. But that was to be expected, and now that
Potts had protection from the admiral, Potts had made sure that
the story of the urine got out. Petes's boss, Admiral McWhorter,
was also standing at the end of the desk. Admirals, even his new
mentor McWhorter, made him jumpy. They could send you
anywhere, in anything, for any amount of time. A Navy submarine off New Guinea came nightmarishly to mind. Or worse,
a return to Labrador.

Another grim bystander had introduced himself as chief of the
Secret Service. He frequently lowered himself over Potts's shoul-
der to check progress and uttered things like "Hurry, Lieutenant.
You're dawdling."

Next to the chief was an Irish-looking Secret Service agent.
Oily black hair and a dimple on the jaw. O'Brien, Potts thought
he had heard.

And then, for Christ's sake, Secretary of the Treasury Henry
Morgenthau had showed up and took turns kibitzing over Potts's
deciphering chart. Potts wanted to yell that the pressure was
killing him. How could he work with half the government staring
at him? Then the Quonset hut's vicious mosquitoes and hard
milking stool came back to him. He wouldn't say a word.

Twelve other sailors in the room were working on the latest
intercepted message to Kurt Monck, but the crowd believed Potts
would be the one who cracked it. Potts shared the belief, but
their floating about did nothing to help.

There was another Secret Service agent watching him. The
latest arrival hadn't said a word, but had lowered himself into a
chair across from the desk. He hadn't removed his eyes from
Potts. The lieutenant stole another glance at him and wondered
why he was wearing a bandage across his left cheek. God, he
looked hard-boiled, even with the dressing. Sunken eyes that ate
into you, a boxer's protective, prominent cheekbones, a flat nose,
a knobby, stubbled jaw, and a dangerous cast to all of it. The
guy was on the verge of murdering someone, Potts thought.

"Enough eyeballing the room, Lieutenant," the Secret Service
chief ordered. "Get on with it."

"Aye aye, sir." Potts returned to the mathematical combina-
tions. He'd crack this. It was the same multiple substitution using
the same key numbers. He just needed to trip onto the right
order.

"Was there any evidence Monck and the woman spent any
time inside the Eleanor Avenue house?" Morgenthau asked. "Were
they staying there, and we just missed them?"

Wilson shook his head, his eyes still on Potts's scribbling. "Monck entered the house only to set the spring gun. We found his prints on the frame near the basement window he broke to get in, on the door where he wired the string to the triggers, and on the Stevens itself. Nowhere else. He didn't even use the bathroom."

Morgenthau wiped his forehead with an engraved handkerchief. His mouth worked several times before he asked, "So where did they stay in Louisville?"

"At the Kozy Kat Inn, just across the Ohio River in Indiana. They ate twice at Art's Cafe nearby. The waitress said they were quite attentive to each other, frequently smiling. She did all the ordering from the menu."

"And the waitress didn't recognize him?"

"The waitress doesn't read the papers. And in any event, Monck was wearing a black wig and a mustache. The waitress doesn't remember a scar, either."

Morgenthau rocked on his heels, taking a moment to glower at John Wren. "So how did you discover Margarete Bayerlein's daughter is in Mexico?"

"We don't know that for sure," Wilson said. "My people found a photo of the girl in the Bainbridge Island home and started showing it to train and bus employees at all West Coast stations. A bus driver recalls her being on his coach, and that she got off at the terminal in San Diego."

"Anybody meet her?"

Mike O'Brien answered, "He didn't see anybody. He had driven her from San Francisco. He recalls she was traveling alone and that she was deathly quiet, unlike most kids that age. She didn't ask for anything. Didn't eat. Didn't ask when the bus would get there. As Mary was getting off the Greyhound, the driver asked her if someone was meeting her. She nodded her head, but didn't offer a name."

"Has her mother just abandoned her?"

"We've had the things in her Bainbridge Island house analyzed by our psychiatrists. It was a loving home, they've concluded. They say there is almost no chance Margarete Bayerlein would forsake the child."

"Then why did she?" the Treasury Secretary asked angrily.

"She must have had a gun to her head," John Wren answered coldly. "She wouldn't have done it otherwise."

These were his first words of the meeting. They were slurred, and Gordon Potts wondered if the agent might be drunk. Then he remembered the wound.

Morgenthau said, "Monck is wearing disguises now. Why didn't he wear one in Louisville, at the salvage company where he bought the wet suit?"

"He deliberately let his location be known," Wren answered, bitterness coloring his words. "Just in case we hadn't yet discovered Margarete Bayerlein's sister's home in Louisville, he wanted to give us a clue. It was part of his plan to lead us to the spring gun."

"And setting up the shotgun trap was the only reason he visited Louisville?"

"Sure. He could have purchased the wet suit in a lot of other cities."

"So how do you know Monck is in Washington?" Morgenthau asked, his voice bordering on the shrill.

Wilson answered, "A DeSoto stolen in Louisville was found in Lexington, Kentucky, with his prints all over it. Then yesterday a Plymouth reported missing in Lexington was discovered in Charleston, West Virginia, again with his prints in it."

Admiral McWhorter continued, "And finally, this morning, we intercepted a very brief radio transmission, and when we slowed it down we found it had Monck's fist."

"Slowed it down?"

"We couldn't get a fix on it, because it was a spurt transmission. This is the first time Monck has used that new equipment and that frequency, so we assume he has found his Washington contact."

"How are you sure the contact is here?"

"We've heard this equipment before," the admiral answered. "The background noise leaves a telltale trace. But in weeks past we've not been able to crack the contact's cipher or precisely locate it. Monck used the same speed-up and sending equipment this morning, but sent his own recognition code."

Potts interrupted politely, "I think I've got it."

All heads bent as one over the lieutenant's work.

He said, "It'll take me a while to be sure."

"Lieutenant, don't..."

"No, sir, I wouldn't think of dawdling."

Morgenthau paced, confiding, "I've had dreadful nightmares of this Kurt Monck, in the form of a series of photographs. The first snapshot shows him at a distance and is very blurry. In the next, he's a bit closer and a bit more distinct. In the next, closer still, and now I can make out some of his face, including the scar. And the next, well, he's almost on top of me, evil leer, wire garrote, and all. And it doesn't seem that I can do anything to stop the rolling of these photographs one after the other."

Over the clicking of page printers, Mike O'Brien said in measured tones, "Sir, there is one thing you can do. Release to the newspapers the fact the POW is in Washington. Same thing we did in Seattle and Chicago and Louisville. We came close all those times. We can..."

"Absolutely not," Morgenthau said, his voice shaking with anger he could not turn on anyone. "That would send the goddam city up in panic. And it would make the president appear to be reacting in fright to rumors of an assassin. His trips to Hyde Park and San Diego would be interpreted as attempts to run from the German."

Wilson backed up his White House Detail chief. "I'm going to override you, Henry."

Morgenthau flushed. "Sure, you could veto me. But I'll be goddamned if you'll cancel Franklin Roosevelt's direct order given to me forty minutes ago. No release to the press, Frank. Don't make that mistake."

Potts jumped from his chair, an awkward maneuver as his

head remained in place over his papers. "It's a bank. U.S. Commerce Bank on Pennsylvania Avenue and..."

"What else?" Wilson asked, gripping Potts's arm.

"It's followed by numbers, looks like a safe deposit number. Four zero two."

"A bank?" the Secretary asked, his hands locked together in front of him. "Why? What do we do next?"

Wilson said, "Monck's contact, or maybe Monck himself, is going to try to pick up some money." He nodded toward Room 1649's door. John Wren was already running through it. "He'll know."

"He didn't last time," Morgenthau said accusingly. "And you lost an agent."

Wilson repeated stubbornly, "He'll know."

Seen through binoculars, which narrowed the range of vision and blocked out the street clutter, the U.S. Commerce Bank appeared austere, even ominous. Its four fluted Ionic pillars supported an enormous entablature. Between the scroll-shaped volutes at the top of each column were distinctive echinus moldings with egg-and-dart ornamentations. The bank had apparently spent all its building fund on the columns and the sculpture-laden frieze, as the side of the bank building was made of simple unpainted brick.

Kurt Monck abruptly lowered the binoculars. There was an edge of irritation in his voice. "Unbelievable. That's John Wren."

"Which one?" They were sitting in a Ford coupe a block west of the bank on M Street. The ignition wiring hung under the dashboard, and two wires had been spliced together with black electrician's tape.

"The big fellow who just got out of the passenger side of that green car in front of the bank. He's got a wrap on his cheek, and he's running into the bank now."

Margarete Bayerlein said, "You sound like you weren't expecting him."

Monck showed his teeth, a mean grin of concentration. "I

344

wasn't. I thought we'd left him in Louisville for good."

"How do you know that was him?"

"I spent some time a little earlier this afternoon in the library of the *Washington Post*. Their story index led me to a wedding photo of him on the newspaper's society page. Married quite a prominent woman four years ago. And the only other mention of him was when his wife died two years later. Murdered. 'Survived by her husband, John Wren,' it said."

"How awful," she said, and meant it. "I feel sorry for him. You can recognize him from an old photo?"

"Barely," he replied, raising the binoculars again. "He's done a lot of hardening since then, it looks like." Monck's mouth pulled into its contorted smile. "I picked up the safe-deposit-box key from Otto Stroop and practiced his signature until I got it right. I didn't have any problem getting into the box. Wren isn't going to appreciate discovering we've already been to the bank."

A packet of money lay on the car seat between them. Other cars arrived in front of the bank. Men wearing the studiously blank expressions of plainclothes policemen entered the building between the columns.

Margarete said quietly, "It's now a duel between you and him, isn't it? You've got a face to latch onto, a person to think about and plan around. Your mission is much more rewarding now."

Monck didn't appear to be listening. Needlessly, he whispered, "There he is again, coming out of the bank. Those will be Secret Service agents gathering around him. It looks like he's giving instructions." He laughed, an unpracticed sound. " I don't think he's got many to give."

The crowd around Wren dissipated as the other agents headed off in a number of directions. Wren leaned toward his driver, nodded several times, and the green Ford drove east on M Street. Monck lowered his head as it passed. John Wren put his foot against the base of one of the columns and leaned back against it, his hands in his pockets. He lowered his head farther.

"Look at him," Monck said. "He doesn't have a clue."

Hands still deep in his pockets, Wren began to amble down

the sidewalk on the other side of the street from Monck's parked car. He held up his hand at two men hurrying along the sidewalk toward him, undoubtedly more agents on their way to the bank. They conversed for a moment, and when they parted the agents walked away without speed or conviction. Wren continued down the sidewalk, pausing once to stare into a window. His head hung with defeat, he slowly drew abreast of Monck's car on the other side of M Street.

"I've never seen anyone with fewer places to go and fewer things to do," Monck said jubilantly. "He's almost given up."

Not quite yet. The move is a peculiarly American skill. The country's sports stress it. It's the move of a football lineman at the snap or a baseball runner stealing second. It's the ability to launch oneself, utterly without warning, from standing to a dead run.

The first Monck knew of it was when Margarete suddenly shouted an unintelligible warning. The German looked up. Directly across M Street, John Wren was leaping between the fenders of two parked cars and simultaneously drawing his pistol from under his jacket. His furious expression was one of a dog running a rabbit to ground.

"*Scheiss*," Monck shouted. He flattened the Ford's starter and gripped the steering wheel almost hard enough to snap it. Time unfolded, and it seemed to take a full minute for the engine to catch. It was a mere second, but long enough to bring Wren halfway across the street. He half-stepped to avoid a passing taxi. Then the agent closed the distance.

The Ford howled into life. Slamming the gearshift into reverse, Monck released the clutch. The rear tires screamed and spun smoke, and the coupe vaulted into the sedan behind it, crushing the sedan's fenders and grille, and pushing it in turn into the panel delivery truck behind it.

The tires reversed, and the Ford swerved away from the curb and shot toward the center of the road. Not quite clearing the Plymouth in front of it, the Ford's fender ripped off and clung to the Plymouth.

Ten yards from the careening Ford, his legs still churning, Wren brought up the .45.

She stared through the window at it in horror.

The agent tried to lead the car like a pheasant as it roared in its tight semicircle to escape its parking place. Wren could not get a clear shot at the German, whose face maddeningly mixed with Margarete Bayerlein's. One bullet from the pistol would pass through the car and everything in it.

Wren stopped a few feet from the accelerating car and peered down the barrel. Light reflecting off the Ford's window created a montage of faces. Tilted by the force of its turn, the Ford lunged from the parking spot and rushed by him, leaving its fender behind.

The gunsight followed the car, but their heads were now low behind the seat, and the coupe swerved violently as it found the center of the road. There was no shot.

His face drained of color, Kurt Monck glanced into the rear-view mirror at the receding Wren, who stood in the middle of M Street, his hands at his side, the pistol still clearly visible.

Monck took a long breath and said, "You mentioned the other day that John Wren and I are alike."

Still low in the seat and clinging to the armrest, Margarete dared to open her eyes. She said nothing.

"You're wrong," Monck breathed. "Had that been me chasing this car, I would have emptied the pistol at it. The duel would be over."

29

MONCK PULLED THE CAR TO A STOP IN front of a drugstore in Hackettstown, New Jersey. When he opened his door, Margarete woke and lifted her head from the blouse she had wadded against the window to use as a pillow. They had driven from Washington, leaving at four-thirty in the morning. He had stolen another car, shortly after they left the city, this time another Ford. She yawned and blinked the sleep out of her eyes.

The stores along the street were just opening for the day. As Monck walked to the front of the Ford, the druggist opened his store's front door to sweep the step. He smiled absently at her, his attention never fully leaving the broom. Monck opened the Ford's hood and leaned over the radiator. A few seconds later, he lowered the hood and returned to the car. He wiped bits of rubber from a pocketknife before slipping it into his pocket.

"Something wrong with the car?"

"There is now." He smiled. He was wearing the tortoiseshell glasses and a mustache. She had helped him try to cover the scar with makeup. It was still visible, but no longer glaring. "And good morning, again."

He started the engine, and they drove another block and a half to the Hackettstown Ford dealer. He pulled the car into the garage, over a service pit. The garage acted as a local metal depot for the war effort. Over a nearly full collection bin near the back wall was a poster that read "Get in the Scrap." The mechanic was standing near the parts bin wiping his hands on a rag. He stepped over a portable jack toward their car.

"Morning, folks," he said, tucking the rag into the back pocket of his pants. He was wearing a blue shirt and the same color pants. There was a spot of grease low on the left lens of his wire-rim glasses. He was in his mid-thirties and was balding, front to back. He must have shaved that morning, but it already looked like he needed another. "Problems with the rig?"

Monck left the car and opened the hood. "I think it's the fan belt." He had practiced the sentence. There was no accent.

The mechanic stuck his hand behind the radiator and ran it along the belt. "You're not kidding. This is almost ready to pop off there. Take a look."

The mechanic did not notice the German study his face carefully. Then Monck bent low, nodding when the mechanic showed him a shredded spot on the belt.

"I've got a replacement belt for you. It's a used one, but it'll do. Can't get new ones these days. Won't take but two minutes."

It took just that, two minutes, for the mechanic to replace the belt. Monck paid him and said thanks. A few minutes later they were back on the road leading out of Hackettstown.

Margarete said, "It appears we drove all the way from Washington to New Jersey to change a fan belt."

"We did."

He did not volunteer any more information, and she knew better than to ask. She balled the blouse again and tried to return to sleep. She could not. A hundred questions kept her awake, and she knew he wouldn't answer any of them.

Otto Stroop looked quickly up and down 20th Street several blocks north of George Washington University. The sidewalks were filled with federal workers returning home after their day's work. With Kurt Monck standing next to him, Stroop felt conspicuous.

They were a few feet from the entrance to the Hampshire Restaurant, notable only for its all-night poker games in the basement. The Hampshire had been raided five times in the past two years, but the game was always afloat several days later.

"You sure this is his game?" Monck asked. He had altered his appearance again. His brown hair was shaved above his temples so that he appeared to be balding. The hair remaining on his crown had been thinned with scissors. The sun-stained spots on his forehead and his scar were covered with makeup. The scar was still visible, but not with a passing glance. He was wearing wire-rimmed spectacles.

"The doorman said he lost about half of the thousand I gave him yesterday after work, and guessed he'd be back today to lose the rest of it."

A noisy bus passed them. The city was so crowded that bus seats had been removed and "stand-sits" had been installed, against which the riders leaned.

"Jesus, Monck," Stroop went on, now in a victorious whisper, "I can't believe all the money in your envelope. Twenty thousand dollars." He laughed. "You know, I was mailed that safe-deposit key a couple years ago, and I had no idea the box had that much money. I don't suppose Berlin had any idea what they'd use it for at the time. I suppose they thought that if they'd given me the box number I might have taken the cash and run. Argentina, Paraguay, who knows."

"It'd be tempting, all right," Monck said unconvincingly, his eyes flitting over the pedestrians, mostly women. The ratio of men to women in Washington during the war years was said to be one to five.

He said, "They'll be waiting for you at your home. You know that, don't you?"

"What?" Stroop turned fully to the German. "What are you saying?"

"The police showed up at the bank a few moments after I got the money. They knew the bank's name, and they probably knew your box number."

"That means . . . they've broken your code." Stroop's face slackened. "Oh, Christ, Berlin sent you my name over the airwaves by the same code."

Monck nodded. "They either have known it for quite a while and were seeing who would show up at your door, or they'd just deciphered the message. In any event, it looks like you're through in this city, and in this country."

Stroop wobbled on his feet. He looked stricken, and his words were barely audible. "But I've worked so hard. My job, my home." He looked with hope at the German. "What am I going to do?"

Monck took the envelope from his pocket and gave it to him. "You've made your deal with the mechanic. The rest of the money is yours."

He stared with disbelief at Monck, then grabbed the money as if it were a life rope. "God, Monck, thank you. I might be able to salvage something out of this."

A gangly, world-worn worker in splotched overalls arrived with the wave of pedestrians, then stepped out of the stream toward the Hampshire's door. Stroop quickly blocked his way, then led him by an elbow to the corner of the building.

"Hello, Mr. Smith," he said to Stroop, his face twitching in what might have been an attempt to smile. "I wasn't expecting to find you here." When his gaze fell on Kurt Monck, George Bell took a step back.

The mechanic was visibly nervous, wetting his lips and glancing repeatedly at the passing pedestrians. He asked timidly, "Your partner?"

Stroop said, "He's come a long way just to check you out. It's his money, and it's his errand you'll be on."

Bell's rubbery lips chewed on nothing for a moment. "I've got it all figured out. Took me quite a bit of thinking, too."

"It must be done tonight."

"Tonight? You never said anything about tonight."

"It's now, or you're out of a job," Stroop said flatly.

Bell again looked at Monck. "Well, sure, I suppose tonight's as good a time as any. Won't take me long, neither." The nearness of the passing pedestrians gave him courage. "Does your friend talk, Smith?"

Monck leaned toward Bell and said in words made flinty by his accent, "If you fail tonight, we will meet again. I assure you, it won't be as pleasant as this."

Bell jumped back. "Jesus, Smith here has already threatened me enough. I'll do it proper. Don't worry."

"Then do it now," Stroop ordered, tapping into Monck's reservoir of austerity.

For the first time in his life, George Bell turned away from a poker game. He backstepped, his eyes never leaving Monck. "You bet. I'm on my way." He turned and fairly ran down the street.

The garage was a short distance from the Blue Eagle. Bell rang the buzzer and waited until the uniformed night watchman let him in. "You back, George?" the guard asked, chewing an apple and turning away. "What's up?"

"I took my wristwatch off doing that lube job and forgot it. It's on the grease barrel in the second bay."

The guard strolled to his office. "Pull hard on the door when you leave. Sometimes it sticks and doesn't lock."

"Will do," Bell called after him.

He entered the garage. Three work bays were surrounded by Secret Service automobiles. The president's green armored Ford was parked against the wall opposite the auto entrance. Meager light was provided by a single bulb over the door to the guard's office. One of the new gasoline pumps, with a rollover meter, stood near the street exit. A half-dozen fifty-five-gallon drums of lubricants were behind it. Along a wood rail platform above the parked cars was a row of new Goodyears, a luxury unheard of in any other auto garage. Two of the bays had cement service pits dug into the floor. One had a built-in hydraulic lift.

Moving quickly, George Bell rolled a portable jack across the garage to the armored Ford. The jack was five feet long, with a pumping handle at one end and a lift pad at another. He stationed it behind the Ford's left front wheel, closed the release latch, and began working the handle up and down. The lift carriage rose slowly. As it neared the car, he felt under the frame for a sturdy spot to locate the pad. He pumped again until the pad began to lift the Ford. The automobile, weighing twice what any other car does, resisted the lift, and Bell had to climb onto the pumping handle to raise the wheel off the floor.

Checking over his shoulder for the guard, Bell used a screwdriver to pop off the hubcap. He jammed the wheel-bearing seal until it came loose, then pulled off the bearing cap. He used his fingers to scoop out the grease. Not satisfied, he crossed the garage to the supply bin for a can of degreaser, which he poured into the bearing. He wiped it clean with a rag, then replaced the seal and the hubcap.

With another rag he cleaned the wheel rim and the garage floor. He dropped the rags into the bin on his way out. He remembered to pull hard on the door, and he heard the bolt catch. Bell had been inside the garage less than five minutes.

Wren rapped loudly on the door, number 32, third floor of the fleabag apartment building near the B&O tracks and the orphan asylum. He stood to the side of the door. The hallway smelled of cat urine and mothballs, and the only light came through a sooty window at the end of the hall. Through the window was the vague outline of a fire escape.

"Who is it?" came an agitated, fearful voice behind the door. Wren heard a window open.

"May I speak with you, Mr. Lyman?"

"You the cops?"

"There's some money in opening the door, Lyman."

A long pause, then the bolt was thrown back. The door inched open. "What money?"

"I need to buy something from you."

The door opened farther. Behind it was Ralph Lyman, burglar, fence, and auto thief, whose first convictions were for running booze out of the West Virginia hills during prohibition. He was a tubercular alcoholic, whose hands shook so much he lacerated himself each time he shaved, about monthly. His new beard was growing around nicks and cuts. His nose was a network of burst capillaries. His eyes were rheumy, and it seemed to be an effort for him to blink them. His hair was lumpy with dirt and oil. He scratched bedbug bites on his arm and asked, "Money? What've you got in mind?"

"I need a car."

"Shit, don't we all, and..." Lyman's mouth dropped open, and he emitted a high-pitched croak, as if in Wren he had suddenly seen the devil incarnate. He rushed for the open window.

Wren moved after him, grabbing him by both spindly shoulders and roughly turning him around. Lyman tried to struggle out of the agent's grasp, a weak effort ending in a fit of coughing.

"You're Wren," he wheezed. "Not me, I'm begging you. I had nothing to do with it. I didn't even hear from Wiley all those years he was in prison. Jesus, we weren't friends. He just paid me to stick up for him. Please..."

"All I want to do is buy a car, Lyman," Wren said, backing away from the spray as another coughing spasm swept over the thief.

Lyman doubled over as he spouted and gasped. He managed to right himself, wiping away the saliva. The burglar was shaking. "I had nothing to do with it, I swear."

Ralph Lyman had been Wiley Sullivan's alibi witness during Sullivan's trial for counterfeiting. Lyman had sworn he and Sullivan had been in New York when the bogus twenties were being passed in Washington. In light of the twenty-dollar engraved plates Wren had found in Sullivan's basement, the jury hadn't bought the alibi.

"What are you talking about?" Wren asked, knowing full well.

"Your wife," Lyman rattled. "Sullivan was crazy, I knew that.

But he never got in touch with me when he showed up in Washington that day. I didn't even know he was up for parole. First I heard about it was when they found his body tied to that cactus in Arizona. I still don't believe it, though. To a cactus, for Christ's sake?"

"How do you know about that?"

"For a month the D.C. police were telling everybody they arrested about Sullivan's death. Scaring the crap out of us on purpose. His killer was never caught, but I knew it was you who had..." Lyman's voice dwindled. "And then you show up here now, and I figured you were going to do the same thing to me."

"I want to buy a car, that's all."

"A car? There's a dozen legit car dealers around here. Why from me?" He walked across the room and sank into a torn and sprung chair.

The apartment looked as though a grenade had gone off in it. A pile of whiskey bottles lay at the foot of the bed. Encrusted dishes filled the sink and spilled over onto the counter. The broken door of the icebox hung open. Moisture had loosened the plaster, and layers of it drooped from the ceiling. The bed was rumpled, and the sheets were brown. Six new radios lined the dining-nook table. Lyman would have been hard pressed to come up with a receipt for any of them.

Wren remained standing. "I want a reliable car that hasn't been reported as hot."

"That's asking a lot," Lyman said.

"The car has to have clean plates, but none from D.C. or Maryland or Virginia."

"A government worker like you doesn't make big enough bucks to buy one of those." Lyman poured himself a double shot into a glass so grimy it was opaque.

"And I need it today."

The thief whistled. He stared at the ceiling, apparently lost in thought. "It's going to cost you eight hundred dollars."

"All I've got is six hundred." Wren pulled fifty-dollar bills from his pocket.

Lyman swallowed whiskey and shook his head. "Can't do it for that. Too much risk, too much work with the license plates."

Wren asked, "Ever hear of a saguaro, Lyman?"

Instantly alert at the metallic tone of Wren's last words, the thief carefully shook his head.

"They sometimes grow two stories tall, look a little like a cross, but with ends upturned. You can find them all over Arizona. Sometimes two, three in a row, and..."

"Six hundred it is," Lyman injected. "Delivered in three hours right out front."

Wren threw the bills onto the mound of whiskey bottles on his way out of the apartment.

They had arrived at the Lakes Hotel in Hackettstown at a few minutes before midnight Wednesday. She was tired and had gone right to bed. Monck left to look around, as he put it. He returned at one in the morning, waking her with light taps on the door. They embraced quickly and led each other to the bed.

Her hunger for him the past two days had been unexpected, rushing, overwhelming, and exhausting. Sleep and lovemaking seemed to merge and made the nights wondrously endless and dreamlike. In his arms, the little clues about him—his cunning, determination, cruelty—she had been collecting as they crossed the continent made no sense.

Monck confided in her of his childhood in Schwabia, of his schooling in Birmingham, of North Africa, and of the Fort Lewis POW camp. He told her of a life she found bereft of affection and tenderness, and wondered at his absence of self-pity.

He spoke of the first man he had killed, a British sentry who had stumbled onto him and his men when they were planting *Tellerminen* on the Via Balbia in Libya. Monck had shoved a knife into the boy's stomach and had never thought of it again until that night, a disassociation she found unnerving, even as she lay next to him.

And she found herself speaking of her past, of her once-in-a-century love for Georg Bayerlein, of their frivolous, laughing, tender, loving times together, of the crushing loss of his death. Of her daughter Mary and their home on Bainbridge Island. All the confidences and intimacies that had built up like water behind a dam now poured forth in a torrent.

During these few hours in the Hackettstown hotel, she felt his urgency and his finality, and knew their time together was ending soon. He would leave her, perhaps in this very town, and she would again be on her own. Somehow she would find her daughter. And she might never know whether Monck was successful. She held him fiercely as he moved against her. She kissed his mouth as she remembered a kiss should be, silently telling him that for these few days and nights, she loved him.

Later she drifted into sleep, and it seemed only moments before he gently nudged her shoulder "Come on, tourist," he said, smiling down at her. "We've got work to do."

She blearily looked at her wristwatch. It was four in the morning. He was dressed, and as she hurriedly put on her cotton dress, he thumbed through the ring of skeleton keys he had purchased in Chicago. On the table next to him were the roll of telephone wire and the dental picks.

Morning had not yet lightened the eastern sky as they left the hotel and to her surprise walked only thirty yards across a weedy vacant lot to a one-story brick building that had "Hackettstown Ford" painted on it.

They walked around an abandoned, rusting harrow to the rear of the building. They found the back door, framed between two empty oil barrels. Monck knelt near the keyhole. Across the alley behind them, a cat hissed and was answered with a long yowl from another tom.

"Good. I won't have to use the picks."

He tried several of the skeleton keys, seeming to know which few of the two dozen might work. After only a few seconds, he jiggled a key in the lock, and the door swung open. He took that key off the ring, closed the door, and relocked it.

"Now you try." He gave her the key.

She easily unlocked the door.

"You're going to open this door twenty-four hours from now. Think you'll have any problems?"

When she shook her head, he led her into the building. They passed through the parts room and a small showroom into the manager's office. Seeing only by moonlight, Monck used a small screwdriver to remove the cover of the telephone. "Watch me. Two screws, nothing to it. Tomorrow night, I want you to take the cover off, then use a scissors to cut these two wires. They're the bell leads, and when they're clipped, the phone will work just fine, except that it won't ring when someone calls. Got it?"

"Doesn't look hard."

Monck replaced the phone cover and led her back through the display room and parts department to the back door. He locked it behind them. He rolled one of the oil drums on its end to the corner of the building near the electricity meter. High on the building's brick wall was the telephone terminal, a nine-by-sixteen-inch metal box painted silver. He stood on the barrel and lifted the box's latch.

"Some luck tonight. I was afraid the terminal would be on a telephone pole."

The terminal contained sixteen copper lugs, but only two of them had wires connected to them. Monck unscrewed those two lugs, brought the wire from his jacket pocket, and with his fingernail stripped a half inch from each end of the double wire. He twisted one wire around each of the lugs, laying them over the wires already in place. He screwed down the lugs, then played out the wire from his roll as he stepped down from the barrel.

The first light of false dawn was purpling the sky as they recrossed the vacant lot. Monck laid the wire out behind him, stopping frequently to conceal it among the weeds. When they reached the window of their room, he pried it open and threw the roll inside. Moments later, he had cut the room's telephone connection and had attached the new wires to it.

"You'll be able to listen in on anybody who calls the Ford dealer now, as the calls will ring both over there and here. After you cut the bell leads tomorrow night, it will only ring here."

They sat on the bed as he told her what she was to say to the caller tomorrow morning. She repeated it several times, and he altered the dialogue, directing her responses.

When he was satisfied, he said, "Everything we've been working for for the past two weeks depends on you tomorrow."

She nodded.

"My life does, too."

"I know that."

He stood, took her hand, and brought her up to him. "I must say goodbye now, Meg."

She took a long breath. "I won't be seeing you again." It wasn't a question.

"I'm leaving you the rest of the money. I'm sorry I couldn't make plans to get you back to the West Coast. In a message to the controllers, I asked that your San Diego contact have a passport for you and Mary. I think it'll be ready." He smiled, sadly, she knew. "The Americans will be looking for you. But you're tough. You'll make it."

"What about you?"

"They'll be hard pressed to stop me from getting away, I think."

She thought it a lie, a kind one, one that would let her think he had some hope. She had begun to know him, and she knew he had not complicated his mission by figuring in an escape.

She came into his arms, and they held each other. He looked into her eyes. He smiled tenderly. "Despite your scalpel, I have loved you these past weeks. In my own way, as best I could."

"I know that, too," she whispered.

He pulled away from her and walked through the hotel door.

30

THE TWO SOUTHERN 1400 STEAM EN-
gines filled the Virginia Avenue Station. For security reasons, other locomotives had been removed that
afternoon. It was Thursday, July 13, 1944. The president was
scheduled to leave the White House for the train in three hours,
beginning his long journey to the Democratic Convention in San
Diego. Secret Service agents, each with restless eyes, surrounded
the engines and the nine sleeper and lounge cars behind it.

In the new diesel age, Franklin Roosevelt insisted on steam
engines, and the Southern 1400s were the Goliaths of a fading
breed. From the cowcatchers to the tenders' rear couplings, they
were ninety-two feet long and almost fifteen feet high from the
rails to the top of the stacks. The locomotives were 4-6-2s, meaning that the pilot truck had four small wheels (two on each side
of the locomotive), followed by the six large, spoked driving
wheels, and finally by two wheels on the trailing truck.

Mike O'Brien tapped the casing above the wheels of the front
truck. "What's in here?"

"Those're the cylinders," Art Blake answered, running his

hand along the rim of his striped engineer's cap.

"Could a man hide in there?"

"Not even if he were only an inch high. Those cylinders go like a bat out of hell, and they don't leave any room for anything else."

John Wren followed them toward the rear of the engine. "And the center portion is the boiler?"

Blake nodded. "Right ahead of the cab is the firebox, then the boiler tubes, and finally, near the front under the stack, is the smokebox. Nobody could hide in there, either. Burn to a cinder."

Blake wore an unevenly clipped mustache centered in a puffy face. His eyes were large and watery, as if he were constantly getting coal cinders in them. He puffed his plump cheeks with indignation at each question. The huge Baldwin engine was his territory, and the Secret Service agents' inquiries lessened the vast mystery of his domain.

Delighted to be holding center stage, he said, "This baby's got feedwater heaters and a Walschaerts valve gear. She weighs 304,000 pounds and has a tractive effort of 47,500 pounds."

"Can you think of anywhere in all those pounds where a man could hide?" Wren asked, irritated at his lack of knowledge of things mechanical.

"In the cab with me, but I'd probably notice him." Blake laughed confidently.

They climbed the metal ladder in front of the cylinder, then walked along the boiler on a narrow catwalk. The Southern was painted a light olive green, and its wheels and catwalks were trimmed in silver. The corporate name, painted on the tender, and the locomotive's number—this one was 1407—were in gold. The cab roof and the roof of the tender were russet brown. All in all, a color scheme much loved by railroad buffs and called the most brilliantly styled steam engine of its time.

"That's the smokestack?" O'Brien asked. It was surprisingly small, testifying to the engine's coal-burning efficiency.

Blake nodded, and they walked farther, single-file on the metal grid. "The next bulge on top here is the sandbox, filled with sand that drops along pipes to be deposited in front of the drive wheels when the tracks are icy."

"Open it, please," Wren ordered. After Blake had done so, Wren dug his hand down as far as he could into the gray sand.

"It's only two feet deep," Blake said in tones indicating Wren had just violated his locomotive. "Nobody's in there."

They walked farther, placing one foot carefully in front of the other. Blake said, "And the last hump on top of the engine is the dome."

"What's in there?" O'Brien asked, rapping it with his knuckles.

"It's an inverted siphon to prevent water from leaving the boiler with the steam." He anticipated the agent: "Too much piping for anybody to be in there. And they'd be parboiled anyway."

They climbed down. Wren glanced at his hands. Not a trace of oil or dirt on them. The Southerns had been cleaned with toothbrushes for this trip. Blake led them into the locomotive's cab. There was scarcely enough room for the three of them behind the bank of dials and levers.

With enormous satisfaction, Blake set himself apart from the unknowing by pointing at various instruments and intoning, "Boiler-pressure gauge, feedwater heater gauge, water-level indicator, steam-heat gauge, booster steam gauge, stoker fine-coal gauge, stoker-jet gauge..."

When he had run out of gauges, he pointed to the controls and began again: "Automatic brake, independent brake, water-column valve, washout plug, gauge cocks, sander valve, throttle, injector overflow..."

Wren found it difficult not to be impressed. O'Brien indicated the housing below the firewall and asked, "What's in here?"

"That's the stoker conveyer screw. It's an automatic coal feeder, and nobody could possibly be in there, not without being pushed into the firebox like by a meat grinder."

"It's going to be crowded in here, Mike," Wren said.

"Just three of us, and we're used to it," the engineer responded.

"Six of you, as I'm posting three of my agents in here," O'Brien said with some satisfaction.

"Horseshit," Blake objected loudly. "This is our turf. We can handle anything up here."

Wren smiled gravely. "Art, that's the first time today you've said something on a topic you don't know a damned thing about."

They dropped from the cab and walked to the tender, a car mounted on two trucks of six wheels each. Wren and O'Brien followed the engineer to the rear of the tender, then climbed after him to its roof.

"You fellows know anything about tenders?"

O'Brien shook his head, a slight movement designed to avoid a lengthy lecture.

"It holds coal in the front part and water in the back part. That bulge a third of the way back is the scoop hump, which is a wall that slants forward and down, so as to make the coal fall forward toward the conveyor screw. Everything behind that bulkhead is water."

They moved slowly along the side of the roof toward the coal bin. Wren asked, "When was the coal loaded into this tender?"

"About three o'clock this afternoon, just four hours ago or so."

"Unload it. I want to look inside the bin."

Art Blake's face went blank, then crimsoned. "Are you shitting me? Unload the coal? That's the craziest damned idea I've... We're pulling the hell out of here in an hour." He looked beseechingly at Mike O'Brien.

O'Brien's face was cast in cement.

"Ah, goddammit it, you guys are going to screw things up."

They walked to the rear of the tender. Wren asked, "And this is the water portal?"

Fearing the worst, the engineer nodded weakly.

The tank lid was the size of a manhole cover. Wren lifted it. The black water was a foot below the lid. He said, "And empty this water. I want to look down in there. And when you're done, empty the other tender."

"Goddammit," Blake whined, "you guys think you can just drop by and..."

Wren and O'Brien didn't stay to hear Blake's plaint. They descended to the track, where O'Brien signaled two agents, each of whom had a German shepherd on a leash. The black-and-tan shepherd was an explosives hunter, and it and his agent began at the cowcatcher, the dog's tail wildly wagging with excitement.

The second agent opened a bag containing Kurt Monck's shirt—discarded at Margarete Bayerlein's Bainbridge Island home—and held it to his dog's nose. It buried its damp black snout in the fabric for several seconds, then pulled at its lead, anxious to begin at the locomotive's front truck. The dogs would quickly search both locomotives and tenders, then all the Pullmans.

Wren and O'Brien walked along the sleepers. In dusk's melting light, the Pullmans were brightly lit from within. They were filled with Secret Service agents. They joined the search for an hour, opening toilets, lifting mattresses, peering into closets.

The president's guests began to arrive. A seat on POTUS was the most coveted ticket in town, and the Secret Service expected early arrivals. Unlike in times past, the VIPs were asked to step through a portable metal detector called an Alnor door, then to join a line near a table where agents thumbed through their suitcases and purses. To check the work of the Alnor door, a translucent screen had been erected near the table, and the guests were asked to step inside for a body search. A female agent patted down the women.

The agents were instructed to allow on board only those passengers whose name was on the guest list and whose faces matched their photographs, quickly gathered by the Secret Service in the prior two days. They were also asked to listen to statements which might give something away. None did, but the comments were far from friendly.

Treasury Secretary Morgenthau did not say a word as he was patted down.

Wren and O'Brien stopped again at the locomotives and tenders. Agent Richard Adams was already in the cab of the lead engine, pushing rounds into a grease gun's clip. On the ground next to both tenders were mounds of coal, surrounded by shallow pools of water. In a huff, Blake had ordered his men to unload the tenders on the spot. A dozen exhausted B&O workers leaned against a loading platform west of the locomotives.

Wren borrowed a flashlight from O'Brien and climbed again to the top of the tender. The water lid was to one side on its hinge, and he aimed the light beam through the hatch into the tank. Nothing but a sheen of black water on the bottom.

"Empty," he called.

He moved forward to the coal bin. A layer of black coal dust as fine as talcum powder covered the hopper. Using the light, he could see down the sloping wall to the conveyor screw. "Empty here, too."

After Wren searched the coal crib and water tank of the other tender, a third locomotive slowly approached the Southerns, ready to push them again under the water and coal spouts. O'Brien posted agents on the top of each tender to oversee the operation.

Thirty minutes later the agents arrived at the Bureau of Engraving siding, a few yards from the Tidal Basin, just northeast of the Thomas Jefferson Memorial. On the siding were the aft nine cars of the train, including the president's Pullman, the Ferdinand Magellan. Secret Service agents swarmed in and over the cars.

Wren and O'Brien boarded the Ferdinand Magellan, stepping across the rear platform with its elevators and through the three-quarter-ton rear door. Confident the car had been thoroughly searched by man and animal, they began searching anyway. The aftmost compartment was the sitting room, containing six plush chairs and a davenport, all done in soft green and gray. All pieces of furniture were firmly attached to the deck, allowing secure handholds for passengers in the event of a wreck. A telephone sat atop a cabinet radio. The carpet was new but thin, allowing Roosevelt to roll his wheelchair over it easily.

In cupboards were gas masks, fire extinguishers, life jackets, an inflatable raft, first-aid kits, a folding litter, emergency C rations, and bottled water.

The car had three sleeping compartments. The president's chamber was the center compartment, which was connected by an interior door to a spacious bathroom, large enough to turn a wheelchair in. Across the tub was a bathing board, and the toilet had a riser, enabling the president to transfer back and forth. Each room had a handset telephone.

They continued to search, moving from the compartments to the conference room, the largest area on the Ferdinand Magellan. An oak table was surrounded by ten office chairs. An agent was passing a metal detector over the chairs' fabric.

At the front of the Pullman was a small crew compartment and a galley, tiny compared with the president's quarters. Each had an agent probing and poking. Another dog appeared, this one a bloodhound with red-shot eyes and dewlaps almost to the ground. Unlike the German shepherds, this dog was all business—no tail-swaying, no jumping at the leash—anxious only to find another source of the scent he had been tempted with. Lifted by the agent to the countertop, the bloodhound ignored a tray of quail breasts—the president's favorite food, other than perhaps oysters—preferring to sniff at a bag of potatoes, then inside the pot cupboard.

Chief Wilson arrived as the search was ending. The weary agents had unearthed nothing. Wilson ordered them to begin again. He found Wren and O'Brien at the Ferdinand Magellan's forward door, a modified battleship bulkhead.

"I'm surprised to see you here, John," he said with one of his enigmatic smiles. "Shouldn't you be on the German's trail?"

The question dripped with irony, as Wren and Wilson had spoken over the telephone four times that day, and the chief knew of each of Wren's dead ends.

Wren took a sharp breath. "He doesn't leave a trail. At least, none that I can find. He's in Washington, but I have no idea where."

"And we haven't been able to locate Monck's Washington contact." Wilson wrinkled his lips in a grimace of thought. "Then we're completely on the defensive? Just waiting for Monck to strike, with no chance of hitting first?"

"That about sums it up."

The chief said gloomily, "Yes, well, so it does."

The search of the Pequest River near Allamuchy, under the railroad bridge POTUS would cross early the next morning, was typical of all river searches conducted that day along the B&O and Lehigh and Hudson tracks.

The sergeant ordered his soldiers to strip to their skivvies, start forty yards upstream, and feel the bottom of the shallow river along its course until they were forty yards below the bridge.

"Sarge, I signed up for Intelligence School," a private yelled from the center of the river. Mud encased his arms up to the elbows. "Now look at me."

Lying in the late sun, Sergeant Sam Blacker took his cigar from his mouth long enough to yell, "You'll be a lot more intelligent when you get done with this river, Pike. I like to think that every Army experience makes you just that much smarter."

"Sarge," another hollered from the bank, where he was squishing mud through his fingers like a child, "it'd help if you'd tell us what we're looking for."

"I want you boys to bring me anything bigger than a pencil that doesn't have hair on it. So, Smathers, that leaves out anything you've got."

The soldiers hooted and even Smathers laughed, and in truth they were having a high old time. This cool stream at the end of a hot day was as close to a picnic as the U.S. Army would ever offer, and they knew it. Sergeant Blacker had been told they were looking for explosives, but did not know the reason. The platoon searched the underpinnings of the bridge just as carefully as they did the water.

They ended their search as night fell, and the sergeant filled out a form listing the items they had found in descending order of interest: a three-pack of condoms wrapped in foil, a set of false teeth, a Boy Scout knife, five fishing lures and one reel, a pair of spectacles with a lens missing, a horseshoe, four frogs, and a rat's skull.

No explosives under the Long Bridge over the Pequest River at Allamuchy. And none of the other eighty-two search teams found explosives under any of the bridges.

At the same time the sergeant and his soldiers were scouring the bottom of the Pequest River, Lucy Mercer Rutherfurd walked from Tranquility's formal sitting room toward the front entrance.

"I'll get it, Elaine," she called. Her voice's melody was picked up and enhanced by the silver pipes of a grandfather clock in the entrance.

She opened the door to a large German shepherd with its tongue hanging out the side of its mouth.

"I remember you, Dobbs," she said, patting the animal on the head.

His trainer, a Secret Service agent wearing a tan jacket and a hunting cap, said, "Once again, Mrs. Rutherfurd, we've got to inconvenience you a bit."

The dog and his master had come from a pickup truck parked to one side of the mansion. A line of vehicles was rolling into the pebbled circular driveway, and agents emerged from all doors. Three of them pulled wet suits and scuba tanks from a truck. She recognized several of them from their prior visits.

"You're Special Agent Jeb Stuart Hall, if I remember," she said, smiling in such a way that even the dog closed his mouth.

"Yes, ma'am. I take it you remember me because my dog here

seemed to enjoy browsing in your clothes closets."

Another smile as she stepped aside for them. "Canine saliva often enhances designer clothes."

Hall glanced quickly to see if she was jesting, saw her puckish expression, and laughed. Dobbs disobediently pulled at his leash, wanting to get to work. A line of agents made their way through the front door, each removing his hat as he entered.

God, she was beautiful. And so refined. She was the only woman Hall had ever met whom he'd trade Dobbs for, straight across.

"Mr. Hall, you and the rest make yourself at home. Don't be shy in your looking, as if I need to tell you that. I've asked the cooks to prepare a little something for you and the others."

"Don't go to all the trouble, ma'am," Hall said, utterly without conviction. Last time "a little something" had proved to be beef Wellington, a first for most of the agents. "Mrs. Rutherfurd, we've been told to station men all over the house this time, not just at the doors. It's going to be a real inconvenience for you and..."

She waved away his explanation, a movement as graceful as a ballerina's. "I understand. You do what you have to. I'll be in the second-floor den if you need me."

The search of the mansion and the pond behind it lasted two hours. When it was over, the team gathered for prime rib, which Jeb Stuart Hall guessed had cost three hundred ration points.

When the meal was over, they started at the front doors and began the search again, working long into the night.

The agents found nothing. And then they staked out the rooms to wait for Kurt Monck.

At the garage, the Ford limousine had gone through its ten-minute search, and another search had been conducted upon its arrival at the White House. It now waited for the president at the north portico. Mike O'Brien stood near the passenger door, next to Pancho Villa Smythe. Their eyes never rested. Eight other agents waited at the portico. The Army scout car's machine guns pointed at the east gate.

John Wren chewed his lower lip as he waited at the east gate, his foot on the running board of the lead car. His stomach had a life of its own, rolling and tossing. He noticed his fierce grip on the door handle only when his fingers began to ache.

What had the Secret Service forgotten? Where was the gap in their protection? And where was Kurt Monck?

The two-hour meeting with Chief Wilson and Mike O'Brien, ending fifteen minutes ago, had not answered any of these bitter questions. The very need to ask them was a clear indication, Wilson had unhelpfully pointed out, that the Service had already failed.

Wren scanned the trees, the Treasury Building's windows, and the White House grounds. Uniformed D.C. policemen were posted every thirty feet along the iron fence. In the dark sky just above the Treasury Building, Wren glimpsed the muzzle of Lefty Jones's rifle. Behind Jones, on an elevated platform, was a Bell Telephone Victory Siren, powered by an automobile engine, which could be heard for ten square miles in the event of an air raid.

People began pouring from the White House: the president's secretary, William Hasset; Dr. McIntire: Admiral Leahy; two social secretaries, Edith Helm and Adrian Tolley; Harry Hopkins; and the director of war mobilization, James F. Byrnes. Wren saw only Roosevelt's feet, resting on the wheelchair brackets, before the agents none too politely brushed the others aside and surrounded the president. The practiced maneuver left none of him exposed. Arthur Prettyman's black hair stood out amid the gray hats. Fala must have been on Roosevelt's lap, as the president laughed approvingly at a bark.

Wren's chest tightened. In Washington, the president would never be more exposed than this. Wren automatically scanned the trees, the Treasury Building, the grounds. The human shield paused for only seconds at the Ford, and Roosevelt slipped into the backseat. His chair was folded and pushed inside after him.

Wren jumped into the lead car. Another agent named Jenks, an Oklahoman whom Wren once had seen eat a beer glass, faced the rear window on a portable seat. A Thompson submachine gun lay across his lap. Wilbur Gottschalk, the swimmer, was behind the wheel. Next to him was the rope ladder that he carried behind the president wherever he went. To the north, East Executive Avenue had been blocked off by police cars. Gottschalk, a big-boned blond with hands as large as bear claws and, it was rumored, webbed feet, waited until the armored Ford was within a car length before pulling through the east gate and turning south.

Wren worked his head like an owl's, sweeping his vision left and right. They turned right on E Street, skirting the Ellipse.

"Wren, this is Number One." It was the president's driver, his voice made small by the radio. "I've got problems with the car. Front wheel, I think."

"Keep it moving," Wren said tensely over the radio. He ordered in a loud voice, "Gottschalk, drop back to the Ford. Jenks, pull out the window."

Jenks crawled forward and pulled a strap on the rear window, lowering it onto the panel. He quickly kneeled on the backseat and raised the Thompson.

"This is Number Three," O'Brien said over the box. "We're pulling up tight. Step on it, everybody."

The president's driver radioed, "The Ford is trying to pull to the right. I think it's the wheel bearing. I can hear it."

A wheel bearing that is failing emits a grinding soprano squeal, the shriek of metal on metal. There were a few people out for evening walks, enjoying the view of the Washington Monument from 15th Street. The president's car passed them quickly. Not one of them heard the screech of a dry wheel bearing. There was no sound to be heard, except the soft whir of the Ford's engine.

"Anything back there?" Wren barked into the microphone.

From the trailing Secret Service automobile, O'Brien said, "Nothing. Not a thing. I can hear the wheel from here, though."

The entourage turned south on 14th Street, then crossed Constitution Avenue. The streets had been cleared by police barricades. The Washington Monument, darkened for the duration, approached on their right.

"Are we going to make it to the train?" O'Brien radioed.

The driver replied, "I think so. It's got a few miles left in it."

The box formation around the armored Ford continued until the automobiles were parked at the Bureau of Engraving. Wren ran back to the armored Ford. He passed his fingers over the hubcap, as if seeing if it was hot.

O'Brien hurried to the car. "It'd be hot, wouldn't it?"

Wren nodded.

Agents draped themselves around Franklin Roosevelt as he transferred into his wheelchair. Arthur Prettyman pushed the chair toward the Pullman's rear platform, where an elevator had been lowered. Wren caught only a glimpse of the president, his black Bakelite holder gripped between his teeth, displayed in a magnificent smile, as if he enjoyed the Secret Service's extra attention.

Agents crowded around the wheelchair as it rolled onto the platform. The electric lift whirred, and the elevator rose, carrying the president and six agents, who had to stand so close on the small platform that they pressed in on him.

Wren heard the president invoke one of his favorite sayings: "Looks like everything's clicking beautifully."

John Wren loved that voice, and he had a precise memory of every time he had heard it. So had O'Brien.

Pancho Smythe and Wilbur Gottschalk followed the president and his valet into the Pullman. Moving with solemnity and purpose, the steel door slowly swung closed. It fit against its frame with a single dull thud. Wren heard the bolts sliding home.

The armored limousine was driven eight cars forward and up a ramp into the automobile carrier. The ramp was then shoved under the carrier, and the carrier's metal door rolled shut.

The Southern 1400s and the VIP cars had earlier been backed down from the Virginia Street Station. Those cars, along with the Ferdinand Magellan and the Secret Service cars, made this the longest train ever to take the president on a journey.

At exactly 10:45 P.M., the enormous locomotives hissed and bled steam. A whistle cut the night as sharply as a knife, and the pounding of the huge pistons began. POTUS inched forward, then quickly picked up speed. It cleared the Bureau of Engraving and disappeared under the shroud of night. Within two miles, the sweeper and trailing trains would be in place.

"I feel better," O'Brien said.

"Not yet you don't," Wren answered, starting back to the car. "The German hasn't made his play."

31

CARL SANDBURG SAID THE LAND OF A farmer wishes him back again. But the fields of tomatoes and beans around Allamuchy would not wish the Secret Service's return. They swarmed over the ground, flushing each plant, carelessly breaking vines and exposing roots, walking each row, probing the clumps of trees at the edge of the fields.

A few minutes ago the sweeper train had come slowly down the valley. And now, when the throaty rhythm of another train began reverberating between the hills, the agents turned for a glimpse of POTUS, and of the Ferdinand Magellan, the green, unmarked Southern Pullman at the rear of the train. They squinted against the early-morning sun. Right on time, of course. He was thirty minutes late for Josef Stalin, but never for her.

The fifty Secret Service agents who had swamped Allamuchy gave away the president's secret stop. He'd been there before, and the townspeople knew what to expect. Three dozen town-folks had gathered at the Allamuchy train station, and more were arriving each minute. The sun was already warming the valley, and most wore shirts and simple frocks. None had dressed up, as the president was becoming one of them. A few hoped he would recognize them from his last visit. A child held a small American flag on a stick.

The spectators were to be disappointed. Chief Wilson had ordered the train not to risk delivering Roosevelt to the Allamuchy station. Instead, Art Blake began slowing his train as it left Independence Township, and it came to a stop at the Long Bridge Road crossing, where trains usually only stopped to load dairy goods from the white creamery. Across the road from the creamery was a cornfield.

Wren and O'Brien had driven to Allamuchy that night and had directed the positioning of Secret Service agents along the tracks. Agents wearing red-checkered hunting shirts roamed the oak and birch trees that lined the tracks for the mile to the Allamuchy station. Sergeant Blacker and his platoon were still along the banks of the Pequest River, which the train had just passed over. Trout floated belly-up in the water, victims of Blacker's explosive charges set off moments before.

Several windows on the forward Pullmans were pushed down, and passengers asked the agents why they had stopped in the country. From their cars, surrounded on both sides by trees, they could see neither the crossing nor the Allamuchy station a mile northeast. The agents smiled politely at the inquiries, but didn't take the time to answer. Their eyes dug into the brush and trees.

At O'Brien's signal, agents climbed to the rear platform of the Ferdinand Magellan. The bolts of the door were thrown from the inside by Pancho Smythe, and the president emerged. He was blanketed by guards. Wren heard him laugh at the phalanx of agents, all wearing raincoats on a hot morning to further reduce glimpses of the president.

The armored Ford was unloaded and driven alongside the track to the president's Pullman. The elevator descended, and Roosevelt slid into the limousine's backseat. The agents had called ahead from the train, and Lucy Mercer Rutherfurd's Cadillac limousine was at the siding, in case the Ford's bearing gave out completely. There was no question of using the Cadillac unless the Ford was totally incapacitated, as it had no armor.

Wren caught a quick view of the president's powerful face. Those who saw him every day, as O'Brien and Smythe did, claimed that he was looking worn and anxious, that the pouches under his eyes were increasingly colored, and that he didn't hold his head as erect as he once did. He looked like an old man. Not now, not with Tranquility a few miles away. The president beamed good health and cheer. Normally he found his Secret Service protection an annoyance. Today he nodded at the agents, his smile never faltering. He tossed a joke at Arthur Prettyman, something about all his friends having the chance to enjoy the summer sun for a while in Allamuchy.

The route to Tranquility had been carefully arranged. O'Brien and Wren got into a trailing car and followed the limousine along Alphano Road a mile. The cars turned right between two red barns and along a dirt farm road that joined a short side street in Allamuchy.

Edith Cramer, whose husband was Lucy Mercer Rutherfurd's chauffeur and who had been consulted on the route, was one of the few in Allamuchy who knew Roosevelt would use the side street. She was sitting on a lawn chair in front of her small white home. She waved at the president. He grinned and waved back.

They climbed the small hill above the town and entered the wide brick gate to the estate, passing carefully placed birch and evergreen trees.

She was waiting for him, standing under the mansion's entranceway, wearing a white cotton dress with a bold red belt. Her hands were clasped in front, and her shoulders were bowed to glimpse him in the dark car. Agents in the fields a quarter mile away could see her blazing smile.

Wren and O'Brien emerged from their car and walked to the mansion. Agents were in almost every window and along the wood fence to the north. Another stood on the deck above the east wing, a rifle across his chest. The wheelchair was passed from the limousine, and she unfolded it.

Agents had been milling in the driveway, and they now closed around the president as he pushed himself from the car.

O'Brien said softly, "I'll be damned."

Wren's hand quickly went inside his coat.

The detail chief held up his hand, halting Wren's draw. "I just saw her touch his arm. She's never done that before in public."

"It's late for both of them," Wren said. "And love makes you careless."

O'Brien smiled quizzically at Wren. "That from you?"

"Let's go see what the German has in mind."

Wren followed the president and Lucy Mercer Rutherfurd as they entered the mansion, but only as far as the entryway telephone. He phoned the nearest Ford dealer, in Hackettstown. He asked that a repairman immediately bring a bearing for a 1937 Ford to the Allamuchy station.

The woman at the dealership said the repairman was on another call, but she would contact him and have him arrive at the Allamuchy station as soon as possible.

After she hung up, Wren held the phone for a long moment, his gaze out the entryway window across the valley. His mouth turned down, as if the sight saddened him.

Wren and O'Brien returned to POTUS, which had moved along the track to the Allamuchy station. Even though they were told the president was not on the train, the townspeople remained at the station. The crowd grew, all hoping for a glimpse of their president, or at least of Fala. Children wandered along the train until asked by Secret Service agents to stay away. Several high school boys trotted over to the lead locomotive and yelled questions at Art Blake. He climbed down to regale them of his years behind the firewall. An agent in the cab told them to leave.

Wren signaled Lefty Jones, who had been sitting on his haunches under the shade of a red oak tree near the tracks.

With his rifle in the crook of his arm, Jones joined the two agents.

"Lefty, there's going to be a Ford mechanic here in a few minutes," Wren said. "The agents down there are going to send him into the carrier. Until he gets inside the carrier, I want your crosshairs on him. And I don't want him to see you. If he takes a quick step, if he puts his hand inside his shirt, if he sneezes, if he scratches his ass, put a bullet through him."

Jones eyed down the track toward the auto carrier, which had its loading platform angled to the ground. "Fine with me," he said in his reedy voice. He moved back across the track and quickly disappeared behind a hedge.

The agents waited, along with the puzzled VIPs, for over an hour. The search was unceasing, again of the train and the fields, the town, the pond behind the mansion, the Pequest River, and everything else within deer-rifle range of the POTUS and Tranquility.

The sun rose over the hill to the east of the town. The birds and insects warmed to the day, surrounding the station with their sounds. The judges and generals emerged from the train, found there was nowhere to go and nothing to do, so they sat around the tiny station, swatting at flies and speculating. Their wives flapped magazines at their faces and sipped Orange Nehi through straws. Rumor was that the train had a hot box and that parts were being flown in from Philadelphia. Mike O'Brien rubbed his thumb raw on his money clip.

Then the station telephone rang. The president had said good-bye to Lucy Mercer Rutherfurd and was leaving Tranquility. He would arrive at the train in a few minutes.

The limousine pulled alongside the Ferdinand Magellan. The agents formed around the President. Within moments he was once again surrounded by the Pullman's bulletproof glass and steel. The massive door swung closed.

At that moment, the mechanic arrived. His pickup truck, a 1937 Ford with sweeping front fenders and a grille that looked like an elongated Rolls-Royce's, stopped near the auto carrier. As the mechanic stepped from the truck, the armored limousine was driven up the gangway onto the railroad car.

"You sure he knows your face?" O'Brien asked, glancing quickly at the pickup. The limousine driver jumped from the bed of the auto carrier.

"He didn't have much time to study it. Coming back from the bank, I happened to glance across M Street, and there they were. I bolted for them immediately. But it must have seemed like ten minutes to him, what with me charging across the street at his car, waving my pistol, like an idiot. He'd recognize me. I don't want to spook him by getting too close."

They both stared at the mechanic as he stepped off the pickup's running board. He was a medium-size man, with a very high forehead, balding front to back. The few wisps of brown hair remaining on his head waved in the breeze. He wore rimless spectacles. Even at this time of morning, the man had a heavy five-o'clock shadow.

"We had a break on this one, John," O'Brien said, tension raising his voice half an octave.

Wren signaled a man leaning against the station platform. His hands stuffed in his pants pockets, the man walked toward them. Wren said, "Yeah, we finally got a break."

Private First Class William Bell had been their break. Six weeks ago he had landed with General Gerow's U.S. V Corps as the first wave on Omaha Beach near Pointe de la Percée. He made it thirty yards up the sand before he was cut in two. The Army had buried him in France.

And now his brother, George Bell, hated Germans with an anger that in its intensity and breadth surpassed any emotion he had ever known. He hated them more than he hated working for a living.

Smith had never mentioned it, but Bell had assumed the information about the Secret Service automobiles he had given him in 1940 and 1941 was somehow ending up in Germany. He hadn't cared much at the time. George Bell would have taken that Mr. Smith's money and never told anybody, and prayed that Smith would never reveal his work for him years ago, had his brother made it off Omaha Beach. But this time, when Smith approached him again in the Blue Eagle, his new-found rage was ignited. The murderers of his brother were up to something. And now he had a chance to avenge Bill.

The following morning he had visited the Secret Service office in Washington and had told them the entire story. He didn't bargain for immunity. He didn't give a damn. He wanted to drop his own bomb on Germany, and this was the only way he could. The Secret Service's interest was immediate and intense. Bell never felt better in his life.

After a hastily arranged conference with Chief Frank Wilson and White House Detail Chief Mike O'Brien, Bell had been told to go along with everything Smith suggested. Tell the Secret Service of every contact. They would take it from there.

At the first meeting in the Blue Eagle, Smith had not told Bell when he would contact Bell again to tell him what to do and to give him the money. The mechanic had been surprised to see Smith again at the Hampshire two nights ago. The Blue Eagle was under Secret Service surveillance, but the agents did not know of the Hampshire. And when Smith and the other fellow, the one with the accent, had told him to tamper with the armored Ford's wheel bearing, Bell went along with them, just as the Secret Service had told him to. Then he had telephoned Chief Wilson at home and told him what had happened. Wilson said he had done good work. Another bomb on Germany.

Bell didn't know that the Secret Service had repacked the bearing the next morning, and that the two-way radio conversation between Roosevelt's chauffeur and the other Secret Service agents on the way from the White House to the Bureau of En-graving siding was faked in the event Monck or Smith was listening, as Monck had done in Chicago.

George Bell ambled up to Wren. Wren asked, "Is that the man you saw at the tavern?"

Bell craned his long head toward the car carrier. "Well, you told me he had been wearing a disguise that day when he gave me the order." Bell squinted. "He's a ways away. I can't really see him too good. But I'd have to say that's him, all right. Same fellow."

Wren felt himself building. His hands were damp and his breath was rapid. Dust seemed to be coating his tongue. So close so often. And, finally, here the POW was.

Their quarry was at that moment pulling a tool box from the bed of the pickup.

Hoover's warning came back to him. Do it at a distance. Don't give him a chance.

But Wren had convinced Wilson and O'Brien that it would be too dangerous to pick him off in the midst of Secret Service agents, VIPs, and train engineers. It would look suspicious if no one was near the train. If Monck thought he was detected he would open fire, or detonate a bomb prematurely.

All elaborate rationale. Wren wanted to talk to the man. They all did. How'd he get this far? How did he escape the Seattle–Bremerton cordon? How did he possibly think he could succeed? What good would the death of President Roosevelt do for the collapsing Third Reich? And he wanted to look into the eyes of the man who had killed Tom Garvin.

Wren would ignore Hoover's warning. They'd take him alive.

At the auto carrier, nine cars forward of Wren and O'Brien, a Secret Service agent pointed up the ramp. The mechanic nodded and began up the incline, his wood tool box in one hand and a wheel bearing in the other. They started along the siding toward the auto carrier just as the mechanic disappeared inside. Their footfalls sounded peculiarly loud in the gravel alongside the ties. The Southerns spewed steam. Behind them they heard a small crowd cheer. Roosevelt must have waved to the townfolks from a window. A Southern's whistle echoed off the hills.

They increased their pace. The agent who had gestured the

mechanic into the car looked at them for a signal. Wren and O'Brien broke into a run, passing the Secret Service car and the communications car.

Wren took huge breaths as he ran. The train began to roll when Wren and O'Brien were two cars away from the carrier, which was the tenth car of the eighteen-car train. Wren signaled the agent with his hand, and he began to push the auto carrier's sliding door closed. Wren reached the auto carrier, a B&O car with the number 748 on its side, and helped slide the door shut. It slammed against the frame, and Wren fit the latch onto the slot and threw the bolt.

Slowing their pace to match the train, the agents jumped onto the steps of the trailing Pullman crew car. Lefty Jones boarded at the other end of the car. They walked through the coupling vestibule, which swayed under their feet. The crew car's door opened, and Lefty Jones passed Wren a red container the size of a baseball. On the ball's smooth surface was a knob that looked like a bottle cap.

"This job is getting more fun by the moment," O'Brien said with an evil grin. "Toss it in."

As did all POTUS's cars, the auto carrier's connecting door had a gun port, covered with a sliding metal grille. Earlier that day Wren had knocked the lock off the inside of it. He twisted the ball's trigger, slid back the grille, and threw the container inside.

"Five seconds, then it blows," Wren said. His words wavered with his impending triumph. He had stalked Kurt Monck across the country. It would end in moments.

Jones passed them gas masks, which they pulled over their heads and pushed tight against their skin. The tin canisters on the front of them and the large plastic eye covers made them look like insects.

The ball was a tear-gas bomb which would incapacitate anyone inside in a few seconds.

They heard a subdued explosion, sounding like a bag of flour falling onto its side.

"Give it two minutes, about as long as anybody can hold his breath," Wren said. He watched the second hand on his watch. They pulled out their weapons.

"Let's go."

Wren slid the bolt, bounced the door open with his shoulder, and sprinted into the carrier, O'Brien and Jones on his heels.

Wren had expected a wafting cloud, but the gas was colorless. As a result, everything inside the auto carrier seemed that much clearer, as if he were viewing it with binoculars. The limousine was enormous inside the narrow car, looking more like a tank than a passenger car. They rushed around the fenders to its side.

The mechanic was sitting on the Ford's running board, his feet splayed out in front of him, and his face was between his knees. His arms dangled below him. A pool of vomit lay on the wood floor. Wren was tempted to laugh. An awkward, ignominious, humiliating capture for a hardened Afrika Korps soldier and would-be assassin.

He kept the gun in front of him as he rolled the mechanic onto his side on the running board so he could look at the fearsome German's face.

The balding head. The wire-rimmed glasses. Wren put his hand under the mechanic's chin to lift his head. There should have been heavy makeup over a scar. He wiped his thumb across the chin. There was no makeup, and no scar.

This man had a few age lines around his eyes. And his forehead was too wide, his lips too curved. Perhaps the lenses were distorting the German's face. With shaking fingers, Wren fiddled with his mask.

The features obstinately remained wrong. Semiconscious and drooling, a man the Secret Service would later identify as a Hackettstown Ford mechanic named Robert Comstock stared sightlessly up at the agents.

"Who the hell is he?" O'Brien asked sharply.

Wren couldn't trust his voice. Understanding seeped into him like an acid. The Ford mechanic was a plant, probably an unwitting one. He was an artifice by the German designed to consume their attention and energy. Wren had been so sure, almost smug as he had closed his trap around . . . around bait.

The certainty of an impending disaster exploded within Wren, blowing him against the Ford.

"Wren, where is Monck?" O'Brien demanded.

There was only one place Kurt Monck could be. Closing in on the president.

Wren spun, pushed past O'Brien and Jones, and ran through the walkway into the crew car. He pulled off his mask and lifted the handset telephone that was directly connected to the Ferdinand Magellan.

It was dead.

Fear and hopelessness pushed his eyes closed for an instant. Then John Wren began a desperate sprint, car to car, toward the rear of the train.

32

WREN HAD LOOKED, BUT HE HAD NOT
seen.

As POTUS began rolling away from Allamuchy, the locomotives filled the valley with their piercing steam whistles. Kurt
Monck had been waiting for the sound.

The water-tank lid slowly opened. The German gripped the rim
and pulled himself higher. From the tender behind the second
Southern locomotive, he saw the roofs of eighteen train cars sway
as the cars rolled over the uneven rails. He threw the lid back and
levered himself up through the hatch. He was wearing the black
wet suit, with a snorkel hanging from his face mask. His face was
blackened with tar. He squinted against the afternoon light.

Monck had entered the tender tank at ten in the morning on
Thursday, almost twenty-four hours before, hours before the
Secret Service surrounded the train to begin searching it. The
wet suit had prevented the dogs from finding his scent. He had
expected Wren to drain the tender. When the water level neared
the bottom of the tank as it was being drained, Monck had
emptied his ink bottles, blackening the remaining five or six
inches of water. The ink was not otherwise detectable in the

dark tender tank. Then he had squeezed himself against the sloping bulkhead that divided the water and coal compartments. Monck knew Wren's angle of vision through the hatch, down and forward at a sharp cant, would be partly blocked by the hatch rim.

In his black wet suit and blackface, partly covered with the inky water, breathing silently through the snorkel, and lying with the stillness of death, Monck merged with the tank bottom and the dividing bulkhead.

While the tender was again filled, he had floated with the rising water level and resumed his wait. During that night's trip, across Maryland and Delaware and into New Jersey, he had bobbed and pitched with each roll of the train. Monck had clung to the rim, fighting surges of motion sickness. Sometime that night, the water level fell enough so that he could stand on the bottom of the tender. During the hour and a half in Allamuchy, the tender was like a steam bath. He had eaten a bag of raisins, checked his equipment, and waited in the dark.

Margarete Bayerlein had waited an hour and fifteen minutes before forwarding Wren's phone call to the Ford dealer. She had telephoned the shoe repair shop across the street from the dealer, said the dealer's phone was not working, and that the mechanic was needed at the Allamuchy station because President Roosevelt's Ford was having trouble with a wheel bearing. The cobbler had sprinted over to the dealership with the message, and the mechanic was dispatched at once.

Monck knew Wren would never accept a suddenly faulty wheel bearing as coincidental. Wren would believe the attempt was somehow coming by way of the limousine repair. The Secret Service would spring their trap around the mechanic.

And when the train pulled out of Allamuchy, he knew John Wren had fallen for his feint with the Hackettstown mechanic, that the Secret Service agents would be occupied.

Monck pulled his wax-and-oil-treated canvas pack from the tender, then dropped the snorkel and mask back into the tank. The wet-suit boots securely gripped the tender's roof, and he bent his legs like a sailor to accommodate the train's rocking. He unrolled the pack to pull out the revolver. With the pack held on his back by shoulder straps, he jumped across the coupling to the first Pullman.

When he saw a soldier standing near the track, he dropped to the sleeper's roof. Then he realized that even if the track guards saw him, they would be unable to forward a warning. He stood and began to run, car to car.

His legs were rubbery after all the hours in the tender, but the pain in his pierced leg had been reduced to a dull ache. As he ran, he looked quickly at the passing New Jersey countryside. He thought of the fertile loess valleys northeast of Berlin, land as carefully and as lovingly tended as this valley. Land undoubtedly soon to be occupied by the Soviets. Maybe this would make a difference. But maybe not. It was of no concern to Monck.

All that mattered was that he beat John Wren into the Ferdinand Magellan.

He ran along the roof of one Pullman to another. He hadn't expected the train to be this long. A lot of political favors being repaid by a trip with the president. He smiled quickly when he crossed the auto carrier's roof. The mechanic was below.

He jumped across the vestibule to a Southern baggage car, then to the radio car. He extracted a pair of wire cutters from his pack, then cautiously slid to the edge of the car. He felt along the roof edge for several feet, coming again to the front of the car. He found a rope of telephone wires. Pushing himself nearer the edge, he quickly bit into the wire with the blades, taking six or seven jabs to completely sever the communications line. He rose to his feet, almost falling as the car dipped on a sunken rail. He began running again, jumping onto the lounge car called the Hillcrest Club, then onto a six-compartment sleeping car. The Ferdinand Magellan was two cars away.

The Secret Service would conclude that Kurt Monck was already on the roof of the Secret Service command car, the seven-compartment lounge car named the Conneaut, the car directly in front of the president's Pullman, when Monck's ruse was discovered and John Wren's frantic dash began.

The auto carrier was the tenth car in the train, with all the VIP Pullmans ahead of it and the Secret Service cars and the Ferdinand Magellan behind. Wren sprinted through the baggage car and into a crew sleeper. Its handset was also dead. The next car, the radio car, was a secured area, and he had to pound frantically on the door and identify himself before he was allowed in. Wren brushed by the agents, running past the humming telex, monitors, link-up machines, and shortwave broadcasters. His gun was out, and other agents fell in behind O'Brien and Lefty Jones.

"Goddammit, hurry up," he ordered the agent fumbling with the lock of the radio car's aft door. The young agent knew of Wren, and his hands were shaking.

The pulse throbbed in Wren's temples. He was certain he was a helpless spectator, that a catastrophic moment that would echo down American history for centuries was occurring a hundred yards away, and he was no part of it. He would be another Major Reno. Too little, too late.

"There," the agent said weakly, throwing the bolt.

Wren jerked the door open and ran through the vestibule into the Hillcrest Club. Startled agents looked up from their copies of the *Sporting News* and the *Washington Post*. They pulled their weapons and joined the file. Wren yelled at one of them to try the handset, and was already in the next car, a Secret Service sleeper, when he learned it too was silent.

He spun past agents who had heard the incoming commotion and were rising to their feet. Wren swore at himself as he sprinted down the narrow passageway. His broad shoulders brushed against the windows as he skirted the lavatory.

Wren sprinted into the Southern dining car. A few guests were eating late breakfasts, not having found anything in Allamuchy to their tastes. Roosevelt's long-time adviser Pa Watson stopped his fork in midair to watch Wren run down the aisle, followed by O'Brien and Lefty Jones. Across from Watson, Secretary Morgenthau, a wad of cinnamon roll in his cheek, instantly realized that a catastrophe was at hand. He slumped back against the seat. White tablecloths flapped after the agents.

A waiter carrying juice on a serving platter did not move aside fast enough. He tumbled onto a table, and his glasses spilled over Admiral McIntire's waffles. McIntire opened his mouth to protest, but saw Jones's rifle, threw down his napkin, and followed them.

Somehow Kurt Monck was at this moment closing in on Franklin Roosevelt. Wren knew it as an article of faith, and after dogging him for two weeks, he had great faith in the POW. Wren felt the same strangling sensation in his chest he had suffered when he arrived at his Washington apartment two years ago and found six police cars and an ambulance below his window.

He would be too late.

Kurt Monck leaped from the lounge car to POTUS's last car, the Ferdinand Magellan. Unlike other Pullmans, the Ferdinand Magellan had three airtight hatches protruding from its roof. Monck ran along the narrow center of the roof, which was raised twelve inches above the roof's sloping sides. He quickly came to the overhang above the rear platform. He tucked the pistol into the wet suit, then slid down the slanted roof, using the car's loudspeaker to brake himself. He turned onto his stomach, gripped the ledge, and pushed away.

His legs swung in space. He released his grip and dropped onto the elevator deck Roosevelt used for boarding and for giving whistle-stop speeches. It was an eight-foot drop, and Monck hit harder than he had anticipated, twisting his ankle sharply against the Pullman's rear wall.

For an instant he feared the Pullman's occupants might have felt his landing. But his drop wouldn't have budged the heaviest passenger car in railroad history.

He had landed to one side of the door and its window. He had prepared himself to resist the temptation to peer inside, to confirm that his target was six feet away.

Just as the German slipped the backpack from his shoulder, his shoulder went cold, then hot, and blood bubbled up from his wet suit. He glanced at the wound. A graze, not enough to slow him.

And he wasted five seconds looking down the track. A soldier, one of thousands posted along POTUS's entire course, had seen him drop from the Pullman's roof and had loosed a shot at the trespasser. In the time it took for the soldier to determine he had not downed his target, the train had pulled out of rifle range. Monck saw him running after the train, yelling a warning that was lost in the train's rattle.

The bullet had seared through a half inch of skin, slammed into the bulkhead, and fallen to the platform. The German could only hope the car's occupants had not heard the bullet's impact through the wall's foot of steel. He tested his right arm. It worked. So intent was he on the door, he couldn't feel the wound.

Monck opened his pack and pulled out a small packet of mixed aluminum powder and pigment. His plastic explosives would not dent the armored skin of the car if just planted on it. The blueprints he had stolen from the River Iron Works had told him there was not a hole or crevice in which to plant the explosives. The plastic needed a confined space for it to have much effect. Otherwise the blast would spend itself in the air. He needed to create a hole in the steel. And do it quickly.

Mixed together, aluminum powder and chromium oxide, which is used as a paint pigment, form thermite. When ignited, the exothermic reaction reaches temperatures of 2,500 degrees, hot enough to eat into steel.

As Monck had seen on the blueprints, the armored door extended from the wall several inches, forming a ledge on the top of the door. He poured the powder into several piles on the ledge, careful that his arm couldn't be seen from inside the

Pullman. He lost some of it to the wind that swirled behind the car.

A match would not be hot enough to ignite the thermite. He dug into the pack for the magnesium strip, tore it into four lengths, and stabbed a piece into each thermite pile. He found a sulfur match in his pack, cupped his hand around it, and scratched it against the door.

It sputtered into flame. He quickly placed the fire against the magnesium strips, one at a time, making sure each was sparkling to life before moving the match to the next. The magnesium strips were as bright as arc welders, and the glows consumed the strips until they burned into the piles of powder.

Monck knew nothing visible would happen for a short while. He glanced over his shoulder. The Ferdinand Magellan passed another soldier, who was saluting the president. Monck waved cheerfully at him.

The thermite began shimmering. It threw off enough heat that Monck had to back away from the door. The powder turned to liquid and settled into the steel lip. Monck stepped to the edge of the platform and glanced around the side of the car. POTUS was on a wide turn, and the locomotives and tenders and the eighteen cars ranged in a long curve to his left. Untold dozens might have been gazing with reverence on their president's car from their Pullman windows. Monck yanked his head back.

The thermite was now pools of liquid fire, eating into the door's steel rim. Monck removed a serving spoon from his pack. He waited. He knew John Wren was coming.

Four minutes after he lit the strips, he judged the thermite had dug sufficiently deep into the steel. With the spoon he scooped out each pocket, letting the smoldering orange-white molten gobs of thermite and steel fall to the platform.

Again he waited, letting the pockets cool. From the pack he withdrew four balls of plastic explosive. They were a malleable gray putty, appearing entirely innocent. He stuffed a ball into each hole, jamming them down as far as they would go. Then he withdrew the blasting caps from the bag and stuck one into each gray lump. The caps were connected by several feet of wire to the battery, which Monck now pulled from the pack.

He stepped over the guard rail to the left side of the Pullman and, holding the rail by one hand and the battery with the other, leaned as far around the car as he could. He could be seen by anyone caring to look from the train or from the ground, perhaps even by those inside the Ferdinand Magellan.

It was too late for them to do anything.

He pressed the battery's key, igniting the plastic.

John Wren sprinted through the coupler to the Conneaut, the last car before the Ferdinand Magellan. The vestibule floor shifted under his feet. The car was secured. He pressed the signal switch near the door and waited for what seemed like thirty minutes, but was actually thirty seconds.

The view latch slid open. A young agent Wren recognized as one of the president's human shields at Tranquility put his eyes to the port.

"Open the door. Hurry."

"You're supposed to call first," the agent said importantly.

"The line's been cut," Wren yelled. "Open the goddam door."

From behind Wren, Mike O'Brien yelled, "Higgens, I'm ordering you to throw that latch, and do it now, or your ass is out of here at the next stop."

Unruffled, Higgens asked, "What's the password?"

"You idiot," Wren bellowed. He jammed his .45 through the grate until it bounced off Higgens's nose. "You open this door or I'm going to put a password through your pea brain."

"Close enough," Higgens replied.

Wren heard the scrape of the latch. He threw himself at the door, bouncing Higgens onto the floor. Long steps took him through the lounge car to its aft door, already opened by another agent. Others were quickly putting on their jackets, and when they saw Wren and O'Brien, they drew their handguns, looking questioningly at each other. They'd all heard of John Wren. He didn't fool around. They joined the long line of agents hurrying after him.

Wren rushed through the last vestibule to the bulletproof glass window on the Ferdinand Magellan's door. He could see only down the short galley passageway to where the aisle turned to round the crews' quarters. This time there wasn't even a Higgens to open the door.

He stabbed his finger at the buzzer. Wren's throat was so tight with fear that he had to force air into his lungs.

The buzz was answered with the deep crack of an explosion, heard clearly above the train's rumble. The blast had an odd metallic ring to it, sounding like an anvil dropped on a metal floor. The coupler floor shifted under him, and the Ferdinand Magellan seemed to jiggle like gelatin in a bowl.

O'Brien's defeated whisper was just audible over the clatter of the train. "Monck is inside."

John Wren lunged at the door through the vestibule curtain. He pushed it open against the wind. There was no catwalk or ladder outside. He looked skyward.

"Help me up, Mike," he shouted over the noise, returning his pistol to the shoulder holster.

O'Brien and Jones grabbed Wren's legs and hoisted him out the door and onto the vestibule roof. Wren scrambled for purchase on the canvas, and found it on the connecting rim. The agents below pushed him higher, and Wren pulled himself up hand over hand. He brought his knees under him and crouched to retain his balance on the unstable roof. He duckwalked across the canvas accordion to the Ferdinand Magellan's steel roof.

His heart beating against his rib cage like a mallet, he began to run, tracing the German's path along the Pullman's roof.

The explosion had almost blown Kurt Monck's hands off the safety rail. He fought for a grip, ignoring the flash burns across the tops of his fingers. He climbed over the rail to the Ferdinand Magellan's aft platform.

The train's trailing wind had immediately cleared away smoke from the blast. The enormous slab of a door had been peeled from its hinges, and it lay at an angle across the platform, leaning against the overhang's support pillar, which looked as if it were about to give way. The top of the door was streaked with black and orange from the blast.

The German pulled the .38 Special from his wet suit and jumped through the narrow opening into the Pullman.

Monck ignored the man in the wheelchair, sitting with his back to the wrenched door.

Pancho Villa Smythe had been knocked to his knees by the plastic explosive. He was caught with one foot under him, raising his submachine gun. Kurt Monck's first shot entered his heart. The second one widened the entrance hole. Smythe sat down and died.

Wilbur Gottschalk had been using the toilet in the first compartment. At the sound of the detonation, he lurched from compartment. He had thought the sound came from the Pullman's front door. He swung his pistol that way, and by the time he realized his mistake, Monck had pulled the trigger again.

A bullet passed in one of Gottschalk's ears and out the other.

The man in the wheelchair gripped the wheel rims and slowly turned the chair to meet the attacker face on. The explosion had knocked the cigarette holder onto the floor.

"So," said the voice Kurt Monck had heard many times on the POW camp radio. "I should have listened to Chief Wilson more closely." A man who believes himself controlled by destiny can remain calm in any crisis.

The German pulled the long wire from the wet-suit sleeve. It glistened with water and perspiration. He put the pistol back under his wet suit, then, holding the wire taut like a rifle at inspection, he stepped across Smythe's body to the president.

Scottish terriers are courageous to the point of foolhardiness. They have a gladiator's heart trapped in a miniature body. Fala launched himself at Monck and sank his teeth through the wet suit into the German's already frayed calf. Monck started with pain, but ignored the dog.

Roosevelt simply closed his eyes.

The garrote slipped around the president's neck as Monck walked around the wheelchair for better leverage. He drew the handles across each other. The great head bent forward.

Monck hadn't heard John Wren land on the aft platform. The German pulled his mouth back in anticipation of the neck's resistance to the wire. And in doing so he looked up to see Wren's Colt.

Wren's smile froze the German. The pistol barrel moved fractionally, searching out Monck's right eye.

They stared at each other for one second. It might have been an instant of pity, surely one of understanding.

Monck suddenly dipped behind the president, trying to gain seconds to draw his pistol. Roosevelt and his chair completely blocked Wren's view of the German.

"You wish," Wren said. He took one step sideways and pulled the trigger.

The bullet rammed through Kurt Monck's eye and disintegrated the back of his head, spraying Gottschalk's body with bone and brain. The German's body slumped behind the chair. The wire fell harmlessly onto the president's collar.

Franklin Roosevelt opened his eyes. His color was a ghastly white, making the bags under his eyes look like black tattoos. But he calmly turned his chair to look at the German. Fala gaily jumped into his lap.

Wren walked to the German's body. Blood from the socket of his eye covered his face.

"You and I will feel better if you give him one for Tom Garvin," Roosevelt said.

Surprised the president knew anything about his partner, Wren glanced at Roosevelt, who nodded knowingly.

Wren aimed the pistol at Monck's still chest and fired again. The percussion filled the Pullman and disappeared just as quickly.

He took a long breath. "You're right, Mr. President. I do feel better."

Powder from Wren's first bullet had singed the president's earlobe. He gently touched it. Then he chuckled appreciatively and said in his fireside voice, "Election year, and the Republicans are desperate again."

33

WREN FOUND HER AT THE SUNRISE
Restaurant, which doubled as Hackettstown's
Greyhound terminal. She was standing near an elderly couple
on the curb, anxiously looking down the street, her suitcase
gripped in both hands in front of her. She bit on her upper lip
and brushed her hair back. Margarete Bayerlein was lovelier than
her photographs.

The agent pulled the Chevrolet to the curb. He leaned across
the seat and waited until he caught her eye. He pushed open the
passenger-side door.

"Get in." His words were thick, strained through an incomprehensible emotion.

Her eyes grew and her lips parted, as if she might protest.
The flush on her cheeks faded, and a look of terror rippled
over her face, contorting her mouth. She glanced quickly up
the road.

Margarete took a step backward, panic jerking her head left
and right as she searched for help. When she began to turn
away from the Chevrolet, Wren brought up the pistol.

"He's not coming. Get in."

The fear and resolve drained out of her. She swayed as if blown by a strong wind. Her eyes clouded with despair, and her words were dark with sorrow and resentment. "My daughter—who'll take care of her?"

Wren lowered his pistol only when she pushed her suitcase into the backseat and slipped into the car. She was so exhausted she could not swing the door hard enough to close it. Wren reached across her and slammed it shut.

They were a mile down the road to Great Meadows before he said, "We didn't find Mary."

Her head snapped to him as if she had been slapped. "No? ...He told me the article in the Cincinnati newspaper was a fake, and..." Her words died in the wind rushing through the windows.

"He was right."

They slowed for a cow that had escaped its fence. It walked happily down the center of the road, its full udder swinging. Wren steered the car onto the shoulder to get around it.

"What did Monck tell you to do today?"

She took a long breath. "To answer the telephone as if I were the Ford dealer's secretary. To wait another hour and fifteen minutes, then forward the message by way of a neighboring business that a mechanic and a wheel bearing were needed at the Allamuchy train station. I don't really know why I was supposed to do that, other than to make the mechanic late."

Wren did not ask her if she knew Monck's target, if she knew President Roosevelt had been in Allamuchy that day.

"This car is untraceable," he said quietly, his eyes not leaving the road. "Its registration numbers on the engine block and frame have been scraped off. It came from North Carolina, so there won't be anybody looking for it up here. And the license plates are clean. There's a fair-looking registration certificate for the Chevy stuck on the sun visor."

She looked at him, bewildered.

"There are enough gasoline ration coupons in the glove compartment to get you to the West Coast, if that's where Mary is. I'd give you a little money, but I spent it all on the car."

Understanding opened her face. After a moment she asked, "You are John Wren?"

He nodded and said out the window, "I figured Monck knew my name. It became personal between him and me."

"Why are you doing this?"

They passed a green John Deere tractor pulling a raised plow along the road. "I wouldn't if I thought you knew anything about Tom Garvin's death."

He looked at her quickly. Her face was young and unguarded. She hadn't known. But suddenly she did, and her features paled in blotches. Kurt Monck had killed another.

She sat silently for a moment, not volunteering information. Wren finally said, "Your eyes."

She looked at him. "Pardon me?"

"They're green."

As if she understood, she replied, "Yes. Yes, they are."

Wren pulled the car onto the shoulder behind a Secret Service Dodge. He yanked back on the emergency brake and pulled the key from the ignition and dropped it into her hand.

He opened the door and climbed out. He waited for her to slide over to the driver's side before he leaned in the window. He was wearing the slightest of smiles. "My wife's were blue."

Without another word, he walked to the Dodge and started the engine. He turned the car around on the country road and started back to Allamuchy.

A thin strip of light seeped under the steel door, and he had stared at it through the darkness for hours. Occasionally a scream wafted into the tiny room, but other than that, he was alone.

Theodor Paeffgen had been in the cell twenty-four hours, he believed. But it might have been only twelve. He had no way of knowing, as he hadn't been fed dinner or breakfast. The only water allowed him was in a tin can near the door. He was carefully rationing it to himself. Near the back wall was a hole in the cement floor that served as a privy. The cot was the only furniture in the cell. A blanket had been thrown at him as he entered, and it was wrapped around his shoulders. He could not stop shivering, and he constantly blew air through his hands.

He leaped from the bed when a key was pushed into the lock. The door opened, and SS Colonel Heinz Freissner stood in the doorway, backlit by the hall light, one fist on a hip and a thick document in the other hand. He was wearing his black SS uniform, and Paeffgen could make out only his silhouette.

"Ah, Dr. Paeffgen," Freissner said in his unctuous voice. "This must be a terrible mistake. A man with your record, arrested, and brought here. It is ... ah ... inconceivable." He made a show of flipping through the documents. "These charges. How can Himmler be serious? Providing aid and comfort to the enemy, dereliction of duty, insubordination. They certainly don't sound like you."

"I thought not, too," Paeffgen said, knowing his sarcasm was lost on Freissner. Paeffgen had been certain of his fate since the rebroadcast on the English propaganda channel of President Roosevelt's campaign speech given in Chicago on his way to San Diego.

Freissner remained framed by the door. "I am working diligently for your release and expect the papers shortly. Don't let this upset you. You'll surely be back in your office by morning."

Paeffgen warmed his hands with his breath and said nothing.

"There is something you could do to expedite this matter, Herr Doctor. We are trying to gather all the witnesses on your behalf, but we can't find your subordinate, SS Major Friedrich Carstenn. He seems to have ... ah ... disappeared. Would you have any idea ..."

Paeffgen's belly laugh chopped into Freissner's words. Freissner waited for it to end, but it went on and on, echoing in the small room and escaping into the hallway.

Freissner tried to cut him off. "Herr Doctor, these noises are inappropriate here."

But Paeffgen laughed on, even when Freissner angrily closed the door and threw the lock. The laugh chased him down the Prinz Albrechtstrasse building's hallway.

Margarete Bayerlein had sent the letter from Belvidere, New Jersey, six days ago to her San Diego contact. She had no way of knowing whether he had received it, or whether he was still active, or whether her daughter was in the city. But she had no other idea how to reach Mary. And she knew nothing about the man she had entrusted her daughter to. He was an anonymous mail drop. She had written that Mary should meet her at the San Diego train station today.

She parked the car on Kettner Boulevard near the San Diego train station's front door. A swarm of sailors came and went. She had never seen so many of them, not even at the Bremerton Shipyard. They carried duffel bags over their shoulders. Sweethearts clung to a few departing sailors, but most were arriving, ready for the Pacific war, their white caps pushed back insolently and their walks cocky.

She searched through them, looking for her little girl. Had the Secret Service in their search for her Mary perhaps frightened the man into Mexico? Or had he somehow known that Monck was dead, and had that alone chased him over the border? Or maybe the increasingly successful Federal Bureau of Investigation had swept him up. Or maybe he had had a heart attack and died.

These tumbled thoughts, ranging from the possible to the absurd, had tormented her for the entire cross-country journey. Her Bainbridge Island home, which she could never return to, meant nothing to her. Nor her job at the shipyard hospital. Nor her ship-spotting duty. All she wanted was her daughter. She squeezed her eyes shut. Just this one thing. Just this...

"Hi, Mom," yelled the girl.

Mary threw her arms through the window frame and around her mother's neck, pressing her against the door, choking off her cry of surprise and delight and thanks. They hugged each other wildly, separated by the unyielding car door.

"Oh God, Mary," Margarete whispered. "If you only knew how much I've missed you."

"I missed you, too, Mommy." She jumped up and down, still clinging to her mother. In one of her hands was an envelope. "Mr. Randolph said you'd be back, and I believed him. I knew you were coming."

"Did he treat you all right?"

She giggled. "I got all the ice cream I wanted for the first time in my life. I'll go and say goodbye to him."

The girl turned from the car and looked around the station entrance. She lifted herself to her tiptoes for a better view. "He's gone, Mom," she said sadly.

"You climb into the car and tell me all about your vacation."

"Vacation?" she exclaimed, running around the Chevrolet to get into the passenger side. "I worked, worked, worked. Mr. Randolph taught me Chopin's Fifth Etude. I can hardly wait to play it for you."

In the envelope was a passport, listing both mother and daughter. To her amazement, the photo of her looked as if it had been taken recently. The car pulled away from the station. A mile away, Franklin Roosevelt was about to accept the Democratic nomination for his fourth term.

The girl talked all the way to Ensenada.

John Wren pulled the middle drawer from his desk and dumped its few contents into the cardboard box. It was the noon hour, and most other employees in the Federal Building had walked down to the waterfront to celebrate a sunny day. He had been in Seattle four days, but this was his first day back. He wouldn't regret leaving.

On the desk was a telex from the Washington office. Based on George Bell's description, a Georgetown University professor named Otto Stroop had been arrested as he tried to cross into Canada at Buffalo.

Also on the desk next to the box was the letter from Kaiser

Industries in Los Angeles. It had been carefully spread out flat, its envelope positioned squarely above it. It offered him the position of senior security adviser at Kaiser's Los Angeles shipyard. He could use a change of scenery and some sun. And after years of working for the federal government, Wren was almost embarrassed by the generous salary Kaiser was offering.

The hole in his cheek had healed to a small pucker, though he incessantly played with the inside of the wound with his tongue, making him look as if he had a jawbreaker in his mouth. The receptionist had greeted him that morning by saying how sorry she was about Tom Garvin, and also saying Wren had lost weight. He had. His jacket was loose and his belt was up a notch.

He wished Garvin would walk in the door, late, as always. But the door remained closed.

He dropped a stapler into the box. Despite his partner's death, Wren felt better these days. Something about meeting Margarete Bayerlein for those moments had lifted a sorrowful yoke from him. He knew now that by searching for her, by reconstructing her from her photos and letters, he had been trying to resurrect Linda. It hadn't worked, and he was glad of it. Not that he'd ever stop missing his wife. But he had learned that the piercing, bone-shaking sadness could be handled. Maybe that would be all he could ever do. Handle it. Manage it.

His wife's photograph was the only item in the last drawer. He pulled it out and stared at it. He smiled slowly and put it carefully into the box.

To Wren's amazement and amusement, his translator, Mary Anderson, all pert and perky and undoubtedly beautifully flushed, had called that morning baldly asking him to take her to a sorority dance. A sorority dance, for God's sake.

Wren controlled himself long enough to tell her he was flattered, but he was leaving Seattle that day. He had thanked the young girl too profusely. After he hung up, he had laughed loud enough for his secretary to rush in. She had never heard him laugh before. He was astounded at how good that call made him feel.

Wren threw the last of his things into the box and put it under his arm. He pulled Chief Wilson's letter from his jacket. It informed him of his transfer to the White House Detail to replace Max Smythe as O'Brien's assistant.

Wren wadded up the Kaiser letter and tossed it into the wastebasket. He walked from the office without looking back.